Bestselling Author Of _Touched By Moonlight_

NOBLE INTENTIONS

I wouldn't ever hurt you, Ivy. You know that, don't you?
Had the boy Noble spoken those words to her, so very
long ago? Did Noble the man know how many times and
how many ways he had hurt her since? Did Noble the man
know just how wonderful she felt nonetheless, sheltered in
his arms?

Ivy breathed deeply again. Noble smelled of cedar and of
something warm and sweet that she could identify only as
uniquely him. She hoped he would not soon let her go.
Despite everything that had driven them apart over the years,
there was still something genuine and perfect about Noble
Smith's embrace. Her body, much to her own surprise, had
not forgotten the sensation. She wondered if his had.

Carole Howey
Noble And Ivy

LEISURE BOOKS **NEW YORK CITY**

For everyone who's ever sacrificed for a child.
There's a special place in heaven for you.

A LEISURE BOOK®

December 1996

Published by

Dorchester Publishing Co., Inc.
276 Fifth Avenue
New York, NY 10001

ACKNOWLEDGMENTS

Endless thanks to Terri Garrett and her parents, the Meekers of Lovell, Wyoming. Without their input—everything from the way sagebrush looks, feels, and burns, to wildflowers, to the smell of air around Thermopolis—Nobel and Ivy might just as well have negotiated the Delaware.

Noble And Ivy

Chapter One

Of all the people Ivy Wingate might have expected to show up at her schoolhouse that fine, spring afternoon, Noble Smith was at the end of the list, way behind President Benjamin Harrison and possibly a few other folks who were known to be dead. She hadn't seen Noble except at a distance in nearly ten years, although his towering, rugged silhouette was imprinted on her memory as clearly as the constant blue-gray shadow of the Tetons that embraced the town of Peaceful.

She most emphatically did not want to see him now, especially as his dark eyes were aimed at her across the distance of the schoolhouse like a pair of primed Colts.

"Good afternoon, Mr. Smith." Ivy was formal, despite the fact that she'd grown up two miles down the road from the Smiths. "Have you come for Charity's school work?" Charity was Noble's

11

younger sister, a bright, spirited girl of fifteen whose yellow braids encouraged smitten young men to pull them and dip them in inkwells. Much like Ivy herself had been a decade ago, when a young man named Noble Smith had sat behind her in Miss Woolson's classroom and taken the same liberties.

"I've come for Charity." His words, in a deep, mature baritone, were clipped, as if he regretted having to spend any on a Wingate at all. Ivy forced herself to maintain her gaze without flinching, although she was torn between a desire to offer up a rude remark or to run from the room crying. Her third alternative was honest surprise. She judged it as the safest course, as well as the quickest way to get him to leave. She had no desire to spend a minute longer than necessary in his presence and, judging by the black look on his angular but handsome face, she was sure the feeling was mutual.

"Charity isn't here."

"What do you mean, she isn't here?" His stoic, granite composure cracked for an instant before he mastered it again, but his anthracite eyes remained wide as they continued to bore into her. Ivy met his hostile glare, determined to not so much as blink in the face of it.

"I mean that she is not here," she repeated deliberately. She hoped her sarcasm would infuriate him; surely he recognized it as such. Noble was no idiot. Quite the contrary, in fact. He'd always been one of the smartest people she knew. He'd meant to become a doctor, before . . .

"Then where is she?" Noble's voice rose in pitch, a painful echo of the sweet young man he'd been, the boy she'd loved a decade before. She blinked once and thrust the bittersweet memory aside, compelled to avert her stare and concentrate upon the pile of slates stacked upon her desk. That he did not address her by name hurt her even more than the coldness in his tone.

"I am a teacher," she reminded him, keeping her voice low so it would not betray her emotional state by shaking. "I am responsible for my students only while they are in my care. Charity did not attend school today; I assumed she was ill at home. There have been several cases of influenza recently."

If Charity had indeed played hooky, Ivy mused, Noble, her legal guardian since the death of their mother, Hannah, two years earlier, would pin her hide to a fence. She restrained a shudder: When had he become so cold? But she knew the answer to that. The timing coincided with the frost about her own heart.

"Where's your brother?" Noble ignored her question. His voice was a feral growl again.

Ivy didn't like Noble's curt inquiry. It triggered a bad feeling in her stomach, an unpleasant memory she'd tried hard, and without success, to forget. She was tempted to lie to him, but she couldn't, even if she knew where Stephen was, which she didn't. She wished she could tell Noble to go to hell, but she couldn't do that either, not without compromising her position as Peaceful, Wyoming's respectable schoolteacher. It wasn't much of a position, but it supported her and enabled her to hold on to the family home, for all that meant, with no family left to hold it for. Maintaining a rigid posture, she made herself meet his cold stare again.

"Stephen and I have nothing to do with one another." She forced the words from her mouth. She was sure Noble was aware of the rift between her and her brother, and she resented the fact that he'd made her say the words aloud. The whole town knew it. Stephen had left Peaceful nearly a year before, following their father's death. She had argued with him after the funeral, and he, all of seventeen and convinced he knew what was best for him, had taken a horse, the small inheritance his father had left him, and ridden off. Since that time he had made no attempt whatever to contact her, nor she him.

Rumors around Peaceful abounded: that he'd joined a band of outlaws down Laramie way; that he'd taken to gambling down in Reno; that he'd speculated and lost everything on a silver mine in Colorado. He'd drifted in and out of town from time to time, but never to see Ivy. She always heard about his visits after he'd long gone. That Noble Smith should charge into her classroom inquiring as to Stephen's whereabouts after not having spoken a word to her in a decade both insulted and infuriated her.

"I have told you all I know, Mr. Smith, which is far more than you deserve."

She hoped her hostile gaze matched his, but she doubted such a thing was possible. She stood up behind her desk. Maybe he would take her gesture as a sign of dismissal and leave. Any other man would have. Any gentleman, that is. Noble Smith, however, stayed where he was.

"He was out at my place last night." It was the first information he'd imparted to her in the interview, and it surprised her because she hadn't asked. "I chased him off and told him not to come back. He . . ." Noble paused, and for a fleeting instant Ivy saw the earnest young man he'd been, the sweet, sensitive boy who'd professed undying love for her on a spring day a decade before. Her heart ached in that instant for the boy who no longer was, and for the wounded young girl who had vanished with him.

Noble regained his icy demeanor as if he'd never lost it.

"He cursed me," he went on grimly. "He made threats I didn't like."

"And have you come looking to me for protection from him?" It was an absurd question. Noble, she remembered all too clearly, was more than capable of taking care of himself in any situation. He was fiercely protective of his baby sister, besides. Ivy had heard all about how he'd stood up to Enoch Witherspoon when the latter had tried to buy out less fortunate landowners after the hard winter of '86. Even the Wingate ranch had been spared as a result of his fearless and indefatigable efforts.

That had been three years ago, and she had never thanked him personally for it. By all reports, Noble was a formidable enemy to anyone who dared to cross him, and he possessed a very rigid code of ethics by which he lived his life and expected everyone else, including Stephen Wingate, to live theirs.

Ivy drew in a short breath in sudden dread: did Noble mean to imply, by coming to the schoolhouse, that the appearance of Stephen and the disappearance of Charity had something to do with one another?

"Is there something you're not telling me?" Noble's voice was sharp. Ivy met his piercing stare, heat filling her cheeks. He'd read her inner distress, she realized, chagrined. He'd always been able to read her when they were children, but it had been so long since they'd met or even spoken that she was surprised he could still do it. *There are many things I haven't told you,* she thought, pressing her lips together. *Things I will never tell you. Things I pray you never learn . . .*

"How dare you, Noble Smith?" She clenched her hands at her sides. "We haven't exchanged a word in ten years. How dare you stampede into my classroom now without so much as a 'Good Afternoon' and start barking questions at me as if I were a common criminal? As if I had any obligation whatever to answer to you, except as your sister's teacher?"

"As one of the citizens of Peaceful, I pay your salary," he retorted, planting his fists at his hips as his scowl of concentration deepened. The gesture reminded her that Noble Smith had, indeed, become a man in the interim. His remark was intended, she was certain, to remind her that he was powerful enough to make trouble for her, possibly even to have her dismissed, if she displeased him in any way. For a long moment it seemed as if not Noble but his imposing father stood before her in that suddenly cramped classroom. The memory frightened her so, that she could scarcely draw a breath.

She rallied. Benjamin Smith was gone, she told herself, meeting the cold, dark eyes of his son. It was not Benjamin but Noble Smith who stood before her, the same Noble Smith she'd swam naked with in the creek on sultry summer afternoons. The same Noble Smith who'd given her a mouse for a pet when her brother was born to ease the sting of being ignored. The same Noble Smith she hadn't spoken to for a month because he hadn't picked her for his partner in the three-legged race at the church picnic, even though he was a head taller than she and it would have been an absurd match.

The same Noble Smith who'd dared her to walk

Witherspoon's fence rail that blessed, cursed spring afternoon . . .

Ivy hitched up the hem of her pinafore and scampered up the four-foot rail fence as deftly as any boy in trousers. Her high-laced shoes pinched, but she hadn't remembered that until it was too late. She'd already accepted Noble's challenge at the schoolhouse earlier. To say now that her shoes were too tight would make it sound like she had turned lily-livered on him. Like she wanted to back out. Everyone had heard her say she'd do it. She wouldn't have it said that Ivy Wingate welshed on a dare.

"I'll hold your lunch bucket, if you like."

"No, thanks," she retorted. She looked over her shoulder at Noble, squinting against the late afternoon sun. Noble looked so much like his pa right then that it made Ivy nervous. It wasn't that she didn't like Benjamin Smith. She liked all the Smiths well enough, but there was something about Noble's pa . . . It was as if he were a fairytale king who'd been enchanted by a sorceress and made to live among his subjects instead of in a palace where he rightfully belonged. Noble had that same look about him right there next to her at the fence, only in Noble's face, the look didn't scare her. It kind of made her feel like a fairytale queen. . . .

"You don't frighten me." She closed her mind to the rest of the unwanted memory, retreating until the back of her knees, in layers of crinoline, bumped into the edge of the seat of her chair. "How typical of a bully, to threaten my livelihood!"

"Ivy, I—"

He stopped. The room was still, so still Ivy heard the birds pecking at the feeder mounted outside on the windowsill. She had not heard Noble Smith speak her name since they were children. Judging by the wide-eyed look on his rawboned face, Ivy supposed that Noble was as surprised as she that he'd uttered it.

"I didn't come here to bully you," he said gruffly after a long, painful moment, looking down at his hands. "Dammit, I . . . I came here looking for my sister." He'd almost said her name again. She'd felt it. Suddenly she wanted him to say it. After ten long, confusing, lonely years, she felt as if she needed to hear her name in his deep, grown-up voice that sounded, blessedly, nothing like his father's. But she'd rather die than ask him even for that.

He proceeded up the aisle toward her between the rows of students' slant-top desks. His long legs covered the distance in an easy stride and his dusty work boots made distinct, soft thuds on the plank floor. His arms swung easily at his sides. He was not the lanky, somewhat awkward youth he'd been ten years earlier. In fact, today his effortless yet disconcertingly feral grace mesmerized her. Another nick against the backs of her knees told her she'd tried to retreat from him again, but by then the chair was against the wall and there was no place else for her to go unless she wanted to turn and run. Part of her did want that, but pride stubbornly welded her feet to the floor.

"She isn't here," Ivy heard herself say, although the sound of her voice was unfamiliar. "I don't know where—"

"Look at this."

Noble had reached her desk and he stood before it, barely an arm's length in front of her. Ivy realized that her gaze was fixed on the belt buckle at his trim waist. She raised it reluctantly, up the lapel of his cream-colored muslin shirt with tiny brown stripes. The shirt had no collar, but it was obvious nevertheless that he had washed recently and put it on fresh, probably just for this interview. The idea aroused an unwanted tremor along Ivy's skin. The shirt was open at the throat, and a fascinating suggestion of the dark hair that no doubt covered his chest peeked out at the vee. She forced her stare up the stark angle of his jaw, over his wide, shockingly sensual but unsmiling mouth. She stopped at last at his naked dark eyes. There was a hint of pain in their chocolate depths that called out unexpectedly to a kindred emotion within her. For a perilous instant she thought she might actually cry.

She lifted her chin an inch. She had shed her last tear over a Smith.

His arm was outstretched. At the end of it, in his long, strong fingers, was a bit of paper. She took it, glad of an excuse to look away from him. She read:

I'll be all right. I love him. Don't be angry.

"It's Charity's handwriting," Ivy murmured, feeling stupid. Of course it was. Noble must already know that. She braced herself against a rude retort from him.

"I know," was all he said. His voice was sad. Hurt. He sucked in a breath, and when he let it out, the pain was replaced by fury. "It's your brother. She's run off with your damned brother!"

Looking across the narrow gulf between her and Noble Smith's stormy face, she was sure she was going to faint. Those who do not learn from history, she could almost hear Miss Woolson saying, are doomed to repeat it. She was sitting down, suddenly.

"No," she moaned as the room shrank around her. Of all the calamities she could envision, and since that day ten years ago she'd been able to envision quite a number of them, none equalled the scenario Noble had outlined for sheer catastrophe. Charity was underage. So was Stephen, but to a court of law, that would not matter. If they were found, Noble could have Stephen arrested for kidnapping, or worse. And given the animosity that had existed between the Smith family and the Wingate family for a decade, Noble would no doubt take great pleasure in doing so.

Ivy clenched her teeth. If it were true, she could not allow Noble Smith to find them. Not without her being there, in any event. Stephen was a headstrong and rebellious young man, but she was sure he had not abducted Charity Smith against her will. She was equally sure that he would not allow Noble Smith to take him without a fight. She could not bear the thought that the resulting confrontation might end in at least one death.

The Smith family had caused enough heartache in Ivy's life. She would do everything she could to prevent them, any of them, from causing more.

"I'm going after them," Noble said in a quiet, menacing tone. He'd read her thoughts again, and it unnerved her even more than before. She wished to keep her own counsel regarding Stephen and his alleged misconduct. She needed to purchase time if she were to avert a tragedy. Another one.

"Let me drive out to my—the ranch before you go off half-cocked," she got out in a muffled tone, not daring to sustain his gaze. "He may be staying out there. He may have nothing to do with this."

"I'll go with you."

"You most certainly will not." She mustered her coldest tone. "You've caused quite a bit of talk already, no doubt, just by coming here this afternoon. It's all well and good for you; you live outside of town and far away from the hurtful gossip. I'll have every busybody from Chicago to the Great Divide asking me for the next month just why Noble Smith wanted to talk to me privately, and each of them thinking they've a right to a candid reply."

"You think you're the only one who's ever been hurt by gossip?" There was a chilly bravado in Noble's question, as if an injured boy were hiding behind his bold manner.

Ivy bit her lip. She had no doubt that Noble knew the sting of malicious gossip. He'd been engaged to marry two different girls in recent years. Both engagements had been called off, she recalled, with the bride's change of heart being generally credited for the cancellation of the nuptials. Noble had appeared in public afterward as if nothing were amiss. However, broad, unguarded public speculation ensued when the young ladies, contrary to his nonchalant example, secluded themselves for weeks as if recovering from broken hearts.

But Ivy had been hurt by more than gossip. Far deeper than she would ever allow anyone to guess, even Noble. Especially Noble.

"I'll drive out tonight, alone," she told him, plastering a mask of indifference on her face before she met his uncompromising gaze again. "I won't have my brother wrongly persecuted. Especially not by you. I'll send a message out to you to let you know what I find."

"I'll come back here tomorrow and ask you myself," he said, as if he didn't trust her. Her face burned, because she knew that he shouldn't. Not this time, anyway.

Chapter Two

Penelope Quinlan was a nosy and garrulous woman with frankly Irish features and a pair of startling blue eyes. They always made Ivy think of the spirited young girl she must once have been, now imprisoned in a sluggish, aging body. Mrs. Quinlan ran the boarding house with a keen eye and a firm hand, ever watchful for any impropriety her lodgers might exhibit. As Ivy expected, Mrs. Quinlan was waiting for her at the front door when she walked in, those bright sapphire eyes of hers brimming with grim but eager conjecture that made Ivy feel exposed.

"Sophie Paul said Noble Smith was over to the schoolhouse today."

Ivy could not help but admire Mrs. Quinlan's directness as well as the lightning speed with which the gossip had travelled from the dry goods emporium adjacent to the schoolhouse to the boarding house at the opposite end of town. Words, it seemed, had wings that outpaced even her brisk young step.

"Good evening, Mrs. Quinlan." Ivy tried to edge past the large woman with that polite but discouraging greeting. She wanted to retreat to her room to recover from the unsettling encounter with Noble, and to make her plans. Mrs. Quinlan, however, with a deftness belying her bulk, moved into her path in the narrow foyer, giving Ivy no choice but to stop and meet her speculative gaze.

"I expect he wanted to speak with you about that sister of his?" the landlady persisted, folding her arms across her massive, aproned bosom.

"I really shouldn't say, Mrs. Quinlan," Ivy reproved her, sure that her censure would have no effect whatever on the woman's inquisitiveness. It never did.

"That Charity Smith is as wild a girl as her brother is steady. And a sight too pretty for her own good, if you ask me." Mrs. Quinlan was never reticent about speaking her mind, whether asked or not. "That's the first time you've spoke to Noble since the trouble, isn't it?"

Ivy mastered a scowl. Mrs. Quinlan knew that. Sophie Paul knew that. As far as Ivy could tell, there wasn't a person in or around Peaceful, possibly in the whole Wyoming territory, thanks to Penelope Quinlan and her ilk, who didn't know that. Considering, it was a wonder Ivy had been able to guard her other secrets so closely over the years. She didn't mind Mrs. Quinlan being the biggest snoop ever to walk on two legs, but she refused to abet her landlady in her dubious hobby.

"I won't be sitting at dinner this evening," Ivy replied. She immediately regretted her hasty, abrupt words, but knew they were irretrievable. In

23

atonement she forced herself to offer her landlady a reason for her absence.

"I must go out to the ranch," she explained, forcing an offhand lightness to her tone she was far from feeling. "I have reason to believe my brother may have been there recently, and may still be there."

"You think he's run off with Charity, then?"

Mrs. Quinlan was too canny for Ivy's liking.

"I think he might know who did," Ivy corrected her, aware of a tightness in her neck and jaw.

"But it'll be dark soon," Mrs. Quinlan observed with a frown. "It isn't safe for a lady to be so far afield after dark. Suppose the gig loses a wheel?"

A lady. Ivy mastered a familiar, searing guilt. "I'll be riding."

"All the worse," Mrs. Quinlan insisted. "Suppose the horse goes lame, or—"

"Mrs. Quinlan . . ."

"Very well," the landlady grumbled. "But what do you expect to come of your meeting, even if you do find Stephen? You haven't spoken to your brother since your pa died. What makes you think he'll tell you anything?"

Ivy flinched. The rift between Stephen and her was painful enough without an outsider's callous observations. Once again she mastered her anger and hurt.

"Regardless, I must see him. I—" Ivy stopped, considering her landlady. It was possible, even likely, that Mrs. Quinlan knew more about her brother's whereabouts than she did.

"Have *you* seen him, Mrs. Quinlan?" It cost her quite a lot of pride to ask, but Stephen was worth it. No matter what had passed between them, he was still her brother, and she still loved him. She felt certain that, in spite of everything, he loved her as well.

Penelope Quinlan squared her immense shoulders and lifted her bread-dough chin an inch.

"*I* haven't," she allowed. "But Sophie Paul said she'd heard from Mr. Gentile over at the livery that Stephen was there yesterday. Bought a flashy mare, cash. Gold, in fact."

Ivy stared. Stephen? Gold? Good horses did not come cheaply, she knew, and Albert Gentile was a tight fist with a bargain. Where had Stephen gotten such means? Her heart sank like a stone as she thought of the possibilities, none of them legitimate. A dozen fresh questions leapt into her mind, but she quickly schooled herself. She did not want to appear too eager for more information. A cautious, if not indifferent, approach was best, she knew, if she did not want to stir up a hornet's nest of public speculation, beginning right here with Penelope Quinlan. Stephen and Charity would hardly benefit from such a result. Neither would she. Or Noble.

"I don't suppose you know where he might have gone afterward, do you?" Ivy tried to sound politely interested, if not downright indifferent. "Or where he'd come from?"

Mrs. Quinlan's raised eyebrow indicated the failure of Ivy's effort. "No, and no," she said crisply, looking very satisfied. "Mr. Gentile said he was dressed to the nines in spit-shined boots and a spanking new Stetson, besides. Yessirree, sounds like Stephen Wingate found his pot o' gold."

Or someone else's, Ivy thought grimly.

"I always thought it was a shame about your brother, Ivy," Mrs. Quinlan went on, running an idle finger along the trim about the door. "He'd been such a sweet little boy before your ma up and left you all. Afterward he turned sour right fast, always actin' as if the world owed him something for his pain. You were never that way. In fact, if anything, folks said as how you'd got sweeter to make up for it, if you don't mind my sayin'." She examined the dust on the end of her finger, then flicked it away and brushed her hand against her apron. "And your ma, she was always kind and friendly, right up to the day she and Ben Smith—"

Mrs. Quinlan broke off as if she realized she'd said more than she should have. Ivy mastered a grimace with great effort. Mrs. Quinlan didn't mean to be unkind, she knew. It was just that it still hurt so terribly when Ivy thought about that awful day and what it had done to both families . . .

"It looks a lot higher from on top, don't it?" Noble teased Ivy from the ground.

If she hadn't been holding onto the fence rail and balancing herself, she'd have swung her lunch bucket at his head. She paused again, meaning to stick out her tongue at him. She was halfway up the fence, and Noble, to her surprise, was looking right into her eyes across from her. His eyes were the color of sweet chocolate fudge. He'd always been taller than she, but the winter had grown him some, too, as if all that snow had stretched his body out like a fast-growing weed. His shoulders were broad as railroad ties, and his neck seemed to rise up from the open buttons of his collarless striped shirt like the trunk of a sapling. Lord, she thought, with a funny, squirmy feeling way down inside of her. He'd all but turned into a man! How could she not have noticed it before this?

"Scared?"

His taunt, along with the disparaging smirk on his handsome face, reminded her to stop staring at him and move on up the rails again. She had a fence to walk. And she knew she'd better stop thinking about the funny feeling she got lately from looking into Noble Smith's big brown eyes, or she'd slip off the rail and fall for sure. A dare wasn't worth breaking a leg over. Neither were Noble Smith's eyes, no matter how nice they were.

"Not of you," she mumbled with a shiver. It was a lie, of course. She was more scared of him right then than she'd ever been of walking any old fence rail, although she couldn't guess why, and would rather cut off her finger than admit it to him.

"You should be, you know," he said conversationally. "You're so scrawny, I could squash you like a bug." He pinched his thumb and forefinger together to demonstrate.

She couldn't tell if he was teasing her or not, but she was sure he meant to make her anxious. His brash talk didn't trouble her as much as the fact that he had obviously noticed her slim figure. Noble wasn't the only one of them who'd done some sprouting over the cold winter months, she realized, her cheeks heating. Her bosom, small but distinct in the snug pinafore, tingled as if it had been exposed naked to his gaze. Flustered, she ignored him, pretending to concentrate on the length of fence rail before her as she sat atop the post. . . .

"Ivy?"

Ivy started. "I'm sorry, Mrs. Quinlan. My thoughts strayed. What did you say?"

The look in Penelope Quinlan's eyes was harder to take than her earlier forthright observations. Ivy knew a moment of terror. Did she know? Had she guessed?

"I'll wrap up some supper for you to take along," Mrs. Quinlan said, her tone so soft it might have been Mama's ghost talking to her. "It's a long way, and it'll sure be late when you get back."

Yes, Ivy thought, awash with relief. Later than either of us can imagine.

Ivy's hands shook as she folded the letter she'd just finished writing. It wasn't cold in her little third-floor room on that April night, but she felt chilled nonetheless. The letter in her hands spelled the end of any chance she had for a quiet, respectable life in Peaceful. She meant to leave it in her room, where it would be found the following morning. Mrs. Quinlan would come looking for her when she didn't come down to breakfast. She would find the letter instead, and Ivy's quiet, carefully obscure existence would be a memory.

She shivered at the idea that a Wingate was about to provide Peaceful with yet another scandal, and she cursed her brother and Noble Smith for forcing such a bleak choice on her. She looked around at the room she'd lived in for the past three years since Papa had died and Stephen had run off from the ranch. It was just a room. There was nothing in it that spoke of Ivy or her life, save the few plain dresses she owned. She'd left everything of sentimental value at the ranch, where it mostly collected dust. Those things belonged there. They didn't belong in a tiny room at a boarding house, any more than Ivy did. But Ivy didn't have a choice.

Sheriff Doman had warned her that she was inviting squatters, leaving the place empty like that, but she hadn't been able to care, any more than she'd been able to let go of it. Well, if there were squatters on the old place, she'd find out tonight. She'd assess their character and their intentions, and quickly decide what to do about them before she headed out after Stephen.

And maybe, if there were squatters, they'd have seen him, and could give her a lead as to his destination.

She pressed the rough paper against her lips and closed her eyes, fighting a heaviness behind them that threatened tears. Stephen himself wouldn't be there. She knew that, as surely as she knew Stephen could not have come by his windfall honorably. Stephen would never willingly go back to the ranch. She had just invented that tale to appease Noble, to buy herself a head start. She was going to have to go after her brother and Charity Smith, pray she could put enough distance between Noble and herself, and hope she could find the runaway lovers before Noble caught up with the lot of them.

She left a small pouch on the bed beside the note. In it was fifty dollars. The note instructed Mrs. Quinlan to give the money to Mr. Gentile on deposit for the horse she'd be borrowing for an unknown amount of time. The horse would be worth more than that, she knew, but that was all she had on hand. She could only hope that the penurious Mr. Gentile would understand her plight and allow her to pay off the rest when she returned. She'd have enough on her mind between Stephen, Charity and Noble without having to worry about the law coming after her for horse-theft.

Ivy had no need to practice secrecy when she left the boarding house just before dusk. Mrs. Quinlan knew where she was going, and why. At least, the landlady thought she knew. Ivy almost wished she could be there in the morning to see Penelope Quinlan's face when she read the note. Tomorrow she would learn the truth of Ivy's disappearance. And the town of Peaceful, and Noble Smith, would learn it right along with her.

If luck were with her, Ivy realized, taking a last

good-bye look at her old room and her old life, she had perhaps a twelve-hour head start on Armageddon.

Ivy smelled like violets, just like she always had. Noble was both amazed and irritated that he'd noticed it in the schoolhouse earlier. The scent was as faint and beguiling as a whisper of spring, yet as steady as the love he had once borne her. Now he couldn't get her out of his mind.

"Damn." He swore under his breath and hunched his shoulders up against a sudden cool evening breeze, sharp with the tang of sagebrush. He often thought out loud, as there was no one left, not even Charity, to listen to his musings any more. He felt foolish for doing it here behind the livery stable, but there was no one to hear him other than his horse. Besides, the sound of his own voice distracted him from the persistent, tormenting memory that his visit to the schoolhouse had reawakened.

"I'm to be a doctor, you know," he boasted to the woman-child who sat on the fence post cocking her head at him like a curious young bird. He wanted so awfully to impress Ivy Wingate, although he couldn't say why. Maybe it was the shy way she'd taken to looking at him, with her head low, peering through those ripe-wheat gold eyelashes of hers. Maybe it was the way her blue pinafore hugged her blossoming body, so different from the way it had fit her last October. Or maybe it was something inside of him, something that had taken hold of him whenever he'd thought about her during the long, cold months of winter, like a bear trap that would not let him go.

"I'm to go to school back east." He swallowed.

*Damn his quivering voice! Say something, Ivy, he
pleaded with her in the silence that followed. He fixed
his stare on her plain black high-laced boots because
he was afraid to look in her eyes. He couldn't say
why he was afraid, exactly, but he thought it might
be because he expected she'd laugh at him, or worse,
that she'd shrug with indifference. Either result, he
knew, would crush him.*

"A doctor," she echoed, sounding not so much im-
pressed as disbelieving. "Who'd want you touching
them if they sick or hurt? Not me."

*Disdain wasn't what he'd had in mind as a posi-
tive response, either. He felt like she'd stepped on his
heart. Or like he'd carelessly shoved it under her feet,
like some fellow named Walter Raleigh that Miss
Woolson had once told them about in class. Disappointment swelled in him like the sick feeling he got
from eating too many of his ma's sugar cakes.*

"Ivy." *He growled her name. Sometimes she made
him so mad! He wanted to kiss her, suddenly, to see
if he could make her mad, too.*

"What?"

*He looked up, into her face. The single word held
such a confusion of emotions. He hoped a glimpse
of her features might give him a clue as to her feelings about his announcement. He wasn't exactly
sure what he was looking for, but he found himself
wishing that Ivy would at least say she would miss
him. He realized, watching her wide, grass-green eyes
fill with dew, that one word from her would be
enough to make him stay.*

There was a noise at the other end of the livery
stable, the sound of a metal bolt being thrown. Noble pressed his ear against the splintered planks of
the wall and listened hard.

"You'll be drivin'." The gravel-rough voice of Al-

31

bert Gentile, livery proprietor, was low. Conversational. He was speaking to someone. Noble held his breath, hoping to hear the respondent, whoever it might be. He expected it was Ivy. He hoped it was. He could not make out a reply, but there must have been one, for a moment later he heard Gentile speak again, this time in wonder.

"Ridin'? But Miss Ivy, it ain't—" The stableman's protest was cut short, but again Noble could not hear the interruption. He didn't need to, this time. He knew it was Ivy in there, now. The mere knowledge that Ivy Wingate stood on the other side of the wall caused a peculiar feeling in his chest, as if he'd been run through bloodlessly by a cavalry saber.

"Damn," he muttered, even softer than the first time. Was that violets he smelled? Again?

Just as he began to despair of breaking free from the insidious spell, he heard more movement inside the stable. Albert Gentile was leading a horse out. Apparently Ivy had convinced the stable man of whatever it was he'd doubted. Noble grimaced, remembering his own long-ago experiences with Ivy Wingate's sweet powers of persuasion.

He found himself envisioning Ivy's pale eyes, the color of spring grass. Her eyelashes were long, fringed curtains that veiled her moods; at least they had when they were children. Today at the schoolhouse, Noble had found himself trying to search behind those veils, looking for any hint of the sweet, pretty, somewhat quiet girl he'd lost his heart to. He was amazed, and a little alarmed, to discover that she'd become a beautiful but strong woman. She still had a small mouth, with its full, round, lower lip, and he was able to remember all too clearly kissing that mouth. He could still taste its sweet nectar, as he imagined a bee always remembered the taste of its favorite flower.

Violets. The delicate yet distinctive aroma had been Ivy's signature for as long as he'd known her. It had gotten so he could not separate the two: tiny, fragile, brave purple flowers peeking up through the first shoots of spring grass, struggling in their brief but lovely lives to bring the first bit of beauty and color into a cold world. Bettina Kraus, to whom he'd been engaged a few years back, took to wearing violet water while he'd been courting her. Noble often wondered to himself if that might have been one reason why he'd called off their engagement.

Ivy's ma had worn violet water too, he recalled suddenly, with a quick wrench in his gut. He recalled father remarking on it more than once. And his own mother had never liked the scent.

Ivy was talking to Al Gentile again. Noble remained very still, straining his ears so hard that he would have sworn he could hear his own blood pulsing through his veins. He couldn't hear what she was saying, only the melodious sound of her voice, like distant glass wind chimes on a gentle evening breeze. He heard Gentile laugh in reply and bid her good evening.

Noble pressed himself hard against the back wall of the livery stable. He didn't want to be seen, not by Al Gentile, and certainly not by Ivy Wingate. She'd told him earlier that she was heading for the Wingate ranch to see if Stephen might be there, with or without Charity. He'd agreed to wait until the following day to find out what she'd learned, but at the last minute he'd decided that where Stephen or Charity were concerned, he couldn't trust Ivy.

And where Ivy was concerned, he couldn't trust himself.

Chapter Three

Three times on the six-mile ride to the Wingate ranch, Ivy reined Al Gentile's prized piebald gelding up and paused, listening hard. She could not rid herself of the feeling that she was being followed. But each time she stopped, she heard nothing more than the ordinary sounds of a Star Valley spring night. Surely it was her guilty conscience troubling her, nothing more. Although why it should bother her that she was deliberately deceiving Noble Smith, she could not imagine. After all, it was not the first time she had done so.

The spirited animal tossed his head with impatience, but she held firmly to the rein at the crossroads. There was nothing remarkable about the spot, nor were there any landmarks by which an ordinary traveller would identify it. It was merely the intersection of the main road to Peaceful and the path to the old deserted Wingate ranch.

It was the very spot whereon her life had taken a fateful turn a decade earlier.

Ivy chucked to her eager mount, unwilling to dwell on her dark thoughts of the past on this moonlit April night. She had a mission to perform, and she could ill afford the distraction of bitter reminiscence.

It was with mixed emotions that Ivy saw there were no lights in the windows of the run-down ranch house. The small clapboard structure took on an unearthly aspect in the pale moonlight, and it was eerily quiet. Ivy drew the piebald up once again when she reached the front yard but could not bring herself to dismount right away. There are ghosts about the place, a childish, frightened voice inside of her warned. The woman in her longed to take that child firmly in hand and lead her about, illustrating the absurdity of that immature fancy. But the woman in her remembered all too much, and remained unconvinced that the child was not right after all.

There were ghosts, she knew. But they were ghosts Ivy had brought right along with her from town, ghosts she carried with her always, every day of her life. They only seemed more real to her out here at the ranch, she reasoned, pulling off her riding gloves finger by finger. The phantoms were more real here because there were no distractions of everyday life to keep them in check. Out here at the ranch, it was just her, the house, and her memories.

From atop the piebald, she looked from one dark window to the other, as if they were great eyes that would blink at her first if she stared at them long enough. She had to go inside; she knew she did. The realization was not a pleasant one, but it was the only way she could determine whether Stephen had been there at all, and if so, when.

She dismounted and made her way to the dark house, leading the gelding. She patted her vest pocket for a box of matches. Her fingers felt strange to her, as if they'd turned to rubber. She realized, walking toward the broken-down hitching rail, that her legs felt the same way. Her mouth was dry and there was a tightness in her chest that made breathing difficult. Indeed, she could hear her every breath, as if there were two of her there in that dark, overrun yard instead of only one. That the darkened windows monitored her approach without blinking did nothing to ease her mounting apprehension. With fumbling fingers she secured the gelding's rein to the rail.

The first fall of her boot upon the warped planks of the porch caused her to start. She glanced behind at the piebald, but he was safely tethered. His spotted neck was bowed, and he was already tugging at a tuft of new grass poking up from the ground, utterly unconcerned by her or the noise she'd made. His steady, ruminative sounds were oddly soothing. Bucking up her courage, she proceeded along the porch in a soft, even step to the front door.

It wasn't locked, she knew. It had never been kept locked, even while the Wingates lived there. Peaceful, and Star Valley, were temperate places in the otherwise wild Wyoming territory, and there had never been a need for the Wingates or any other residents to bolt their doors against evil that threatened from without. Their evils, she reflected grimly, had come from within themselves.

She gripped the rusted lever. It felt cold and gritty. Unfamiliar. Rallying herself against such foolish fancies, she tipped it down. It gave reluctantly. Metal grated against wood with a dry squeal

and the door slowly opened, revealing the thick
blackness inside the house.

Ivy was about to step into the menacing void
when the cold hand of fear gripped her shoulder
once again and held her back.

"Stephen?" she made herself call out. She was
dismayed that her voice sounded so small and girlish. She swallowed, then tried again. "Stephen?
Are you here?"

From inside the house came a tiny, strangled cry
that might have been a human sound, or that of a
timid, trespassing animal that had decided to flee
rather than to defend its borrowed home. Ivy could
not be sure. The only thing she knew for certain
was that the sound did nothing to allay her renewed trepidation. She licked her lips, although
her tongue was dry as dust and did not help.

"Stephen?" Her repeated call was no more than
a whisper.

The darkness beckoned to her. Fascinated, she
took a step forward, into the house.

The door slammed closed behind her, shutting
out what little light the moon had previously
granted. She didn't even have enough time to
scream before a strong, gloved hand clasped over
her mouth, effectively stifling her. The leather
tasted of salt, sweat and horse. That alone was
enough to convince her that she was not entangled
with a ghost, but with a flesh-and-blood man. And
judging by his size and strength, the man was not
Stephen. She choked on the revolting combination
even as she struggled to free herself from her bru-
tally powerful captor.

Her struggle won her additional restraints as
more invisible hands effectively pinned her flailing
arms against her sides. The odor of unwashed men
surrounded her like a flea-ridden blanket. She

Carole Howey

gagged at the stench and at the rough hand that
pressed hard into her mouth like a bridle bit.

"Quit it, girl," an unfamiliar voice grated at her
ear even as the hold about her arms tightened
painfully. "You can't get loose. We aim to keep you
'til we're through with you, so you might as well
keep still. And it won't do you no good to scream,
'cause there ain't but us to hear you. Unnerstand?"

Ivy went rigid with sheer terror at the sound of
the unfamiliar disembodied voice, and the term
"us." How many of them were there? She could not
even think to breathe, much less reply.

"Unnerstand?" Her captor punctuated his repeated question with a brutal shake of her shoulder. His face was next to hers; his beard beside her
cheek was as scratchy as dried straw. His breath
smelled of rotting teeth.

Ivy felt faint. She managed to nod her head with
a quivering motion. This must have satisfied her
captor, because in a moment she was free again.
Instantly she made a blind dash in what she hoped
was the direction of the front door. From behind
her came a ripe curse, and she tripped over something she could not see.

She was flat on her stomach, dizzy, gasping,
choking on dust. In the next instant she heard an
oath, then felt a crushing force on top of her. The
pressure robbed her of breath and flattened her
against the filthy floor. She thought of apples in a
cider press. She could see them, blood red and
gleaming, dancing before her eyes, surrounded by
darkness. She thought it absurd in the extreme
that she would think of such a thing just then, as
she was very obviously about to die of suffocation.

Then there was nothing.

*   *   *

A dim yellow light throbbed beyond Ivy's eyelids. She turned her head to escape it.

"She's comin' around," a strange, male voice observed in a disinterested drawl.

She realized she was lying on her side on the floor. Something, probably the smell of the air, told her she was still in the ranch house. Her body ached, and she remembered the fall she'd taken, and the crushing force afterward. Every breath hurt; perhaps she had broken a rib or two. She could not tell, nor did she think it mattered much; she was going to die.

She tried to get up but realized that her hands were secured behind her. Her ankles, too, were bound. The only thing she could move was her eyelids, and she lifted them fearfully. It took a moment to focus her eyes in the weak light, and when she did, she beheld three pairs of dirty, worn-out boots, none more than an arm's length away from her nose.

"Who are you?" she croaked. "What do you want of me?"

"I'll ask the questions, girl," a harsh male voice informed her. "Where's your brother? You come here to get somethin' for him, didn't ya?"

"Why don't you ask her one question at a time, Jack?" A rational but equally chilling voice chided him. "She can't hardly breathe, yet."

"Why don't you shut the hell up, Carl?" Jack growled. "Set 'er up. She ain't gonna run far, now. 'Sides, I wanna see her when I talk to 'er. And I want her to see me."

Ivy didn't care for the sound of that. Nevertheless, she was helpless to resist as someone grasped her shoulders with a bruising grip and sat her up with her back to a wall. Grateful as she was for the prop, and to be reclined in a less vulnerable position, she was frightened anew by the aspect of not three but five men before her. The lamp was behind them; she could see only their dark silhouettes. Their very presence polluted the familiar trappings of the family greatroom, and mocked the sense of security she'd always felt in the house.

"Purdy thing, ain't she?" one of the shadows opined.

"Anything in a skirt looks good to you, Moss," another observed. A third man chuckled, but it was not a pleasant sound. She shrank back, wishing she could evaporate into the faded pattern on the wallpaper.

"We ain't gonna hurt you, gal," Carl told her. "We jus' wanna akse you some questions."

Ivy started, then looked down. Stephen's gold! she thought, fear gripping her throat. That had to be what this was about!

"Look at 'er lookin' away," Moss grumbled. "She knows what we want. She knows somethin', too, or she wouldn't be here. Make 'er talk now, Carl, or let's take 'er with us. We been here too long, already."

"Relax, Moss." Jack was calm, but it was a threatening calm, the kind of calm that sent a slow crawl up Ivy's spine, like a big, hairy spider. "Nobody knows we're here 'cept Miss Ivy. And I guess Miss Schoolteacher's real anxious for us to leave her alone." A big, calloused hand came out of the darkness and pulled a long curl out of her neat bun. "She'll tell us what we want to know. You bet she will."

Another pair of legs moved forward in a slow swagger and halted in front of her. Their owner crouched down, reached for her chin, then jerked it up with a quick, rough gesture that hurt her neck.

"Where's yer brother, Missy?" Carl hissed.

Ivy had to make herself breathe. It seemed to her, as she stared into the ominous shadow, that she'd forgotten how.

"I don't know," she whispered, glad that it was the truth.

A bolt of lightning whipped her face, although she was not so much hurt as she was stunned by the force of the effortless blow. It happened so quickly that she could not even cry out.

"Don't lie to me, girl," Carl warned, his faint Southern drawl crackling like a whip. "We trailed him all the way to Peaceful. You're his only kin. Where're you hidin' him?"

Terrified afresh, Ivy choked back her urge to blurt out what she suspected about Stephen and Charity. She wanted the men to vanish, taking their stench and their awful voices and frightening words with them. As eager as she was to be quit of these men, though, she could not put her brother and Noble's sister in jeopardy. She pressed her lips together and shook her head. Hard, strong fingers grasped her face, threatening to crush the bones inside with their mean force.

"I spent six years of my life in the territorial prison for that gold, lady," Jack warned, "and I aim to get it one way or the other. I'd rather have it in my pocket, but I'll take it in trade right here, if I have to." His other hand shot out and seized Ivy's lapel. In the time it took her to gasp, he'd yanked it back and ripped open her shirt, sending bone buttons pinging everywhere. The top of her left breast was exposed down to the ribbon trim of her chemise.

Ivy couldn't cover herself, as her hands were tied fast behind her. She tried to pray, for she knew screaming would not avail her, but a mad thought

41

occurred to her suddenly—maybe lying would.

"Wait!"

Carl put a restraining hand on Jack's arm, and his grip relaxed. "Now you're bein' sensible," he said. "Where's your baby brother?"

Ivy, free of all threatening hands, tried to think. She had to send them someplace believable and far enough away to buy her sufficient time to get away. And she had to hope it was someplace Stephen hadn't thought of taking Charity.

"Canada," she said evenly, hoping the men could not hear the deceit in her voice. "He took the gold and headed north. Saskatchewan, I think." Stephen had always hated the cold, and his choice, she knew, were one forced upon him, would have been to head south, which was exactly the direction she herself was going to go as soon as she was free of these brutal men.

Carl hooted a laugh. "See?" he said. "I knew she knew about the gold!"

Ivy hoped she hadn't overplayed herself, but it was too late to worry about it. She had made her decision. There was no recanting her story.

"She's lyin'." Jack sounded skeptical.

"Why should I lie?" Ivy argued, finding renewed strength in her mounting desperation. "Stephen's been nothing but trouble to me for years, and he washed his hands of Peaceful long ago. If he's done something wrong now, well, he'll just have to face up to it on his own. I don't owe him anything. He said he'd found that gold. Did he steal it from you?"

"Never you mind," Jack told her. "It's ours. He has it. We aim to get it back."

"Let's take her with us," Moss said brightly. "It'd be nice to have us a woman to do the cookin' and cleanin' up after."

"I bet she makes up a real fine bed," Jack drawled

in agreement, still holding her torn garment. The others laughed cautiously. Apparently Jack was the man they most feared. Ivy had no trouble understanding why.

She pressed her lips together. This was not going at all as she had hoped. But then, improvisation had never been one of her strengths. She found herself looking up at the shadow that was Jack, wishing she could see his face yet somehow relieved that she could not.

"I think she likes you, Jack," Moss volunteered. The other men laughed at his remark, but Jack did not. Ivy looked down again quickly. She could feel Jack's gaze on her like a case of small pox, and she wished she could cover herself up again to hide from it. Among decent men, she always felt like soiled linen. Among these men, she felt like an outhouse.

"Let's go." Carl's voice was terse. Apparently he didn't like the way Jack looked at her, either. "We got miles to cover."

"We ought to stay here for the night," Jack told him, fingering Ivy's collar with a strange tenderness she found terrifying. "We can't make no time 'til daylight, anyway. 'Sides, I want to bed down with somethin' soft, tonight. Somethin' sweet. Somethin' that smells like violets."

Ivy's stomach lurched as Jack's rough fingers grazed her throat. She wondered, in a detached way, how Jack could even smell her violet water, surrounded as he was by his own foul reek. Did she wear some sort of a mark, she wondered, that proclaimed her soiled state? Had she duped herself into believing that all of Peaceful had not perceived it?

The silence in the small room pounded in Ivy's ears. She was going numb, she realized, from her

43

feet up. Her future, thanks to Stephen and her concern for him, was utterly out of her hands. If she were capable of feeling anything she would probably cry, but as she would rather die than to allow these creatures to see her break down, she was glad her senses had been deadened. She closed her eyes.

"There's five of us, Jack," Carl reminded the man whose fingers toyed with her neck and the top of her bosom. "The rule is we share. Everything. So don't be thinkin' you're gonna keep her all to yourself."

Dear God, wasn't it enough that one of these animals was going to use her? A sob caught in her throat, but she swallowed it quickly. If she thought about it, she would surely go mad. She wished she could hate Stephen for his part in this ghastly drama, but she could no more hate him than she could hate Noble Smith.

She rallied. There were five of them, and only one of her. But they hadn't had her yet. Fighting would not avail her, she knew. But perhaps her wit would prevail where her physical strength was found wanting.

"Come on, gal." Jack took hold of her arms and hauled her to her feet with frightening, painful, ease. He hoisted her onto his shoulder with no more concern than he would have for a sack of grain. "I'll be about an hour," he told Carl in a laconic tone that seemed to dare the other man to argue. "It's gonna get a might loud in there, so some o' you ladies might want to clear out."

Ivy stiffened with fear at his words and tried to shut out the crude chorus of laughter from Jack's comrades. If her resourcefulness failed her, there was every chance that each of them would have more than a nodding acquaintance with her by morning. She had only her wits to prevent that growing certainty from becoming a reality.

Chapter Four

Jack dumped Ivy unceremoniously on the bed and threw the bolt on the door. Ivy watched from her helpless position, coughing up dust as the big man lit the lamp on the nightstand. Tied as she was she could scarcely move, except to rub her cheek against the musty but familiar patchwork quilt beneath her. The light grew brighter as Jack replaced the glass chimney, and Ivy wished at once that he had left the room dark.

It was her very own room he'd brought her to, the one place in her life where she had known peace and innocence, the place where she had wept and healed and could still pretend that none of it had ever happened, the place to which she still retreated, in her mind, when she could no longer endure the pain of her memories.

Now, thanks to Stephen and Noble, even that sanctuary woud be denied her.

Jack was as large as his shadow had suggested, and as repulsive as every ugly deed he had no doubt committed to consign him to half a dozen years in the penitentiary. His face might at one time have been pleasant enough, but there was a stone hardness to his sharp, aging features that the shadows cast by the small lamp only enhanced, giving him a distinctly demonic aspect. His looks, in any case, were irrelevant: He was a cruel and vicious degenerate. Bedding him would be no easier or more pleasant for her if he were an Adonis.

By force of will alone, Ivy restrained a shudder. This was going to be difficult. Quite possibly the most difficult thing she had ever done, even though she'd thought she'd already done the impossible.

Laurel.

Thinking of Laurel somehow gave her new strength, and new resolve. She forced herself to look at Jack, who was standing by the bed leering down at her, unfastening his trousers, and she managed to see Laurel instead.

She smiled.

Jack smiled too, but it was not a comforting expression. Indeed, it was anything but.

"You think you smile at me, I'll go easy on you," he said, his gravelly voice thick with lurid anticipation. "But I got just enough meanness in me, after six years in prison, to take it all out on you, pretty lady. Your brother, he's gone with that gold. I doubt I'll ever see him or it again. But right now, I don't even mind that so much, because I got you in trade for it. And I intend to take it, schoolmarm. Every last dime of it."

Ivy swallowed her fear. "But you—we only have an hour," she murmured, keeping her voice low and steady but for a single betraying tremor. "Carl said—"

46

"You think I give a damn what Carl or any o' them other shitfaces say?" he interrupted with a hearty, unpleasant laugh. "Let one of 'em think they can two-step on in here and take you away from me before I'm good 'n ready. He'll see right quick who he's dealin' with. But Carl ain't stupid. He knows I'm the best gun he's got, and I got more sand than all them others put together. 'Sides," he added, giving her a sideways look meant, no doubt, to frighten her, and succeeding. "By the time I'm finished, likely none a' them boys'll even want to look at you."

Jack pulled her up by her shoulders again as if she were a rag doll rather than a human being and smothered her with his kiss. She had hoped to lure Jack in, to make him think she wanted him, and thus to purchase herself some additional time in which to find a way out of her plight. She realized, as the outlaw pushed her back on the bed and fell on top of her, that he didn't care whether she pretended to want him or not. He seemed actually to delight in the fact that he could abuse and humiliate her, and that there was nothing she could do to prevent him from having his way.

She tried to envision Laurel while the monster clawed at her clothing, but the sweet, dark-haired wood sprite had never seemed farther away.

"Scream!"

It seemed that the whispered command had come from within her own head.

"Scream, Ivy!"

It was not her imagination but a voice.

The weight of her attacker was yanked away. Her eyes misted and she greedily gulped in new air.

"Scream, dammit!" the oddly familiar voice insisted again.

47

Her vision cleared. The voice, she realized, belonged to Noble Smith. He was standing above the bed, brandishing the butt end of a big Colt revolver. She was never so glad to see anyone in her whole life.

She screamed.

"Again!"

It was easy to obey his command. She was terrified anew, for they were both in serious danger, should any of those men choose to come through the door. Jack's limp bulk slipped to the floor with a loud thump, an exclamation point at the end of Ivy's calamitous noise.

There was a sharp rapping at the door, and the sound of the latch being tried unsuccessfully.

"Jack!" It was Carl's voice on the other side. Ivy recognized it. "You all right in there?"

Noble slapped his hand over Ivy's mouth before she could utter another sound.

"Go 'way!" he growled in a passable imitation of the rough voice of the man who now lay on the floor at their feet, unconscious.

Noble relaxed his tense grip on Ivy's mouth, but he did not release her entirely. She searched his face in wonder. He sent her a look of warning with his dark eyes and pursed his mouth in a silent "shh."

A moment of quiet followed. It seemed to last forever.

"Jack?" The muffled inquiry was more tentative, this time.

Noble arched one eyebrow at Ivy and his hand fell away from her mouth at last.

"Carl," she supplied in a trembling whisper.

"I said go 'way, Carl!" Noble insisted, once again aping the fallen man's voice. Ivy whimpered helpfully.

"If you say so."

Noble drew in and released a carefully silent sigh. He met Ivy's gaze again, but his features demonstrated no relief.

"Keep making noises," he advised under his breath. "Maybe bounce the bed a little. I'll get the horses."

"Noble!" she hissed at his back.

He turned to her. "What?"

Thank you, she wanted to say, but the look in his eyes, angry, almost cold, stopped her. Besides, she wasn't free yet.

"Untie me!"

He started to say something, then appeared to think better of it. He shook his head twice and disappeared out of the window.

Ivy alternately cursed Noble Smith for leaving her there bound and helpless, and prayed for his safe and swift return. An eternity crawled by until Noble hopped back in again. She was hoarse from crying out and from sheer terror that Jack would revive, or that the men in the greatroom would break down the door.

Without once glancing at Ivy, Noble thumped the prone outlaw on the back of the head again so hard that she heard the crack of Jack's skull. He was bleeding from the wound Noble had given him, she noticed, but she could not spare any pity for the man. He would have beaten and raped her but for Noble's intervention, she knew.

And they were not out of danger yet, either of them.

Noble sliced through the rawhide thongs binding her wrists and ankles without comment. Ivy had little time to note the soreness of her joints, and Noble seemed far more interested in getting her safely out of the window than in the condition of her injuries. He was as cold and remote as he had been in the schoolhouse that afternoon, and she wanted to strike him for his indifference even as she wanted to hug him for his intervention. That contradiction confused her sufficiently to persuade her to obey each of his instructions without challenge until they were safely out of the window and some distance away from the house.

He pulled her along by the arm as if she were a pet on a leash, into the darkness. Her blouse was in tatters; she wanted to effect some sort of repair for modesty's sake. She yanked her arm away from Noble's insistent grip and paused as they gained the corral, trying to adjust the shreds into at least a decent covering of her bosom.

"What the hell are you doing?"

She couldn't see Noble's face in the darkness, but his voice was taut with irritation.

"Trying to fix my blouse!" she snapped at him, feeling as frayed and tattered as the garment about her. "I can't even cover my—"

"Damn it, Ivy, if we wait here another thirty seconds, you won't have to worry about covering anything! Now come on!" He took hold of her again, his fingers digging pitilessly into the yielding flesh of her upper arm.

"You'll ride with me," he said shortly, in a tone that brooked no protest. "We'll lead the pie. I've loosened all their cinches; they'll have a hell of a time following us if they try. Leg up?" He bent over and linked his fingers, providing a stepping stool for her to mount his waiting mare.

Annoyance edged out the last trace of her fear.

"I can ride myself, on the piebald," she argued, taking a step backward.

In the darkness, she saw Noble's broad shoulders square themselves.

"And get lost in the dark trying to follow me? Don't be an idiot, Ivy. We can't risk it. Get on the mare. Now."

Ivy was nettled, and she felt very peculiar, besides. She had just been rescued moments before from a truly hopeless and harrowing circumstance, and here she was arguing with her savior. She should be grateful and acquiescent, but instead she was shaking and livid. She felt as if she had no control whatever over her actions or her words. It was just Noble's ill luck that he was the handy scapegoat. Perhaps later she would feel sorry for him, but just now she was indignant.

"By what right do you presume to order me about, Noble Smith?" she demanded in a whisper. "I said I would ride the piebald, and I—"

"Dammit, Ivy!" Noble took two lunging steps toward her, his head down. Before she could think, he caught her full in the stomach with his shoulder and lifted her off the ground. Had the wind not been knocked out of her, she would have screamed. She was still gasping for air when he deposited her across the front of his saddle, face down. Her bruised ribs protested the treatment with a shock of pain, but she still could not cry out.

In a moment, Noble was in the saddle, one knee pressed against the back of her legs, the other across her shoulders. No! she wanted to shout, her terror renewed at the thought of being bounced along in that manner as Noble galloped them off into the night. But there was not enough breath in her lungs to accomplish even a feeble protest. Noble's legs jerked as he dug his heels into the mare's sides, and the animal was off at a dead run.

Ivy's side throbbed with each cadence of the mare's stride, and in the reeling darkness she lost her sense of right side up and upside down. The most expedient thing to do, under the circumstances, she thought, was to faint. She wished she could, but the constant, mounting ache in her body combined with the sheer terror inspired by the blind, precarious gallop made such relief unlikely. She bit down hard on her lip to keep herself from sobbing. Noble Smith would regret his treatment of her, she vowed in silence, closing her eyes tightly. She would make sure of it, even if it was the last thing she did in this life.

The report of gunfire pursuing them did not surprise Noble. The nearness of it, however, did. He'd hoped to be out of range before the men at the Wingate ranch discovered the escape, especially since Ivy was draped down on either side of the mare, a perfect mark for a wild, lucky shot. A bullet hummed by his ear like a dangerous, stinging insect and he hunkered down to make himself as small a target as possible. He breathed a silent curse. *If either of us gets shot on account of your stubbornness, Ivy Wingate . . .*

The sound of the shots grew dimmer, though, and soon ceased altogether. Noble suspected, grinning in spite of himself, that the men were discovering that their saddles had been tampered with. He breathed a sigh of relief and relaxed his tense hold on the rein.

The mare slowed in response to his body's commands. There was no need to maintain a breakneck pace anymore. By the time the men adjusted their saddles, there would be no chance that they could track them in the darkness. Noble knew the area; he doubted their assailants did. He also knew he hadn't been seen, so he could just double on back to his place and act like he didn't know anything, even if the strangers came to call after daybreak asking questions. There was nothing to tie him to the business out at the Wingate ranch. Nothing, that is, except for Ivy.

Ivy!

Noble reined the mare to a stop and slid from the saddle. Ivy remained in her dangling, prone position, unmoving. Noble hesitated. It was too dark to see if she'd been hurt, and there wasn't much he could do for her there in the woods even if she was. Looking at her, he felt a twinge of regret that he'd tackled her and slung her across the back of the horse the way he had. When she came to, she wouldn't thank him for it, that was sure. But dammit, she hadn't really given him a choice.

"Ivy?" he said softly, touching her limp shoulder. "Can you hear me?"

He slid his fingers lightly along down her neck until they touched her cheek. "God, you're still so soft."

The new grass around Witherspoon's fence smelled of spring. His thumb etched lazy circles against her cheek.

"You're so soft," he marvelled in a cracked whisper, wanting to cry somehow. "Just like a cloud, I expect."

"You never touched a cloud," she chided him.

"Not 'til now."

Noble sucked in a deep draught of chilly night air and drew his hand away from her cheek, mortified at the betrayal of his own flesh. He hadn't wanted to touch her. He knew nothing good could come of it. But he didn't seem able to stop himself. He pressed his forehead against the warmth of his saddle and closed his eyes.

"What happened to us, Ivy?" he whispered to the

leather as a familiar ache descended in his gut. "We should have been married, and had babies. I loved you so much, so much. . . ."

The pain swelled until it stabbed at the very backs of his eyes, as if Satan himself were prodding them with his pitchfork. He jerked his head up and squared his shoulders into stiff right angles with his body, staring hard into the darkness to fight off unwanted tears. Damn me, he thought. Damn me, my eyes and my hands. Damn Pa, and damn Ivy's ma. Damn Ma, and Ivy's pa. Damn Stephen, and Charity. Damn—damn everything.

He wanted to include Ivy in his comprehensive denunciation, but he was unable to fit her name in, somehow. He straightened and shook his head, wishing he could dislodge the thoughts running around inside of it. He took in a deep breath of cool, sweet air and felt better for it. Encouraged, he took in another. This one, however, yielded a faint trace of violets.

Noble carried Ivy into his house, deliberately thinking nothing. She was still out cold, so she couldn't fight him or ask a lot of questions that he had no wish to answer. He laid her on his own bed and stayed with her just long enough to ascertain that she had no serious injuries, then he escaped to the barn to tend to their horses.

He risked a small light, deeming it safe and knowing he could not perform his chore without one. Unsaddling and grooming a horse was a mindless task, but bone weary as he was, it was enough to keep his mind off of the woman in his bed. He tended his mare first, as Gentile's piebald seemed contented to stick his nose in the feed bucket. It didn't take long. He decided she could wait until morning to have her hooves picked out.

Giving the mare a last, fond pat, he turned to the gelding.

The first thing he noticed was the bedroll, then the saddlebags. They were full, and secured for a long, hard ride.

Odd, he thought, reaching for them. Ivy was to have returned to town that same evening. What could be in the saddlebags?

His curiosity piqued, Noble worked the buckle on one. Ivy would be furious, he knew, if she guessed that he'd looked inside, but she was safely abed in the house. She need never know. He flipped the bag open and thrust his hand inside.

Clothing. Extra shirts, stockings and underthings, and several clean handkerchiefs. The idea that Ivy would not think of making a trip, even a short one, without spare handkerchiefs made him smile. Purest white, all neatly pressed and folded into squares, they seemed hopelessly incongruous to their rough surroundings. He felt foolish for his impulse, but he held them against his cheek for a moment anyway. Somehow it satisfied him, even comforted him, to discover that they smelled of violets.

She won't miss one. As if of their own volition, Noble's fingers peeled off the top handkerchiefs and pulled out the one in the middle. *It will hold the scent the longest.* He stuffed it quickly into his shirt, feeling like a kid who'd just swiped an apple from the general store even though he had a pocket full of pennies. Shaking off a brief spasm of guilt, he jammed the rest of Ivy's things willy-nilly back into the pouch.

Noble suddenly wondered why she had packed them in the first place. It looked as if she planned on being gone for a spell. It looked as if she were making a getaway, in fact, and not thinking about

Carole Howey

returning to town at all. He frowned as he opened
the other bag, half-knowing what he'd find inside.

A pocket knife, a tin of matches, a small wallet
containing a few coins, probably all the money the
schoolteacher could get her hands on at short notice. A small bundle wrapped in brown paper and
tied with string, dark with grease stains: Food. His
gaze strayed once again to the tight bedroll secured behind the gelding's saddle.

Fury seized him as he totaled the evidence at
hand.

Chapter Five

Ivy felt as if a mule had kicked her high in the side, just beneath her right breast. The pain was so clear she could see it even with her eyes closed and taste it even though her mouth was dry as sand. A blessing disguised as agony. Far easier to endure physical pain, she knew, than to be plagued by memories.

The pressure of her corset was torture. She wished she could loosen it, or take it off completely. She did not want to breathe, for she knew the pain would be redoubled with each breath, but neither could she stop herself from doing so. She experimented, trying first many shallow breaths, then, finding it to be uncomfortable, one deep breath. That, she quickly discovered, was agony, a sharp, poisoned arrow piercing her lung.

She cried out loud, a single, plaintive sob.

"It hurts, does it, Ivy?" Noble's voice startled her.

57

He sounded cold and remote, even for Noble.

Ivy opened her eyes. When the room stopped spinning, she was able to focus on Noble's tall, lean form, standing by her. His big hands were at his hips, their long fingers splayed and tense. She could not bring herself to look at his face, sure that what she would see there would only increase her pain.

"N-Noble," she managed. "What happened? Where are we?"

"We're at my place, which is all you need to know at the moment. I'll ask the questions, for now."

Ivy knew Noble meant to sound uncompromising, and she had to admit that he was succeeding. For the moment, though, except for her side being on fire, she knew she was safe, warm and as comfortable as she could expect to be, under the circumstances. She merely nodded in acquiescence and closed her eyes again.

Looking down at Ivy, Noble grew suddenly hesitant. He had not noticed that stain on the side of her face, and he could not tell if it was dirt or a bruise. And her clothing was—well, ruined. His gaze drifted downward. It lingered on the soft swelling of her bared breast capped by a teasing hint of the white eyelet lace of her chemise. She drew a shallow breath and the swelling rose, taking his heart with it.

He looked away quickly, ashamed. He was no better than those men who had bound her hand and foot, meaning to rape her. His shame was doubly branding because he'd thought, at first, listening outside the Wingate ranch house, that Ivy had gone to the place knowing that those men were waiting for her, or for Stephen. It hadn't taken long for him to discover the truth, and then only a little longer to decide what to do about it.

He fumbled with the blanket, folded at the foot of the bed. His hands trembled as he shook it out and laid it on top of her. He could not think clearly with that delicate vista before his eyes. Beneath the blanket, Ivy sighed.

"Thank you, Noble," she murmured, and her soft voice sent a shimmer of heat along his spine. "What—" She winced. "What did you want to ask me?"

What had he wanted to ask her? He couldn't think.

"You're hurt," he got out at last. "Is it the bruise on your face? Or is it—is it somewhere else?"

She was the one on the bed; why did he feel like the one in distress?

Ivy pressed her fingers to her cheek. Their whiteness emphasized the discoloration of the flesh beneath, and her gesture told him she had not thought about her face at all.

"No," she said quietly, as if it would pain her to speak any louder. "My side. I think my—my ribs might be broken."

And he had pitched her across his saddle face first!

"God, Ivy," he muttered swiftly, kneeling beside the bed. "I might have killed you! Why didn't you say something?" He pushed the covers aside and probed the area gently, ever so gently, with his fingers. Doc had taught him how. Doc had taught him lots of things, after his pa had left, taking with him any hope Noble had had of attending medical school.

Ivy's quick gasp commanded his attention, abbreviating his fleeting, unwanted reverie.

"Right there." She whispered a sob as his fingers rested lightly against the third and fourth ribs.

"Is it bad?"

She closed her mouth tightly, but a film of glistening perspiration above her lip gave her away.

"I'm probably just being a baby," she said in a light tone that didn't fool Noble for a minute. "You know I never could stand pain." She looked up at him, apology written in her remarkable green eyes.

Noble realized just how close they were, and that he was touching her in a very intimate place. His face heated, and he was glad there was only one small lamp lit. He swallowed and withdrew his hands.

"Broken ribs hurt like hell." He tried to keep his tone light, if not indifferent. "My pa broke his once, and you should have heard him yell. In fact, maybe you did."

Dammit, why did he have to bring up his father? He sensed a curtain between them all of a sudden, a heavy, black drape that did not allow light to pass either way. Ivy's pretty features went rigid, as if they'd frozen solid at his words. Noble looked away. He smothered a curse aimed at his father, even though for all he knew, the old man was long dead.

"There's nothing I can do for you if they're broken," he said woodenly. "Your corset will work just the same as a plaster, maybe better. The only thing that fixes bruised or broken ribs is time. Time and rest."

Time and rest. Ivy sighed, although the exercise caused fresh anguish. Noble might as well have told her to drink liquid gold. Time and rest were two things she could not afford.

"There's a fresh shirt in my saddlebags," she breathed, drawing the blanket up about her chin. "You didn't bring them in, did you?"

Noble got to his feet. The bed was only as high

as his knees. It reminded her of how very tall he was.

"I saw them," he answered, ignoring her question on purpose, it seemed to her. "That wasn't all I saw."

Ivy wished she could hide from the iciness in Noble's voice. She stared at the hem stitching on the blanket. She did not answer him.

"You weren't aiming to go back to town again once you'd been out to the ranch, were you, Ivy?"

A new pain tore at her insides, one that had nothing whatever to do with her sore ribs. She could not speak, nor could she meet his gaze. She could, however, feel his accusing stare upon her like a searing brand. She heard him sigh, and the sound of the breath leaving his body drew tears to the back of her eyes.

"I just want to know one thing, Ivy, although why I should trust your answer, I don't know."

She waited, her face burning.

"Do you know where Stephen took Charity?"

"No," she whispered, feeling empty.

"Look at me."

Anger, shame and fear battled within her, but she obeyed his gentle command. His wide mouth was set in a firm, tense line, but his dark eyes revealed a glimmer of softness. Of sadness. She thought at once of Laurel. *Oh, Noble, if only you knew. If only I could tell you. . . .*

"Why were you going to run away?" he demanded quietly. "Just because that's what a Wingate does?"

Ivy saw red.

"It wasn't a Wingate that ran off with my mother, was it?" She couldn't hold back. How dared Noble look down his nose at her, when it had been his own father, Ben Smith, who had deprived her of her mother when she'd most needed a mother's care? She was equal to his gaze, then. More than equal to it. It was his turn to look away.

"I'm sorry. I shouldn't have said that." His apology was formal, as if she were nothing more than a stranger he'd accidentally bumped into on the street.

"I don't know why I should expect any better of you," she retorted, wanting to hurt him with her words as he had hurt her.

"Damn it, I said I'm sorry, Ivy! If you expect me to fawn over you just because you're hurt—"

"I don't expect anything from you, Noble Smith, but simple courtesy. And maybe a little respect. I don't like this situation any more than you do. I wish Stephen and Charity hadn't run off together, but they have. I can't help that, any more than I could help—help what happened ten years ago. Neither can you. And the sooner you stop pretending to be God—"

"Me?" he exploded. "Me, pretending to be God? That's not how I see it. I'm not the one holing myself up in a schoolhouse and looking down my nose at everyone else in town, as if nobody's quite good enough for me to waste my time on. I'm not the one who set myself up to be some damn paragon of virtue trying to make up for the loose ways of my ma, and the fact that she abandoned her own husband and two children and ran off with a respected family man—"

"Damn you, Noble Smith!" Ivy shot up from the bed, ignoring the sharp stab of pain in her side, and hurled the pillow at Noble with as much force as she could muster. "Damn you!"

To her outrage, he caught the object with ease, although he did take two steps backward. She looked about desperately, but there was nothing else she could throw at him. He knew nothing of the shame and the disgrace that were hers and hers alone. How she wished she could tell him, just to see the look of horror on his face. She wished she could kill him. She wished she could die.

But she would do none of those things. Instead she flailed her fists, raining furious but ineffectual blows against his hard, unyielding chest. Each swing caused a stab in her own side, but she didn't care. That pain meant nothing, compared to the hurt inspired by Noble's cruel pronouncement.

"Ivy—" Noble caught her wrists in a grip that was as firm as his voice. She struggled. He brought her arms down to her sides, grunting from the effort.

"Let me go! You—you—"

"Ivy!"

"You awful man! I hate you!" she sobbed. The pain grew worse, and her face was wet with hot tears.

"Ivy, stop it. You mean to hurt me, but you'll hurt yourself worse."

Noble's arms surrounded her, bands of warmth that brought her storm of fury to an abrupt end. Ivy, exhausted by her exhibition, laid her head against the soft lapel of his shirt, savoring the heat of his chest beneath it, and uttered a broken sigh.

I wouldn't ever hurt you, Ivy. You know that, don't you?

Had the boy Noble spoken those words to her, so very long ago? Did Noble the man know how many times, and how many ways, he had hurt her since? Did Noble the man know just how wonderful she felt, nonetheless, sheltered in his arms?

Ivy breathed deeply again. Noble smelled of cedar and of something warm and sweet that she could only identify as him. She hoped he would not soon let her go. Despite everything that had driven them apart over the years, there was still something genuine and perfect about Noble's embrace. Her body, much to her own surprise, had not forgotten the sensation. She wondered if his had.

His arms remained secure about her for a time. She did not move. She scarcely dared to breathe. Noble's chest, against her cheek, expanded and contracted three times. His heart thumped a strong, steady rhythm. She felt a light pressure against the top of her head. She heard him gasp in a quick breath, and the gentle weight lifted.

"Damn," he muttered. His arms released her from their tender prison. She backed away, unable to look him in the face.

"What you said about my ma, that wasn't fair, Noble," she accused, striving to keep her voice from shaking. "And you know it."

He let out a hard breath and turned away from her.

"Nothing's fair in this life," he declared bitterly. "Haven't you learned that by now, Ivy? If you're expecting it to start with me, you'll be waiting a damn long time. I've been disappointed once or twice myself, you know, and I don't set much store in fairness anymore. Sometimes I can't believe I ever did. Deep down, I don't guess you do either. Or am I wrong?"

Ivy continued to stare at Noble's boots. He wasn't wrong. He was more right than he knew. At least, she would have thought so even as recently as an hour ago. But just as she had begun to despair at the ranch of escaping Jack and the others, Noble had appeared. There, in that desperate circumstance, stripped of all the encumbrances of their tangled past, Noble and she had fallen with alarming ease into their familiar, almost mystical childhood union. Understanding without words, as if speech were far too clumsy a method for them to convey their thoughts to one another, or, indeed, as if communicating by discourse might actually baffle or deceive them as it seemed to confuse everyone else.

And he had prevented those men from using her. He had saved her . . . that time.

"I didn't believe in it for a long time," she whispered, so heavy with fatigue that she needed to sit down on Noble's bed again. "But I think it might be time to reconsider."

She found the courage to look him in the face again, only to discover that he quickly looked away from her.

"We'll have to get you back to town." His tone was curt, his features blank as stone. "It won't do to have it get about that you spent the night here at my place."

"I'm not going back to Peaceful."

His head jerked up, sending a shock of sable hair into his face. "What?"

"I made my good-byes." She gingerly eased herself back into a reclining position and closed her eyes. "I meant to go looking for Stephen and Charity. I wanted to go myself. I hoped to find them before you caught up to us, to try and work things out so you and Stephen wouldn't kill each other when you did meet."

"Well, things have changed." Noble's voice was frosty as winter. "I followed you out there and found you, and now—"

"And just why did you do that?" Ivy opened one eye to regard him again. "I meant to ask you before."

Looking down at her, Noble felt a rush of telling

warmth fill his face. "Never you mind, why I did that!" he snapped. "Could be I didn't trust you. And it's a good thing I didn't, as it turns out, or you'd have been dinner for five hungry men, wouldn't you?"

"Don't you trust me, Noble?"

She would ignore his question, damn her. Well, two could play at that game.

"I'm going after Charity and Stephen," he insisted, directing what he hoped was an uncompromising look at her as she lay on his bed. "And I'm not taking you with me."

"Did I ask you to?"

Her question was tranquil as a spring afternoon on a soft green meadow, and it set up a whole host of alarms in Noble's mind. He pressed his lips tightly together, hoping to keep his emotions in check.

"You're going back to town." He employed the tone he always used on Charity when she behaved foolishly, hoping it would work on Ivy. "You're hurt. You can't ride with broken ribs anyway."

"Who says they're broken? They hurt, sure. I won't deny that. But I just need a night's rest."

Lord, he wanted to shake her!

"Oh, and then you'll be ready for a long, hard ride to God knows where?" he challenged her. "With a few dollars, a tin of matches, a couple spare shirts and five hankies?"

"You went through my bags? You only said you saw them!"

Good. At least he could get a rise out of her.

"Leave Stephen and Charity to me, Ivy." He stared her down, although with that pilfered handkerchief in his shirt burning into his chest, it was a great temptation to look away. "I won't kill him, if he hasn't hurt Charity. I promise."

Her green eyes narrowed. "But how can I be sure he won't kill you?"

Several thoughts occurred to Noble at her question, and he gave her a quick, whimsical grin. "Would that bother you so much?"

Why did his heart do a two-step when she looked away from him in confusion?

"You needn't worry," she told him in a firm, quiet voice. "I won't be going with you. Since I know my brother a bit better than you do, I'm sure I'll have more success doing this my own way rather than following your instruction. I am going, Noble."

"Like hell, you are!"

She closed her eyes as if she were closing the subject along with them.

"I don't see how you can prevent me."

Noble stared at her hard. He didn't either, at the moment. But he was not about to let her know that. And he sure as hell was going to try.

Chapter Six

The shaved pine rail was worn smooth by time and the elements, and Ivy's shoe pinched unbearably. She'd walked this rail, or one like it, dozens of times. She couldn't say why this time was different, but it was. She licked her dry lips, wondering why the ground had never seemed so far away before.

She glanced to her right, the public side of the Witherspoon fence, and saw the back of a tall young man. Somehow, in her dream, she knew it was Noble. Not the grown up Noble who had faced her with such cold contempt in the schoolhouse, but the boy Noble, intense and tender, mocking and confident. The Noble she loved. The Noble she'd been born to love, and would die loving.

She balanced herself and stood up, filled with the most peculiar sensation that she'd done this very same thing before, under the very same circumstances. She could even predict, as she stepped care-

fully, arms outstretched, along the narrow rail, precisely when she would hear Noble's startled young voice calling her name. Precisely when her foot would lose its way and send her tumbling from the fence, toward the new grass, toward Noble's outstretched arms.

"Ivy! Ivy Wingate, if you don't wake snakes!"

Wake . . . wake . . .

She fell.

Wake.

Ivy opened her eyes to pale daylight. The dream had disoriented her, as it usually did, but in a few seconds she remembered that she was at Noble's ranch, in Noble's room. In Noble's bed.

But Noble was not there.

Remembering her tender ribs, she sat up slowly. She was surprised and pleased to discover that the pain had diminished. Perhaps they were not broken after all. Encouraged, she lowered her feet to the floor and felt the cold, splintered planks through her stockings.

Odd. She did not recall having removed her boots, nor having Noble do it for her.

Outside, a rooster uttered a half-hearted attempt at heralding the sun.

"You're a little late," Ivy observed aloud with a small laugh. The sound of her voice echoed in the plain, austere room. Ivy listened until all was still again. She shivered.

"Noble?" she called tentatively, then waited.

No response. Wondering why she was not surprised, Ivy got to her feet. All things considered, she felt remarkably fine, if a little hungry. Well, that was to be expected. She never had eaten the supper Mrs. Quinlan had wrapped up for her. If Noble would not accommodate her with some breakfast, she would have to manage something else, and soon. She sniffed. Noble was not cooking anything right now, not even coffee. Nor had he, any time recently.

The house, she decided, was far too quiet.

She looked about for her boots, but they were nowhere in evidence. That was odd, and a little disturbing. Despite the angry protest of her sore ribs, she got down to look under the bed. Along with a collection of dust bolls were what looked like Noble's best shoes, shining even through a thin layer of fine, gritty dirt. They were far too big for her, but they would serve to keep her from getting splinters as she went from room to room in search of Noble and her own boots.

She was not too surprised to discover that the house was neat and clean, for the most part, except for the same dust lightly coating Noble's shoes. The pale, golden-brown film was a fact of life in this part of the country, though, and had been the bane of every housewife Ivy had ever known for as long as she could recall. The furnishings were exactly as Ivy had remembered. Hannah Smith had been proud of her heirloom Philadelphia furniture, keeping it polished and oiled to almost-new condition.

Hannah had been dead for nearly two years, but obviously someone, either Noble or Charity, maintained her rigid routine of preservation. From what Ivy knew of Charity, having been her teacher for better than five years, she somehow doubted that it was her.

Charity was pretty and smart, with a sunny disposition. But she was also somewhat vain and self-centered, and by all reports her older brother indulged her recklessly. Ivy could not imagine the girl exerting herself over much more than braiding her hair or sewing lace on her pinafores. Nor could she imagine Noble constraining her to do more than that.

It was immediately obvious to Ivy that neither Noble nor his mother had seen fit to ever change a thing about the rooms she remembered so clearly from her childhood, when the Smiths and the Wingates had visited one another with congenial regularity. The Queen Anne settee facing the fireplace, its claret satin-ribbon upholstery faded with age, still dominated the front parlor. The benevolent old grandfather clock, notorious for keeping atrocious time, stood silent sentry by the front door. Obviously, it no longer kept any time at all. Numerous other familiar pieces greeted her gaze, eerie reminders of happier times. Ivy drew a sigh and, realizing that she had no wish to encourage further memories, proceeded back toward the kitchen.

Noble was not there, either. Nor had the kitchen been used recently. Hannah's old Staffordshire dishes, some now venerably chipped, stood lined up in blue-and-white regiments in the open cupboard. The huge, black, cast-iron stove was cold, and the enamel coffeepot was still hanging amid the jungle of pans and kettles above it. Her ma had always envied Hannah Smith's kitchen, Ivy remembered with a phantom spasm of pain, for its size and modern conveniences. Pa had always had a distrust of such fripperies. Funny though, that he'd purchased and installed a cooking stove less than a year after Ma and Ben Smith had eloped together. He never said anything about it, but Ivy, who quickly became accustomed to its wondrous ways, suspected that he'd done it less for her convenience in preparing the family meals than to spite his runaway wife.

A noise outside drew her attention, and she

pushed back the blue gingham curtains of the window above the sink. A quick perusal of the yard revealed nothing unusual, but the noise had sounded suspiciously like the throwing of a recalcitrant bolt of a big door, perhaps the barn. Relieved to be out of the lonely house, Ivy hurried outside, scuffling along in Noble's big shoes, to investigate.

The early morning breeze rustled the rangy pines, drowning any noise Ivy might have made as she moved along the garden fence toward the dark, weathered barn. She rounded the side to find the door was open wide. The stink of fresh horse dung nearly overwhelmed the sweet aroma of hay.

It had been a long time since Ivy had been around animals; she'd sold off their remaining stock after Pa's death, when Stephen left home. She could not have maintained the place herself, nor could she have afforded to hire help and expect to earn enough to keep it going. Besides, she'd all but left ranch life behind when she'd taken the teaching position in Peaceful. She missed the close contact with horses and other creatures she'd learned to respect, if not exactly love, but the strong odor wafting forth from the Smith barn quickly reminded her of how easy it had been to get out of the habit. She resisted the impulse to hold her nose and walked in.

Noble was nowhere about, but his chestnut mare and Albert Gentile's piebald gelding stood in the middle of the barn. Both were fitted out and tethered, as if awaiting only a command to depart. Noble's Henry rifle, which he'd gotten as a birthday gift when he was twelve, was oiled and waiting in its sheath against the mare's saddle. Secured to the saddlebags of the pie were her own boots, empty and limp. Neither horse acknowledged her presence by noise or movement. A calico cat wove its bold way between their long legs, batting here and there at the straw, no doubt foraging for breakfast.

Something, instinct or fear, prevented Ivy from calling out to Noble. She approached the tethered animals and stroked them on their muzzles, whispering sounds of appeasement. Waiting between them, she saw Noble emerge from the tack room ten feet away with a length of bridle leather coiled over his shoulder. He was wearing the same clothing he'd had on the night before; Ivy suspected he'd never gotten undressed. His stark, angular jaw was covered with an overnight growth of beard. His eyes were wide and unfocused, possibly from lack of sleep. His generous mouth was slack, as if he were lost in reflection of some past or future event over which he had no control. He took several long steps in her direction before he looked up at her.

"Ivy!" He stopped abruptly, as if the very sight of her had robbed him of his ability to move.

"You were going to leave me here." The words materialized on her lips at the same time as the thought solidified in her brain. A thread of pain laced along her breast like the bindings of a corset.

Noble pressed his lips together, widening his already broad mouth. His throat bobbed. His dark eyebrows, tapered like the wings of a hawk in flight, met for an instant above the bridge of his small nose, and his bright, coffee-colored eyes wore a hooded look. He glanced beyond her, out of the opening.

"It's still early," he offered, fingering the ends of the bridle leather that dangled from his shoulder. "You could make it back to Peaceful in time for school, I bet. No one even needs to know you were gone."

A flash of anger chased the pain up and out.

"Was I to have accomplished this without my boots? Without a horse?" She wanted to sound cool and condemning, but she could hear the high, tight strain in her voice, a combination of anger and hurt.

Noble's shoulders dropped. He uttered a brief oath and looked up at the rafters as if they might bestow upon him a means of keeping himself in check.

"You're not going with me, Ivy. I told you that last night."

"And as I recall, I didn't argue the point."

Noble let out a hard breath. "Ivy—"

"You're a high-handed bully," Ivy cut in, doing her best to bite back the fullness of her sudden fury. "You always have been, and you always will be. You delight in trying to boss people about. It's a wonder to me that Charity stood for it as long as she did. She's no fool, you know, and she has as much spunk as you ever did. Maybe more."

"Keep Charity out of this!" His eyes flashed and his deep voice trembled with warning. "This is just between you and me, right now!"

"You're wrong, Noble," she flung at him, emboldened by his telling response. "There isn't anything 'between' you and me. There hasn't been for a very long time. And if you think I'll bow to your wishes just on your say-so, you'd best think again. I never did before, even when we—when we meant something to one another. There's no reason why I should start now."

Noble was shaking his head by the end of her speech, and there was a faint smile on his lips that she took to be derisive.

"You always were a pigheaded thing, even when we were kids. I swear, I never knew a person—boy, girl, man or woman, who'd slice off their own nose to fret their face quicker! You haven't changed one bit, Ivy Wingate. You'd spit in the wind on a dare, wouldn't you? It doesn't matter that your safety or your life might be in danger. Just like the time you walked old Witherspoon's fence."

Noble's jeering tirade ended right there, although Ivy suspected he'd meant to say a lot more. His last word echoed in the cavernous barn like the final bang of a judge's gavel. Ivy felt a vast emptiness deep inside of her, as if Noble had reached in with one of his big hands and, like the most skilled of surgeons, removed her very soul. She longed to look away, but she forced herself to stare him down. He paled suddenly, and his eyes grew wide with dismay. She felt a shiver of satisfaction.

One of my bigger mistakes, she wanted to hurl back at him, but her tongue refused to move. Laurel had come of that mistake. Laurel, hundreds of miles away, who knew her only as Aunt Ivy. Laurel, who wrote her letters in a careful, childish hand and had seen her twice in her life.

Laurel, who had been the very image of Noble since the day she was born, over nine years ago.

"Go on back to town, Ivy," Noble urged her in a growl, looking away. "You've done all you can. There's no point in you losing your job, and your place in the community, on account of a couple of wild, foolish kids. I swear I won't go hard on them. After all, I was once—" Noble broke off, unwilling, or unable, to continue. Ivy swallowed a lump in her own throat as a result.

"It's too late," she told him, her gaze fixed on the dangling stirrup of the pie's saddle. "By now, Mrs. Quinlan knows I'm not there, and she knows where I've gone. I left a note in my room. I burned my bridges, Noble. I can't go back. I can only go forward."

Noble did not want to look at her, but the quiet resolve in her pretty voice forced his gaze her way. A rosy petal of sunshine caressed the curve of her throat, and in the pale light she looked so much like the girl he'd lost his heart to that it was all he could do to keep from reaching for her.

It's too late, she had said.

He clenched his fists at his sides until his fingernails bit into the calloused flesh on his palms. It was too late. It was ten years too late. He had locked up his heart, and he had hidden the key so well that he doubted he'd ever find it again. Bettina Kraus hadn't found it. Neither had Mary Boyd, although for a time Noble had deluded himself into thinking they each, in turn, might. He realized, listening to Ivy's quiet, measured breaths, that all the while it had been in her keeping. He knew that it always would be. Closing his eyes, he knew then that he didn't even want to have it back again unless Ivy herself was willing to open the lock with a tender hand.

He could not have her running about exposing herself to dangers she was incapable of imagining. He could stand anything, endure any personal hell, as long as he knew she would be safe. He tried again.

"Those men at the ranch," he began. "Carl, Jack, and the others. They're looking for Stephen, aren't they? They'll be looking for you, too, since you gave them the slip last night. By now they figure you know where your brother is, and they'll be on your trail. And if you think they were rough on you last night, I guarantee they'll be ten times worse when they catch up with you."

"Don't you think I know that?" Ivy's head jerked up unexpectedly and her green eyes flashed like a cornered cat's. "Do you honestly believe that I want any part of this adventure? I don't, Noble, but I have no choice. You forced it on me when you came into my schoolroom yesterday afternoon and all but told me that Stephen had abducted Charity. It was the talk of the town by nightfall.

"I've lived through too much scandal." Ivy met his gaze with challenge. "I've had a belly full of it, and I'm not about to stay around Peaceful and endure any more of it. I don't care if it ruins me once and for all, as it very likely will. I don't care if Stephen has done something terrible, although I can't bring myself to believe he really has. He's my brother, and he's the only kin I have left. What kind of sister would I be if I allowed him to face this threat on his own? What kind of teacher, or friend, would I be of Charity's, to abandon her over a foolish mistake? After all, as you pointed out just a few moments ago, I committed an error of shortsightedness when I was only a little younger than she. I continue to pay for it to this very day. I expect, in one way or another, I always will. So you see, I can't afford to allow concern for my own welfare to prejudice my decision about looking for them."

Noble found himself standing before her, staring into uncompromising green eyes that seemed to beg him to understand. He could only guess what it had cost her to make such a declaration, especially to him. She was strong, he marvelled. And loyal. Just as she had always been. And oh, God, how he loved her for it!

Noble would have done anything to keep himself from touching her after that, even chop off his arm at the elbow, but his hand paid no heed either to his pride, or to his common sense. His fingers needed to touch her cheek again as they had last night. If she were to slap them away, well, he would bear it. He could, he suspected, bear anything, if only it meant keeping Ivy near to him, always.

"Don't, Noble."

Anything, that is, except her icy contempt.

His hand fell to his side like a child's abandoned toy. He cursed himself in silence as he forced himself to maintain her stare.

"You mean to go on, then, no matter what I say?" he persisted in an urgent whisper. "No matter that you're placing your own life and welfare in danger?"

A faint smile traced her lips, like a hesitant kiss. It made him feel as if the floor had vanished beneath him.

"Would you allow that to stop you?"

He averted his stare. "What I'd do doesn't matter."

When had it ever mattered? He heard Ivy sigh. He turned away and made a show of examining his horse's front right shoe.

"I don't give a damn," he muttered. "Come. Go. Do whatever you damned well please. Just don't get in my way." He hoped she couldn't hear the lie in his gruff voice, and he damned himself for telling it.

"May I have my boots, please?"

"What?" He dropped the hoof.

"My boots."

He yanked them from the pie's saddle and tossed them at her feet.

"There. Damned poor boots for a trip like you're about to take, too. I hope you know that."

"I do." Her voice was smaller.

"Hmph. I expect so." He adjusted his bridle. "You're Ivy Wingate, and a schoolteacher to boot. You know everything. Well, since you're up and about, and you owe me for saving your skin, not to mention putting you up for the night, go on inside and scare us up some breakfast. I guess you know how to do that, too."

He felt able to look at her again. She clutched her boots to her bosom. Her pretty green eyes were like flint arrowheads.

"Are you trying to give me the slip?"

He arched a brow. "Afraid I'll steal your horse?"

"You tried to steal my boots, why not my horse, as well?"

"The day's wasting." He ignored her question and nodded toward the stable door. "Let's go together, since you're so worried."

He took two steps that brought him right beside her. She drew herself in with a flinch. It pained him that she thought he might do her some injury and he considered her, wondering if she could really believe him capable of it. Her wide eyes and quivering lower lip convinced him. And intrigued him.

"What do you have on your feet now?" he asked.

Ivy's cheeks went as crimson as the blush of a summer sunrise and she looked down in answer. He followed her gaze and recognized the toes of his best shoes, which were far too big for her, protruding absurdly from under the hem of her muslin skirt. A laugh tickled the back of his throat.

"Ivy girl, if you don't wake snakes," he declared with a shake of his head.

Her scowl was replaced by a look of wonder and Noble lost his urge to chuckle. He remembered happier times when he often used those very same teasing words on her. She remembered, too. He knew she did. The water filling her eyes as she held him captive with her gaze told him so.

He was falling, yet he stood on solid ground. His

mouth said her name, but no sound came from his throat.

And she touched him.

It was a simple touch. He thought she meant to touch his lower lip with the tip of her finger, but her hand faltered before she reached it and her finger brushed the placket of his shirt, instead. But it was a touch.

"Ivy." This time a sound did come out, but it was a small one. It had to be, for there was but a little time before his lips joined with hers.

Ah, God, her sweet softness! She didn't fight him, didn't stiffen and try to break away as he slipped his arms about her and settled his mouth more firmly against hers. Her arms were trapped between them, but she didn't use them as a wedge. She scarcely moved at all, except her mouth, which was most definitely kissing him back.

This is wrong, Ivy's conscience told her, even as she welcomed Noble's long-overdue kiss. But how could something that felt so extraordinarily right be wrong? There could be only one answer to that: It wasn't wrong. It wasn't wrong at all.

It was the past ten years that had been wrong. They slipped away as if they had never been at all. Noble held her up close to him and for a glorious moment she was the young girl Noble had kissed with such ardor and tenderness just before they'd made love on the spring grass by Witherspoon's fence.

And what of the child who had come of that love?

Chapter Seven

Ivy broke free of Noble's kiss, but she could not give up his closeness yet. She turned her head aside and pressed her temple to his collarbone. She ought to speak, but she couldn't. What could she say to him that wouldn't utterly destroy what had just been reborn between them?

"Noble?" she managed at last.

He cleared his throat. "What?"

"How did this happen?"

"Don't know." Rubbing his cheek against her hair, he let out a sigh. "Don't care. Do you?"

"No." she admitted. "I just wish . . ."

"What?"

I wish everything could be right between us. But it can't be. And you can never know why.

"Make a wish, today," he urged at her silence, pressing her close to him. "I'd reckon today's a good day for it."

Noble had always had a way of talking that wasn't like anyone else's. He could talk magic spells, it seemed to her. And she loved his voice when it spoke so tenderly. He didn't have to try anymore to keep his voice in that low register, that sonorous baritone, like he'd had to when he was seventeen. It had settled there very nicely all on its own.

"Why?" She wanted him to talk some more, to drive away the dark fringe about her joy with his words.

He pushed away from her just far enough to tilt her face upward.

"Because I got my wish, today," he breathed, with as much love in his dark eyes as she'd ever hoped to see there.

Tears burned behind her eyes as he kissed her again. His kiss was almost enough to make her forget every reason why she shouldn't yield to its pleasures.

Maybe, she thought, *maybe if I wish . . .*

To Ivy's surprise, Noble broke off his kiss abruptly. He let her go and took a step back, and she could see the heat in his face as he looked away from her.

He remembers what happened the last time we kissed like that, she thought, feeling her own face burn.

"Tell you what I wish, now." His tone was just short of jaunty. He dragged the back of his sleeve across his forehead, pushing aside a lock of dark hair that had fallen.

"What?" Anything to ease the sudden, renewed swell of tension between them.

Even though he couldn't meet her eyes for more than a second, he found her a quick grin. She wondered how hard he'd had to look for it.

"I wish you'd make me some breakfast," he said with a light little laugh.

At the house, Ivy shooed Noble off to shave, promising that she would make breakfast for them both while he was gone. He demanded, and received, another kiss for his concession, but Ivy was unable to abandon herself to it as she had its predecessors. Holding her emotions at bay, she put on coffee and a pot of porridge and set herself to the mindless chore of stirring the cereal.

The truth was, she wanted to be alone. She could not think clearly with Noble about, exuding his maleness and the youthful high spirits she remembered from their childhood. Not when she herself had plummeted into renewed despair.

Noble must be told.

The very thought sent a cold stab of terror down her spine. Told what? That he was the father of a nine-year-old girl who had been left by her mother for another family to raise?

It had been simple, though not easy, to keep it from him before. The Smiths and the Wingates, or what was left of them, had no truck with one another after that terrible day.

Pa was a proud man. He withdrew from everyone in the valley when Ma and Ben Smith ran off together, and he'd pulled Ivy and Stephen right along with him. Pity was for beggars, he often told them, with a hard set to his mouth that Ivy could vividly recall. He would have none of it, nor did he care to subject himself or his children to the scorn and ridicule of the neighbors on account of Ben Smith having stolen his wife away from him. He took Ivy out of school and made her teach young Stephen at home. He forbade her or Stephen from even speaking Noble's name, or indeed the name Smith, in his hearing, ever again.

83

Ivy closed her eyes, trying to shut out the awful memory of the aftermath. But suddenly she was fifteen again, and as helpless as she'd been then . . .

The privy stank, and the cold went through Ivy like an iced railroad spike. She leaned over the splintered seat and retched again. Tears soaked her eyes, from the combination of the smell and the force of her act. She wished she would die right there. She wondered if Noble would hear of her death, and if he would feel sorry. She wondered if he was suffering as much as she.

She was sick so much, lately. The mornings were the worst, and she didn't dare let Pa see how sick she was. He'd seen her crying two weeks earlier over the supper she was fixing, and had shaken her for it. Her ma wasn't worth their spit, let alone her tears, he told her, his voice like rusted iron. And she'd better not be crying over a Smith, or he'd take it out of her hide right quick.

Pa was a hard man, and never particularly loving, not even toward his children. One look at his face as he laid that law out to her had been enough. Ivy had held her breath and willed herself to stop crying right then and there. She never cried again in Pa's presence. She thought to save up her tears for the nighttime when Pa and Stephen slept, but she found that by then she was unable to release them. Instead they sat like a stone weight in her breast, allowing her no relief, reminding her constantly of her loneliness. She missed her mother, and she missed Noble. And the one person who might come closest to understanding that had forbidden her to mention either one to him.

Her stomach heaved again, but there was nothing left to bring up. Her chest ached, her throat was raw and foul and she was sweating in spite of the cold. Outside, Pa would be about his morning chores ex-

pecting breakfast on his table, a breakfast she was supposed to be inside fixing right this minute. The very thought of bacon frying was enough to cause a new revolt in her insides. Oh, why couldn't she just die?

The privy door swung open, admitting bright, blinding sunlight and a brisk May breeze. Ivy, on her knees, jerked around in anger, expecting to find that seven-year-old Stephen had once again not bothered to knock.

To her dismay, a tall shadow appeared in the doorway instead.

"Get up, girl." It was Pa. Ivy shielded her eyes with her arm, but she could not see his face, only the dark, ominous outline of his silhouette against the spring morning. Fear introduced a new revolt into her stomach, but she clenched her fist at her waist, where her apron was bound, and pressed her lips together to hold back the tide. She scrambled to obey the terse command, but not quickly enough to satisfy her father.

"I said, get up!" He punctuated his repetition with a hard yank of her arm and Ivy cried out, more in fear than in pain. She doubted anything her father might do to her could compound her physical or mental misery.

She was wrong.

"You come out here four, five times every mornin' when you should be gettin' my breakfast," Pa growled, sounding more like a grizzly bear than a father. "I been watchin' you for nigh on two weeks, now. Once should be enough for a healthy young girl. You comin' out here to bawl? Or are you keepin' some other secret from me?"

"N-no, Pa," she whispered, longing to pull her arm from his bruising grip but not daring to move lest he think she was trying to sass him. She knew she'd *be feeling the back of his hand besides, if she did.*

Her brief, respectful answer did not seem to satisfy him, for he tightened his hold.

"You sick, Ivy?" he persisted with another savage shake.

Ivy would have given an eye to be able to run from that cramped, stinking privy, but Pa held her fast.

"No," she choked back another assault of rising bile. "I mean, I—" She could no longer hold it in. Wrenching away from Pa, she doubled over the privy once more. Through her renewed misery, she felt a spark of hope; perhaps Pa would take some pity on her in her state. She expected at any moment to feel his hand on her shoulder, this time not in anger but in tenderness, and to hear his softened voice urge her back to bed. She was thus startled when she was once again jerked to her feet amid a virulent stream of obscenities she'd never before heard him utter.

"Whore!" Pa exclaimed at the end of them, shaking her by the shoulders. "Filthy slut! Whose is it? Answer me!"

But Ivy could not answer. She was dazed from the shaking, paralyzed with fear at her father's outburst, and the words he hurled at her made no sense in any case. Slut? Whore? She had only a vague idea of what those things were; Pa had used them in a tirade against her mother on the day she'd left them, and she knew by the context that they were not complimentary. But 'whose is it'? She stared at her father in mute amazement. What was he ranting about?

Then they were out in the blinding sunlight, leaving the stronger stench of the privy behind. Pa had hold of the bib of her apron, and she could see his face at last. It was ugly with an emotion that more closely resembled hatred than rage.

"Pa!" Ivy tried again, terror clogging her throat. "Pa, please! I-I don't—"

Noble and Ivy

"By God, I ought to horsewhip you!" Pa screamed, a big vein bulging purple beside his eye. "You've shamed yourself and your family, as if one shame wasn't enough! Some no-account boy put his seed in your belly, and I'm bettin' it was Noble Smith! Was it? Tell me!"

Noble . . . Ivy remembered Witherspoon's fence and the sweet spring grass beneath them. She could almost see Noble's earnest, angular face above her own. She could almost feel his heat penetrate her, bringing first a burning stab of pain, then a brief, shuddering sweetness, like the running sap of a sugar maple. She closed her eyes and swallowed a breath, her face scorching from the memory.

Was it shame, as Pa said? Truly? It hadn't felt so very wrong when they'd been lying together afterward on Witherspoon's grass, their hands loosely linked. She had felt a little strange, sort of stretched and sore, as they'd walked toward home together in silence, not touching. And it was not until later that evening, long after she'd made the awful discovery that Ma had gone, that she realized she had bled. She'd gotten scared then, and had wished for Ma so hard it hurt. But Ma had gone, almost as if she'd known that Ivy had been made a woman that day, able to shoulder every burden associated with the title.

Still, Ivy did not understand Pa's words. Seed? Did Pa mean to tell her that—that she was going to have a child as a result of what she and Noble had done on Witherspoon's grass? But how could that be? They'd only been together once, and it hadn't lasted very long . . .

Her breath caught: It never lasted long with the bulls and stallions, either, but there were always calves, colts and fillies, come spring.

Pa released her shoulders and took her face in his

87

hands. His grasp was gentle, but for some reason she feared that demonstration more than she had his ferocity.

"Did he force you, Ivy?" Pa breathed, pain and hope mingling like whiskey and water in his breath. "Was that it? He made you do it, didn't he? That filthy pig whoreson bastard! I'll kill him with my own hands! My—my little girl!"

Pa's voice became a tender whine of agony at the end of his harangue, and his blue eyes, wet with tears, begged her to admit that she'd been coerced by Noble Smith into a grownup act she'd neither understood nor consented to.

But she had understood it. She had wanted it. In fact, she had all but begged Noble to go on, even when he'd offered to stop. She regretted her recklessness daily since Ma had gone, but she could not deny it now and add a cowardly deception to her sin. It wouldn't be fair to Noble. To say that the babe inside of her was the result of an act of violence was to allow a horrible injustice to the three of them: Noble, herself and the child.

She hung her head. The truth would shatter Pa, but a lie was unthinkable. Her heart rose a little at a sudden thought: If she confessed to her complicity in the deed, Pa might drag her over to the Smiths and insist that Noble marry her. After all, Bettina Kraus had told her that very thing had happened to Mary Boyd's older sister only last year. It had been a scandal for a time, but the gossip had eventually died out. The baby had been born in October, the first grandchild for both families. There was such general rejoicing at the time that no one seemed to remember that the marriage of Catherine and Brian Mercer had had such a disgraceful beginning.

But Pa was angry at the entire Smith family, and hurt by her mother's betrayal. There was no telling what he'd do, just out of spite.

"Ivy?" There was less hope in Pa's tone this time than worry. Ivy took a deep breath and made herself look into her father's probing eyes.

"I . . . we love each other, Pa," she said, just above a fearful whisper. "Noble and me. We didn't mean to—"

She was cut off by the sound of Pa's hard gasp.

"No!" he exclaimed, shaking her again. "I won't listen! First my wife, then my daughter—"

"Pa, you're hurting me!"

"I won't have it, Ivy, do you hear? I won't have any bastard grandchild of Ben Smith's around to remind me every day of who it was took your ma away! You have that baby, and I swear, I'll drown it in the trough!"

"Pa!" Ivy broke his hold at last and backed away from him. Her stomach was clenched in a knot, as if the muscles were gathering together to protect the child inside her from her father's blind rage.

Ivy didn't clearly remember what had happened during the time following that exchange, except that it resulted in her being sent away. Pa's cousin Ciely and her husband, Tom MacDonald, lived down south, outside of a modest railroad town called Rawlins. They were older, like Pa, but their marriage hadn't been blessed with children. The plan was for Ivy to stay with them, far from the gossiping tongues of Peaceful and the influences of Noble Smith, until the baby was born. Pa let out that she'd travelled south to help out her cousin who'd just had a child. The baby was to be raised by the MacDonalds as their own.

Ivy was welcome to visit them, of course. But in the intervening years, she'd only been able to make the long trip once, and then only after a long and heated dispute with Pa. The experience had almost

Carole Howey

been enough to make her wish she'd heeded Pa's advice not to go. She could still remember the staggering pain in her breast when Cousin Ciely had nudged Laurel, then a shy five, forward from behind the protection of her skirt to say hello to her aunt Ivy . . .

"That looks like the slop I give to the pigs." Noble's teasing baritone, just behind her ear, startled Ivy from her unpleasant reverie. "And it doesn't smell much better."

Ivy didn't answer. She couldn't. She looked down before her at the pot. She'd forgotten completely about the porridge, and it was bubbling angrily, spewing gray lumps up like fountains. Flustered, she sniffed. Sure enough, it was burned.

She burst into tears.

"Hey!" Noble touched her shoulder, no doubt to comfort her, but its effect was just the opposite. Ivy felt herself breaking into little pieces. She feared she would soon be nothing but a pile of shards at his feet.

She had to pull herself together.

"N-Noble," she managed, ducking her shoulder out from under his touch. "I was—I was thinking. You startled me." She abandoned the spoon in the pot—its usefulness had long been outlived, in any case—and brushed the back of her wrists across her cheeks.

"What is it, Ivy-Over?" His hands grasped her shoulders again, both of them, more firmly, as if to prevent her further escape. "You can't have changed so much in ten years that you'd cry over a burned breakfast! And you used to treat me to the tart side of your tongue whenever I teased you. What's wrong?"

Noble gently turned her to face him and she did not resist. Another rebellious tear leaked out of her eye, but before she could blot it, Noble stroked it

90

away with the side of his thumb. The tender gesture begged her to yield her secrets to him.

"I . . ." The confession caught in her throat. Noble was concerned about Charity, just now. He would not thank her for distracting him with more bad news as he hunted for his sister, especially not with five desperate men on the same trail. Surely, a better time would come, a time when they would be unencumbered by family responsibilities.

Had there ever been such a time, for her and Noble?

"Nothing," she said, shoving aside her self-pity and regret. "I was—you startled me, that's all. I'm all right." She sniffled, blinked her eyes hard and forced a smile to her lips. She risked a look at his face, knowing that she could never convince him if she did not.

His dark eyes probed her, and she sensed he was not deceived by her performance. The feeling was unsettling, yet oddly comforting.

"Now, now," Noble said in a soft, singsong way as he gathered her into his arms. "You don't have to put up a brave front for me, you know. I guess everything from last night just caught up to you and kind of took you by surprise. What you went through was enough to shake anybody up, and at first you came out of it storming, just like you used to." He held her close, and she savored the strength and the surety of his embrace. It held nothing back from her. "I should have guessed it affected you more than you let on," he continued, his fingers playing with the braid of hair that fell down her back.

"I'm all right," she repeated into his lapel, reluctant to leave the succor of his embrace. "Truly, I am."

Noble made a clucking sound and he pushed her back a bit.

"You know, it's all right for you to cry," he told her, lifting her chin with a gentle hand until she was constrained to meet his indulgent gaze again. "I wouldn't mind at all if you did. In fact, I kind of wish you would. You see, Miss Wingate," he went on, his voice as hushed as a breeze through the cottonwoods outside, "it happens I got an itch to comfort you."

The unguarded tenderness in his tone and the love in his eyes undid her resolve. Before she quite knew what she was doing, she was sobbing like a child once again, right there in Noble's arms.

Noble wasn't quite prepared for Ivy's utter breakdown, but he was glad of it nonetheless. It gave him an excuse to keep her close, to let his body reacquaint itself with the feel of her next to him. She felt so good, so damn good in his arms that he wondered how he'd managed to go ten long years without holding her. She belonged there, he realized, pressing his cheek to her soft, fragrant hair. Just as she belonged in his kitchen, fixing their breakfast. Just as she'd belonged in his bed last night. Last night, and every night . . .

He was utterly baffled by Ivy's mysterious feminine underthings and silently, enormously grateful to her for saving him from the embarrassment of admitting to that fact. She untied ties, unlaced laces and unbuttoned buttons while he watched in fascination. She revealed herself to him shyly and he accepted the revelation as a precious gift, feeling humble and thrilled in the same instant.

Noble was amazed to discover that the buttons of his trousers, which he undid every day without so much as a thought, had become objects of immense frustration. They seemed to have swollen to twice their original size while their accompanying holes had shrunk. He cursed under his breath. Ivy waited for him on the grass, her hands joined as a modest shield of her own nakedness. If she laughed at him, he would die. Finally, after a painful eternity, he kicked his trousers off and away. A slight breeze blew up, teasing and chilling the backs of his naked thighs. He shivered. Ivy smiled shyly, and he was lost.

Ivy was around him. His rigid flesh pierced a barrier he had not expected. She cried out in a small voice, and he knew he had hurt her. And he had sworn, only a moment before, that he would not. He could not look at her, fearing the reproach he might see in her smoky eyes. He wanted to stop, to not hurt her anymore, but he was amazed, and a little frightened, to discover that his body was no longer under his dominion.

Her heat enveloped him. It lured him deeper with a power that passed his understanding. Beneath him Ivy whimpered, but he realized she was holding him fast to his mission, not allowing him to retreat far, although some part of him wanted to, told him he should. It was as if the lower regions of his body were possessed by a dark, pagan, hungry spirit. He pressed his face against Ivy's neck. He knew he was crying. She was crying too: He could taste the salt of her tears on the tender flesh of her neck. He took in the flavor with the tip of his tongue, wanting to reassure her.

In a few quick movements, it ended in a brilliant, if brief, release, unlike anything he'd ever experienced. Breathless, bewildered, utterly exhausted, he rolled off of her, closing his eyes against the chaos of thought that pursued him. The sunlight pulsed through his eyelids and slowly he came back to himself.

Oh God, what had they done? What had he done?
"Ivy—" he began, but his voice, only lately
changed to a manly baritone, cracked at once. What
could he say to her? What did she expect to hear from
him?

Her answer was the intake of a choppy breath and
the release of a single sigh.

"Noble?" she called softly after a moment, as if
afraid he'd abandoned her. The thought lanced him
and he groped for her hand, beside him in the tender
grass. He found it and entwined his fingers with her
own, loosely, so she could pull away from him if she
so chose. He hoped she wouldn't.

He breathed a shuddering sigh of relief when she
squeezed his hand . . .

"Noble?"

Noble stirred, aware of an odd, sick feeling in
his stomach.

"What?"

"I'm all right, now."

Noble opened his eyes and realized they were in
the kitchen. His kitchen. His arms, and his heart,
were full of Ivy Wingate. Only she wasn't afraid
and confused, like they'd both been ten years ago.
Amazed, still lingering in his reverie, he looked
down at her. He was disconcerted to find that she
was gazing up at him. He felt as if his face were a
nickelodeon, and she had just watched the memory there.

Chapter Eight

Ivy served breakfast in silence. She pushed the mess around her bowl as Noble ate without looking at her. When he finished, he made a great show of setting the empty bowl away with one hand while he pushed himself back from the table.

"Best breakfast I ever ate," he declared with a very convincing smile.

Ivy attempted a wilting look. "You're a liar," she said, holding in her own smile. "Lying's a sin, and you'll go to hell for it." She cleared away the dishes, relieved that whatever had inspired that uncomfortable silence between them earlier had passed. "And if you ever went to church, you would know that."

Noble laughed. He caught her about the waist and pulled her into his lap with no more effort than he might a child. Ivy cherished the playful gesture, deliberately putting her darker thoughts out of her mind. Long years of having Laurel dwell on the fringes of her consciousness enabled her to do that. She made a sound of annoyance with her tongue against her teeth, but she could not help smiling at him. Noble caressed her with his gaze even as he secured his arms around her.

"All right," he conceded, wearing a grin of his own that would melt granite. "I've had better, but I guess the company made me forget that. And who says I don't go to church?"

"Driving Charity every Sunday doesn't count," she told him, looping her dishtowel around his neck. "You actually have to come in to the building for the exercise to do you any good."

Noble considered her with a sober expression, although his dark eyes sparkled. He rubbed his freshly shaven chin with one hand.

"I do, huh?"

She nodded.

"And are you personally going to undertake my salvation?"

Ivy felt a warmth flood her cheeks under his tender scrutiny, and she found herself staring at his dimpled chin.

"That isn't my job," she told him, feeling suddenly awkward and shy.

"Suppose I make it your job?" Noble's baritone became husky.

His words startled her into meeting his gaze again. This time he seemed obliged to look away.

"There isn't any way around it, Ivy," he said, sounding resigned yet entreating. "I've known forever that I wanted you for my wife. Remember, when we were kids, I said it? Oh, I strung myself along a few times since then, thinking I could get over you if I just married somebody else. But each time I backed out of it, because I knew it was wrong. It wasn't fair to them, or to me. Or you, either. I guess I broke a couple of hearts in the process." He looked at her again without any suggestion of pride or vanity. "My own not the least. But there's still plenty of time for us to make it right, I think. That is . . ." He cleared his throat. "If you're—if you're willing?"

Ivy could not move. For a moment she wondered if she'd forgotten how to breathe. Noble went on gazing at her, his dark eyes wide and earnest.

"Noble," she ventured, then moistened her lips. "Are you asking me to marry you?"

He gave a small, self-conscious laugh and colored slightly about the neckline of his shirt.

"That's the way it looks, doesn't it?" he agreed, breathless.

She looked down. She should feel wonderful, she knew. She should feel light as air and laughter, for there was nothing she'd ever wanted more in this life than to marry Noble Smith, to live with him as his wife and to have his children. Instead she felt chained to the earth, weighted down in every part of her body. *Yes,* she wanted to be able to answer him, then to lay her head upon his shoulder in contentment. *I will marry you. I want to marry you.*

But what of Laurel?

She made herself look at him and was immediately sorry, for he wore such an expression of love and hopefulness that it tore at her heart. And he was waiting for her answer.

"We aren't children anymore," she said softly, touching the faint cleft in his chin with the tip of her finger. "So much has happened to us both since then. How do we know what we feel now is love?"

Noble made a grimace, but his eyes kept smiling.

"You know what your problem is, Miss School-

97

teacher Ivy Wingate?" he teased in a sensuous, honeyed drawl. "You talk too much."

As if to prevent her from compounding her error, Noble caught her lower lip with his mouth. He drew upon it gently, finding all the places of her secret delight with the tip of his tongue. A small sigh escaped her as he performed the same artful maneuver on her upper lip, then for good measure he took her whole mouth with languid deliberation. She shivered with reluctant pleasure, her protest temporarily deferred. She marvelled at the contrast of his mature, accomplished kisses to the tenuous efforts she remembered from their youth.

"Where did you learn how to do that?" she murmured in awe, presenting her throat to him.

"Don't remember," he replied in a growl, obliging her by nibbling it. "Marry me."

A fresh blade of sweet fire plunged down her spine.

"But Noble," she argued, with what little rationality remained amid the growing haze in her brain. "We shouldn't—"

"Dammit, Ivy!" He set her back at arm's length and gazed into her eyes while still holding her tightly. "My whole life has been 'shouldn't,' ever since my pa left us. I was so turned around, what with losing my chance to go to school, having to take care of Ma, Charity and the ranch, and on top of it all, not being able to see you and set things right."

Noble paused, looking past her, as if seeing what had been, instead of what was. He closed his eyes tightly then opened them wide, and Ivy could see they were wet. She looked away, wanting to say something to console him, but unable to speak for her own heartache. She knew precisely his pain.

She also knew that he could not begin to guess hers.

"Ma was bitter," he said, his voice muffled and sounding very much as if it belonged to a seventeen-year old boy instead of a twenty-seven-year old man. "She was broken. You should have seen her, Ivy. The life went right out of her when Pa went, and she put everything on me: the ranch, the house, Charity. I'd thought I was a man that day, after we—Well, I found out soon enough what being a man really meant. A lot sooner than I should have. And it didn't have anything to do with—with what happened between us that day in Witherspoon's field."

Ivy said nothing. Her own memory of it was as fresh as the sting of a bee, and it paralyzed her.

"I know," she whispered.

"I tried to see you." He went on as if she had not spoken. "Even though Ma forbade it, and I was working so hard I scarcely had the strength to eat the supper I'd made at the end of the day. I tried to come to you." His words were quiet and heavy. "But I knew your pa was bitter too, and he chased me off more than once with his shotgun. Folks whispered about the Smiths and the Wingates behind their hands whenever I went into town. It got so I hated going there, even for supplies. But Ma wouldn't leave the house. It was like I was in a prison, Ivy. I was chained to this place, to working it, like a dog. Then I heard you'd gone away south. I didn't know whether to be glad you were out of my reach, or to do myself, or somebody else, some harm."

Noble laid his forehead against her shoulder, as if the very telling of the story exacted a weighty toll upon him.

"While you were gone, Ma . . . said things to

me," he said, just above a whisper. "She was so full of bitter poison, I guess, that some of it was bound to spill over. By the time I heard you'd come home, I was convinced that you—that you were just like your ma, and that it was best I stayed away from you. I spent the next ten years of my life trying to learn how to unlove you. And all that came of it was that when I saw you in the schoolhouse yesterday, I realized that I love you more now than I ever did. Even now, with this business of Stephen and Charity. . . ." He trailed off into silence, as if overwhelmed by the clutter of emotions that he'd allowed her to glimpse.

Ivy slipped her arms about his neck and held him close, as much for her own comfort as for his. *Tell him about Laurel,* her conscience schooled her sternly. *You may not get another chance like this.* She opened her mouth to do just that, but quickly closed it again: Charity was foremost in Noble's thoughts at the moment. His little sister's welfare and safety were his primary concern. What good would be accomplished by revealing Laurel's existence to him now, especially since the child no longer belonged to her? To them? It would surely complicate matters further between them. Besides, it would create another distraction that neither she nor Noble could afford: They had to concentrate their efforts on finding the two runaways who, with an irate gang of desperate men pursuing them, were in even more trouble than they suspected.

But how could she accept Noble's proposal of marriage without being completely honest with him? And how could she refuse it, knowing, as she did without doubt, that she loved him, and he her?

Noble brought his head up with a sigh and Ivy found herself looking at his handsome face once again. He offered her a lopsided grin, but his eyes remained sober and intense.

"All I need in this world is to know that you love me," he said, his baritone light and hopeful. He said nothing more.

Her eyes burned and her heart was heavy.

"I do love you, Noble," she said quietly. "And I always have. Never doubt that. And never forget it."

His smile widened and he touched her brow with the side of a gentle, crooked finger.

"Why does saying that make you look like you just bit into a lemon?"

She laughed, more out of nervousness than amusement.

"Maybe because my mouth isn't used to saying it."

Noble closed his eyes as if he himself had just tasted a favorite sweet.

"Well, my ears could sure get used to hearing it," he declared, bundling her close in his arms again. "And I know just the thing to get your mouth into practice."

He caught her lips with his again before she could protest, and she could not help but be glad. Noble had always managed to find his winsome way around her, but the man seemed to know her better, even, than the boy ever had, despite their years of separation. And, she realized, parting her lips to welcome his tongue, she would not have wanted things any other way.

Noble drank from her as if she were a pitcher of cool, fresh water and he'd just come out of the desert. She had never been kissed by anyone but Noble, and he hadn't kissed that way when he was younger. She wished it would never end.

His embrace tightened.

"Ivy, sweetheart," he murmured, his voice husky as he nuzzled her neck. "You smell so good . . . God, I want you."

Noble felt his control rush away from him like a storm-swollen freshet. He hated the feeling, nearly as much as he loved the sweet, tempting woman who had caused it. He had lost control with her once, and the price had been ten years of bitterness and regret.

A sharp, brisk series of knocks on the front door saved Noble from having to decide what to do next.

Ivy leaped up from his lap and pressed her fist against her mouth, staring in the direction of the front room, wearing a wide-eyed expression of terror. Noble got up quickly and moved the kitchen table aside. The floor rasped in protest.

"Noble?" Ivy's whisper was a plea. He pressed a finger against her kiss-swollen lips and pointed to the trap door of the cellar.

"Hide down there," he whispered as a cold sweat trickled down his back. He was not expecting company, and his only thought was that it was the men from out at the Wingate ranch who had nearly raped her the night before. Even if it wasn't them, neither he nor Ivy could afford for anyone to find them alone together at his place.

He swung the trap door open, and it creaked on its unoiled hinges. Without looking at him, Ivy scrambled down the ladder-like steps into the dark hole. Noble closed the door behind her and moved the table back into place above it.

The blows on the door rained again and Noble calmed himself. It couldn't be the men who were looking for Stephen: Surely they would not be so mannerly as to knock a second time. They probably never would have knocked at all.

"Who's there?" he mustered the will to call out

as he made his way to the front door.

"Gentile, from the livery," came the curt reply.

Noble started. What the hell could Al Gentile want with him? And why was he coming to call just now? Annoyed and bewildered, Noble threw the latch on the front door and pulled it wide.

Gentile took a step backward and met Noble's stare wearing a look of wonder on his chiseled, ageless features. He was a short man, but efficiently built and remarkably well-groomed for a keeper of horses. Noble had known him all of his life, just as he did most of the other inhabitants of Peaceful, and he had never known Gentile to be anything other than businesslike and utterly dry in his dealings with everyone, himself included. That the usually imperturbable man reacted in such a telling manner to Noble's abruptness left Noble temporarily abashed.

Gentile, however, seemed to recover from his shock at once. He arched a salt-and-pepper eyebrow at Noble, and the expression spoke volumes.

"Morning, Noble," he greeted him with a hint of wry amusement in his tone. "You look like you might have been expecting the devil. Sorry to disappoint."

The talk in town, when there was nothing more interesting to say, was that Gentile had been a schoolmaster once, and a captain during the war. He had no family that anyone knew. The more gossipy citizens of Peaceful speculated that the liveryman was too exacting to be satisfied with the way a wife might launder his drawers to be troubled by one. He had a way of looking at people as if he couldn't decide whether he was amused or annoyed by them. Neither notion appealed to Noble, especially with Ivy Wingate hiding out in his cellar and her violet scent clinging to his own collar.

Noble held on to the door and did not invite the older man in.

"What brings you out here, sir?"

He winced when he said it. He'd been calling Gentile "sir" since he was old enough to talk, and he'd never been able to shake the habit.

Gentile sent him a brief grin, as if he knew exactly what Noble had been thinking. "A cup of coffee would bring me in to tell you."

Noble lowered his gaze momentarily, then stepped aside with a wave of his hand. He mumbled an apology for his rudeness and invited Gentile to sit in the front parlor while he got the coffee. Gentile declined, following him instead into the kitchen. Noble restrained himself from ordering him back into the parlor, praying that Ivy would stay put and keep quiet down below.

There were already two mugs on the sideboard. Surely Gentile's hawk eyes had noticed. Noble cursed under his breath.

"I heard Charity was missing." Gentile lowered himself into one of the spindled chairs with efficient, military grace. "Were you expecting some company?"

Noble chose to ignore the question. He filled both mugs from the fresh pot and carried them to the table. "What can I do for you?" he asked, taking the chair across from his guest.

Gentile considered him for a long, uncomfortable moment. Noble forced himself to meet the older man's scrutiny without blinking, although his face grew warm with the effort. Finally Gentile leaned back in his chair and rootled his thumb and forefinger in the breast pocket of his brown leather vest. Noble watched, mesmerized, swearing that he could hear Ivy's heartbeat through the floor that separated them. Gentile withdrew a folded bit of paper, smoothed it open on the table and pushed it across to him. His actions seemed to take forever.

"Ivy Wingate left that at Mrs. Quinlan's last night," he informed Noble laconically. "She left a schoolhouse full of kids without so much as a by-your-leave and took my best horse, besides." Gentile hooked his forefinger through the handle of the mug and drew it to his mouth for a sip. The way he did it was an unspoken condemnation of Ivy's actions.

Noble restrained an urge to argue on Ivy's behalf. As far as Gentile knew, he and Ivy were still at odds, and Noble preferred to keep it that way. Instead, he studied the note for a moment without touching it. He recognized Ivy's neat handwriting at once. He bit his lip to keep his mounting agitation in check and planted his elbows before him on the table.

"Says there she left you fifty dollars for him," he observed, leaving his own mug on the table in favor of steepling his hands. "Anyway, what's this to do with me?"

Al Gentile raised one eyebrow as if to say he suspected Noble knew exactly what it was to do with him. Noble ignored the look as best he could.

"Fifty dollars isn't enough for the animal she took by half," Gentile informed him, his tone pained. "And I mean to get the rest of the money, or the gelding, back. Word has it you were over at the schoolhouse visiting her yesterday. I thought you might know where she is. Or at least where she went."

Noble considered him. The piebald was an exceptional horse, it was true. Ivy had good taste, if not good sense. But while fifty dollars might be a little on the low side, he doubted the animal would fetch as much as Gentile's inflated ideas. He frowned.

"Ivy Wingate doesn't discuss her travel plans with me," he said dryly, satisfied that his declaration was at least partly true: If he had his say, Ivy would remain behind, safe in town. "If you've got it in your mind that she stole the horse from you, shouldn't you report it to Sheriff Doman?"

That was a risk, Noble knew, although a calculated one. Gentile and Doman were not known for their fondness for one another, and Noble suspected that Gentile would not relish reporting to the lawman that the well-liked schoolteacher had stolen his horse. Especially since she'd left him a hefty deposit.

Gentile leaned back in his chair until it creaked and crossed his polished boot over his knee. Noble heard the steady tap of the older man's other foot and prayed that Ivy would not take it as a sign that she should come up out of hiding prematurely.

"I thought I'd see what I could find out on my own, first." Gentile made a show of looking apologetic, if not downright sheepish. Noble wondered if he might not also have been an actor during his eclectic career. "I'd hate to see Miss Ivy set herself up to get hanged over what might prove to be no more than a misunderstanding."

Noble scowled.

"You're saying you'd have her arrested and maybe hanged over a difference of a few dollars? It says right there she left you fifty and promises the rest as soon as she can. And I don't care if the horse she took was Pegasus; you don't have a nag in that stable worth more than seventy-five dollars on his best day." Noble stopped himself before he said more, although his hands itched to throttle the covetous old muleskinner.

Gentile raised an eyebrow at him and nosed his coffee as if it were a fine brandy. "She took the pie."

Noble stopped himself before he blurted out "I know," remembering only at the last instant that Gentile had not previously mentioned the fact. He shrugged.

"So?"

Gentile took several more considered draughts of the coffee Ivy had prepared half an hour ago.

"This brew's a lot better than your usual swill." He issued an approving nod.

"I don't have time to socialize." Noble stood up. "You have a horse to hunt down. I have a sister to find. I should have left at sunup."

"Why didn't you?" Gentile kept the cup to his lips, but did not drink.

Noble avoided his sharp gray eyes. "I think you'd better go." He found himself studying the seam in the floor, where the trap door to the cellar was.

Gentile set his cup down.

"I think you're buying yourself some trouble, boy," he said. "But at least if you buy it, you'll own it fair and square. Tell Miss Ivy, if you see her, that she has ten days to bring back the pie, else I pay a call on the sheriff. Then he'll put it out on the wire and she's sure to get caught." He sighed as if he regretted the inevitable, and Noble recognized the expression for the fraud that it was.

"I like Miss Ivy," he went on. "Always have. But I have my business to think of, and she needs to be taught a lesson. 'Course, not every sheriff is as soft—that is to say kindly—as Bill Doman. She's liable to get hurt, or worse. I'd hate for it to come to that, Noble." With a last, knowing look, he got up. "Thanks for the coffee. I'd best be getting back to town."

Noble bit his lip. "Wait, Gentile," he said, keeping his voice low.

Chapter Nine

Ivy knew it was Gentile with Noble in the kitchen above her. She could not make out their words, but the timbre of their voices was unmistakable. Al Gentile was not a menacing man, but his seriousness always frightened her. Of course, with the piebald in Noble's barn only partially paid for, she had reason to fear the grim liveryman at the moment.

The men conversed for what seemed hours while Ivy shivered in the blackness below. She crouched on the ladder and clasped her arms about her, not wanting to discover what other creatures might be sharing the cellar. Finally the voices stopped and two pairs of footsteps clattered from the room in a weird, irregular rhythm. She waited for one of them to return. Just as she began to fear that she'd been left alone, trapped, in the cellar, the drumming of a single set of footsteps running across the kitchen floor reassured her. It was all she could do to keep from calling out to Noble to free her from her dungeon which, thanks to her busy imagination, had suddenly become a terrifying place.

The daylight blinded her when Noble opened the trap door. She shielded her face with her arm and scrambled up the ladder. She tripped once in her haste, but Noble caught her and lifted her out as easily as if she were a child. What a wonderful father he would make, she marvelled, staring as he set her down on her feet. He is a father, her conscience reminded her. She blanched, but forced herself to look at him.

"You look spooked, Honey." Noble concentrated his gaze on her shoulders as he brushed away the dirt of the cellar from them.

"What did Mr. Gentile want?" she asked, ignoring his comment.

Noble glanced at her, and she was startled to note the seriousness of his gaze. He gave her a quick grin meant, she was certain, to be reassuring and skimmed the tip of her nose with one finger.

"Just to pass the time of day." He turned away from her to close up the cellarway again. "I told him I was busy, that I had to get out and look for Charity."

"It sure seemed as if he had a lot of day to pass the time of."

Noble leaned on the table for a moment before he lifted it back into place.

"What do you mean?" he inquired lightly, turning away.

She walked around the kitchen until she could see his face. He seemed uneasy, and he was making her feel that way too. Uneasiness quickly gave way to irritation.

"I mean it sounded like you both had a lot more

109

to say to one another than just 'howdy'!" she snapped.

"Did you hear us?" Noble jerked his head up. His dark eyes narrowed with suspicion.

"I heard your voices, sure, but I couldn't hear what you were saying," she retorted. "I'm not an eavesdropper." Not that she hadn't tried to be one. She stared at his big hands as they clenched and flexed.

One of those hands reached for her. The tips of his fingers grazed her cheek.

"Is there anything you think you should tell me?" he asked unexpectedly, his tone low and even, like a patient parent's.

Ivy's face boiled. Gentile, she surmised, had revealed what amounted to her theft of the piebald, and Noble had chosen to protect her rather than to give her up. She looked away, choked by Noble's loyalty. It made her own greater deceit seem even more ugly to her.

"I left him money," she answered, unable to face him. "I meant it as a deposit on the pie. I told him in a letter that I'd give him the rest, but he'd have to wait until I got back to Peaceful, or I'd see that he got it somehow."

"How much?"

"What?"

"How much money did you leave?"

"Fifty dollars." She felt as if her last breath had left her body. She hurt so.

Noble considered Ivy's slumped shoulders and her bowed head. She looked miserable. His heart ached for her, and for what he and Gentile were about to do to her. But it was for her own good, he reminded himself. He wished he could take more comfort from that thought.

*   *   *

Noble fussed and frowned and argued, but Ivy still thought he gave in a bit too easily to her insistence on coming, especially when she'd admitted to taking Gentile's horse under false pretenses. He'd said he understood, and that everything would work out. She was a little alarmed at how easily she trusted him, and how readily she capitulated to his strength and conviction. He was up to something, and she guessed she'd better watch him. She loved him beyond reason, but that did not alter the fact that Noble Smith was high-handed and willing to go to great lengths to get his own way.

Just like her.

She smiled at his back. It was midday, and the sun was high. They'd left on their quest several hours earlier, and the day had already become quite warm, for April. Noble watered his mare in Witherspoon Creek. The swift water, swollen by the spring thaw in the mountains around them, formed white bubbles around the placid animal's fetlocks. Ivy watched as Noble pulled his arms from the sleeves of his old brown coat, revealing a dark, uneven stripe of perspiration down the back of his shirt. The sight of it, coupled with the play of his muscles, warmed her more than the sunshine. He looked over his shoulder at her and grinned, as if she were a willing confederate in some childish mischief.

"When are you going to tell me where we're going?" he called back to her over the din of the rushing water.

"As soon as we're too far along for you to find a way to send me home." She might as well be as honest with him as she could. Lord knew, she was keeping enough from him as it was.

111

No, she would not think of Laurel. She could not afford that luxury.

"You're worried, aren't you?"

Ivy started at Noble's candid remark. She felt the sensation drain from her face, as if a tap had been opened somewhere around her gut. "What do you mean?"

Noble yanked the blue checkered neckerchief from his throat and pushed back the brim of his dusty old black Stetson. He mopped his brow with a casual enough gesture, but there was a shrewdness in his dark-eyed gaze that was no comfort to Ivy. She felt as if her deceit were a bright red mark she wore upon her breast, like Hester Prynne's Scarlet Letter. She was sorely tempted to avert her gaze from his, but tried instead to brave it out. She was doubly distressed when his sober gaze transformed into a puckish, knowing grin.

"Come on, Ivy. You can't keep secrets from me. You never could. Your face is like a slate, with everything written all over it."

If only you knew, she thought. She pressed her lips together, smothering her regret. Her vision clouded.

"What's wrong?" Noble dismounted. He came to stand beside her and touched her leg. He looked up at her, his chocolate eyes brimming with concern. "It's those men, isn't it? They didn't—God, you're trembling!"

"I'm fine," she managed in a small voice, both overcome by his concern and relieved by his misinterpretation. "I don't . . . I mean—"

"Get down," he ordered, his curtness softened by entreaty. She was about to protest, but he held out his arms in an offer of assistance and she found herself complying with his gentle demand before she realized it. She stood before him and cherished the warm comfort of his hands on her shoulders.

"Did they hurt you, those men at your ranch? Other than the bruises, I mean? I assumed they hadn't, but I never really asked you, did I? I guess I didn't really want to know."

Ivy closed her eyes and allowed the sweet urgency of Noble's chivalrous inquiry to shelter her from her own demons. She shook her head.

"Then what is it? Are you worried they might follow us?"

She shook her head again, unable, unwilling to compose herself to answer him.

"Are you afraid they might find Stephen and Charity before we do?"

Tell him, a stern voice in her head commanded. Tell him about Laurel! The voice sounded so much like her father's that her heart resisted. She opened her eyes and beheld undisguised distress in Noble's handsome, angular features. The sight opened old wounds and inflicted new ones. The terrible lie of omission was growing within her like an unwanted seed.

"We found each other again, Ivy," he reminded her, his baritone cracking once, as if he'd strained it somehow. He moved his hands along the slope of her narrow shoulders to the soft part of her arm and gave her a gentle, reminding massage. "No matter what else happens from here on out, we have that. And nobody can take that away from us, ever. Never again. Right?"

Ivy could not answer him. She searched his face and found, to her surprise, that he was seeking reassurance, just as she was. She had to give to him what comfort she could, even though the price was her continued secrecy.

"Nobody," she echoed softly, wondering if he could hear the whisper of deceit and irony underlying her reply. Noble is right, that voice jeered at her again. Nobody can part you again. Nobody, that is, except for yourselves—and your secrets.

Noble's lips brushed against the sensitive skin beside her mouth and a long, slow growl was born in his throat. She answered with a muffled sob as he captured her mouth with his own. His fingers played in the braid of hair secured at the base of her neck until they freed it from its bindings, then they raked through it like a loving comb. She marvelled at his mastery. She melted against the firmness of his chest beneath the softness of his shirt. Her loins responded with a needy cry of their own that terrified and amazed her.

She wanted him. That was the single, crystalline fact she was capable of understanding at that moment, and she knew it would take but a single gesture of encouragement from him to send her plummeting down the wondrous path of destruction they'd both followed so long ago. She thought of Laurel, and she knew at once that she could not put herself through that kind of torment again.

"Noble, stop—"

A gunshot punctuated her breathless exclamation. The bullet buzzed through the tranquil afternoon and stung a sagebrush just behind the piebald. The horse jolted with a neigh of protest. Ivy froze. Noble's right hand shot out to seize the frightened animal's reins while with his left arm he pulled Ivy into a protective embrace. A second shot sent up a spray of dirt at their feet.

"Mount up and ride," Noble ordered her grimly. "Across the creek and down the trail. Don't stop, and don't look back."

"But—"

A third shot was swallowed by the stream.

"Go!" he roared. "I'll hold them off. Don't look back! I'll catch up!"

Ivy mounted the pie and dug in her heels before she was in the saddle. Noble's eyes had never looked more beautiful to her, or more sad. She caught another glance just before he slapped the horse's rump.

"Hee-yaahh!"

The pie bolted. Ivy clung to the rein and leaned far over the animal's neck. Together they raced across the creek, pursued by the sound of more gunfire. She gritted her teeth, expecting at any moment to feel the swift burn of a bullet pierce her body, or for the pie to fall beneath her. She wished for it. She hoped she would draw their fire, so that Noble might escape as well.

But in moments as the creek, then the ground, thundered away beneath them, she realized that the shots remained behind.

Dammit! They had him pinned on all sides. There was no cover except for the mare, and Noble was damned if he'd sacrifice her, except to buy Ivy a few more moments to get away. The scrub pine he was crouched behind was a laughable shield, if he was in the mood for a joke. As bullets sent up geysers of dirt all around him, he knew they were aiming wide on purpose. They couldn't be that bad at shooting that they were aiming for him and missing.

The mare was restive. She was an even-tempered animal, but Noble knew that if she hadn't been tethered, she would have bolted once the shooting started. He briefly thanked his Maker that he'd been smart enough to secure her to the pine he was hiding behind, but he dared not waste time on the prayer. As the bullets continued to sing around him, he reviewed his options.

He couldn't make out the position of the assailants in the surrounding brush and rocks, especially in the glare of the sun. Not that he could have hit any of them if he shot; he was not an especially accurate marksman except with the Henry, and only then when he could see what he was shooting at. Anyway, the Henry was still in its sheath on the mare's saddle. He doubted the men in the ambush would allow him to retrieve it so he could return their fire. His best chance, he figured, was to try and get away from there.

But did he dare to follow Ivy? If his intention was to lead them away from her, surely it would be wiser for him to take a different route to escape. Down the stream a ways, maybe. Far enough to lead them off the scent, but not so far that he couldn't catch up with Ivy again quickly when he'd lost them.

His decision was made. He yanked the mare's rein free and, with a brief, formless prayer, he charged from behind the pine and into the saddle. The mare didn't need his heels in her sides to take off down the creek like a thing possessed. Noble made himself as small as possible against her and braced himself for the inevitable searing pain of a bullet. Where would it strike? he wondered. He'd never been shot, but he'd helped Doc treat enough wounded patients to know the damage a bullet could do to human flesh. He could only hope it wouldn't strike his head, his back, or anywhere else that might affect a vital organ. He was no good to Ivy, or Charity, dead.

He was several dozen yards downstream before he realized that not only was he still unmarked by bullets, but he no longer heard shots flying about him. Emboldened by the realization as much as he was bewildered by it, he reined the mare to a splashing halt and listened.

What he heard inspired first wonder, then panic. There was a dull thunder of many pounding hooves, but they were all heading away from him: The ambushers had wanted to drive him off so that they could pursue Ivy!

Contrary to Noble's instruction, Ivy drew up and paused as soon as she realized the men behind her were still shooting at him. She hadn't liked the idea of leaving him there alone in the first place, and she would not allow him to sacrifice himself for her safety without putting up some kind of fight for him. At the very least, she figured, reining the gelding back where they had come from, she could act as a decoy long enough for Noble to escape.

Assuming he was still alive, that is.

The thought froze her heart. With a cry, she urged her mount back down the road toward the creek, toward the sound of the shots.

But the shots had stopped.

Ivy pulled to a halt again, confused by the sudden silence. Before she could even conjecture what it meant, she became aware of the dull thrum of galloping horses heading in her direction.

Quickly she nosed the impatient gelding off the road, into the sparse cover of the trees. On the slim chance that it might be Noble coming to catch up to her, she wanted to keep a clear view of the road while keeping out of sight herself. If it was Noble, he'd be in a hurry and not expecting to find her waiting for him. If it wasn't Noble, it would be five men looking for her with anger in their eyes and revenge in their hearts.

The thrumming grew nearer. Shaking, weak with terror, she slid from the saddle and scrambled to a thicket. She pulled the gelding behind and hoped that whoever was charging along the road was not looking for her there.

She had not sought cover too soon. Peering through the thicket, she saw five riders surge past as if chased by the very devil himself. They moved far too fast for her to recognize any of them save to know they were men, but she felt certain they were the same ones who had ambushed her at the ranch last night. It could not be a coincidence that there were five of them. As they sped past, her heart hammered in time with the cadence of the pounding hooves. How long would they continue along the road before they realized she had left it? How long before they came back looking for her?

She had no time to speculate. She was between Noble and her pursuers, and time was not her ally. She had to return to the ford and discover what had happened to Noble before she could decide her next course of action.

It was not far back to the ford. Ivy stayed off the road but near enough to see it in the event that Noble might actually be in pursuit. She hoped he was, but as she heard the sound of rushing water announcing the nearness of the creek, she knew.

He would have followed her if he could. He had not. Common sense told her that he could not have survived that fusillade.

She hardened herself: Noble was dead.

Chapter Ten

Ivy felt cold and empty as she entered the clearing at the ford, despite the warm, full April sunshine that blinded her. She no longer cared that the men might double back and find her there, alone and helpless. Nothing mattered anymore. Any instinct for self-preservation she'd possessed had been swallowed whole by the realization that Noble was gone. God had allowed them to find one another again for the time it took Him to blink, then He had taken him away from her again forever.

She was too devastated even to cry.

The creek rushed along in mindless merriment, a cruel ostinato to her bleak mood. A congregation of killdeer sang like a faulty but enthusiastic church choir in a cathedral of nearby scrub pine. The piebald pushed ahead through water that reached his knees. He carried her all the way to the other side before the import of the scene struck her.

The scrub pine that now provided hospitality for the killdeer had also lately served as the hitching post for Noble's mare. And neither the mare nor Noble was presently anywhere in evidence.

Her heart rising, Ivy did not wait for the pie to reach the bank before she dismounted to have a closer look. She was filled with doubt and disbelief, even as her boots took on water up to her ankles. Perhaps she was not in the same place at all. Perhaps she was much farther downstream than where she'd been when she left Noble behind.

There was a confusion of footprints all around in the soft dirt, trampled by a small cavalry of hoofprints. Near the pine, she recognized the impression left by her own boots, along with Noble's larger, heavier ones.

A thrill coursed through her that she tried to temper with reason as she knelt down for a closer look. She could make out nothing among the dirt, stones and bits of broken-off twigs that indicated Noble had been hurt or dragged away—no blood or bits of torn cloth. And it would have taken a far stronger current than Witherspoon Creek to wash away a man of his size. She straightened, tallying the evidence before her.

Somehow Noble had escaped alive.

A cry of wordless joy left Ivy's lips. The sound of it startled both her and the birds in the bush, who took flight as one in protest. Quickly Ivy looked about, nonplussed by her imprudence. What if those outlaws had already doubled back and heard her?

She stood up and looked about one more time, not certain what she was looking for, not knowing what she should do next. There was no clue as to where Noble might have gone. But at least he had gotten away.

But which way had he gone? She had not passed him when she'd doubled back to the ford.

Disconcerted, Ivy sat atop the waiting piebald. She must decide which way to go to find Noble, and soon, for it was not wise for her to remain in the open. If she had time to think, she might be able to guess with some accuracy which direction Noble had taken. But time was not her ally.

She paused: Neither, strictly speaking, was Noble. Noble had openly admitted to wanting her to remain behind, and to being interested in finding a way to force her to do just that. And he was up to something, she was sure of it.

Ivy sat up straight in the saddle, filled with a bold, new plan: This was the perfect opportunity for her to strike out in a new direction entirely and pursue Stephen and Charity, alone!

But what of Noble's distress when he could not find her?

She set her jaw. Noble would know she had escaped. Noble would know she was all right somehow, wouldn't he?

But she had believed him to be dead, she realized as the pie grew restless beneath her. What sense would guide Noble into believing she was all right?

She stiffened again. Pursuing Stephen and Charity alone was the lesser of two evils, at least as far as the runaways were concerned. And that opportunity was sliding away from her with every moment she delayed.

Her decision was made. She nudged the pie farther up the bank. No sooner had she started upon the road than she heard a horse approach from downstream. She looked around. The road was straight; she judged she could not follow it and be out of sight by the time the rider reached her. Her only choice was to hide and hope whoever was coming upstream in a hurry was not looking for her.

The pie shied from the thicket of sagebrush and scrub pine. God alone knew what dangers the animal sensed, but she had no time to sweet-talk him. She slid from the saddle and yanked his rein, hoping the bushes were tall enough to hide them from view.

"I won't tolerate craven behavior," she scolded in a low tone, wishing she had a carrot or an apple wedge with which to tempt him. "I haven't got time for it. I suspect you'd make a lovely sofa, if you prefer to stay out here in the open by yourself."

That last seemed to motivate the recalcitrant gelding. No sooner had she drawn him in and quieted his restive nickering than the lone rider came into view. Ivy held her breath as he reined his bay to a halt.

It was Noble.

Holding her breath, she watched him slow his mare to a trot. He did not appear to be hurt. Call to him, a voice inside her advised. But she pressed her lips together.

Noble stayed on the mare and looked around. His hat, drawn low over his brow, shaded his face from the westering sun. She could not see his features, but she felt the intensity of his gaze as he surveyed the area. He turned his head, slowly, from one side to the other, as if making careful note of everything that moved around him. Ivy felt lightheaded, but she dared not take a breath for fear of attracting his attention.

The pie flicked his tail. The family of killdeer, which had retreated to the surrounding sagebrush, took flight again. Noble jerked his head in their direction and drew his Colt from its holster with a quick, easy motion. The clean, metallic click of the cocked hammer startled her as much as if he had actually fired a shot.

"Come out of there," he ordered crisply. "Real slow. And keep both hands where I can see 'em."

She could not force her feet to move.

"N-Noble," she managed in a small voice, disappointed by the failure of her most recent plan. "Don't shoot. It's me."

Noble lowered his gun at once.

"Ivy?" His voice was hollow with amazement. "How did you get back here? Are you all right? Why are you hiding?"

She could not confess to the truth, that she'd meant to go on without him.

Noble reined toward her. "No, don't answer me now." He eliminated the need for a lie. "We've got to get away from here. South? Shall we go south?"

Ivy stared up at him, feeling as if her limbs had turned to granite. She could make out his face clearly, and it was strained with worry.

"I know you don't want to tell me, Ivy, but I think it's time you started trusting me. We can't wait here for those men to come back. You meant to head south, didn't you?"

When she did not answer him right away, Noble breathed a quiet oath and glanced up at the sky.

"I figured it out a ways back," he said, impatience lacing his quiet tone. "You were going to get us to Greybull, and I guess you thought to aim south after that to Riverton. You think Stephen's headed for the train, don't you? Maybe in Rawlins, or Rock Springs?"

Ivy lowered her head, amazed by Noble's perception. Rawlins would be Stephen's destination if he were headed for Chicago, Rock Springs the junction of choice if her brother's aim were San

Francisco. If Stephen knew the danger following him—and he was no fool; how could he not?—He would want to head east, where there were more people among whom they could hide. He and Charity could easily take up new names and lose themselves together in a city the size of Chicago. He would head for Rawlins.

Rawlins was where the MacDonald cousins lived, with Laurel.

"Come on, Ivy. We have to make tracks. We can talk about this when we get to Basin," he said, mentioning the name of the nearest town.

Noble was right beside her, looking down at her from atop the mare. She could not bear to know what he was thinking, and she knew if she met his gaze, she would see it very clearly. Without risking another word, she emerged from the cover of the scrub and mounted the pie.

Rawlins. You're going to Rawlins. Stephen will be there, or he will have been. Ceily will be worried, and Tom will probably be angry. And Laurel . . . Laurel will be Laurel. Noble's daughter, living a good and happy life with two people who adore her, people who have given her love and stability for nearly ten years. People she knows as Ma and Pa. People who love her fiercely, as you do, and who, also like you, would do anything to keep her from being hurt, either physically or emotionally. A man and a woman, your own kin, who would fight to keep the child they view as a very special gift from God.

"You've been awful quiet," Noble observed.

It was late. The sun was setting beyond the Tetons, but they hadn't made camp. Noble wanted to press on, to make Basin, so they wouldn't have to camp out with those five desperate characters on their trail.

Ivy did not answer. She had thought of nothing but Laurel all afternoon, throughout the long, punishing ride. Watching Noble's broad, ramrod back as the miles thundered away, she admitted to herself for the very first time the real reason why she had so far been unable to tell him about their daughter: She was terrified. Not for herself; even if Noble took it in his heart to hate her for her monumental betrayal, and there was every chance that he would, she would endure it. Her terror was for the MacDonalds, and for Laurel herself.

Not that Noble would hurt them, any of them, intentionally. But she knew Noble: He would not brook any obstacle to acknowledging a child long denied him. No matter that Ivy had freely, if reluctantly, given Tom and Ceily her daughter, knowing that to have done otherwise was to expose the child to hardship and shame, or worse. With the MacDonalds, Laurel had enjoyed advantages that she, Ivy, could never have hoped to give her at the time, namely, a mother and a father who wanted her and were able to care for her. For Laurel to be forced to accept the fact, now, that her life was a lie and that she was only on this earth through an accident of nature was the most unforgivable cruelty Ivy could imagine, surpassing even the cruelty of having had to give up Laurel in the first place.

The only logical course of action open to her, Ivy realized, was never to let Noble know about his daughter. It was an injustice to him, but the revelation would bring greater injustice to Laurel, who alone was innocent of any wrongdoing, and who deserved whatever happiness Ivy and her loving adoptive parents could provide her.

"Ivy?"

"What?" She stirred and noticed, for the first time, an ache in her legs and back.

Carole Howey

"I said, you've been quiet." Noble sounded kind of stretched, himself. "What are you thinking about, back there?"

"Nothing," she murmured, and regretted it at once: As a schoolteacher, she knew that the only time a student responded to an inquiry such as Noble's by saying "nothing" was when they meant everything.

"See that dust over the rise?" With a sweep of his arm, he pointed toward a dirty cloud just above the horizon. "I'm pretty sure that's Basin. We can make it by nightfall."

He seemed not to notice her clumsy falsehood. Ivy breathed a prayer of thanks.

"Do you think we should spend the night there?" she asked. If Noble wanted to change the subject, she was only too happy to oblige him.

Noble reined to a halt, intending, it seemed, for Ivy to catch up with him. He pushed his black Stetson back off his forehead, and as Ivy drew beside him she could see the creases of worry in his brow. She knew at once why he hadn't marked her evasive answer. He had other things on his mind that he obviously did not care to share with her. She was not certain that she even wanted to know what they were.

"I think it's the safest thing," he replied without looking at her. Then he heaved a big sigh. A moment later he flashed her an unexpected grin, although his coffee-colored eyes remained sober.

"Are you sorry you came along, now?" he wanted to know. "You look done in. And I bet you're hungry, too, wishing you were about to sit down to one of Penelope Quinlan's suppers at the boarding house instead of out here in the wild."

Ivy bridled.

"I'm not so weak and soft as you think!" she retorted, glad of an excuse to speak sharply to him.

His grin widened, although his gaze still seemed guarded.

"No need to bite my head off," he observed in a wry tone. "I'm just saying that because I know it's how I feel, right about now. It's no insult to be accused of having common sense. Besides—" he sent a sideways look her way that persuaded a warm blush to her cheeks—"though I'd never make the mistake of thinking you weak, I actually kind of prefer you soft, just the way God intended."

Good Lord, she felt as if she were coming down with a fever, just on a look and a few flirtatious words from Noble Smith. What an extraordinary feeling!

"Tongue-tied?"

She was. The realization made her face feel warmer still.

"Well, now, that's got to be a first," he declared with a gentle, teasing laugh, sidling his mare closer to the piebald. "Ivy Wingate, speechless. They ought to make it a national holiday."

She found the will, despite her deepening chagrin, to look up at him. Her intended retort, however, was taken away by Noble's kiss.

He took his time with it, too, and her rebuttal, by and by, was forgotten. She closed her eyes and gripped the horn of her saddle. Noble's kiss sent a tickle to the tips of her toes, as well as to the tips of her breasts.

She was not sure how long his kiss actually lasted, but he was no longer kissing her when she felt his hand perform a languorous massage on the back of her neck.

"I love you, Ivy-girl." His whisper was like a mystical chant, and she was under its spell. "And I would never hurt you, if I could help it. You know that, don't you?"

A smile teased Ivy's lips, and she opened her eyes.

"Why do you say that as if you expect to at any moment?"

To her wonder, Noble's own fond, lazy grin suddenly sagged. He looked away.

"I'll buy you dinner," he offered in a tight voice, as if something were constricting his throat. "It may be the last good meal either of us has for a long time."

Without further comment, Noble nudged the mare to a canter. Ivy stayed behind, sensing his sudden pensive mood. Her own humor had darkened considerably in the last few moments, since the withdrawal of Noble's kiss. The stain of her secret, she sensed, keeping pace behind the mare, was deepening.

Chapter Eleven

"I only have eight dollars," Ivy whispered as they reined to a halt before the Basin Hotel.

"Never mind." Noble was terse. "We only need one room. I'll sleep in a chair."

"But, Noble—"

"I said, never mind!"

Ivy stared as Noble dismounted. He did not look at her. His motions were quick and jerky, as if he wanted to punch someone. Her, maybe.

Noble was signing the register by the time Ivy followed him into the hotel. The round-faced woman at the desk looked at Ivy and frowned. Her bold stare reminded Ivy of the bruise on her face. Ivy put her hand to her cheek, but it was too late to hide the mark from the critical innkeeper. Chagrined, Ivy allowed her hand to drop to her side once more. She felt exposed, as if she were guilty of some awful crime. It was obvious that the woman held her in contempt. No doubt she believed Noble to be responsible for the bruise, and for Ivy's overall deplorable condition. Noble had surely registered them as man and wife; the woman probably did not believe that they were married, either.

Ivy looked down at her dusty, rumpled skirt. She didn't look any too respectable, she had to admit, after everything she'd been through that day. She pushed an errant lock of hair back into the failing braid at the base of her neck and stared at the floor, flustered by the silent censure of the woman staring at her, annoyed with herself for feeling that way.

"I've ordered a bath sent up for you." Noble, finished with the register, stood before her without touching her. "Go on and get cleaned up. I'll take the horses over to the livery. I'll be back as soon as I can and we'll get some supper. Stay in the room until I come for you. Don't go running off anywhere, Ivy. I mean it."

She wanted to take exception to his overbearing tone, but she was so tired and achy that she couldn't. She could, however, scowl at him, and she did, but he had already walked away from her as if she and her feelings were of no consequence. She stared after him, her face filling with heat, feeling the curious, pitying gaze of the woman behind the desk.

What had gotten into him?

The bath was a welcome refreshment. Ivy washed her hair, too, since she doubted she'd have the chance again for a long time. It was still damp when she dressed in a clean shirtwaist and her riding skirt. Afterward, she sat on the creaking bed in the small but neat room and pulled her comb through the tangles. She welcomed the pain.

"Ivy."

She started and turned around. In the open doorway of the room was a rangy young man standing with his legs wide apart and the tips of his fingers grazing the handles of his twin Colts. His holsters were tied to his thighs, as if he expected a fight from her, or else expected her to try and escape. His jade green eyes studied her, and his full auburn mustache curled as his mouth turned down in a half-smile, half-sneer.

"Who are you?" Ivy demanded coldly, in a bold attempt to mask her fear. "How do you know my name?"

He laughed quietly. The sound was disconcertingly familiar.

"Don't you recognize me?"

Stephen!

With a cry, she leapt from the bed and flung her arms around him. He hesitated as if he had not been expecting so fond a greeting, and for a moment Ivy feared he would not return her affection. She held him tighter, afraid he would try to pull away from her.

"I-I didn't figure you'd be this happy to see me." His voice was gruff, but she knew it nevertheless as Stephen's, and wondered how she could not have recognized it at once. It had deepened, of course, but nevertheless it retained a familiar burr, a holdover from his slight childhood lisp. It was a long way from fifteen to seventeen for a young man, she knew. As a schoolteacher, she watched such changes take place gradually in her students. Seeing Stephen after two years, however, she was stunned by the contrast.

"Stephen," she murmured, as the words backed up in her throat. "Stephen, oh, Stephen, I'm so glad to see you!" There was much she wanted to ask him, but at the moment, none of it seemed important.

"Same here, Sis."

He placed his arms about her awkwardly, as if she were a cumbersome but precious heirloom. That, Ivy supposed, was as close to an expression of fondness as she would ever get from him.

"I won't break," she teased him. "I'll bet you squeeze Charity tighter than that!"

He released her at once. She took a step back and did not look at him. Her mention of Charity was what had wedged them apart, and she did not know how to reach for him again across that gap.

"That's why I come here looking for you."

"Came," the schoolteacher in her corrected.

"Charity doesn't want to go back." He ignored her amendment. "That's why I'm here. I—" his green-eyed gaze narrowed, and he reached for her face. "What happened to you? The side of your face is six shades of blue."

Ivy's hand went to her cheek. She had forgotten about the souvenir from last night's encounter. She wanted to blurt its cause to him, but she held herself back, for reasons she did not know herself.

"I fell. Now what—"

"Noble do that to you?" Stephen's young voice was hostile with challenge, as if he meant to do something about it if she said yes.

"No!" she retorted in Noble's defense, glaring at her brother. "Noble's not that kind of man. Not like Pa."

"You're sure?" Stephen looked doubtful.

"He never struck Charity, did he?" Ivy only guessed at that, but as Charity never missed a day of school, nor had she ever showed up looking anything but pampered and healthy, she felt it a safe assumption.

Stephen glowered. "He'd better not have."

"He didn't," she dismissed with a wave. "Or you would have heard. So would I. You know Peaceful. Now what were you about to say regarding you and Charity?"

Stephen gave her a doubtful look as if he meant to argue the matter further, but he set his square jaw, instead.

"Charity doesn't want to go back," he repeated, sounding even surer of himself than before. "I wanted to tell you so you would tell Noble, and the two of you would let us be."

"Why don't you tell him yourself?" Ivy inquired with a lift of one eyebrow. "He's here in town."

Stephen scowled at her again, but it was not a hostile expression, this time. It reminded her of when he was younger, when he'd spent the day playing in the dirt and struggled against her admonitions to take a bath.

"I know that," he retorted. "I've been watching you two for a couple of hours, since well before you rode into town. Noble ain't so clever as you or him like to think."

Ivy considered him.

"You've been—then you know about the men at the ford? The men who think you took their gold?"

Stephen lowered his gaze just long enough for her to guess that he knew exactly what she was talking about.

"Did you take their gold?"

Stephen's eyes smoldered.

"Do you think I did?"

Ivy took up her comb once again and applied it to her damp tangles.

"What I think isn't important, is it?" she pointed out dryly. "They said you did. And they seemed pretty upset about it last night out at the ranch.

133

That's how I got this, since you asked. And I would have gotten worse, if Noble hadn't turned up when he did. Apparently it's a great deal of gold, which they no doubt came by through illegal means."

"They stole it."

"And what did you do with it?"

Stephen yanked his tall gray Stetson from his head and slammed it to the floor with a bitter oath.

"I knew you'd think the worst of me! You always did. I swear, I don't know why I even thought that you might—"

He broke off, shaking his head, looking so frustrated that Ivy took hold of his broad shoulders and shook him hard. She could not help but notice that he scarcely moved, for all her effort.

"Stephen, stop it!" she ordered him in a stern tone. "I'm here because I love you, and I want to help you. Surely you must know that! But you have to tell me everything."

"There isn't time!" Stephen was brusque. "Noble will be back soon, and I can't let him find me here." He broke away from her and sidled to the window sash. She watched him poke the curtain aside with one tentative finger. He peered through the gap he had created, careful to stay out of sight.

"I don't know why you don't just sit down with Noble and explain to him. To us both." She tried to reason with him.

Stephen glanced over his shoulder at her, wearing a whimsical grin. " 'Us,' huh? So that's the way things are, now. Looks like my taking off with Charity was good for something, wasn't it?"

Ivy blushed.

"Where is Charity?" She decided it best to change the subject.

"Somewhere safe." Stephen looked out of the window again.

"Do you mean safe from Noble, or safe from those men?"

"Both."

Ivy clenched her jaw. Stephen was cautious and evasive. She found it irritating, but she realized it was probably a good thing, too. Being in possession of a large amount of stolen gold, he had a powerful inducement to such behavior.

"Tell me about the gold," she urged him. "You say you didn't steal it?"

Stephen looked down uneasily.

"I didn't say that—exactly."

Ivy prayed for patience. "Then what, exactly, did you say?"

Stephen paced. "I found it."

"Found it?" Ivy couldn't help sounding doubtful.

He examined his fingernails. "Yes."

"Where?"

"I was prospecting with a fellow down on Horse Creek last year, before the snow. Name was Boyd. He said he knew where we could land a big strike. Said he'd split it with me, fifty-fifty." Stephen sighed as if he could believe neither his luck nor his stupidity. "We found gold, all right. Only it was the loot from some holdup the fellow was in on about seven years ago. He claimed the others were dead or in prison, and that as the statute of limitations had run out, the gold was ours, free and clear."

Ivy narrowed her eyes. "Why did this fellow decide to let you in on it?"

Stephen shrugged. "He was old, Ivy. Older than Pa was, I guess. He wanted my help hauling it down from the mountains, and figured I'd keep my mouth shut for the privilege."

"And you swear you weren't involved with the original robbery?"

"How could I have been?" he retorted hotly. "Seven years ago, I was ten years old! Criminy, Ivy!"

Ivy pondered his naive response. Stephen was too literal to be able to dissemble about such a point. She decided she believed him. "Where's this other fellow now?"

Stephen sighed. "Dead. Killed by a rockslide on our way to Dubois. Except now that I've had some time to think about it, I'm betting that rockslide was no accident."

Ivy's heart rose in her throat, and she strove to keep her tone even. "So you're saying you think that man's confederates killed him."

"Yes." Stephen's voice was casual, but she could hear the strain behind it.

"And now they're after you," Ivy said.

Stephen said nothing. He looked out into the street again.

"You," Ivy repeated, training her stare on him, "and Charity."

Stephen jerked his head up. His eyes were cold, his jaw tense.

"I have sixty thousand dollars in gold," he told her, as if he really meant he had God in his hip pocket. "All the gold there was. It's mine, legally. I can buy all the protection Charity needs."

"If you live long enough!" Ivy snapped, her patience at an end. "How do you expect to move such a cargo in secret? You can't possibly move as fast as you need to, to avoid those men. Can't you appreciate the position you're in? The danger you've placed Charity in?"

"I love Charity," he argued, his eyes flashing. "I'd never do anything that would cause her harm!"

So very like the words Noble had spoken to her mere hours earlier. How easily Stephen uttered them! How easily they had come from Noble's lips, as well. She had no doubt that both men truly believed them. That was the real tragedy of it.

"You already have," she murmured. "Where is she, Stephen?"

Stephen shook his head. "I can't tell you that. All you need to know is, she's safe, and she's where she wants to be, with me. I asked her if she wanted to write a note to Noble, but she said no, she'd already written one and she wasn't ready to write another."

Ivy found it easy to imagine the reckless, petulant Charity Smith saying such a thing. No doubt the girl had been a trial to Noble since the death of their mother. In fact, they'd probably been a trial to one another.

"She's but fifteen years old," she whispered, more to herself than to Stephen.

"Sixteen," Stephen corrected her, as if that made a world of difference.

"Noble is her brother. He's concerned for her. Besides, he's her legal guardian."

"Not anymore," Stephen declared with a note of prideful challenge. "We're married."

Ivy felt the floor fall away from her. Then as if from a distance, she heard Stephen laugh.

"Ivy? Criminy, I didn't think you'd go and faint on me!"

A warm strength supported her, and she realized that he was holding onto her arms. She hadn't thought about how big he'd gotten. The top of her head scarcely reached his shoulders. Why, he was as tall as Noble!

"I'm all right," she insisted, but did not pull away from his hold. "Married? When? Where? Oh, this is going to crush Noble! He'll have it annulled, if he can."

"Aren't you going to congratulate me?" Stephen asked her with a raffish grin.

Ivy felt faint again.

"Congratulate you?" she echoed, staring at him. "For having virtually kidnapped a girl, possessing stolen gold and for having five desperate men on your trail? Have you lost your mind?"

Stephen's smile evaporated and he released her from his grip.

"I might have known you'd take that view," he said, backing away. "You're just like Pa. Nothing but the straight and narrow for you. Either of you. Never take a chance. Better to stay safe at home, like a couple of prisoners of that damned ranch that Pa made a hell out of for us after Ma ran off. Now he's dead, and you ain't changed. Well, that's fine. I guess you deserve whatever hell he's left to you. But I don't plan on keeping you company there."

His words stung so deeply that Ivy burned to respond in kind. She found, however, that she could not, for in Stephen's hard, ugly words, she realized, there was more than a grain of truth. And that hurt most of all.

She went to the window. "Where are you going to go?" she asked.

There was a cold silence. "Can I trust you with the answer to that?" he asked at last. "I'd really like for you to know, Ivy. I mean, you're my only kin, and all. But I guess you come all this way with Noble for a reason, and I don't think that reason is to bid me and Charity a fond farewell. 'Sides, I guess you know where I'm headed."

"San Francisco? Or Chicago?"

She looked at him once more. He was grinning again, but he already looked more like a man and less like a boy. She almost didn't know him anymore.

"Near enough," he told her, nodding. "I expect I can pretty much do what I want wherever I go, with sixty thousand in gold."

"If you make it there alive," she agreed. She covered her mouth with her hand: The alternative was too awful to consider. "Stephen, I wish I could make you—"

"You can't." He bit the words off like the bitter rind of some sour fruit. "Any more than I can make you understand, I guess. So there's no sense in trying. Maybe someday, when we're both older . . ."

If by God's grace you get any older, Ivy could not help thinking.

She looked away from him, out of the window, afraid of seeing the shadow of death in Stephen's young face. She was not superstitious, but she was frightened. She wished he would leave, yet she desperately wanted him to stay. He had broken her heart, but she suspected she had helped him along in that endeavor, and she did not want to be left alone. Down the street, there was a freighter in front of the General Store with eight teams of mules, and a roly-poly man with a dark beard and a misshapen hat directing the workers as they unloaded the goods. Across from the hotel, Noble emerged from the sheriff's office and made his way back.

"Noble is coming," she said.

Stephen did not reply.

She turned from the window. "Will you tell him, or—"

But Stephen was no longer there.

Noble's head ached. It might have been because he was hungry, ravenous, in fact, but he suspected it had more to do with the chat he'd just had with the sheriff. The lawman had eyed him with more than a little distaste as Noble laid out his plan to him, but he ultimately agreed to it. The sheriff was the law; he really had no choice. And neither did Noble. He wished he didn't feel so much like Judas: It was for Ivy's own good.

Ivy Wingate sure as hell wouldn't see it that way.

Climbing the stairs to their room, he felt as if his boots were full of lead, just like his heart. He wanted to feel nothing, but that was hard, since he hurt so much he wanted to die. He wondered, approaching the door, if Ivy would ever forgive him for it. He wondered if he would ever forgive himself.

He knocked.

"Ivy?" he called softly. Would she be able to hear the betrayal in his voice? Read it in his eyes? He started to tremble at the thought of it, but willed himself to be still.

The door squeaked open in answer to his summons, but Ivy did not wait there to greet him. She was hurrying away from him, toward the window even as he entered the room, her hands busy in front of her face, as if she had only just washed it and was toweling it dry.

He could not help but notice the graceful rhythm of her slender figure in motion. Her pretty auburn hair was damp and hung like a wild cloak to the small of her back. When he realized he was wondering what her back might look like naked, draped with all of that hair, Noble closed his eyes and shook his head hard.

"Just let me wash up," he said, glad that he'd thought of something to say, and that she was not looking at him. "Then I'll take you to dinner. The fellow at the livery says they make good food here."

"What did the sheriff say?"

It don't matter, I guess, that I think it's a pretty mean trick to pull on anybody, let alone your woman, does it? That's what the sheriff had said.

Noble hadn't meant for her to know he'd been to see the sheriff. But more surprising than her observation was the muffled, unsteady quality of her voice.

"Oh, the sheriff—I went there to see if he knew anything about Stephen and Charity. To find out if they'd been this way." He prayed that sounded natural to her. It had, in fact, been part of his mission. But only a part of it. "Ivy, are you all right?"

She nodded quickly, still not facing him. "Had they?"

Her voice quivered like a frightened child's. It made him forget for a moment that she'd asked him a question.

"Had they what?"

She turned to face him, reluctantly, it seemed to him. She did not meet his gaze. She was flushed, her cheeks were smudged and her eyes were rimmed in red. She'd been crying, but she seemed not to want him to know it. The fact so distressed him that he obliged her by ignoring it.

"Had they been seen? Stephen and Charity, I mean," she said.

"Frankly, the sheriff doesn't strike me as being a man who notices much, although I can't imagine Stephen and Charity escaping anyone's notice. You know how Charity is." Noble felt a twinge in his stomach at his disloyalty to his sister, but the truth was she was vain and liked to be noticed. Surely Ivy, having been Charity's teacher, knew that.

Ivy said nothing. She stood in the center of the small room twisting her russet hair on itself. Noble

141

watched her wrap the bounteous mass into a neat package at the nape of her neck. He felt drawn to her, as if she were pulling him. But he sensed a danger, too, as if she might actually be leading him to the edge of an abyss.

He was standing beside her with no clear idea of how he'd gotten there. It seemed the most natural thing in the world for him to put his arms around her and burrow his face in the fragrant, damp hair by her ear, and not being a man given to defying nature, he did just that. She felt so good in his arms, so damned good. He hated himself for what he was about to do to her. I'm sorry, he thought, holding her so tightly he could feel her heart racing against his.

Chapter Twelve

Noble plastered a cheerful smile onto his face as he escorted Ivy downstairs, even though he felt at any moment as if that plaster was going to crack. Ivy's small hand was secured in the crook of his arm, and he could not deny the sense of pride he felt, knowing she was beside him, even though there was no one in the tiny hotel dining room to see them. *Thank God,* he thought, straining to keep his smile intact. *At least I won't be shaming Ivy before a crowd of spectators.*

"I hope the food's good," he said, guiding her to one of half a dozen gingham-covered tables. "'Course, I'm hungry enough to eat dirt." He doubted he could eat a mouthful of even the finest steak.

"You're always hungry," she murmured as he held her chair out for her. "Just like Stephen."

"What's that?" The inquiry popped out automatically, although he'd heard her quite clearly. The mention of her brother's name drew him up short, probably because his mind, at the moment, was not on Charity and Stephen but on Ivy, and Albert Gentile. Ivy had gone pale, and she stared at a bunch of greens stuck in a bottle that served as a centerpiece for one of the tables. Noble recognized it as a variety of Indian paintbrush, a common wildflower. It didn't look anywhere near to blooming, and neither did Ivy.

"Stephen." She muttered the repetition, as if she'd rather have choked on it.

Ivy sat down, but glanced up at him wearing a pained look as he slid her chair up to the table. Noble's heart froze, and for a moment he was unable to force his feet to move. Did she know of his plan? Had she guessed, or had he accidentally allowed something to slip?

He rallied. *Ivy knows nothing*, Noble told himself. *It's only your guilty conscience taunting you*. He affected a sauntering gait to his own place at the small table across from her. He even managed a little smile, to his amazement. Ivy did not return his expression. If anything, she looked even more desolate. He shifted his gaze out of the nearby window and found himself staring at the sheriff's office across the street. Heat filled his face, and he hoped once more that the sheriff would remember every aspect of their bargain. His time was growing short, like the wick in the lamp on the table.

And he still needed something from Ivy. He fidgeted.

"Something wrong with your chair?" Ivy asked.

"No. No." He sat still, abashed. "I guess you just got me started thinking about Stephen and Charity again. You said you think they'll be headed for Rawlins," he prompted her.

144

"Just to get the train for Chicago," she answered, staring at the bent silverware. "Stephen always meant to go to the city. He always talks—talked about it."

Mrs. Kimmerle, the proprietress, emerged from the kitchen door, wearing a stern scowl on her weathered features.

"Got what's left of a son-of-a-gun stew back there. It'll have to do you," she announced, as if she meant to shove it down their throats if they refused her bounty. "And maybe some biscuits." The last was added grudgingly, as if she'd meant to hoard the things for herself but was at the last moment overcome by an uncharacteristic and entirely unexpected spirit of benevolence. She disappeared again without awaiting their acknowledgment of her largesse. In spite of his nervousness, Noble chuckled.

"Real warm, our Mrs. Kimmerle," he said in a low tone, stealing a glance at Ivy again. "Makes you feel right at home, doesn't she?"

Ivy's laugh was brief and reluctant, but it nevertheless made him feel like a cur, as if the deed he was about to do was written in his eyes. He was forced to look away from her again, and his mirth was swallowed by his guilt.

Mrs. Kimmerle dealt the stew before them like a bad hand of stud poker. It smelled right enough, but Noble's stomach was already in mild revolt, thanks to what he was about to pull on the woman he loved. It was all he could do to chew up and swallow a few mouthfuls while he tried to look hungry. Ivy was watching him, he knew. He could not afford to demonstrate any suspicious behavior.

He could not help but notice, watching her watch him, that she scarcely did more than move the contents of her own plate from one side to the other. He took another mouthful, hoping she hadn't noticed his scrutiny.

"Noble?" Her quiet voice was accusing, or seemed so.

Damn it, she knows! his conscience screamed. He tried to swallow, but the stew stuck in his throat the first two times. He made himself meet her gaze.

"What?"

She looked so forlorn that he wanted to jump up, yank her from the room and confess that it had all been a terrible mistake and that they had to leave, now. He kept silent and waited.

"I saw Stephen."

Noble jumped to his feet with such energy that he knocked his chair over.

"What! You saw . . . Where? When?" If Stephen were here, in Basin, he could be apprehended at once, and there would be no need for him, Noble, to execute the plan that he and Al Gentile had concocted in his kitchen. Then Ivy need never know what he'd meant to do!

"Just before dinner," Ivy was saying softly, and he made himself listen to her through the growing din in his ears. "He came to the room. He said that—"

"Where did he go? Was Charity with him?"

"Noble, sit down."

"Damn it, Ivy—"

"Sit down and listen to me, or I won't say another word!"

Noble righted his chair and sat, but not before glancing once more at the sheriff's office across the street. Time was against him. He hoped she would talk fast.

"Okay, I'm sitting. Now, where—"

"Noble."

Damn it, she sounded just like his ma when she said his name like that. He pressed his lips together, chastened, and prayed that the sheriff would stay put for a few more minutes.

"He's hiding out somewhere nearby, he wouldn't say where," she told him, just when he was sure he could stand no more of the stillness. "He has—" she lowered her voice and leaned over the table, although there was no one in the small dining room who might have overheard them—"sixty-four thousand dollars in gold. Charity is with him." She anticipated his question. "Those men who followed us from Peaceful—they're after the gold. Apparently someone Stephen met prospecting at Horse Creek—"

"Charity!" Noble burst forth, unable to contain himself any longer. "Is she all right? Has she—"

"She's fine. But—Noble, they're married."

Noble sank back in his chair, thinking, for an instant, that he'd been shot. That one word from Ivy's lips was like a jolt of hot steel in the center of his chest. Ivy was going on, but Noble could not hear her.

"Married!" he echoed in weak interruption. "For God's sake, Ivy, she's just a child! And Stephen—Stephen isn't much more than one!" He felt, suddenly, as ancient as Methuselah. He wondered if he would ever be able to stand again. He wondered if he would ever be able to look at Stephen Wingate and repress his urge to kill the boy with his bare hands.

"Noble, calm down." Ivy met his gaze with direct, sober green eyes. She squared her narrow shoulders and raised her chin an inch. He felt his own back straighten in answer. "It won't do any good to lose your temper now. They're married; it's not as bad as it might have been. But there are five desperate men on their trail, after that gold. They need our help, not our anger. We can't let them spend their lives on the run, and that's exactly what will happen to them if we don't keep our wits about us now. You don't want to lose Charity, and I don't want to lose my brother. I've lost—we've both lost too much already."

Noble closed his eyes against the unspeakable rage that filled him. Coupled with an enormous sense of utter helplessness, it made him want to break things. *Restraint,* he told himself, clenching his jaw. *Your whole miserable life has been restraint, from the day Pa ran off. Noble, the steady, sensible one. Noble, the man of the house at seventeen. Noble, who undertook a man's responsibilities for two people who'd never thanked him for it, thereby sentencing himself to ten long years of bitter regret and loneliness . . .*

In the darkness of his mind, a beacon of clarity blazed suddenly: He was angry. He was angry at Charity, furious at Stephen, for having the courage to challenge what was "right" and "respectable" to make new rules for their own happiness. But mostly he was angry with himself for having denied himself, and Ivy, the happiness they deserved in favor of the burdensome yoke of family responsibility.

It was about time he took responsibility for his own happiness.

"Miss Ivy Wingate?"

Noble started at the sound of the new, gruff voice beside him. He opened his eyes to see the sheriff standing by the table between him and Ivy.

"Yes?" Ivy, pale, looked from the sheriff to Noble, and back again. Sudden panic robbed Noble of his ability to speak.

"Ma'am, it is my unpleasant duty—" he paused

for a long, acid look at Noble—"to place you under arrest for the theft of a horse belongin' to one Albert Gentile of the town of Peaceful in the territory of Wyomin'—"

"Wait a minute, Sheriff." Noble found his tongue. He prayed he had not found it too late.

Ivy sat as still and as white as a statue. The sheriff sent Noble an undisguised glare. "What have you got to say now? Change your mind?"

Noble's face burned, and he could not look at Ivy. He felt as if a sword were hanging over his head. Nevertheless, he swallowed his dread and plunged on.

"I want to pay Miss Wingate's debt."

"Noble!" There was shock in Ivy's exclamation, shock and outrage. Noble fixed his gaze on the sheriff, who merely raised one snowy eyebrow.

"You don't say?" The man sounded skeptical. "That's right funny, mister. Half an hour ago you came into my office tellin' me to come over here and arrest this lady, now you're tellin' me you want to bail her out?"

Noble shook his head. "No, Sheriff. I want to settle the debt with Gentile and have the charge dropped altogether. I have an account at the Bank of Peaceful, and I can have a draft—"

"Well, now, it ain't that simple." The sheriff narrowed watery blue eyes at him and looked smug.

Noble fought his growing desperation.

"Why not?" he demanded.

"Noble, how could you?" Ivy's accusation was plaintive. Mrs. Kimmerle emerged from the kitchen wearing a look of great interest on her harsh features, the commotion apparently having captured her attention. Noble ignored them both.

"Why can't I just pay her debt?" he persisted, standing. "That's all Gentile really wants. You're

149

not going to be hard-nosed about this now, are you?"

"Me?" The sheriff laughed once, but it was not an expression of amusement. "I didn't like it right from the get go, and I b'lieve I told you as much. I sent that wire, just like you said, and Sheriff Doman confirmed it. It was your call, Smith, and there ain't no way to skirt around it, unless—" He stopped.

"Unless what?" Noble prompted.

The sheriff levelled a long, appraising stare at him, then at Ivy. Noble risked a glance at her for the first time. Her face had gone from white to scarlet. No doubt she was mortified by the whole proceeding. He felt like kicking himself.

"Accordin' to the law, only way you can assume Miss Wingate's legal debt so's she ain't liable for prosecution is if she's your wife."

"Now, just a—" Ivy began.

"No, wait a minute, Ivy!" Noble overrode her protest, seeing a glimmer of hope. "You mean if I marry Iv—Miss Wingate, I can square her debt with Gentile and he can't prosecute her?"

"Noble Smith, if you think I'll marry you after this contemptible exhibition, you had better think ag—"

"Dammit, Ivy—"

"Whoa, whoa!" The sheriff stepped back, both of his hands out before him. "I don't aim to get caught in this crossfire! You"—he pointed a finger at Ivy—"had better think about this, Miss. You're in a heap o' trouble; it's best you know that. Even if you can make restitution on your own, you could still face charges, if this Gentile presses. And accordin' to Bill Doman, he's a regular 'by-the-book' sort. I wouldn't put it past him to take this thing as far as it'll go. Now, I admit this here fellow—" he gestured to Noble with a jerk of his thumb—"don't seem like prime husband material at the moment, seein' as he was the one as turned you in, and all. But I been married, and I seen the inside of prison, and I can guarantee that bein' in jail is plenty worse than bein' rightly hitched."

"Could you give us a minute to talk this out?" Noble wanted to shut the sheriff up before he could manage to set Ivy completely against him.

"I have nothing to say to you!" Ivy stood up, wearing her indignation so clearly that Noble winced. "And there is nothing you can say to me that—"

"Ivy, listen to me."

"Why?" she challenged him, backing away. "So you can talk me into trusting you? Again? 'Fool me once, shame on you. Fool me twice, shame on me.' I can't believe I allowed you to do this to me, Noble. I can't believe you think I'm fool enough to let you dupe me again!"

Her words hurt as if she'd struck him. The worst of it, Noble knew, meeting her gaze reluctantly, was that he deserved them, every one. He pressed his lips together and drew several deep, even breaths. Feeling three pairs of eyes on him like a case of smallpox, he swallowed a desperate curse and tried once more.

"Ivy." He took a step toward her. She took two steps back.

"May as well hear him out, Miss," the sheriff advised, and Noble blessed him for his reasonable tone. "It can't hurt. If it helps any, I think he meant well. He just went about it in a high-handed way."

"As usual!" Ivy snapped. But she did not, Noble noticed with relief, back away any further. Taking that as a good sign, he closed the distance between them. He took hold of her arms gently.

"Ivy, I—"

"Take your hands off of me!"

He tightened his grip instead.

"No," he said firmly. "Listen to me." He trained her gaze to his and was dismayed by the hurt he read in her green eyes. He made himself go on. "I know you won't believe this, but I really did go to the sheriff for your own good." He loosened his hold; she was so tender, and he had no wish to hurt her any more than he already had. He moistened his lips, buying time to order his thoughts. He would only get one chance at this, he sensed, and he could not afford to ruin it.

"I know what this looks like to you," he began, aware of his interested audience, keeping his voice low on account of it. "But you have to believe me when I say I was only thinking of you."

"How dare—"

"No, Ivy, please. Hear me out. There—" He glanced over his shoulder at the sheriff, who looked stern. He preferred Ivy's cold, angry look. "There isn't much time. You can't know how scared I was when those men—when you were out at the ranch last night. I kept thinking you could be killed, or worse. Then you said you were going after Stephen—"

"I meant it, Noble!"

"I know you did. God help me, I know it! And I was desperate to do anything to keep you from getting into the middle of all this. When Gentile came by this morning, we talked this over. I figured having you arrested and put in jail was the best way to keep you safe in spite of yourself, and to keep you from getting in between Stephen and those men. I swear, if I'd thought there was any other way to do it, I would have."

Ivy's glare was unchanged. "Is that supposed to be an apology?"

"You want me to apologize for trying to save your life?" Noble felt the small hairs go up on the back of his neck.

Ivy made a sound of disgust.

"No, I expect you to apologize for humiliating me here and in Peaceful!" she retorted, not looking at all mollified by his explanation. "And all for the sake of an excuse for a devious way of 'protecting' me! Even the sheriff said it—you're high-handed, Noble. Nothing excuses such despicable behavior. Nothing!"

She tried to pull away from him again, but Noble was determined to try once more.

"Listen, Ivy!" he insisted, giving her another small shake. "Suppose our positions were reversed. Now, you know me as well as I know you. If you'd told me to stay behind where it was safe, would I have done it?"

Her eyes narrowed suspiciously. "No."

"Would you have tried to stop me from coming along?"

"Yes."

"Would you have done just about anything to keep me here, where it was safe?"

She did not answer him.

"Would you," he said softly, sensing her capitulation, "have had me put in jail to save my life?"

She no longer seemed able to look him in the face. He crept his hands down her arms until he found her fingers, and he laced his own with them.

"Is there a justice that can marry us?" he called to the sheriff, keeping his gaze on Ivy.

She glanced up at him wearing a mutinous expression. "I said I understood," she reminded him in a hiss. "I didn't say I would marry you. I didn't even say I forgave you."

"Basin ain't but a small town," the sheriff replied genially from behind him, ignoring Ivy's retort. "I wear a couple o' hats. You want me to marry you now? Mrs. Kimmerle here can be a witness and we can get all this nonsense over lickety-split."

"But I—"

"Look here, Miss." To Noble's surprise, the sheriff came forward and addressed Ivy in a lecturing tone. "You don't want to go to jail any more than I want to put you there. And unless I'm dead wrong, and you can tell me if I am, you'd a sight rather be married to this here fellow than not, even if he is a mite high-handed. So if you want my advice, don't go lookin' to clip off that pretty nose just to spite your face. Marry him."

Ivy got a look on her face that said she'd sooner eat dirt than admit that the sheriff was right. Noble held his breath.

Chapter Thirteen

Ivy wanted to shake off Noble's tender hold on her hands and tell him to go to the devil. The words stung her tongue like hot coffee drunk too quickly, but it was for that very reason that she hesitated. His explanation was reasonable enough, even, in some ways, laudable. And the tactic was so like him that, had it happened to someone else, she might have laughed out loud and applauded his ingenuity.

"Ivy?" Damn him, he would use that tender, coaxing tone with her, and, damn her, she would surrender to it. But how could she accept him, when he'd treated her in such an abominably deceitful manner? And yet, how could she reject him, when she knew that she loved him in spite of it? Moreover, that it was the only reasonable course open to her?

She held her breath to keep her answer locked

155

inside of her while she considered him. His dark-eyed gaze was steady and as sober as a judge's. His broad shoulders rose and fell with his rapid, nervous breaths, and he moistened his lips with the tip of his tongue.

"You didn't bother to propose properly," she ventured, not wanting to sound like a surly child, but knowing that was exactly the effect. If he smiled, she would kill him. Then the sheriff would have a real reason to lock her up, not some flimsy excuse trumped up by Noble Smith and Albert Gentile.

But he did not smile. He did quite the opposite: He went a bit red about his neckline and glanced back over his shoulder once at the sheriff.

"Dammit, Ivy," he muttered, his voice low and gruff. "I did this morning, and you didn't answer me."

"Well, if I embarrass you so much that you have to whisper now, maybe it's best we forget the whole idea!" Her anger, righteous and irrational, kindled all over again and she yanked her hands away from his grasp. "Sheriff!"

"Ivy, you're acting like a child! Stop it!" Noble was stern.

"I'm acting like a child? And what shall we call what you've done?" Her irritation mounted. She wanted to remain calm and reasonable, but she could not seem to control herself. "Suppose I said I would rather go to jail, to face up to whatever I may or may not have done wrong, than to marry you just to avoid it? You've already made a shambles of my character, you and Albert Gentile! Now am I to have it spread throughout Wyoming that you offered to marry me just to keep me from going to jail? And that I accepted your proposal for little better reason?"

"Dammit, Ivy, you know it's not like that!" Noble

shouted his retort, his rawboned face gone entirely crimson. "Trust you to twist it around that way!"

"And trust you to make such a contortion necessary!"

"I, uh, hate to get in the middle of a lover's quarrel," the sheriff interrupted in a calm, wry tone. "But Sheriff Doman's waitin' on my reply back at the Peaceful telegraph. As interestin' as this is, I got to get back to him. You two gonna get hitched now, or not?"

The note of amusement in the older man's voice angered Ivy all the more. She answered simultaneously with Noble.

"No!"

"Yes!"

Noble glared at her again. "Ivy!"

She stared back coolly. "Aren't you going to say 'dammit' again? It seems to be a favorite expression of yours, lately."

"I got supper to clean up," Mrs. Kimmerle complained in a whine that cut the air like a straight-razor.

"Go 'head, Olga." The sheriff pulled his pocket watch out of his vest with a resigned sigh. "It don't look like these two is gonna decide this anytime soon. I give 'em about thirty more seconds 'til I march this lady over to one 'o my cells."

His glance darting from one face to the next, Noble looked close to panic. Ivy was somewhat mollified by the notion, although not enough to relent.

"No, wait," he pleaded after a swallow, returning his petitioning gaze to Ivy. "I apologize, Iv—Miss Wingate. It was a mean, underhanded thing to do to you, even if I only meant to protect your life by doing it."

His abrupt, formal apology stunned Ivy even more than the act that had precipitated it. Her jaw unhinged and her mouth hung open. Unsmiling, Noble went on.

"I can't hope that you would forgive me for such behavior, but I do ask that you allow me to begin to make it up to you in some measure by doing me the very great courtesy of becoming my wife."

Ivy knew she was staring, but she could no more help that than she could fly. If she could fly, she would surely have launched herself from the spot to some remote place where she would never again have occasion to see the two people before whom Noble had so thoroughly mortified her. She was certain that only she could detect the note of irony and humor in Noble's self-effacing declaration. She was equally certain that to refuse him in the wake of it would not only look like the height of stupidity to Mrs. Kimmerle and the sheriff, but the most vulgar ingratitude as well.

Her desire to kill Noble redoubled. She found herself, to her complete shame, to be staring at the floor.

"Very well." She forced the concession from her lips even as she considered her revenge. "I will marry you, Mr. Smith. But—"

The remainder of her codicil was truncated by the sound of the sheriff clapping his hands once in an unmistakable sound of glee and triumph. She wondered if he had not been a part of this deplorable conspiracy from the very beginning. She sensed it was not wise to ask him, and she decided she did not really want to know, anyway.

"Hallelujah," the sheriff declared, sounding more weary than jubilant. "If you two'll just step across the street with me to my office, we'll swear out the license right quick. Olga?"

The gentle heat surrounding Ivy's fingers was Noble's hand, she knew. Her cheeks warmed at the

158

feel of it. She knew he was looking at her, too, but she could not bring herself to meet his gaze. She did not want to see his triumph. Not while she was busy plotting her revenge.

The wedding was conducted like a business transaction. Noble had no ring for her, only the promise of one. And afterward, he did not kiss the bride as tradition dictated, but instead wrote out a formal declaration assuming and covering his new wife's debt to the liveryman in Peaceful. When they left the sheriff's office, it was dark in Basin, and they were husband and wife.

"Better, now?" Noble's question was diffident, but gruff. They were the first words he'd spoken directly to her since making his double-edged declaration in the hotel dining room twenty minutes earlier. It was far more than she intended to say to him in the foreseeable future. He could talk to her until hell froze, as far as she was concerned. She would not answer him.

"Ivy?" He slipped his arm about her waist. She did not shake him off, but neither did she encourage him in any way. She wanted to make abundantly clear to him that she was completely ignoring him. That meant not acknowledging anything he did, considerate or not. And if he thought he was going to share her bed tonight . . .

"I'll sleep in the chair tonight, if you like," he said at the end of a sigh.

His simple, quiet pronouncement so took her aback that she did not resist him as he guided her across the quiet street back to the hotel. Didn't he want to share her bed? She stole a sideways look at him. His angular profile was grim in the pale light of the three-quarter moon. He looked more like a pallbearer than a new bridegroom, she

159

thought, stunned. Why that fact should make her feel like crying, especially since she'd had no intention of allowing him to share her bed, she did not care to speculate.

"Are you all right?" He spoke again, quietly, and she realized she had choked back a sob. She nodded, not trusting herself to answer him aloud, even with so much as one word. And he, no doubt, would think she was being stubborn and fractious. As if verifying her belief, he sighed.

"We have a long road ahead of us," he said at the end of it, and she wondered if he were referring to the immediate future or to the rest of their lives. His next words clarified his meaning. "If you don't want anything else, maybe we'd best just go on up to—go get some sleep."

Ivy felt as if she had willingly plunged into a deep, black hole. She wished, not for the first time, that she had behaved more prudently. Why was it, she wondered dismally, that one never thought of prudence until it was far too late?

The room was dark. It had previously been adequate in size in Ivy's estimation, but it seemed to have shrunk while they were at the sheriff's office. It contracted still farther when Noble closed the door, sealing them together in the darkness. Noble did not speak, but Ivy could hear his breathing behind her. Or was that herself she heard?

A light began behind her, and it swelled to a warm golden glow. She heard the clink of glass on metal; Noble was no doubt replacing the glass chimney on the lamp he'd lit. She did not see him perform the action, but she heard every sound, every movement, from the flare of the match to Noble's bottomless sigh. Everything seemed magnified to her, every sound and every shadow. She stood in the middle of the room, unable to move as the walls pressed in about them. She wanted something, she realized, feeling hollow inside. What she wanted was for Noble to touch her.

She would rather die than ask him. She could not even bring herself to look at him, for fear he would easily read the yearning in her eyes.

"I'll get us some water to wash up," Noble offered, just shy of a whisper.

Ivy had taken a bath just before dinner, but it seemed silly to point that out to him. He was obviously in a hurry to escape from her presence. She did not blame him. She had treated him horribly. She would have escaped herself, she realized, if she thought she'd get very far. She listened to the scrape of the ceramic pitcher as Noble took it from the wash stand, then the dull thud of his boots on the thin carpet on the floor.

When the door closed softly, she let out a breath she hadn't even realized she'd been holding. She turned slowly and the first sight that met her eyes was the brass bed, neatly made up with a faded red patchwork quilt and two feather pillows.

Two pillows for two heads. One bed. Against her will, Ivy found herself envisioning herself and Noble in the bed together. It was not a large bed; they would be obliged to lie close to one another, touching one another, all night. She could easily picture Noble's weight creating a canyon in the thin mattress that would inevitably pull her toward him. It required no concentration at all to imagine the heat of his hard, lean body pressed against her . . .

A tremor passed through Ivy's body like a thundering locomotive in the night, leaving a hole as big as a tunnel: Noble would be sleeping in the chair. He'd said so.

She drew the coverlet back with a trembling

hand. Her eyes burned. She thought of Stephen and Charity living as husband and wife. She thought of Ma and Pa, then Ma and Ben Smith.

She thought of Noble, holding her on his lap as if she were a queen, asking her to be his wife. Lord, had that only happened twelve hours before?

And here she was, Mrs. Noble Smith. And her husband, the man she'd waited ten years for, the man who had fathered her child, had offered to sleep in a chair tonight.

"Water's cold," Noble announced, apology in his deep, quiet voice.

Ivy started. She had not heard him return.

"Thought you'd be ready for bed, by now." It sounded as if Noble's collar had gotten too tight, but she remembered that his shirt was open at the throat.

"I haven't a nightgown," she blurted, then fell into awkward silence again.

She longed to look at him. She was sure his face would give her a clue as to what he was thinking, but she could not bring herself to turn around. She felt foolish, and afraid.

She heard Noble heave a sigh that was as big as the shadow he cast in the room. She listened to the heavy tread of his footsteps as he made his way to the lone window. While he looked out into the street, Ivy splashed the water into the bowl at the wash stand, more to cool her face than to wash it.

She couldn't find the towel.

Noble was beside her like a wall of solid heat. "Here."

Her groping fingers tested the length of his long, muscular arm until they finally found the towel at the end of it.

"Thank you," she mumbled, pressing the towel to her eyes as she turned away from him. Her body ached to feel his arms around her. A full minute went by, and she realized, feeling sick, that he was not going to touch her at all.

"Good night," she managed, escaping to the bed.

She stared at the turned-down bed, hating Noble, hating herself.

"I know you're angry, Ivy." Noble sounded old. "Hell, you have a right to be. I did the wrong thing. I did it for the right reasons, but that doesn't mean you have to like it, I guess. I'm not particularly proud of it, myself. And you were right, what you said about me and church, this morning. Maybe if I weren't such a reprobate, I'd never have pulled such a mean trick, no matter what. But you know, I do remember something Reverend McIlhenney said a long time ago in a sermon. Maybe it was at somebody's wedding. He said, 'No matter how angry you get, always kiss good night.'" Noble paused. Ivy swallowed. "I think he'd be pleased to know that at least some of his good advice took on me, don't you?"

Noble stood directly behind her. She felt his soft breath against her neck. It was breaking down her resistance, like a slow tear in old satin, thread by thread.

She clenched her jaw as she turned toward him. If he was smiling at her, she'd slap his face and tell him to go straight to Hades.

But he wasn't.

The glow of the small lamp revealed his stark features. They were rapt with some emotion Ivy did not dare put a name to. He took hold of her arms with a gentle, commanding grip. His midnight eyes searched her face and his wide mouth parted as if he might speak, but he merely swallowed. He bent his neck, bringing his face closer to hers. He hesitated just long enough for Ivy to

163

realize she could not let him stop then, no matter what. Still holding her arms, Noble closed the distance between their lips and joined his mouth to hers, soft as silk, firm as steel.

Liquid waves of warmth rippled down, through Ivy's limbs, through her body. Noble's kiss took its own sweet time awakening her memory and her need. Like vines, Ivy's arms curled up at the elbow and she pressed her palms against Noble's back, savoring the sculpted contours beneath her fingers. He was beautiful. She could feel it. He was a man now, not a boy. His kiss, and the welcoming wall of heated flesh around her reminded her of that.

His arms encompassed her, holding her against him as if he feared she might break away from him. His mouth became more insistent, taking charge, leading her to treacherous heights and untold depths and making sure she followed. She clung to him, utterly overcome.

When he dragged his lips away from hers, it was only to find the tender place just below her ear.

"Ivy, Ivy," he murmured, his hot breath a feather-like caress. "Good night, sweetheart."

"Good night, Noble," she sighed, holding him close as his lips blazed a path from her ear downward.

"Goodnight." He kissed the side of her neck.

"Goodnight." She kissed his collarbone.

He held her close with one arm and slid the other up between them like a benign but cunning serpent. His hand found the buttons of her shirtwaist.

"Goodnight." He kissed the hollow below her throat as the buttons began to yield, one by one, to his undertaking.

"Goodnight." Not to be outdone, Ivy tried her skill with his shirt. Her breath caught as Noble slipped his hand inside her chemise, and she lost her place.

"Let me," he whispered, and she could hear the boyish smile in his husky baritone. "I'll do you first."

"But I . . ." She faltered. "I haven't a nightgown," she said again, feeling foolish this time, and suddenly shy.

"I know."

Noble continued his mission, as if that fact had given him greater impetus. Unable to resist his will, Ivy's hands fell to his waist, where they found purchase at his belt. She submitted to his ministrations, aching to be freed from the last remaining barrier between them. She closed her eyes, waiting, feeling Noble's big but gentle hands deftly perform their task. Her garments fell or were peeled away, one by one, until there was nothing but the slight chill of the room touching her.

"God, Ivy." Noble's pronouncement was hushed.

She trembled. "Is something wrong?" She opened her eyes to find him staring at her, his eyes wide.

"Wrong?" he echoed, not seeming to understand. He looked into her eyes again briefly, but his gaze could not seem to keep from straying to the form he had revealed. She blushed in sudden confusion.

"Noble?" she said in a tentative whisper.

Her prompting stirred him.

"Nothing's—I mean—you're even more beautiful than I remembered," he finished, his voice hollow with awe.

Ivy looked down. She had never thought herself beautiful, and no one else, except for Noble, had ever used the word to describe her. Her breasts, never large, were sloped and bottom-rounded, where once, before Laurel, they'd been high and taut. Even the nipples had changed, during and after her pregnancy, from a fresh strawberry pink to a rosy but distinctly brownish hue. And her stomach had never returned to its former flatness. It was not big, but rounder and fuller, as if the muscles of her abdomen clearly recalled that they had sustained a child within them and now wore that proof as a badge of honor.

Oh, God, she hadn't meant to think of Laurel! Stricken, trembling, Ivy turned away from Noble with a cry.

Chapter Fourteen

"Ivy, sweetheart," Noble's soft words teased her ear even as he enfolded her in his arms from behind. "It's all right."

But it isn't, she wanted to protest. *It can never be all right between us. And you can never know why!* She longed to surrender to the arms that sheltered her. She wished she could forget what lay between her and the man who held her. But she could not. Any more than she could reveal the fact of Laurel to him.

But she was his wife. While that did not change the situation regarding their nine-year-old daughter, it fundamentally and irrefutably altered the bond between herself and Noble.

Noble nuzzled her bare shoulder appreciatively. "You are beautiful," he repeated, convinced, it seemed, that he had guessed the basis of her turmoil. "You're the most beautiful thing I could ever hope to see. So beautiful I could cry. But I won't. I'll just—"

His tribute came to an abrupt halt. He buried his face against her shoulder, finding the tender flesh just below the crest of bone. He teased the tiny spot with his tongue, then sucked upon it until her breasts tingled and her loins ached with dark need. Ivy closed her eyes again and swallowed, humbled by his blatant adoration, and by the knowledge that she would never feel truly worthy of it. This act between them, the act that was supposed to be the most sublime expression imaginable of love and caring between two people, would, for her, forever be bittersweet. She let out a broken sigh.

"Better?" The question rumbled deep in Noble's throat, a primal growl. The sound spoke to her anguish and to something else so deep within her that she could not begin to guess its center. His hands moved upward along her ribs in a strong caress, each finally cupping a breast with an achingly tender touch. His sharp intake of breath matched her own.

"Yes," she lied, writhing, turning in his arms. "Noble, take me. Make love to me. I want you. Now. Please."

Ivy's desperate plea thundered in Noble's ears. It might have been God's own voice, or one of His angels, saying that life had been given him; he had only to reach out with both hands and take it. The need within him wanted him to fling her to the bed and bury himself deep inside of her at once. Indeed, his groin ached and his maleness strained against his better judgment. Still, something about her entreaty held him from a reckless act of blind passion. He held her close, very tightly. As warm and inviting as she was pressed against him, and as hungry as he was to have her, that was the only way he stood any chance of keeping himself in check.

"Ivy," he sang softly, nuzzling her ear to buy himself time to think.

He needed a moment to collect himself, he knew. He'd been clumsy and selfish with her once. This was her wedding night, and by God, he'd make her know this was a man she'd wed, not the callow, overeager boy who had loved her once for thirty seconds on a soft, green meadow. He only had one chance to make love with Ivy—for the first time—as man and wife. They had the rest of their lives to perform the act in haste or at leisure, as they wished.

Oh, but how could he make himself wait, he wondered, gasping as she tugged with ineffective urgency at the buttons of his shirt, when he had waited so long for her already?

Her fingers had found their way beneath his open shirt, and they played upon him. The melody she found made his senses swim.

"I'm going to pick you up, sweetheart." Talk, he told himself. Say anything. That might make it easier for you. . . .

"Why?"

Because I might take you right here on the floor if I don't. "So I can carry you to the bed."

She sighed, quivering in his embrace. "All right."

She lifted her arms, sweet, white, tender columns, and settled them about his neck. His chest tightened at the gesture of infinite trust. Her fingers combed through his hair. Her touch felt so good, so damned good. Too good. He closed his eyes against the dizziness her caresses inspired.

"Your hair is so soft, Noble," Ivy whispered.

All at once, he smelled violets. Their tender roots

169

worked themselves right into him; their seductive aroma enveloped him. He was falling, falling . . . A surge of sudden panic seized him. Talk to her!

"That's because you love me." Lord, did she have any idea at all what she was doing to him?

"Is that why I'm beautiful? Because you love me?"

With Ivy in his arms, Noble reached the bed in a few steps.

"You're beautiful," he answered softly, laying her down on the wrinkled bedsheets, "because that's how God made you for me."

The mattress sagged with their combined weight. With Ivy's arms locked about his neck, Noble sank into it, right on top of her.

"Noble." Her hot breath singed his ear, and her body writhed beneath him, reminding him sharply of his own need. "Take me. Right now."

Noble groaned. Deep in his loins, a part of him longed to answer her demand in a swift and unmistakable manner, but his head, and his heart, prevailed.

"Shh," he advised, squeezing his eyes shut, then opening them. A new thought occurred to him, one that made him feel dull-witted all over again. "Don't be afraid. I—" He had to taste the shadowed hollows of her neck. Her skin was sleek and warm beneath his lips, and the flavor of salt met his tongue. It nearly made him forget what he'd been about to say. She whimpered deep in her throat. Her eyes were shut tight, as if she were preparing for pain.

"It won't hurt, this time," he rasped. "I promise. And we have all night. All night, Ivy!" The very thought sent a wicked, wild tremor down the back of his legs.

With inches between them, Ivy opened her eyes

and looked up. He read doubt in her gaze. His churning ardor cooled, yet at the same time he felt curiously relieved by the idea: Knowing of her anxiety would enable him to help her overcome it. Moreover, it would help him, he was sure, to hold off his own fulfillment until she was ready to receive him.

"Do you love me?"

She nodded, her eyes green and mysterious as a fairytale forest.

"Do you trust me?"

That was a gamble, but having nothing to lose, he took it anyway. He held his breath until she nodded again.

"Then trust me in this."

He eased himself off of her, off of the bed. He watched her while he undid the last buttons of his shirt, and her anxious gaze never left his. He gave her his best, assured smile and was encouraged when she tried to smile back, albeit uncertainly. He peeled off the sweat-dampened shirt and dropped it onto the floor.

"I was almost killed in that shirt," he offered in a low tone, finding her a grin. "And it sure smells like it."

Ivy's sober gaze was on his bared chest, making the hairs on it stand up at attention. Her look had the odd and unsettling effect of making him feel, alternately, like a bumbling, naive idiot and a great beast in rut. His face heated with a flush that was half desire, half shame. Ivy lay motionless on the bed, looking like a shapely ivory statue.

She bit her pouting lower lip and stared, pointedly, at his pants. Suddenly they felt several sizes too small for him.

Say something, he pleaded to her in silence, his hands faltering at his belt. *God, this isn't easy for me, either. You must know that!*

But Ivy remained silent. Irresistibly, bewitchingly mute. Noble pushed his pants down his legs and kicked them away, then stood there naked in the small, soundless, golden room. He felt utterly vulnerable standing there, especially with his maleness jutting forth, full of his need for her. But somehow, he sensed it was that very defenseless exposure that Ivy needed from him, and that he required from himself. Never, in the ten intervening years, had he given over control of himself, and the harsh demands of his deprived body, to anyone. To yield that control now, to Ivy, and to himself, seemed the supreme expression of the love he felt for her, so strong he could hear it humming in his ears.

"Noble?"

"What?"

A little smile played on her luscious mouth.

"Kiss me goodnight?"

He kissed her. Oh, he kissed her. Her throat. Her shoulders. The tender, sensitive skin on the insides of her elbows knew his kisses. Her breasts, those lovely, twin hillocks of creamy perfection with their taut, dark strawberry peaks, full and yielding in his mouth, became intimately, succulently familiar with the bold attention of his kisses. Beside her, half-covering her with his body in the drooping bed, he pressed his hardened length against the sleekness of her thigh as he crooked his leg up, between hers. The heat and wetness of her nether lips branded his own thigh, and as she began, slowly, to move her hips against him, Noble knew a power and a weakness that together set his senses reeling.

"Sweet," he muttered, sliding one hand beneath her, down the hollow of her slender back to the generous swelling of her buttocks. He resumed his suckling of one breast while, with his other hand, he stroked and massaged its partner. She was all curves and valleys and searing heat, and he wanted a lifetime to explore every bit of her.

He moved his hand downward, over the lean contour of her ribs and the tender rise of her white belly. She was his, all his. She was familiar and new all at once. Somehow, he suspected, rejoicing, she always would be that way to him.

When his fingers found the tight, soft curls at the joining of her legs, she gave forth a long, shuddering cry, as if it were some great joy she could no longer keep inside of her. Noble lifted his head, wanting to see her pleasure etched on her face, needing proof of it before he could allow himself even the beginning of his own completion. The solid flame of his erection throbbed against her leg, and he willed himself to keep still, to keep himself from exploding before he should.

"I want it to be good for you," he told her in a jagged voice, finding the nub of her desire beneath the soft shield of her thatch of hair. It came to full, fiery life at the tips of his fingers. Her eyes were smoky and gleaming as they gazed up at him from beneath dark, fringed lashes, and tiny sobs punctuated each panting breath she took, enchanting him.

"You are so beautiful, so damned beautiful," he thought. She was. She was so beautiful, he ached just feeling her beneath him. His mouth came down upon hers and she received him joyfully, playing with him, teasing his probing tongue with hers, sending him to new heights.

His fingers sought deeper and the thick wetness eased their way. Ivy was gasping, moving her hips against him again, coaxing him to give her more.

"Noble!" His name in her hoarse whisper was a plea for release from the exquisite torment his touch visited upon her.

He could wait no longer.

He eased himself between her legs, and she spread them wider to accommodate him. The sweet aroma of her desire mingled with the fainter scent of violets, and both embraced him, enslaved him. He felt as if every bit of feeling was concentrated in the tip of his shaft as it searched for entry. When it found the warm, wet hollow waiting for him, he groaned.

He braced himself above her with his arms and cherished the fear, wonder and want in her face. Suddenly she thrust her hips upward, taking his whole length inside of her. The rush of tight, wet heat around him made him gasp.

"Sweet God, Ivy!"

Ivy wanted to close her eyes with fresh shame at her raw desire, but the sight of Noble above her, his stark, angular features taut with need, his hard, beautiful chest glistening, filled her with a strange, primitive glory she wanted to savor. He was in her, fully, and he remained still for a long moment as if time itself were waiting for them. She was on the grass in the meadow, on the bed in the Basin Hotel, and somewhere in some shadow of the future at precisely the same instant. But she knew that wherever she was, whenever she was, as long as Noble was with her, she was where she belonged. She sobbed.

"Sweet, holy God!" Noble began to move in her, slowly, like a great, smooth engine grinding out its first rotations. He withdrew and advanced with deliberate slowness, wanting, it seemed, to unmask her long-hidden, primal hunger layer by layer, just as he had undressed her earlier. Noble slid to his elbows, bringing his face closer to hers. His dark eyes held nothing back from her.

"I love you, Ivy-girl," he panted, and thrust again. He blinked hard and shivered. Along with the incredible, nameless, answering sensation deep in her loins, Ivy felt a surge of power that was intoxicating. She said his name in a soundless whisper and pulled his head down to taste his reply. The fury of his kisses swallowed her answering cries of wild triumph and utter submission.

Noble's body found a rhythm with her own, and he played it again and again and again until Ivy felt as if she were floating, or falling, into a shimmering star. The room was filled with light, and a sound of human joy like none she had ever heard. With a formless, throaty cry, Noble collapsed upon her at last. Her cheeks were wet and she knew she'd cried, but they had been tears of happiness. She couldn't tell for certain, but she thought Noble might be crying, too.

Noble remained inside her, as if together they made one whole person and he didn't care to change that. After several deep, shuddering breaths, he rolled onto his side, pulling her leg over him so they could remain joined. Eyes closed, Ivy sighed. She wondered at the little waves of pleasure that continued, at intervals, to throb within her, and delighted that Noble shuddered in her arms with each one. They did not speak, and she was glad. Conversation would remind her that time was, indeed, passing, and that there was a world outside of the little room that demanded their attention. Noble kissed the end of her nose and uttered a brief, breathless laugh.

"What is it?" She opened her eyes to his adoring smile and could not resist touching the tiny wrinkles at the corner of his wide, sensuous mouth with her finger. "What's so funny?"

"I'm going to make you mad again," he told her with quiet deviltry in his rumbling baritone.

She tried not to smile back at him, but failed. "How?"

"Reverend McIlhenney?" It was a reminder, not a query. He kissed her chin.

"What about him?"

With a warm, gentle hand, he caressed her back, then her sides, up to the soft part just beneath her tingling breast.

"And the goodnight kiss?" He found the fullness of her breast once again. The kneading motion of his fingers made her giddy with renewed want.

"Yes?" She could scarcely breathe the question.

"Good story, wasn't it?" He nuzzled her cheek. The roughness of his stubble tickled and aroused her.

"Mmhmm." She did not think she could speak, and she didn't even want to try.

"I'll have to tell it to him when we get home. Maybe I should have been a man of the cloth, myself."

She opened her eyes and frowned, confused. "What? What do you mean?"

She tried to break away from him, to sit up, but he held her fast, pressing her breasts against the wall of his chest muscles. His piratical grin widened, as if he were enjoying himself immensely.

"I made it up," he informed her blithely. "He never said any such thing. At least, not as far as I—"

"High-handed, arrogant," Ivy sputtered and struggled to escape his embrace, but to no avail. Noble held her fast, chuckling in a tender, indulgent way.

"Now, now; don't think of it like that," he argued, soothing her with a bold caress of her backside. "I prefer to think of it as a good idea he should have had, only I had it first."

"I don't think it was such a good idea." Ivy pretended to grumble, but she knew her own smile betrayed her amusement. "Deceiving your wife that way! You ought to be ashamed."

"Oh, I am, I am," Noble assured her, sliding his hand down farther. "But I did it for a very good reason."

She rolled her eyes. "Don't you always?"

His fingers found the place where they were still joined and his sable eyes lost their teasing look. Her body responded with a slow, throbbing burn.

"I did it," he murmured, pausing to draw upon her lower lip with his mouth, "because I wanted to kiss and make up with you afterward." He kissed her whole mouth, and she had no thought of protest or complaint. "Forgive me?"

"Mmm," Ivy returned, finding his mouth to finish what he had started. "We'll see."

Chapter Fifteen

It was dawn when the chirp of a meadowlark on the windowsill woke Noble up. He couldn't have gotten much sleep, he reflected with a smile, snuggling closer to Ivy's fragrant warmth. They'd used up all the oil in the little bedside lamp, and afterwards they'd used up a good bit of the darkness as well. He'd gone to sleep exhausted with Ivy—his sweet, warm wife Ivy—in his arms. Still, he felt fresh as a new babe this morning.

Ivy was still asleep. She lay on her side facing away from him, the perfect position for him to fit right behind her as if she were made for him. And she was. Oh, she was.

Lightheaded at the thought of what they'd done together in that bed, and of having her beside him in the light of a new day, Noble stroked her abdomen gently. Her flesh was smooth and supple with youth and her soft skin invited his touch. She did not stir from her sleep. He grew bolder in his caress, fondling the tender undersides of her breasts, drawing lazy circles with the tips of his fingers down the slopes of her figure to the curly nest of hair concealing her womanhood.

Ivy trembled in her sleep and rolled onto her back with a deep, somnolent sigh. Noble hesitated only a moment before drawing the coverlet down with a quick but careful motion. He did not want to awaken her.

Pale, early morning light filtered through the gauze curtains, gilding Ivy's lush form so that it shimmered with the faint, golden light. He thought of the night before, when she had glistened with the heavenly exercise of their passions. He grew hard again at the memory and at the sweet reminder of it in his arms. Dazed with bliss, he laid his head down on her shoulder and gazed at the charming landscape created by the rise of her breasts, the gentle valley of her waist, and the tender swell of her voluptuous white belly.

She had changed. He'd realized it at once, seeing her last night. Her body was the same as he remembered, yet different, as if the ten intervening years since he'd last made her his had effected some slight but fundamental change in her conformation as well as her maturity. The differences were subtle, so subtle he could not put a name to them, or define them in any way except to realize they existed. Ah, but he would have the time of his life, he realized, nuzzling her long, slender neck, exploring those differences with her, and revealing his own.

Ivy stretched and sighed. She felt warm and fluid. She felt sensitive all over, remembering Noble, and their night of magic. She felt sleepy. She felt cherished.

179

She opened her eyes.

Noble was beside her, propped up on one elbow. His angular features were serious, but they blended to a brief half-smile as she met his gaze. He reached over and pushed a lock of hair away from her cheek with his thumb and forefinger.

"Good morning," he greeted her, just above a whisper.

Ivy realized that she was naked, and that the covers had been pulled away from her. Her nakedness was exposed to his adoring gaze. The heat of an errant blush filled her face and she reached for the blanket.

"No, don't." Noble stayed her hand with a firm but gentle hold on her wrist. She realized that he, too, was still unclothed. His body, long and lean, was stretched out beside her like Zeus. He was relaxed and unabashed in his nakedness. It excited her. That fact made her blush all the more, and she avoided his bright eyes.

"Are you all right, this morning?" He spoke in a hushed and intimate tone as he drew invisible wonders with his finger all along her ribs, up to the underside of her breast. "I didn't hurt you last night, did I?"

The tenderness of his strength overwhelmed her, and she could not answer him right away. She trapped his finger with her hand and held it.

"Noble, after all that's happened, do you still think I'm so fragile as that?"

He concentrated on their joined hands, not looking at her face.

"It isn't that," he protested, his neck turning crimson. "It's been so long since we . . . since I . . . since you—" He let out a hard breath and flopped down on his back. "I mean, I guess it has."

She joined him in his blush and looked down

again, along the planes of her body. She felt a tightening in her womb, the phantom of the baby, Noble's baby, who'd been nurtured there so long ago.

"You know it has," she murmured, trying not to think of Laurel. "There was never anyone but you, Noble. Ever. Although I guess . . ." No. She could not ask him. She would not.

"What?"

"Nothing. It doesn't matter." But it did. Terribly. She closed her eyes.

"Look at me, Ivy."

Her eyes burned. She squeezed them closed tighter.

"Ivy." His tone was half-coaxing, half-gruff.

"Noble, don't tell me," she pleaded. "I don't want to know. I don't need to know. I know that men—" She gulped, and made herself go on. "Men need certain things. You were engaged to marry—" She could not bring herself to name the two girls, acquaintances of theirs from childhood, to whom Noble had been betrothed. "You must have. You needn't tell me—"

"There was no one else, Ivy."

Ivy opened her eyes and found Noble gazing into them, so close that her breath caught. An eternity passed as he looked into her soul without blinking.

"No one." He touched her cheek.

Her face burned. She wondered it didn't scorch his finger. She could not look away. She wanted to die.

"Ivy, are you all right?"

"No. Yes." She found his hand with hers and squeezed it. "I'm sorry, Noble. I didn't—I mean, it wasn't any of my business—"

A brief chuckle issued from somewhere deep in his chest, and his gaze was steady and tender.

Carole Howey

"If it isn't your business, I'd like to know whose it is."

His frankness completely undid her.

"I only meant I shouldn't have asked." Ivy could not tell whether her brain was slowing, or her tongue was getting thicker. In either event, speech was becoming a monumental effort.

"You didn't ask. I told you."

Noble punctuated his straightforward declaration with a kiss upon her forehead.

"Noble, I—"

"Shh," he advised. "I hear something." He inclined his head toward her.

"What?"

He put up his finger. "Listen." He stared into her eyes with rapt concentration. "Hear it?"

She shook her head.

"It sounds like your heart." He pressed his ear to her breast. His hair, fine, thick, and too long for polite society, tickled. "It's saying something." He slid one leg over hers, and his need pressed against her thigh. "I can't make out what." His voice dropped to a hoarse whisper. "Can you tell what it is?" He allowed her breasts to pillow his head, and he hooked his arm around her waist as if to make certain she'd stay there with him. But she had no desire to leave. She loved the fact that he was teasing her as lovers did.

"Oh, it's saying a lot of things." She wanted to tease him in return, and she tried to think of an answer. She shuddered with pleasure as he circled one nipple with his tongue.

"Like what?"

Oh, he was a devil, suckling her that way, making her respond! She drew in a short, hard breath.

"It says your face feels like a shaved porcupine," she got out in a panting giggle.

182

"I married me a sassy woman, I see," he grumbled, easing himself between her parted thighs. "What else is it saying?"

She laughed, pleased at having bested him, never an easy thing to do.

"It says—dear God, what are you doing?"

His fingers were performing wicked magic on her. He arched one bold, sable eyebrow. It gave him the look of a rogue.

"Do you like it?" He sounded genuinely pleased.

"Yes, oh yes."

"What else does it say? Your heart, I mean. Tell me." He continued to gaze at her, and he continued his massage, but his smile faded and he gave her a heated look.

"It says it—Oh, God, I—I love you, Noble!" She gasped, tortured, triumphant, her hips finding a new and wonderful rhythm to explore in concert with the movement of his fingers.

He closed his eyes; then he opened them halfway, as if the weight of his desire made them too heavy. His slow, sensuous smile stripped away her sense.

"Now I know how to take every drop of that sass and vinegar of yours and turn it into sweet, sweet honey," he drawled. He thrust inside of her and she welcomed him with a cry.

He took her with a fierce power that drove her to quick, brilliant release. He went on afterward, driving into her, biting, sucking, bruising. It was wonderful, then it was hard, too much. But she welcomed it, all of it, offering the pain to God in atonement for her sin of giving up Laurel and of deceiving Noble. She had wanted such pain the night before, but Noble had instead given her infinite tenderness. This morning he surprised her with pleasurable pain. When it was over, she stifled her sob.

"Oh, God, I did hurt you that time, didn't I?"

Noble's voice was quiet with distress. He pulled away from her at once, and she felt his gentle hands on her legs, drawing them together. "I'm sorry, sweetheart. Ivy. I shouldn't have—I'm sorry. It was too much. Damn me for a brute!"

Noble got out of bed, his anger at himself apparent in his tense, abrupt movements.

"Noble, don't. Come back to bed. It doesn't hurt anymore. Come here. Hold me."

He sent her a guarded look over his shoulder. "I'm surprised you'd even want me touching you again." His tone was heavy with self-reproach. The thought of it saddened Ivy.

"Hold me."

He slipped back into the bed with her. The springs creaked and sagged beneath him, and Ivy fell against him. He drew the coverlet up about them both, cocooning them, face to face. He cradled her cheek in his hand and searched her face.

"Oh, Ivy, I don't want to hurt you like that, ever again. Tell me if I do. Hell, keep a skillet by the bed and whack me with it if I do—"

Ivy placed her finger to his lips. If the price of her penance was Noble's self-recrimination, she would simply have to find another way to punish herself. Noble did not deserve this. He was blameless. The very thought that he was suffering for her wrenched her heart.

"I'm all right." She smiled.

"You're sure?" He traced it with his finger. She nodded, wanting to reassure him.

"I feel as if—" She broke off, suddenly embarrassed. She wanted to tell him how wonderful, how alive he'd made her feel, but it occurred to her

Noble and Ivy

that he might think it a brazen declaration.

"What?" he urged her.

She took another breath, blushing harder still.

"I feel tender in ways I didn't know I could, until now," she allowed, concentrating on his mouth. "But I don't hurt," she added quickly, sensing his renewed concern. "Not really."

Noble slid his arms about her, allowing himself to be cheered and consoled by her words. He had a hell of a lot to learn, he decided, about being a proper husband to a woman he'd known his whole life. He breathed hard and shook his head, hoping to shake off his disquiet in the process.

"I'd forgotten what it was like, being with you," he said. "I'd forgotten what you were like."

"How can you forget what you never really knew but once?"

Her smile was sweet. Girlish. Forgiving. He kissed her nose.

"I love you, Ivy. I hope you're not tired of hearing that, because it makes me feel so good to say it that I expect I'll be saying it a lot."

She made a face. "I'd sooner get tired of breathing."

He lay still and held her close. She was warm and soft, and she smelled of love and fresh violets. Heaven, or damned close to it. He closed his eyes and sighed.

"Noble, I'm warm. Can we take off these covers?"

He opened one eye. "You're not afraid of what might happen, if we do?"

She gave him a reproving look befitting the schoolmarm she'd been, but it became a winsome smile at the last minute. "Maybe we should get up. We'd best get an early start."

He was unwilling to give her up just yet, but he pulled back the blanket.

Carole Howey

"Five more minutes," he entreated, settling back against his pillow. "The sun's just up. Wherever they are, Stephen will have the hell of a time getting Charity up, you can bet."

" 'Like brother; like sister?' " Ivy teased.

He pinched her on the hip. She squealed.

"Sassy woman! Be quiet. It's too nice to just lie here in a real bed, and you're a soft, soft pillow." Against his will, his thoughts took a lustful turn.

She eyed him with enough sternness to set him straight again.

"I'll be good! I promise."

She shifted onto her back, apparently satisfied by his pledge. Noble settled himself beside her, his head on her shoulder, exactly the way he'd started out earlier while she was still asleep. Ivy drew a deep sigh, and he hoped it was one of contentment. Lord only knew, they would have damned few moments of peace like this for some time to come. They had rough days and miles ahead of them, likely ten days or more to Rawlins on horseback, through hard country. Before them were two people trying to elude them; behind them were five desperate men on the trail of Stephen's gold.

Gold and love, Noble thought. Which of the two had, throughout history, been the cause of more strife?

He did not want to think about such weighty philosophical puzzles. Gazing at the captivating swells and hollows of his wife's body, he marvelled once again at his amazing good fortune. Two days earlier, if anyone had told him he'd be waking up with Ivy Wingate—Ivy Wingate Smith—in his arms, he'd have said they were crazy. Now here he was, feasting his eyes, and other parts of himself, on those sumptuous breasts with their full, dark, taut nipples, and that sweet, enticing and very fem-

186

inine roundness of her belly. He could not resist cupping it with his hand.

Something about Ivy was different. He frowned. Was it a shadow, or was there truly something about her body that he had not noticed before?

He stopped breathing and squinted. Prior to last night, he had seen Ivy once before thus, ten years ago. She'd been fifteen, little more than a girl, but already she'd had a woman's body. He vividly remembered the first time he'd ever seen her naked, that sunny afternoon in Witherspoon's field. But the body he recalled was different in small but elemental ways, he realized, from the body he'd made love to, the one he was fondling. He continued to stare along the length of her, amazed that he had not perceived it before.

Over the years, he'd helped Doc White deliver enough babies to recognize when a woman had borne a child. Doc had been clinical in his descriptions of the way pregnancy changed a woman's body. The average man might not even notice such changes in his own wife, he'd said, particularly if he were faithful to her. But to a doctor such signs were obvious.

The size and the overall shape of the breast changed: Ivy's breasts were ample as they had always been, but their fullness seemed to have shifted. The nipples darkened from pink to a dusky shade. The woman's belly, if it had been flat, was flat no more, even if the woman was otherwise rail-skinny. Often it bore residual lines, sometimes faint and ghostly, sometimes deep. They were stretch marks, where the skin had been expanded beyond its elastic limits by the child growing inside.

Noble lay very still. He used to tease Ivy with the name Stringbean, and now her belly fit upward in the curve of his hand. And was it a trick of the light, or were there pale, white markings on her belly?

He was filled with such a nameless ache that he could not move. He had to be wrong. He must have forgotten something that Doc had told him, or he must have misremembered the lessons, or Ivy's body. Ivy could not have borne a child. He would have known if she'd been pregnant. There was no way she could have kept such a secret from him, indeed, from all of Peaceful.

But there was only one way for him to be certain of that.

"Ivy." A whisper was the best he could do, with his chest throbbing as if he'd just been stabbed.

Ivy liked the breathless sound of Noble's voice. It reminded her of the boy he'd been. She sighed again and stretched. "I know, we should get up to get ready for our wedding trip."

She expected him to chuckle at her joke, but he did not. His long silence made her afraid.

"What is it, Noble?"

His fingers played gently on her belly, but otherwise he did not move.

"Ivy, there's something I need to—" He chopped off his sentence. Ivy waited while he took in a shuddering breath. "There's something I need to ask you."

"What?" She was more bewildered than apprehensive, but the choked sound of his voice brought an uneasy rise to her throat.

"There was a baby, wasn't there?"

Chapter Sixteen

Ivy could not convince herself that she'd heard him correctly. A chasm opened up at the bottom of her stomach, and she dropped into it as if through a treacherous trap door to hell.

"God, Ivy." He sounded as if his voice might break under the strain. "Why didn't you ever tell me?"

"T-tell you?" she got out, burning, longing to escape from his painful inquiry, but held fast in the strong circle of his arm.

"About the baby."

About the baby.

Ivy wished with all her might that she could, indeed, disappear into that chasm. She swallowed several times, but there was a lump in her throat. Some time passed; she had no idea how much, except that it seemed like a wretched eternity. He knew. Somehow, he knew. And he knew she had deceived him.

Carole Howey

"Ivy?"

Noble spoke, but it was Laurel's voice she heard, Laurel's face she saw before her, in her mind's eye. And it was Laurel she still needed to be strong for, Laurel she needed to protect, no matter what the forfeit to her own happiness, or Noble's.

"There is no baby, Noble." She forced the words from her mouth. She wasn't lying, not really. Laurel was a growing child, a baby no longer. Ivy wished she could muster the spirit to put on an elaborate show of denial for Noble, but she knew she would have to settle instead for small untruths. Noble knew her too well to be deceived by any other kind.

"But there was," he persisted, sounding stronger, more detached. "I never made it to medical school, but I helped Doc with enough births to recognize when a woman's body has nurtured a child. What-what happened to it, Ivy?"

His question was hesitant, as if he feared her answer. The dread in his voice, blessedly, gave her a lie, where she'd had none moments before.

"She died."

Why had she confessed the baby's true gender to him? As long as she was inventing, why couldn't she have made the baby a boy, or not have mentioned a sex at all?

A strange, fleeting sense of foreboding shook her: It was bad luck to wish someone dead, or even to speak of a person's death. Ma had always said so. Ma had been superstitious, to practical Pa's everlasting annoyance. Ivy had tried never to believe in such foolishness herself, and she had succeeded quite well over the years.

Until this moment.

She shivered as if a ghost had walked across her grave, and the chill did not leave her.

"Died?" There was pain in Noble's echo. "A girl? A baby girl?"

Ivy squeezed her eyes shut. *Forgive me, God,* she thought. *Forgive me, Noble. Forgive me, Laurel.*

"That's why I went away then. When Pa found out I was with child, he . . . he made me go." That part was true. It wasn't so hard for her to say. She gulped a breath, encouraged, wanting to continue before she lost her nerve. "I was to have the baby in Rawlins and give it up for adoption there. I would have kept it, but with Pa so set against you as he was, and with me only fifteen and not married, I didn't have any say." All of that was true, and she thought it best to stick to the truth as long as she could. This was difficult enough as it was. She fought an urge to babble on, wanting some sign from Noble. What if he didn't believe her?

Noble released her. He drew away and sat on the edge of the bed with his elbows braced on his knees. His broad shoulders heaved with each silent breath. He looked like a puma ready to strike.

"Noble?" She reached out to him and succeeded only in grazing his side with her fingertips before he jerked away from her convulsively.

"Don't." That one word was an iceblock of hurt. "I—God, a baby girl!" He whispered the last incredulously, as if to himself. "A daughter! And I never knew . . ."

"Noble." Ivy sat up on her knees behind him, but stopped short of reaching for him again. He had rebuffed her once; she did not want to risk a second, possibly harsher, rejection. She could not endure it. "I'm sorry. I would have told you, if there had been any point to it. But there wasn't. There isn't. There's nothing we can do now for Laurel—"

Ivy covered her mouth, horrified by what she'd

said: How could she have revealed Laurel's name to him?

Noble half turned to look at her, and she flinched at the wounded look in his sable eyes.

"Laurel? You named her? Laurel?" Noble spoke his daughter's name with quiet awe, as if speaking it could give the child back to him, to them both. "God, don't tell me any more." He turned away from her again, and Ivy felt chilled. "Laurel. A daughter. My daughter. God!"

He got up as if he could no longer bear to be near her.

"There wasn't any way for me to tell you." Ivy thought she might strangle on the words, yet Noble's anger made her feel justified in her lie. He was hurt and he was outraged, but he would accept, eventually, that his daughter was dead. He had to. His reaction confirmed her belief: Noble could never tolerate knowing that Laurel lived, but that she belonged, irrefutably, to another father and mother. That was the cross she would have to bear, alone, for the rest of her life.

"Don't say anything else," he said woodenly, snatching his clothes from the floor where they had spent the night, shaking the garments violently as if they were full of sand fleas, or scorpions. He looked at everything but her as he pulled them on with rough energy. "I don't want to hear any more. Get dressed. We'll get some breakfast and be on our way. Stephen and Charity have a head start on us for sure. We'll have to make some miles today, and it'll be hard going. I'll go on down for the horses and some things we'll need."

His hand was on the door lever. He was going, without so much as a look at her. As if he couldn't stand the sight of her. Ivy's throat caught.

"I'm sorry, Noble," she managed to whisper.

Noble paused at the door, without moving, as if there was something more he needed to say to her but could not find the words.

"I know," he muttered at last, his shoulders drooping. "So am I."

The sun set on a day that was hot, unpleasant, and buzzing with biting blackflies. Noble called a halt on a rise between the river and a muddy draw, in the dubious shelter of a couple of old scrub cedars that looked as if they'd sprung out of the solid rock around them.

"I'll tend the horses."

Noble thought hard as he dismounted, and could not remember having addressed a single remark to Ivy all day that consisted of anything more than four clipped words directly related to their mission.

"All right."

Had any of Ivy's replies been longer than two words? He could not recall. He doubted it.

He chucked to the weary animals and drew them a little ways away from the spot he'd chosen as their campsite. There was a patch of new grass nearby where he could hobble them, and they could graze while he removed their saddles.

And Ivy was far enough away that he wouldn't feel obliged to converse with her while she set up supper.

Ivy. Mrs. Noble Smith.

Damn.

Noble removed the bedrolls from behind the saddles and tossed them in the direction of the camp proper. He turned his attention to the cinches. More than at any other time in his life, he wished he was a praying man. He'd ask God for help picking through his feelings, which seemed to have gone through a meat grinder a couple of

times in the last two days. He'd ask Him how he
should talk to Ivy about what she'd endured alone,
because he wanted to know, but he didn't know
how to ask her. He guessed it was too late anyway
to help her, and he guessed it wouldn't be fair to
start up his praying career by asking God for favors. The Almighty was sure to look on it, and on
him, with a more jaundiced eye than usual.

Anyway, he had so many favors to ask, he wasn't
sure he'd be able to decide which one was the most
important. All he knew was that his plate was
pretty full, and he already felt bloated on bad luck.
All he could think about, aside from the daughter
he'd lost, was Al Gentile in his kitchen, talking
about the trouble he was buying. Damn, it was like
the man had a glass ball he looked into, or as if
he'd cursed Noble with those very words.

The worst of it was the strain between him and
Ivy. And the worst part of that was that he didn't
know how to fix it.

A quick sting burned his neck. He slapped it.

"Damn." He looked at the smear that was left of
the blackfly on the palm of his travel-stained glove.

"What's wrong?" Ivy's concern was genuine
enough to make the sting subside.

"Damn blackflies," he muttered. "We can't travel
too near the river from here on out, or they'll eat
us for breakfast, lunch and supper."

Ivy didn't comment. All he heard was the clank
of the coffeepot as she set it on the stones around
their small fire. The smell of burning sagebrush,
then cedar, singed his nostrils. He wondered when
she'd last cooked on an open fire, and opened his
mouth to ask her before he remembered they
weren't conversing.

He wished she would talk. He wished she'd say
something, anything, even make a remark about

the hard ride, the warm weather, or the flies. A
word from her would allow him to jump down her
throat. He wondered if that would ease the raw
wound in his heart. He doubted it.

"Aren't you going to say anything?" he called to
her, hoisting the saddle from the piebald's steam-
ing back. He didn't mean for that to sound conten-
tious, but he knew it did. He carried the saddle to
the clearing. Ivy did not look up from her labor.

"I thought you were angry with me."

Her voice was so pretty, and so sad, it broke his
heart.

"I am," he retorted. "I mean, I'm not. I mean—
hell, Ivy," he wound up, dropping the saddle to the
dirt near the fire. "It's a pretty big belly full, learning that I have—had—a daughter. Didn't you ever
mean to tell me?"

Why had he started down this road? He hadn't
wanted to know this morning, because he felt so
stunned and helpless when she told him. Now he
was unable to think of anything else. He kept pic-
turing the girl Ivy holding, instead of a doll, a
pretty, dead baby in her arms, crying. The picture
made him sick with pain and emptiness.

"There was nothing you could do." Ivy concentrated on opening a tin of beans.

"Not even for you?"

His question must have startled her, because she
looked up at him unexpectedly. Her green eyes had
a hunted look. She scraped the back of her wrist
across her cheekbone. She looked away again, but
her hands shook.

"She was gone, Noble. It was hard. But it was
hard to think of giving her up, too. Harder. Pa
would have hated her. He could barely look at me,
once he knew, until I went away. He said he would
always have thought of her as—" She stopped, as

if she wished she hadn't spoken at all.

"What?" he prompted her, trying to sound as stolid as she did.

She glanced at him once again, measuring him, then quickly looked away and scraped the beans into a pan.

"As Ben Smith's granddaughter," she finished, her voice low with apology. "He couldn't bear the idea. When I came back, alone, he never mentioned the baby at all. He didn't even ask what had happened, as if he wanted to pretend it had never happened at all."

"What did Stephen make of it?" Noble felt a little better for talking, but not much. It still hurt like hell to think that Ivy had kept such a secret from him, whatever her reasons.

"Stephen never knew. He was too young to understand what was happening, and I went away before I got so big that he'd notice."

For some reason, the thought of Ivy big with his child made Noble's throat close up like a drawstring sack. His eyes backed up with water and he had to think of something else quickly, or he knew he'd cry.

The mare. He still had to unsaddle the mare. The tightness eased from his throat, but instead moseyed down into his chest.

"I hope you do better with those beans than you did with that oatmeal yesterday." He turned away from her before she could respond to his lame attempt at a jest and aimed himself for the patient mare.

"Are you still angry?" Ivy's question was tentative, as if she feared either him or his answer. He halted. His eyes burned again, but he attributed it to the clay dust a sudden breeze sent into them.

He pressed his gloved fingers into them as hard as he dared.

"I'm not." He pushed his hat back off his brow. "I wasn't. I just . . . I feel bad. Sick, sort of, like when I found out Pa had run off. I remember thinking then: How could he do that to Ma and to Charity? I didn't really think much about what he'd done to me. Not until later. That's how I feel right now. I feel kind of empty, and I can't stop thinking of you, all alone there with the—with our baby. And I can't stop wishing that I could have been there with you, even if all I could have done was hold on to your hand."

Noble felt as if he'd trapped himself in a small, dark, airless room. More than anything, he wished he hadn't spoken what was on his mind. He hurt like hell, and he realized that there was nothing Ivy could say or do that would not make him weep for the child he'd been, and for the child he'd lost.

"Finish up with the mare. This will be hot in a few minutes. I'm going down to the river to wash." Ivy said nothing except for that.

His eyes dried at once and anger took the place of the pain. She wanted to keep him at arm's length, did she? Well, by God, he'd give her arm's length, and more.

"Wait here for me and we'll go together," he ordered her curtly. "We didn't see anybody all day, but that doesn't mean they're not around. I don't need you disappearing, too."

To his surprise, she was still there when he carried the mare's saddle in to camp minutes later, looking as if she had, indeed, waited per his instruction. Against his will, he softened at the thought. He resisted the temptation to look at her, though, instead striding through the small campsite with his towel slung over his shoulder and a

197

sliver of soap clenched in his fist. If she wanted to share either, she'd have to ask him. By God, he'd not volunteer it.

Noble established himself along a prominence in the bank where the swift water collected in a sheltered eddy. There was enough light from the tail end of the sunset to complete his task, if he didn't tarry over it. He knelt in the damp clay mud and looked down into the pool, hoping he'd spot a trout to tickle. A fresh-caught fish to enhance supper might improve his humor, and impress Ivy, besides.

He laughed to himself and shook his head, wondering at how little he'd really changed, over the last ten years.

There was no trout. With a sigh, he pulled his shirt off over his head, not bothering to unbutton it. He swirled the dusty garment in the pool. The water was cool. Cold, in fact. He considered undressing completely and diving in for a bath, but his private parts shrank at the very idea. He'd have to make do with a spit bath, as Pa used to call it when they'd washed together before supper at the rainbarrel after a hard day of work.

The shirt made a good washrag, and he plied it vigorously on his neck, his chest, under his arms and what part of his back he could reach. The soap was small and didn't bubble up much, but it smelled fresh and would help cut the grime of the day's ride.

"Would you like me to help?"

Ivy spoke directly behind him. The sound of her voice loosened the knots in his tired shoulders.

"Yes," he answered.

He'd meant to say no. Damn his disloyal tongue.

But he couldn't regret his reply when he felt her gentle hands on his back. She took the soaked shirt from his hand and plied it in a firm but gentle massage, a slow, spiraling motion all the way down to his lower back, the part he could not reach. A stray trickle of cool water escaped from the cloth and teased its way along his spine, right into his pants. It might have been the tip of her finger.

"I'm sorry, Noble." Her apology was a soft, low melody that found a harmony deep inside of him. His shoulders shuddered, and he prayed she would think it was because he was cold. He tried to answer her, but his tongue felt too big for his mouth.

"I should have told you about La—about the baby." Ivy did not seem to notice, or if she did, she misinterpreted his silence. "It was wrong of me. You deserved to know."

Noble arched his back, welcoming her touch. He closed his eyes as she traced his spine downward with the wet shirt. He clenched his fists on his knees, praying that she would stop, praying that she would never stop.

The cleansing cloth was withdrawn. Just as he was about to cry out for her to continue, he felt the dry softness of his towel as she patted him dry, starting with his shoulders.

"I won't keep things from you anymore," she said, sounding earnest and innocent. "From now on. I promise. Will you?"

"Will I what?" Lord, he must sound like an idiot! His cheeks heated.

"Will you promise not to keep things from me? From now on, I mean?"

He looked up to see her straighten and hand him his towel.

He was paralyzed by what he saw in the last rays of the fading light. Ivy had unbuttoned her shirt-waist and stripped it away so that it hung about her waist, revealing all of her arms, her neck, and more than a little of her chest. She was cinched at the waist with her corset, but above it the soft, filmy cotton of her chemise was pulled taut by the full roundness of her breasts. Her smooth, white skin looked like sweet cream, so good he could taste it.

"Noble?"

"What?"

"Will you promise? And do you forgive me?"

He wrenched his gaze from her and stared down into the little pool again in an effort to collect himself.

"Yes. Yes." God, yes.

"May I use the soap?"

He nodded. "Take the towel, too."

"Thank you." Her voice was rich with contrition and gratitude. It started a thrumming in his ears.

The next thing he heard was the rustle of Ivy's clothing as she moved away from him, down the bank aways. He heard the quiet splash of water as she washed herself. Not daring to look at her, he imagined the graceful movement of her slender hands as they stroked the length of her arms. He pictured her lifting her thick braid of auburn hair from her neck as she washed her back. He even felt her blush as she squeezed a trickle of cooling water down between her breasts.

The sudden rush of heat that filled him was like the fiery surge from a blast furnace. Without pausing to consider what Ivy might make of his bizarre behavior, he plunged his whole head down, face first, into the brisk water of the Big Horn River.

Chapter Seventeen

Ivy tried not to think about her ambiguous promise to Noble as she served their meager supper on tin plates. From now on, she had said. He had agreed. She stole a glance at him. He was picking at his dinner in abnormal silence. She wondered whether that caveat would mollify him, should he ever learn the truth about Laurel. She doubted it would. But it would enable her to live with herself, and with her lie of omission, at least for the time being. She sighed.

"What? You say something?" Noble, five feet away, looked up from his dish as though glad of an excuse to stop eating. His eyes were like two coals as he scrutinized her.

She shook her head and curled up tighter in her crouch by a fallen cedar branch.

He grunted. "I thought you did. You look like you're thinking about something, that's for sure."

Ivy looked down at her half-eaten plate of beans. "What are you thinking about, Noble?"

It was Noble's turn to sigh. He set his plate aside and tipped his head back to stare at the black sky. He propped one elbow on his knee. With his other hand, he stroked the dark shadow of beard stubble on his neck.

"Something's wrong," he mused, drawing his words out. "You saw Stephen in Basin, and he said he was with Charity, and they were headed for Rawlins. The two of them had to be travelling with over a hundred pounds of gold, as I figure it. That means a pack animal, or mighty slow travel on two horses. Either way, we should have come across them today, or some part of their trail. There hasn't even been any sign of those men who were following us. I should have picked up some sign before now."

Ivy stared. She hadn't thought about the men following them, or about tracking. She'd just assumed she and Noble were trying to catch up with the runaways along the way. How hard could that be? How many ways could there be to get from Basin to Rawlins? Once they got through the Wind River Canyon, there were plenty of passes over the various ranges, but the canyon was still least a day away, maybe two. Surely there'd be some sign of them by then. Surely they wouldn't have to go all the way to Rawlins . . .

The thought made her shiver.

"Cold?" Noble eased over beside her, crossing his long legs out in front of him in a more relaxed posture. He pulled her close with one arm.

If anything, she felt too warm. She was tense in the shelter of his embrace, and she tried to compose herself. A coyote howled in the distance.

Noble grinned at her.

"Nervous?" His voice took on a boyish, mischievous tone. "It's nothing but a coyote, Scaredy-cat. They don't eat much. I guess you've never done much camping out, have you?"

He'd misread her agitation. Thank goodness. She gave him a sideways look.

"If you mean to tease me out here, Noble Smith—"

His chuckle cut short her pretended indignation, and he held her tighter. "You'll what? You'll pick up and leave? Go off by yourself in the dark? The way I look at it, I have ten years of teasing to make up for, Ivy-Girl. So get used to it. Unless you want to sleep by yourself, way over there someplace with the coyotes and the rattlesnakes."

"It's too early for rattlesnakes." She doubted that was true even as she said it, but she could hope.

Noble rubbed his cheek with his free hand. "I'd have thought it was too early for blackflies, too, but there have sure been enough of them. Maybe we should introduce the blackflies to the coyotes and rattlesnakes, and see which gets the better of which."

Ivy laughed.

"I think we've lost our minds, Noble," she declared at the end of it, laying her head against the firm comfort of Noble's solid shoulder. "Here we are, miles from home, miles from anywhere, chasing after Stephen and Charity to keep them safe, and we're laughing together by a cozy camp fire as if we haven't a care in the world, like—" She stopped. She could not go on, and she did not know why.

"Like what?" he asked softly.

"Like a couple of school children on a picnic," she managed to finish, although her voice was fainter than before.

203

His lips were comforting and cool against her forehead, but they inspired a burn inside of her.

"I guess there's a part of us, both of us, that's still those two kids, Ivy," he said thoughtfully, after a long pause. "I sort of hope there always will be. But that's not how I see us now, here."

Noble's arm tightened around her shoulder, and he took hold of his draped wrist with his free hand, locking her to him. It felt so perfect that she did not want to query him. She did not want to speak or to move, ever again.

"What I see," he continued, his voice gentle as the night around them, "are two people, very much grown up, very much in love, who have found each other after a very long time being lost and alone."

Ivy closed her eyes. She saw the same thing, and it made her smile, until the gray shade of a small child-ghost sprang up between the two adult lovers. The image was as real and as disturbing as a vivid dream or a nightmare. She opened her eyes to dispel it, but she discovered, to her dismay, that it was not so easily banished.

She slipped her arm about Noble's waist, assailed by sudden panic. There was only one thing right now that could get in the way of her happiness with Noble, she realized, holding him tightly. And that was Ivy Wingate Smith.

She tried to steady herself before she spoke to him again.

"Noble?"

"Mmm?"

"I want to have a child."

He rubbed her arm with lazy, caressing strokes and pressed another kiss against her forehead. "We'll have a baby," he assured her, just above a whisper. "We'll have lots of babies. You'll see. And they'll all be sweet and pretty like you, or hell in a

204

handbasket, like me. And—"

"No," she protested, holding him closer still so he could not see her face, and read her guilt there. "I want a child. Now."

A low, indulgent chuckle shook his chest.

"Honey, it takes at least nine months."

"Noble!" She didn't know whether to strike him for making such a joke, or to be grateful that he misread her anxiousness.

"I know, I know. I'm teasing again. Mark it against my account."

"Noble, this is serious!" She pulled away from his embrace and sat up, not trusting herself to look him full in the face. "I want a baby. I want your baby. I never had anything in this life that I really wanted until the last two days—"

"So now you want everything, right away," he finished for her in a sigh, with no trace of amusement in his voice. "I know the feeling. God knows, I know the feeling. But there's more to it than that, isn't there?"

Ivy's heart stopped. He knew!

"What do you mean?" She gasped the words.

"Look at me, Ivy."

She did not move.

"Please?"

She bit her lip and turned to him slowly, terrified at the thought of what she would see in his face. When she dared to look, what she saw amazed her.

There was no suggestion of the anger or hatred she expected, or even of pain. There was only Noble's sweet, handsome, angular face, tendering a fond smile, his dark eyes frankly adoring.

"You feel bad about Laurel," he said. Compassion mingled with sadness in his soft baritone, and the combination touched something in Ivy, something old and painful. "And you feel like you need to make it up to me, somehow. I know, because that's how I feel, too, even though I never saw her, never knew her. I wish I could make everything right. To bring Laurel back. Or to make it as if she'd—as if none of it had ever happened.

"You think a baby will take her place, or make up for her, somehow. But it isn't like that. It can't be. It would be as if someone could have come along and said, 'I'll be your Pa, Noble, since yours ran off,' or, 'I'll be your Ma, Ivy.' It might have worked out for Charity or Stephen, since they were so young when it happened, but not for us. It would never have been the same. And it won't be the same for us when we have a child together. We can never make another Laurel, Ivy. And it would be wrong of us, either of us, to think we could."

Ivy stared at him, paralyzed with relief that he had not guessed the truth. He offered her a smile, although it lacked the heart to remain long on his features.

"Come here, sweetheart."

Ivy went to him, glad of both his understanding and his ignorance. She would make him happy, she vowed, slipping her arms about him as he embraced her. And she would make him forget about Laurel, the child they couldn't have, even if it meant that she herself could never forget her.

Noble held her against him, curling a stray lock of her hair at her neck with one lazy finger.

"We should clean up supper, if we aren't going to eat any more," she reminded him at the end of a sigh.

"Are you all right, now?" He kissed her brow.

His tender concern induced a swell of tears behind her eyes, but she held them back.

"I'm fine," she assured him in as bright a tone as she could muster, staring at the fire. "You will think about what I said though, won't you? About a baby? I do want one."

He chuckled again, that deep, rumbling, pleasing sound she remembered and loved so well, even when it made her blush, as it did then.

"There's better ways to make babies than thinking about it, darlin'," he drawled. "I expect we won't have long to wait for one, if we keep on going like we started out."

What a beautiful, simple answer to her prayer!

Noble was uneasy as he checked the horses and set out the bedrolls, but he couldn't tell why. It wasn't a strong sensation; it was more like the nag of a half-remembered warning from the past, or the phantom pain of a bruise long healed. He watched Ivy stow the cleaned utensils from supper, wondering whether his feeling had anything to do with her, or if, indeed, it had any foundation at all beyond their current chancy situation. Either way, he decided, it was best not to mention it to her right off. Not until he'd had time to think about it a little. There was no point in worrying her without cause.

"Are you sleeping all the way over there?" Her incredulous question startled him out of his thoughts. He had set the bedrolls on opposite sides of the fire for several reasons, most of which he preferred not to think about, much less to explain to her. For one thing, he knew he couldn't sleep next to her on this, their second night as man and wife, and not want to have her. The idea of making love out in the open that way made him nervous. He looked across the fire at her and tried to frame an explanation that would not sound asinine.

Damn, she was pretty by the dying light of the fire! Her plain shirtwaist was all buttoned up again, but for a fleeting instant he saw her as she'd been earlier, by the river, with her russet hair all falling out of its bindings and her bare arms plump and white in the moonlight. Gazing at her, he wanted to know what she'd look like by the light of the fire. He imagined she'd look like fire herself, all red and gold, warm, with a measure of danger.

He shook his head as if a bee had buzzed by.

"I thought I'd sit up on watch for a while," he replied at last, maintaining an even tone, although it was an effort to do so. "I wouldn't want to keep you awake."

Ivy shot him a teasing grin before stooping to gather up her own sleeping gear.

"You didn't have that misgiving last night," she reminded him, skirting around the fire to his side with her bundle. His face heated, and other parts of him got uncomfortably warm at the delicious memory, as well. He opened his mouth, but realized too late that he had no answer for her, this time. She looked up at him with a decidedly impish twinkle in her eyes, which were a fairy, forest-green in the darkness.

"Cat got your tongue, Noble?"

He couldn't help smiling at her saucy question, even as the telling heat continued to pump into his face. He wished he had a nickel for every time Ivy had used those words on him in past years. When they were kids, he'd wanted to flatten her when she said it, and once or twice, he'd actually done it. As they grew into their teens, though, he remembered quite a different desire overwhelming him whenever Ivy Wingate's quick tongue got the best of him.

"I'll show you what's got my tongue, Miss Win— Mrs. Smith," he growled, taking hold of her arms with an abruptness that made her cry out.

"Nob—"

He cut off her exclamation by claiming her mouth with his. The knowledge that he'd startled her, and possibly even frightened her, was shockingly satisfying, and it imbued him with brash, new power. She struggled briefly in his arms, but he tightened his embrace. Her surrender was his reward, and he relished it. He teased and plundered her mouth with his lips and his tongue in a wondrous dance that was part taking, part yielding, and the most sublime parts of both. The pressure on the back of his neck, he knew, was her arms holding him to his purpose.

He scooped Ivy's legs from beneath her and dropped to his knees with her secure in his arms. He drank another draught from the sweet silk and fire of her mouth and pressed her to the waiting bedroll. She writhed and whimpered under him, but he knew her response to be a kindred desire this time, not a protest. That was one error he would never make again.

"Ah, God, Ivy," he murmured, loving the feel of her body beneath his, craving more. "This is wicked. Sweet and wicked. What magic makes me want you so much?"

As he took her willing mouth again, he knew the answer to his question. He had always wanted her, just as he had always loved her. Just as he always would. Some things in life, he had learned early, were inescapable.

Wanting to show her to what many good uses his tongue might be applied, he freed her from her clothing, down to the chemise whose dimensions had so intrigued him as they'd washed by the river. That fragile garment, secured by seductive satin ribbons, mounted no defense against his incursion, and soon betrayed its mistress to him like a deserting sentry. Her breast rose and fell rapidly with each panting breath. He allowed himself a long, appreciative gaze at the luscious vista his efforts had revealed.

"Noble . . ." There was a rich plea in her ragged whisper, then it faded.

He grinned.

"Cat got your tongue, Ivy?"

He toyed with one erect nipple, rolling it gently between his thumb and forefinger. Her eyes were half-closed in a slanted, exotic expression he willingly took for encouragement. Her lips were parted, and she moistened them with the tip of her delightful tongue. The one the cat had.

The fire was dying, but the heat between them roared like a brushfire. He tasted it on her skin, on the tender, yielding flesh of her breasts, sweet, yet salty with want. Her fingers ransacked his hair as he journeyed downward along her belly, their activity spurring him on. Tight chestnut curls tickled his chin.

He wanted to explore their hidden cache. Her sweet muskiness told him she wanted him, too.

Her hands tightened in his hair. He heard her take in a gasp of air and hold it. He could not tell whether she meant to stifle a cry of fear, desire or protest. He paused, waiting for a single sign from her that would make him stop, praying it would not come.

She withdrew her hands from his head, leaving the decision entirely up to him.

He undertook his commission with fresh delight and utter abandon.

Ivy lost all sense of herself, except for that part of her upon which Noble was committing acts of unspeakable enchantment. She felt shamelessly stripped, not only of her clothing, but of every sense of propriety she'd ever known, honest or false. She gave herself to Noble in a way she could never have imagined. He took her in a way she could never have dreamed.

When he finally entered her, she cried out in joy to the darkness. He answered her with a shuddering groan. His heat filled her. He held himself above her, his elbows braced on the ground on either side of her. His cheek brushed hers gently with each long, slow thrust of his loins against hers.

"Love you," he muttered, licking her ear. She thought she would go mad. "Love you, Ivy. Sweet. God . . ." The rest of his words became a single, protracted moan. Her body answered in the way Noble's had shown her.

The fire was nearly out. The night air was chilly; Ivy knew she'd be cold but for Noble's possessive embrace. She nudged him with her elbow and he snored softly in answer. The sound filled her with contentment, and she smiled to herself.

She freed her hand from Noble's and slid it down to her bare belly. Her skin prickled with goosebumps. She wondered, feeling all around, if they had started a baby there. She tried to remember what she'd felt like when she was pregnant with Laurel, but could only recall the sickness that seemed interminable. She was surprised to discover that she could remember little else connected with the event. She wondered if she would be ill again, and she realized she did not care. There was nothing she would not endure for the chance at giving Noble another child, a child to replace the one he must never know . . .

"I doubt you could feel anything yet, String-bean." Noble's voice was an amused but serene whisper in her ear. "Maybe if I put my ear against your belly, I could hear something."

Ivy turned in his arms and met his steady, sleepy smile. "You'd hear my stomach for something better than beans," she told him, placing a finger against his parted lips.

He shrugged his eyebrows, as if he hadn't the energy remaining to move anything else.

"You could have stayed behind in a jail cell in Basin," he pointed out to her lazily. "I bet the food was better."

She pulled a lock of his hair that hung over his ear. "I like the company here."

"So do I." He kissed her nose.

"Noble, I'm cold."

"That's because you're all undressed. Now, who did this?" He sat up with a grunt, folding his long legs beneath him. Flushed, dishevelled, sheepish as a schoolboy, Noble drew the lacings of her chemise together with surprisingly awkward fingers. Ivy pretended annoyance and brushed his fingers away.

"Let me," she told him. "The fire's going out. Find some more cedar."

He curled his lower lip in as he got to his feet. "Yes, ma'am."

Ivy felt oddly relieved that Noble's attention was drawn elsewhere while she put her clothes back on. It was one thing to have his blatantly admiring gaze on her while they were engaged in that most private of acts. It seemed indecent, otherwise. She had to think of the act as separate from the rest of her life, and from her relationship with Noble. Otherwise, she was certain she'd walk about with a constant crimson blush on her face. Hardly a desirable state of affairs.

"Ivy."

Noble's hands took hold of hers as she finished

the uppermost buttons of her shirtwaist. Having not marked his approach, she was startled into meeting his gaze. His dark eyes were sober and intense, and there was no hint of a smile about his wide, sensuous mouth. Ivy's heart climbed into her throat at the look.

"I know what you're trying to do," he said, his voice as soft as the night around them. "Don't. Don't hurry this. Any of it. We waited so long to be happy together; we can sure wait out wanting another child. When we make love, I just want it to be you and me. I don't want to feel like there's any reason for it other than the fact that we love each other. It would make me feel—" he tilted his head back as if the sky might provide him with the word he sought, and he pressed his lips together—"I don't know. Used, I think. As if I was no good for anything except putting a baby in you." He looked at her again, and there was a trace of sadness in his expressive eyes that Ivy longed to erase. "I never thought much about it before, but looking back, I think that might be one reason why my pa and your ma did what they did. My ma never seemed to have much time to treat Pa special. Hell, I even remember times he used to catch her at the stove and try to give her a kiss, and she'd chase him off. Not teasing, either. Just—sort of—testy. Like he was a bother. Most times he just went off with a little joke, but I guess it didn't make him feel any too good to be turned aside all the time."

Ivy stared at Noble's hands. They were big and calloused, but they were gentle, and they never used her but with the touch of a lover. Noble's story reminded her of her own mother and father, and she remembered all too clearly the roles being reversed. Only Pa had not merely chased Ma with words or looks. She cringed at the memory.

"Don't look so sad, sweetheart." Noble brushed the underside of her chin with one crooked finger. "Remember what Mrs. Woolson used to tell us? 'That's why we study history, so we don't repeat others' mistakes.'" His mimicry of their old schoolteacher was so precise that Ivy could not help laughing.

"You're so smart, Noble," she pretended to grumble, afterward. "You could be the President, if it wouldn't be such a comedown for you."

"I'd be happy just to be the king of my own little house," he declared, squeezing her hands. "As long as you're there to be my queen. Come on, Stringbean." His tone became brisk and businesslike again, as if he did not want to think overlong about the analogy he'd made. "We need to get to bed. And I mean to sleep, this time. The night isn't getting any longer, and the days are too long as it is."

She fell asleep quickly in his arms and dreamed of being crowned the queen of Wyoming.

It was scarcely light when Ivy opened her eyes. She was cold, but that was not what had awakened her. She rubbed her eyes with her fists and rolled onto her back. The fire was out. Noble was gone.

She sat up with a start of panic. "Noble!"

"Quiet, Stringbean. I'm listening."

She calmed at once and twisted around to see Noble crouched nearby on the rise with his rifle propped like a staff beside him. He was staring down south along the river, apparently scouting the way they'd be travelling.

"Listening to what?" She heard nothing but a few early-rising meadowlarks, and the sound of the Bighorn rushing through its valley.

"I don't know, exactly." He continued to peer southward, not granting her even a glance. "I

214

heard a noise a little while ago as I was lying there with my ear to the ground. It sounded like a lot of horses."

Ivy's heart stilled. The men who were after Stephen's gold, who had almost raped her at the Wingate ranch? A sudden wave of dread made her want to stand up and run, but she could not move.

Noble got to his feet, but remained bent over as he trotted down the rise toward her. His expression was grim.

"Looks like a whole damned parade," he announced in a whisper. "Men. Horses. And a wagon, too, with a team of mules. Probably a freighter, but I don't like the looks of the others, even from here."

"You think it's . . ." She could not bring herself to finish.

Noble grimaced as he nodded twice.

"Looks like five of them," he confirmed. "You collect our things; I'll saddle up the horses."

"Where are we going?"

Ivy wondered how far down inside himself he'd had to look for the grin he flashed her.

"Right into the jaws of death, sweetheart."

He hoisted his saddle and started toward the hobbled animals, with a single-mindedness of purpose on his angular features that frightened Ivy.

"Isn't there someplace we can hide?" Was that her voice? It sounded like the squeak of a mouse.

"Not here. We've left our marks all over. They're south of us, anyway; I guess they picked up Stephen's trail somehow without . . . I don't know. The idea that they might have happened on us last night . . ." He shook his head quickly as if trying to chase a worrisome insect. "We'll have to move fast, get ahead of them somehow, between them and Stephen."

215

Noble's swift, quiet words and even quicker, stealthy movements persuaded Ivy that haste was in order. She found, in his brisk, businesslike manner, the courage to stir. She rolled to her knees, pulling up the bedrolls as she went.

By the time she climbed into the saddle of the waiting pie, the campsite bore no trace of their use except for what evidence of the fire they could not erase, namely the smoke-blackened rocks. Seeming to read her thoughts, Noble said, "We'll leave this as it is. I want them to know we've been here in case they double back, and to know we've gone on."

As his remark faded in the dawn, she heard for herself the distant sound of hooves drumming the earth. Her heart quickened in time. Dear Lord, this was really happening! And here they were, she and Noble, miles from any help. She grasped the saddle horn and began to shake.

"Hell of a way to wake up, isn't it?" Noble's hand was on hers as he leaned across from atop his mare, and he grinned at her recklessly. "Think of the stories we'll be able to tell our grandchildren!"

As if his smile had wrought some good magic, her trembling ceased. She could not manage a smile in response, however, until he'd turned away again. He led the way back down toward the river, and she followed in silence.

It was scarcely sunup, and already the blackflies were buzzing. It was damp by the river, and in no time, Ivy's clothes were sticking to her like a clammy second skin. The sound of the oncoming horses faded, muffled, she supposed, by the rock croppings and swaybacked cedars along the river. Noble was tense and wary. He scarcely shrugged the blackflies away, while she twitched and swatted. Presently he looked over his shoulder and nodded toward a dry rock draw to his left that led up away from the river again.

"This way." He scarcely mouthed the words.

The draw led to a small canyon shaded by cedar and overgrown sage. It appeared to have two exits, which made it a good choice of a place to hole up for a bit. Ivy was glad when Noble dismounted, and she did the same. Her stomach had awakened, and it was not pleased by the fact that they'd taken off without breakfast. It grumbled like a petulant child.

Noble grinned as he led the mare to her, although his coffee-colored eyes still wore a hunted look.

"You'd best grab a bite of jerky," he advised, caressing her cheek with a gloved hand. "That noisy stomach of yours is liable to give us away."

Before she could muster a retort, he handed her the mare's rein.

"Stay here. I'm going up on those rocks to get the lay of things. Keep the horses as quiet as you can. And your stomach, too." He touched the end of her nose. Then, as if he knew that was not enough reassurance for her, or as if he needed some for himself, he pulled her close in an abrupt embrace, brushing her lips with his.

"Don't worry, Ivy-girl," he whispered in her ear. "I'll get us out of this. Stay here."

As comforting as his words and his touch were, their succor lasted only until he disappeared over the crest of the rocks.

Chapter Eighteen

Noble felt like a spider, creeping his way up the wall of rock. He wished he were one, as he was no lover of heights, and he could all too easily envision himself slipping and falling twenty or thirty feet down to the canyon floor. It was neither a steep nor a particularly difficult climb, but he was nervous and his sweaty palms made it more of a challenge than it needed to be. He hated leaving Ivy there alone, but he figured it was the lesser of two evils. If he were spotted, at least he could lead the men away for a time and hope Ivy had the sense to escape in the other direction.

He did not spot his quarry right away, because they were not where he expected them to be. From the dubious shelter of a scruffy sagebrush, he looked out and spied what he had earlier termed a "parade," five men on horseback—doubtless the same men who had been dogging him and Ivy since the Wingate ranch in Peaceful—and a lone freighter driving eight teams of mules and what looked like an empty wagon piled with tarps. The bunch of them were surprisingly close by, perhaps only a hundred yards away, but judging by where they were positioned, Noble doubted they'd come the way he and Ivy had, which meant they hadn't passed through the spot where they'd spent the night. Encouraged, he remained where he was, straining to hear the exchange between the men.

It was impossible, with the sound of the river behind him. He thought up a curse and kept it to himself as he used the cover of the rocks and cedar to get closer to the assembly of men, mules and horses. He withdrew his gun from its place at his hip and prayed he would have no need of it.

At about forty feet, there was nothing closer to hide behind, and Noble stopped. The ragtag lot of riders clustered about the freighter, who looked more like a somber, if dusty, preacher in his black garb than a freight driver. Noble was reminded, oddly, of the "Adventures of Robin Hood," which he'd read when he was younger, and of the character called Friar Tuck. Friar Tuck, Noble recalled, had hoarded his share of secrets, much to Robin Hood's dismay.

The men surrounding the freighter wore expressions of casual distrust on their weathered, unpleasant features. Noble spotted Jack, the man who'd meant to violate Ivy at her ranch three nights before. He felt an icy thrill race through him as he thought of putting a bullet between the man's legs. But if he did that he'd have to kill the others as well, and he doubted he had the stomach for wholesale slaughter. Instead, he kept very still in the brush and listened hard.

In the time it took Noble to blink, a giant materialized, standing in the back of the wagon like the fabled Colossus of Rhodes: long legs apart, shoulders like railroad ties, a wild crop of wiry black hair and a fierce scowl on granite-hewn features. Noble suspected it was not these imposing attributes that gave the five men about them pause, but the cocked Colt revolver leveled square on the leader's chest. Noble held his own breath, as if the gun were fixed on him instead.

"Solly don't want you in wagon," the freighter remarked in a clear, casual, but distinctly accented voice. "Solly don't talk much, and he listen even less. That's what I pay him for."

The man sounded so complacent that Noble was forced to stifle a laugh.

"There's five of us and only one of him," one of the mounted men pointed out. Noble wondered if the man could be as stupid as he sounded, but, noticing that he did not go for his own gun, decided he wasn't.

The driver shrugged his beefy, sloped shoulders. "He have one bullet to spare. Or maybe one of you take two."

Noble could not swear to it, but he thought the giant standing in the wagon delivered a glance in his direction. He tried to make himself as small as possible behind his bush, no easy thing to do.

"Aw, come on, Jack," one of the men entreated with an anxious undertone to his voice. "This Jew muledriver don't know nothin', anyway. We'd best double back and pick up that trail we passed."

Jack didn't answer, merely pinned the freighter with his stare. Noble ached to throttle him.

Noble decided against a confrontation right there, not knowing Solly and not liking the odds one bit. A slow, burning cramp began to worry his leg, and he wished the riders would leave so he could get up and stomp it out.

The riders were none too quick to leave, but leave they did, loping back up what passed for a trail behind the wagon, in the direction of the campsite he and Ivy had recently quitted. Noble waited behind the bush, as still as he could be. Jack and his men obviously did not know he was there, and he wanted to keep it that way. He dared not risk being discovered by a chance look over a shoulder.

The giant, Solly, did not put up his weapon right away. He said something to the driver in a guttural, harsh-sounding language that Noble not only did not understand but could also not identify, except that he knew it wasn't French. The driver laughed. He made a reply in the same exotic tongue, then stared as if the bush shielding Noble did not exist.

"You come out now," he invited in a conversational tone. "Or Solly shoot."

Noble felt like a mouse in a trap. It didn't take long to review his choices. They amounted to one. He grunted as he got to his feet and hoped his cramped leg would not fail him as he walked out from behind his faulty cover, holding his hands over his head. The deadly click of Solly's cocked revolver made him freeze in his tracks. He felt as if he'd swallowed a stick.

"Drop your gun," the driver entreated, as if he were inviting Noble to join him for breakfast. Noble complied, feeling rather stripped. What next? he wondered.

To his surprise, the driver squinted and looked beyond him.

"You, too," he called a trifle louder. "Come out. Hands up, please."

Much as he wanted to keep his eyes on the man holding him at gunpoint, Noble could not prevent

221

himself from turning around. Amazement, terror and anger warred in him as he watched Ivy step forth from behind a stand of cedars several yards behind him. She sent him a piteous look of apology, and he could only hope he was not glaring at her.

" 'Love, honor and obey,' huh?" he muttered as she gained his side.

Through her contrite expression, she grinned fleetingly. "Best two out of three?"

"Stay behind me."

He approached the wagon cautiously as the driver scrambled down. Noble was amazed at the efficiency with which the large man accomplished this feat. Noble stopped a half a dozen feet away, his arms still stretched overhead. As Ivy bumped to a halt behind him, the driver jerked his gloves from his fingers with quick movements. Solly, Noble noticed, did not relax his vigilant pose. The driver waddled toward them, a genial look on his round face and his fleshly hand extended in greeting.

"Moishe Braman," he said, a grin parting his gray-flecked dark beard. Noble was not certain whether it was a greeting or an introduction. He opted for the latter, with a wary eye toward the giant in the wagon.

"Noble Smith." He accepted the proffered hand, wanting to smile, but somehow unable to. "And my wife, Ivy." Something inside of him made him want to babble on, to relate his and Ivy's entire story to Braman on a single breath, if possible, but his mouth refused to allow him to make an idiot out of himself. He swallowed, instead.

"We're looking for two people," Ivy, behind him, blurted, her small voice shaking. "A young couple. My brother and his wife. They were on their way to Rawlins. Have you seen them?"

One of Braman's bushy eyebrows disappeared beneath the brim of his odd, black, flat-brimmed hat. His quizzical look shuttled between Noble and Ivy twice.

"I see you before," he said with slow conviction. "In Basin."

Noble frowned, but Ivy piped up joyously. "Yes, of course! You were the freighter I saw in the street. I suppose you must have seen us two nights ago, when we went back and forth from the hotel to the sheriff's office."

Noble was surprised to discover that the memory of that night, mostly due to circumstances leading up to the event Ivy mentioned, made his face grow warm. Braman laughed again, compounding Noble's discomfort.

"Yes! The wedding!" Braman clapped his hands together and nodded. "Olga Kimmerle tell us about it. Big argument at the hotel. Sheriff Richman want to arrest you." Each embellishment stung Noble worse than the bite of a blackfly. "Then you marry. Solly!" He launched into a stream of alien words whose effect was to make Solly, taciturn, ominous Solly, put away his weapon and grin. Noble, both irritated and relieved, wondered if news of the event had already blanketed the territory. If so, it had no doubt escalated to an epic saga. He could just imagine what Penelope Quinlan, Sophie Paul and all the other Peaceful biddies would make of it. The thought pained him even more.

"We don't have time for friendly chatter," he cut in, mastering a glare. "I don't mean to be rude," he went on with a pointed look at the man who had so recently held them in check at the point of a gun. "But we have ground to cover. If you've seen them, please tell us where, and when. If not, my wife and I will just be on our way. Oh, and we'd appreciate your not mentioning to those other men that you saw us."

Behind him, Ivy's stomach emitted an especially lusty growl. Braman chuckled.

"Breakfast," he said firmly, clapping his hands together once and rubbing them for emphasis. "Solly make *latkes*. We have coffee. We talk. Solly!" he bellowed.

Noble started to protest, but Braman, obviously accustomed to ordering people about and to having his wishes obeyed, was already pulling out a fry pan, a coffeepot and a sack of provisions as if the matter were settled.

"I'm hungry, Noble." Ivy nudged him. "Let's eat with them. Maybe they've seen Stephen and Charity, or know about them. Besides, we shouldn't be rude."

"They held a gun on us a short while ago," he reminded her in a whisper. "I guess your stomach has a short memory, but that strikes me as about as rude as a person can get."

"Noble." That chiding tone, again. He bit his lower lip to hold back a rueful grin. He was hungry, too.

"All right. I'll go back for the horses. You did leave the horses hobbled back there in the gully, didn't you?"

Ivy looked startled.

"Why—no," she remarked, coloring. "I thought you'd want them ready, in case we had to leave quickly."

"I would have, if you'd stayed behind with them! Damn, Ivy, don't tell me you just—just left them there!"

She looked as devastated as if he'd struck her. "But there was nothing to tie them to." Her voice faltered. Both Moishe Braman and Solly paused in their preparation to stare at him. He felt like a criminal. He smothered an apology and turned away.

"Guess I'd better go get them," he snapped. "If they're still there, that is."

He loped off toward the gully, half-hoping the horses would be gone, just to show Ivy the folly of her escapade. They'd be in a fine pickle then, of course, without their horses, but Ivy needed some kind of once-and-for-all lesson to teach her to do as she was told, or they'd both come to grief.

Fortunately, the Lord chose not to send Ivy, or him, a harsh message this time. The horses were placidly milling about the gully, nibbling at tufts of spring grass growing in the rocks, and they demonstrated only indifference to his return.

"Bred for speed and stupidity," Noble muttered to himself as he rounded the animals up. He considered for a moment tethering them and going back to Ivy empty-handed, telling her they had run off. Imagining her horror, he decided that would be taking his teasing one step too far. Maybe even half a mile.

When Noble returned to the freighter's make-shift breakfast fire minutes later, he was surprised, and a little alarmed, to discover that Ivy had, in that short time, apparently made fast friends of Moishe Braman, and his silent giant, Solly, who was tending a sizzling fry pan. Ivy and the robust freighter were chatting in an easy, sociable manner. Solly didn't seem to be saying much, but he was smiling, a surprisingly pleasant expression Noble had not seen upon his stony features before. A succulent but unfamiliar aroma met Noble's appreciative nostrils. His stomach growled low in answer.

"Don't they smell wonderful, Noble?" Ivy's enthusiasm dissolved what little remained of Noble's earlier anger. He never ceased to be amazed at the simple things in which she took delight. "Moishe says they're made from potatoes. He says Solly will teach me how to make them."

"You are lucky man, my friend." Moishe, grinning through his beard, waved Noble toward the fire. He and Ivy were sitting together on a rock, and there was room for one more. "Your wife, she is, as we say in Yiddish, a mensch."

"Moishe and Solly have wives waiting for them in Rawlins," Ivy explained as Noble sat down beside her.

"No, not waiting yet," Moishe corrected her. "Coming on train."

"Oh, yes. Mail-order brides, Noble. That's quite common, I understand, although I never knew anyone in Peaceful who had one, did you?"

Before Noble was able to answer, Moishe spoke up again, his expression pensive.

"We are—how you say?—eager. No, anxious. Five years we live here, five years driving freight to Basin, to Greybull. No wife. No home. No children. But—" He spread his broad hands expressively. "I am not young man, like you. Is too much, this long trip, eight, ten, twelve times a year. Solly and me, we open a dry goods store in Rawlins, now. Build houses. Homes. But what is home without a woman? A wife?" He winked at Noble, then glanced at Ivy.

Noble stared back, wondering about the sanity of a man who'd take a complete stranger as a wife, and the wisdom of a woman who'd travel hundreds, maybe thousands, of miles to marry a man she'd never even seen. It seemed a hell of a risky start to a marriage, for both partners. How lucky he was, he realized as his gaze strayed to Ivy, to have found what he wanted and needed, right within arm's length.

But Braman was most enthusiastic about his and Solly's impending nuptials. It seemed to Noble that the mule driver would happily have kept him and Ivy there for half the day prattling on about the virtues of the two women who had come, via New York City, from Braman's very own village in Russia. At least, Noble thought, they would have that much in common.

After they'd stuffed themselves on the hearty fare, Solly cleaned up the cooking gear and Braman stowed it away, humming to himself as he worked. Noble took his cup of coffee and went in search of Stephen and Charity's trail. He walked slowly, scanning the ground, until he was thirty or forty feet from where the freight wagon waited. The path was definitely the main route he and Ivy had followed since Basin, and the only way by which a wagon pulled by mules could travel. It had been trampled by the outlaw posse that Braman had sent north, and the dust revealed no more than a confusion of hoofprints and wagon ruts. No sign of Stephen and Charity.

The truth was inescapable. He'd lost the trail somehow. Maybe he'd lost it yesterday, when he'd been preoccupied with thoughts of Ivy and the baby she'd had. Thinking back, he couldn't remember the last time he'd actually seen the trail; he'd just assumed that he'd guessed Stephen's plan and the trail was still there. Cursing his stupidity and arrogance, he realized he'd have to backtrack and try to pick it up again. That meant taking Ivy right back into more danger.

"Noble?" Ivy was right behind him. He took a deep breath and tossed off the dregs of his coffee, gathering courage to face her with the news of his costly blunder.

"I lost the trail," he admitted. "We have to go back until I pick it up again. Only . . ." *Only it's more dangerous now than before*. He could not bring himself to say it. He doubted he needed to.

"Noble, I have an idea."

"What?" He turned to her, willing to listen to anything that might mean he could keep her from harm.

Behind them, Braman's humming erupted into a soft but full-blown song in his language, Yiddish. Ivy glanced over her shoulder at the freighter, then back at Noble. Her cheeks were pale. She looked at him through dark, fringed lashes and bit her lip. She swallowed hard and took in a deep breath of the spring morning around them. She looked about as pretty as he'd ever seen her.

"I think I ought to travel with Mr. Braman and Solly in the wagon, and let you go on after Stephen and Charity alone."

Chapter Nineteen

A killdeer lit in a nearby cedar, warbled a brief, plaintive song at Noble, and flew off. Noble remembered to breathe.

"You—what?"

Some of the color came back into Ivy's pale, round cheeks. "I said—"

"I heard you." He cut her off, more abruptly than he meant to.

"I think they know something about Stephen and Charity," she went on in a swift, low tone. "More than they're letting on. Maybe I can get them to tell me what they know. Moishe seems to feel, uh, protective of me."

"Hmph." Noble couldn't argue with Ivy's instincts, only her rating. He'd have put Braman's regard for her somewhat higher than "protective."

"In any case, it's a way for us to look in two places at once. Cover more ground. And even if they haven't seen Stephen and Charity yet, Stephen would be a lot more likely to approach a freight wagon than he would be to make himself known to you and me."

Ivy's train of thought was getting away; he decided to keep up as best he could and throw a log under her wheels when he had to. Her reasoning was impeccable, so far. She'd obviously thought this out. He just wanted to see how far. And to what end.

"If we split up now and I go with them, we can arrange to meet somewhere along the way, maybe in Riverton."

"Or in Rawlins," he interjected.

She jerked upright and her eyes grew wide, as if he'd thrown not just a log under her wheels but a whole forest.

"Y-yes. Rawlins." Her voice was tighter than before. "But I doubt we'll need to go that far."

She lost a child in Rawlins, he reminded himself. *And so did you.* He attributed the burn behind his eyes to the bright sunlight.

"There's Thermopolis," he allowed, rubbing the stubble on his chin. "About a day away. That'd be too soon to do us any good. Jeffrey City's about three or four days south of that, and it's the last town this side of the Divide."

"We're sure to have them by then." Ivy didn't sound convinced so much as hopeful. "If I haven't caught up to them, I'll take a room at the hotel and wait for you. Then we can—"

Noble shook his head.

"That's no good," he muttered. "We stand to lose too much time if they haven't gone that way, and it's too big a risk to let you stay in that town alone. We know they're going to Rawlins. I guess I understand why you'd rather not go there, but it's the only thing that makes any sense."

Ivy stared at the ground and said nothing.

"You seem awfully eager to get away from me."

"Oh, Noble, it's not that I want to!" She seized his arms with such fervor that he could not mistake her dismay. "I don't want to at all! I just think it would be better. I'm no help to you. I've made more mistakes on this trip than I can count, and it fell to you to fix them. Besides, you worry about me, and I'm afraid that makes you less careful for yourself. I couldn't bear it if something bad happened to you, and I couldn't live with myself knowing that my own carelessness might be to blame for it."

"Nothing bad's going to—"

"You know you can't promise me that," she cut in. "Hold me, Noble." She closed the narrow gap between them and he gladly enfolded her in his arms. A faint whiff of violets met his nostrils. He held his breath, trapping her sweet, elusive scent inside him, wishing he could hold it, and her, there with him forever.

"I'm here, Ivy-girl," he murmured against the softness of her ear. "What is it? Tell me. You can tell me anything; you know that, don't you?"

He savored the silkiness of her hair against his lips. Why was he never prepared for the sweet, inescapable way she worked herself straight into his heart? Why was he about to abandon his concern for her welfare and beg her to stay with him, despite knowing she'd be safer with the two freighters? He felt her sigh in his embrace.

"I just want all of this to be over," she whispered. "And I want us to go someplace where we can live quiet lives together and have a family and forget everything unpleasant that's ever happened to us from the very beginning."

231

Noble closed his eyes and held her as tightly as he dared. He understood her wish so thoroughly that it frightened him. He wished the same thing himself. For a treacherous instant he envisioned them out on his porch in the twilight, having gotten the babies to sleep. He saw himself sitting on an old wicker chair, then watched as Ivy came and sat herself on his lap . . . They had too many miles to cover before he could realize such a fantasy, or even allow himself to dream about it. He opened his eyes and held Ivy back once again at arm's length.

Her features betrayed her inner turmoil. He felt a rush of compassion for her that inspired a tightness in his throat.

"I swan, Ivy Smith," he breathed into her ear. "I love you so much, I expect I'll die from it one of these days."

"Don't say such a thing!" Ivy looked as distressed as if he'd struck her, and he immediately regretted his wretched attempt at a joke.

"Oh, hell, Ivy," he said in a hasty, gruff voice. "You know I don't mean . . . have you talked to Braman about this plan of yours?"

"Yes." Ivy fussed with the buttons of his shirt. "He's agreed to take me."

Noble took hold of her hands again to get her attention. "You're sure you trust him?"

She tilted her head with a look of intelligent curiosity. "Don't you?"

He did, he realized in amazement, glancing once more at the singing mule driver, who was checking the back of his wagon with surprising energy. Odd, for Noble realized he was not a man who, in general, trusted easily. His gaze strayed to the taciturn giant helping the driver. "What about Solly?"

"Solly seems a gentle man, despite his silences,"

Ivy observed, tugging her hands away from Noble's grasp. "I think he's just shy, perhaps because he doesn't speak English. And he's a wonderful cook, don't you think?"

"Hmm. Is that why you want to go with them? So you can eat better?" he teased her, realizing, with a sharp twinge of regret, that he was missing her already.

She directed a reproachful look at him.

"Go away with you," she grumbled, tugging on his lapels until he brought his face to hers for a brief kiss. She tasted sweet and salty at the same time.

"We go." Braman's robust announcement startled Noble. The burly freighter was in the driver's seat. Solly, in back, sent Noble a somber nod and drew the tarp over his head in preparation, Noble guessed, for another ambush like the first. Noble took Ivy's hand and walked with her to the driver.

"My wife tells me she's arranged passage with you to Rawlins, Mr. Braman." An invisible hand squeezed Noble's heart as he said it. They were really parting, and it would be another week at least until he saw her again.

The mule driver measured him with a steady, brown-eyed gaze. "I take her to Rawlins," he repeated deliberately, his stare straying once to Ivy as he spoke. "Solly and me look out for her. You no worry. We keep her safe from those men. We keep her safe from everything."

Braman looked so serious that Noble could not doubt him, yet he still felt a dull ache in his gut at the thought of parting from Ivy, his wife of two days.

"I'll take the pie." He turned to Ivy again and spoke briskly, knowing that was the only way he could get out what needed to be said to her without

233

choking up. "He stands out like a tabby in a chicken coop. The mare is pretty ordinary. She won't draw as much attention." As he said it, Noble glanced at the driver. Moishe Braman, he guessed, had already drawn about as much attention as was possible on the stretch between Basin and Rawlins. He doubted there was anything he or Ivy could do to garner more. He took some measure of comfort from that fact.

"You'll be careful?" He searched her face. Her brave smile hurt more than it helped. The time for parting was upon them, and Noble found he wanted to delay it as long as possible.

"I will," she promised. "Remember? I said I didn't want you to worry about me. Where will I meet you in Rawlins?"

Her question reminded him of the uncertain outcome of their mission. He grimaced at the thought.

"I'll get a room at the hotel," he informed her, planning as he spoke. "And if I'm not there, I'll leave a message for you."

Her features darkened as if a storm cloud suddenly threatened a beautiful day. "Why wouldn't you be there?"

Why wouldn't he? he wondered in echo, watching her. If Stephen and Charity had gotten there first and were already on their way to Chicago. Or if he discovered, upon arriving, that they had never been there at all. The myriad possibilities worried him, but for Ivy's benefit he shrugged them all off and gave her a jaunty grin.

"Afraid I'll find me some other woman?"

The darkness on her features became a scowl, which in turn became a sudden, unanticipated swell of tears.

"Ivy, sweetheart, I was only teasing!" He hugged

her fiercely, feeling like a cur for his joke. "Here.
Stop crying, now." God, he felt like crying himself,
and if she didn't stop, he just might start. "Where's
your hankie?"

Ivy, sniffling, squared her narrow little shoulders. "I'm all right." But her hands shook as she
fumbled in her pockets. "I can't . . . I don't . . ." She
came up empty.

He remembered where there was one. "Here."
He reached inside his own shirt for the small,
folded bit of cloth he'd purloined from her saddlebags three days earlier. It was rumpled and slightly
damp, and it certainly no longer smelled of violets.
But it was hers. He put it in her hand and she
looked from it to him, her eyes drying as suspicion
replaced despair.

"This is mine," she intoned slowly. "Where did
you get it?"

Noble felt a sudden rush of heat fill his cheeks
as he remembered separating the handkerchief
from its companions when he'd gone through Ivy's
things in the stable, and his motivations for doing
so. He found himself staring at the damning article
in her hands. Much as he was tempted to lie to save
face, he could not keep the truth locked inside himself.

"It came from your saddlebag that night you
stayed at my place. It smelled so good, and you had
five of them, and—and I figured you wouldn't miss
it." He was babbling like a dopey kid. He couldn't
even look at her.

There was a warm, soft pressure in his hands,
like the head of a kitten that came to be petted. He
looked down to see her hand in his, with the folded
white handkerchief between them.

"Keep it," she whispered. "I'm all right, now."

His throat clogged.

"You're sure?" he managed. He risked a look at her. He was glad, for her smile was worth any embarrassment he felt at having been caught in so sentimental a gesture.

In answer to his question, she slipped her arms about his neck in a gentle embrace.

"I love you, Noble Smith."

"I love you too, Stringbean," Noble replied tenderly. "Now give me a kiss. A big one. It'll have to hold me until I see you in Rawlins."

A wild, frightened look darted across Ivy's face. She pulled him down and pressed a thirsty kiss to his lips that reminded him of the things he'd be missing for the next several days. Each of those days had a night. He began to wonder, fighting a sudden, dull ache in his groin, how he was going to make it through all those nights without her.

"Damn," he growled, burrowing against the softness of Ivy's cheek. "I'm going to miss you, Ivy-girl. You'll take care of yourself, won't you?"

"You said that already," she reminded him with a faint, quivering laugh as she straightened his shirt lapel. "You'd best go. Mr. Braman is waiting for me."

Noble found, in her smile, the strength to grin, himself. "See you."

"See you."

Ivy held her head erect and her chin high as she watched Noble hoist his long, lean form into the waiting pie's saddle. The smile she'd coaxed to her lips was threatened, but she kept it there as she watched Noble nudge the gelding to a jog, then a lope.

"Come, Missus," Braman, behind her, entreated in a tone respectful of her melancholy. "We go, too."

"Wait." Noble would turn around for a final farewell. She was sure of it. She needed to maintain her smile until he did, for once it faded, she doubted her ability to recover it until she saw him again countless days hence.

In a few seconds, he was out of shouting distance. The gelding neared the crest of a small rise, and Ivy knew that in moments horse and rider would disappear on the other side of it. Her heart leapt with every stride the pie took to the top. Her hand left her side, as if it meant to wave at Noble whether she wanted it to or not. Whether Noble turned to see it or not. Thus, when the gelding jolted to a halt at the top of the ridge and Noble finally turned around, her hand was already high in the air.

She could not tell for certain if he was smiling, but somehow she knew he was. And she knew the expression was every bit as hard for him to maintain as it had been for her.

The freight wagon was slow, and built for efficiency rather than comfort. Bumping along on the hard seat beside the bulky Moishe Braman, Ivy decided the reason for the driver's corpulence was to provide greater padding against the unyielding seat. Unfortunately, the springs beneath, whose purpose was to cushion the bumps of the road, had long since succumbed to the added burden of his bulk and were no longer functional except to creak with annoying regularity.

Braman's conversation, over the miles, had grown increasingly more stilted and forced, until finally it lapsed into a diffident silence Ivy found preferable, as it matched her dreary humor. She had the uncomfortable feeling that she knew the reason for Braman's new reserve, and that she was it. She had discovered at breakfast, when Noble had gone back to retrieve the horses she'd left in the gully, that Braman knew of the MacDonalds, and knew where their ranch was outside of Rawlins. She could not prevent herself from asking the garrulous freighter a flood of questions about Tom and Ciely, and about their daughter. He knew little about Laurel, but that did not surprise Ivy: Laurel was of schooling age, and would have had little opportunity to encounter the likes of Braman and Solly.

"Why you no mention your cousins to husband?" Braman had asked bluntly, soon after they'd gotten under way. "Why you no tell him you ask me to take you there for visit before we go to Rawlins?"

She'd met his gaze with some amazement—how did he know, after all, that she had not done just that?—but found that she could neither maintain the level look he gave her, nor further compromise herself with a falsehood.

"I . . . because," she said, feeling lame as a three-legged mule deer. "He doesn't know them."

That was true enough, but it did not prevent a wave of guilt from flooding her nonetheless, forcing her to look away from him.

Ivy told herself repeatedly in the lengthy silences that followed that she'd been honest with Braman, and with Noble, about her reasons for wanting to travel with the freighter and his partner. But that did not prevent her from feeling like a Judas.

Still, it was worth it. Even if things became twenty times worse than they were, it was a small wage to pay. It was worth anything to her to be able to see Laurel again, even if only for a day. After all, it would be the last time.

"Horses," Braman, beside her, muttered.

Ivy emerged from her reverie surprised to discover that the wagon had rolled to a halt. The restive mules swatted at flies with their bristly tails, their dark coats sweating and twitching.

"Horses?" she echoed, feeling stupid. Braman nodded up ahead, and she followed the direction of the brim of his hat. Some distance up ahead, coming through a draw, was a cloud of dust and the dull sound of thunder. Stephen? she wondered, filled with doubt and trepidation. No, he and Charity would be headed the other way. Noble? Too much disturbance for one animal.

Braman reached below and knocked three times on the floor of the wagon. Ivy guessed he meant to alert Solly to expect company.

"Go in back," Braman advised her in a low, thoughtful voice. "And keep quiet, no matter what."

His words sent a nameless chill through her despite the midday heat. No matter what? What was he expecting to happen? Remembering her promise to Noble, she climbed over the seat into the back of the wagon, onto the lumpy tarp. There was a grunt from beneath; Ivy guessed she'd stepped on Solly. A corner of the tarp was drawn back by a hand she could not see.

"Hurry up!" Braman urged her without turning around.

Ivy looked up. The riders were closer, and she counted five. She stifled a cry of dismay. How had they gotten in front of them, and why were they bearing down upon the freighter again?

But she had no time to ask these questions. The hand that had drawn back the tarp yanked her down to the floor of the wagon and threw the tarp back on top of her. It took her a moment to catch her breath and to adjust her eyes to the comparative shade under the stifling cover.

There, beside her, was Stephen. His finger was pressed to his lips and his eyes, a dusky green in

239

the shade, begged her to be silent.

She did not want to be silent, though. She wanted to cry out for Noble, but Noble wasn't there. Then she thought she saw him, but his bold, stark image faded suddenly to blackness.

Chapter Twenty

The water that hit Ivy in the face was tepid, and it smelled like the inside of a barrel. She sputtered and opened her eyes to Charity Smith's pretty, smiling face.

"There, I told you that'd do it," the girl remarked, sounding very pleased with herself. "Are you all right, Miss Wingate? I thought Stephen had hit you in there, and boy, was I mad! I guess you just fainted."

Ivy stared at her, unable to move or to speak. She felt as if she'd been plucked up from where she was and set down in some place she'd never been before. Her vision grew hazy again about the edges, like a fading photograph, and she closed her eyes.

"Stephen! She's going on us, again!" There was panic in Charity's voice this time, only it sounded very far away. Ivy thought of the bad-smelling water and she forced her eyes open again.

"No, no," she heard herself say. "I'm all right. What—what happened?"

Edges began to get sharper for her as she stared at the girl, but she wished she could make the world stop spinning. She felt most queer. It reminded her of a feeling she'd had long ago, but she could not recall when or where, or in connection with what event. She remembered that someone had given her a quantity of whiskey and had demanded she drink it. The disorganized memory made her want to retch. Indeed, her stomach revolted, conjuring an unpleasant recollection of her morning sickness when she'd been pregnant with Laurel. Uttering a low moan, she rolled over in the dirt. She had not even realized until that moment that she'd been lying down on the ground.

"Criminy, Ivy! I musta give you a start, at that!"

She recognized Stephen's voice, and she commanded herself once again. Her stomach obeyed reluctantly. She tried to sit up, and felt several strong hands take hold of her arms and shoulder to assist her. Appalled by her lack of composure, she feigned annoyance and shook them off.

"I'm all right, for heaven's sake!" she snapped. The scene came into crackling focus, as if her own words had jarred her out of her swoon. Before her, crouched about like mischievous stone gargoyles, were Stephen and Charity, wearing expressions of guilty amusement. Behind them, a little farther back, stood the impassive giant Solly and the mule driver, Moishe Braman. Ivy felt like fainting again. To prevent that from happening, she rubbed the back of her neck and fixed her gaze on Stephen.

"I think you'd better tell me what's going on here," she said in as stiff a tone as she could muster.

Stephen looked embarrassed. "We should get

back in the wagon," he told her in a hushed voice. "Carl, Jack and the boys may still be around—"

"You'll tell me here, and you'll tell me now, or I'll scream bloody murder and you can explain it to them, too!" She wouldn't, of course, but she stared daggers at her younger brother and hoped he believed she would.

Stephen looked abashed, and he glanced once at Charity as if to say, see what I've had to deal with all my life? Ivy found that she resented the look, and she resented Stephen as well. She bit her lip to keep herself from exploding with anger.

"Missus." Braman spoke up, sounding serious, but in no way placating, which was a good thing for him. She had a glare to spare for him, as well. How dared he agree to take her with him without having said anything about Stephen and Charity hiding all the while in the back of his wagon?

"I am businessman," the freighter began, ambling forward, eyes downcast. "Your brother, he come to me in Basin three nights ago with plan. I take him and wife to Rawlins, in secret, and he pay one thousand dollars in gold, half in Basin, half in Rawlins. I tell no one, not even a woman who tells me she is his sister." He looked up at her with a quick nod. "Then we find you, and you look so—how you say, upset—that you break my heart." He sighed a sigh Ivy thought a bit melodramatic, but she allowed it to pass without remark. "I want you to know he is safe, him and his wife. But I can't tell you." He sent a look to Stephen the meaning of which Ivy could not grasp. "So I bring you along, and you find out yourself." He shrugged, as if to say the matter was entirely out of his hands.

Ivy thought it a shrewd way of keeping to the letter of his agreement with Stephen, if not the spirit, and try as she might, she could not be as angry as she wanted to be, at any of them. Stephen was here, and Charity, and they were unharmed. Her relief outweighed her anger.

Until she thought of Noble.

"Oh, God," she moaned, closing her eyes again.

"What is it, Sis?" Stephen's hands closed on her arms, and his tone was quietly urgent. "You gonna faint again?"

She wished she had the strength to punch him.

"Noble," she said, as a sickness gripped the pit of her stomach. "He's going to think I knew all along about you two being with Braman. Dear God, how am I going to explain this to him, after he'll have spent the last week scouring the territory?"

"You just let me handle Noble." Charity spoke up, with no small amount of brash assurance. "He's my brother, and I've been handling his temper since I was a little girl."

Ivy opened her eyes again and stared at Charity. Charity Smith—Charity Smith Wingate, she corrected herself—gazed back at her.

Charity was a pretty girl; in some way that Ivy was sure even Charity herself did not realize, the girl was actually beautiful. It was more than the wide innocence of her clear, blue eyes and the peculiar tilt to her nose, so like her brother's. It was greater than the straight, patrician line of her pale brow or the gentle roundness of her chin that hinted, quite falsely, at an acquiescent disposition. And her golden hair, shimmering, abundant, looped back only by a blue satin ribbon and otherwise tumbling down her back like the regal mane of some wild animal, was only a part of the elusive effect.

Ivy suspected that, more than any of these things, it was Charity's bold willfulness combined with her unquenchable gaiety, all the more moving when one considered her unhappy upbringing, that caused men to find her irresistible. Certainly, Ivy thought, stealing a glance at Stephen to find him gazing at his young wife with rapt adoration, he found her so.

Charity had been among her oldest students at the school, and Ivy always suspected that Noble had constrained his sister to continue her education despite the girl's own wishes. Charity was clever as well as attractive, and she had always placed more stock in those two assets, Ivy felt, than they were worth. As her teacher who had known her for many years, Ivy suspected that it had always been Charity's intention to marry young and to marry well, and responsibility be damned. In that regard, Charity could rightfully have been said to be somewhat shallow. Yet withall, she was so lovable that it broke Ivy's heart to think of the responsibilities, and the troubles, the girl had acquired along with Stephen's name.

"Noble likes everyone to think he's a tiger, but he's really a pussycat," Charity explained, demonstrating, to Ivy's surprise, neither guile nor frivolity. "He knows me, and he knows I'm willing to go to any length to have my way. None of this is your fault, Miss Wingate. I'll make him see that."

Ivy started to speak, but Stephen interrupted her.

"She's Mrs. Smith now, remember?" Stephen's grin spanned his young, angular face as he held her gaze. Ivy felt herself blush, to her continued annoyance. She could not help but wonder what else Stephen and Charity had heard of her discourse with Noble, or with Moishe Braman.

"I forgot," Charity murmured, blushing herself, although Ivy suspected the younger girl looked

much more fetching than she herself did on account of it.

"I'm twice your sister-in-law now, so you may
call me Ivy," Ivy told her, amazed that she herself
sounded so much like the schoolteacher she had
been only a few short days ago. "Why have you
both continued to run away from us, when you
both so obviously, and so desperately, need our
help?" she wanted to know.

Stephen shot her a skeptical grimace.

"Funny, it didn't seem like it was help you were
offering, back there in Basin."

Ivy checked herself. Stephen's and her own idea
of helping him were, obviously, two different creatures.

"Let's not quibble over this, Stephen," she said.
"What happened with those men this time? What
did they say to Mr. Braman? Did you hear them?"

Stephen straightened from his crouch and adjusted the brim of his gray Stetson with his thumb
and forefinger as he scanned the landscape to the
south. Then he spoke.

"They didn't stop." He was laconic. "But I don't
like that it was the second time in a day that they
come upon us like that. And, of course, they
couldn't miss the fact that Moishe's towing a horse
along, now."

"We must go," Moishe put in his opinion, as if
he'd only been waiting for someone to mention his
name. "Every minute here is danger. They maybe
watch us. Is yet seven, eight days to Rawlins.
Maybe more."

"Ivy may have had a good idea, though." Stephen
eyed her with an appraising look that made her
uncomfortable. "This Tom and Ciely MacDonald
you talked about. They're Pa's kin, right?"

Ivy nodded hesitantly, not sure where the question led, but sure she would not like it.

"And they live outside Rawlins?"

Stephen's mind worked just like Noble's: Calculating. Direct. Always three or four steps ahead of everyone else's. It was unnerving, most times. Just now it was terrifying. Stephen knew nothing about Laurel, and what had happened ten years ago. Ivy was determined to keep it that way.

"Stephen, we can't—"

"They're nesters, probably dirt-poor, like the rest," Stephen interrupted her, with more than a hint of contempt edging his voice. "I bet they'd be glad for a chance to earn some gold just for hiding us for a few days and keeping their mouths shut—"

"No!" Ivy felt faint all over again, but she could not afford to succumb to the feeling this time. Too much was at risk. Stephen, startled, returned his gaze to her.

"I will not allow you to use the MacDonalds in that manner, to put them at risk," she told him, hoping he could not perceive the guilt that must surely be etched on her face. "I'd sooner see you leave that gold right here on the side of the road than to make them a party to your foolishness and greed."

The light in Stephen's catlike eyes flared. He planted his legs apart and his fist against his hip.

"Oh, you would, would you?" He was sarcastic and overloud. "Well, that's just like you, Ivy. It's just what I expected. Proper, pious, holier-than-thou Ivy, deciding what the rest of the world should do in order to fit with her ideas of what's right and wrong."

"And isn't it just like you to believe that the whole world can be influenced to your way of thinking, if only you just wave a few dollars under their

247

noses?" she retorted, stung by his assessment as well as by his scorn.

"Well, I worked hard for that gold, lady. Damned hard. It's mine. And I'm damned if I'll give it up just because you think it's the thing to do!"

"That's enough! Both of you!" Charity sprang up beside Stephen, a summer blossom braving a tall, angry weed. She seized his arm with both hands and jerked it as if it were a bell-pull. Surprised by the interruption, Ivy stared at the girl, who seemed suddenly to have become a mature woman before her eyes.

"Charity, now don't you—"

"Don't you 'don't you' me!" She did not allow Stephen's protest a foothold.

Ivy admired her instantly. "That's right. Talk some sense to him, Charity," she lauded.

"I'm not defending you, either!" Stephen's wife turned on her hotly, her blue eyes like twin flames. "You're behaving like a pair of fools, and ones who don't care a fig about one another, at that. Can't you two do anything but quarrel?"

Ivy felt instantly ashamed. Stephen glared at his wife, and Ivy would have sworn she saw steam coming out of his ears, but he did not seem able to maintain his angry bearing. His broad shoulders drooped and his chin sank to his chest.

"Char." He growled the syllable, but Ivy could tell right off that he was thoroughly conquered, especially when he sent Charity a look like that of a whipped puppy. Charity budged not an inch, but continued to glare at her husband, who was a good head taller than she was.

Ivy got to her feet and dusted off her hands. "I'm sorry, Charity. You're right, of course. But Stephen and I have been doing battle for so long it seems we've forgotten how to address one another in a civilized way."

"Then learn!" Charity directed. "And it might help if you'd stop talking down to Stephen as if he were still a kid. He isn't, Miss—Ivy. And neither am I."

Staring at Stephen and Charity, Mr. and Mrs. Stephen Wingate, Ivy clamped her mouth shut. She knew that they would accept only her help, not her interference, and that only on their own terms.

She wondered if parents felt as she did then, when their children asserted their independence. She wondered if she would ever know for certain.

She turned away.

"I'm sorry, Iv." The hand that closed upon her shoulder was warm and conciliatory. It was the hand of a man. A man she was meeting for the first time, thanks to his tempestuous and outspoken wife. She suspected the relationship would not be an easy one, but that it had the potential to be even more rewarding than their previous roles as stern guardian and rebellious child. She put her hand on top of his.

"I'm sorry, too, Steph."

Ivy wondered who would speak next.

"There. That's settled, at last. Good." It was Charity, and she sounded more like the schoolgirl Ivy knew than the chiding wife and scolding sister-in-law she'd been moments before.

"It might be settled, for now," Ivy ventured to Charity, testing a grin out on her brother, who tested back warily. "But I can't promise we won't lock horns again. And you can bet we'll both be watching to see how grown-up you and Noble act, when it's your turn."

She noticed that Stephen's grin widened. She guessed he was thinking the same thing.

*   *   *

They bypassed Worland, Kirby, Lucerne and Thermopolis, and by the fourth day they started through the Wind River Canyon. Stephen and Charity continued to travel in the wagon out of sight, and if Moishe or Solly thought there was danger, Ivy joined them. But there was no sign of the men who had dogged their trail in the first days, at least none that Ivy could detect. She found herself looking for signs that Noble had passed that way before them, but saw nothing. For all she knew, he had disappeared from the face of the earth, an event she tried not to consider.

The canyon was a spectacle that was both majestic and frightening in some way Ivy could not fathom. Perhaps it was the tales Moishe had spun for her, stories he said the Shoshoni told. It was a spiritual place, to them. A holy place, but not one, fortunately, that was forbidden for white men to pass through. It was in the Wind River Canyon that the Big Horn River became the Wind River, a section called the Wedding of the Waters. It was said to be a place of great power, and that marriages consummated there would endure throughout time. She found herself wishing, as the wagon wended its way through the narrow, winding pass, that Noble would appear, and that they could realize their love in such a place. She had the growing, uneasy sense, as the band grew nearer to Rawlins and the MacDonald ranch, that her marriage to Noble, and their love, was shortly to have need of every bit of magic that could be conjured on its behalf.

It was near dark when Braman pulled the team to a halt at a secluded rise not far from the roaring water. Solly got out and lurked about, looking for any signs of danger, Ivy guessed. Apparently he was satisfied that there were none, so he waved to

Braman as a signal that they were safe. Ivy fell to helping Solly with supper preparations only to discover that by the time it was ready to eat, Stephen and Charity were nowhere in evidence.

"Now, where can they have gotten to?" she fussed, half to herself, as she glanced about the canyon walls.

"They go off by themselves." Moishe Braman, having washed for supper, patted her arm and nodded in a way no doubt meant to be reassuring.

"By themselves!" she echoed, incredulous. "Don't they have any concept of the danger they're in, every minute?" She did not know which she found more irritating at the moment: Braman's placid demeanor or her brother's characteristic recklessness. "Which way did they go? Did you see them leave? Why didn't you stop them?"

Anger and panic fought for dominance as she stared hard at the portly mule driver. He wore a calm, fatherly look of tolerance on his round, bearded face.

"Is no need for worry," he assured her, not taking his hand from her arm or his gaze from her face. "They are having long, hard trip, those young ones. They are in love. They are wanting time alone."

The meaning of Braman's awkward, earnest words took half a minute for Ivy to fully absorb, then but another three seconds for her to blush with heat. No doubt Stephen and Charity had heard the stories of the Wedding of the Waters themselves, and sought to try out its enchantment on their own love.

"Oh." Her reply was late, she knew, but she had to say something. Braman and Solly were looking at her as if she might need further clarification of the circumstances. She found she was not equal to their stares.

"I'm not very hungry, after all," she murmured through her embarrassment, making purposefully for the back of the wagon. "I think I'll just go to sleep."

But with worry nipping at her heels, sleep played hide-and-seek with her straight through until daybreak, when Stephen walked back into camp wearing a look of distress on his young face and bearing Charity's limp form in his arms.

Chapter Twenty-one

"I know she didn't feel so good last night, even though she tried to pretend she was fine," Stephen reported as he laid his wife on a cushion of blankets Ivy had hastily set up in the back of the wagon. "This morning she was weak, and she feels warm to me."

"He worries over me too much." Charity was undeniably pale as she addressed Ivy. Her voice was small, more of a moan, and her brow was marred by a frown of discomfort. Ivy brushed aside a lock of damp, yellow hair and placed her hand on Charity's forehead.

"I'd say hot." Ivy ignored Charity's remark in favor of Stephen's. Charity was burning up like a sagebrush fire. Ivy could only hope she would not as quickly be extinguished. Charity tried to sit up, but Ivy pushed her shoulders back, gently. She resisted, making an attempt to glare.

"Lie back, Charity. You're sick." Ivy hoped she did not sound as troubled as she felt by her sister-in-law's condition. The girl seemed to be faring none too well, and she relented to Ivy's request with a small sigh.

"Will she be all right?" Stephen stood by the rear of the wagon, his anxious gaze trained on his young wife, shifting his weight from one leg to the other. He pulled at each of his long, strong fingers until the knuckles cracked.

"What happened?" Ivy asked him, feeling as helpless as he looked. "You say she didn't feel well last night?"

Stephen met her gaze for an instant. His cheeks instantly flowered to crimson and he returned his stare to Charity's supine form.

"I—Criminy, Ivy, what do you think happened?" he retorted in a hoarse whisper. "We—last night was our wedding night. We got married in Emblem, five days ago, and Charity had this idea that she wanted to—to wait until we got here to the canyon to—" Stephen's flustered hesitation was nearly as painful to Ivy as her distress over Charity. Respecting it, she fixed her own gaze on the ailing girl. Charity's breathing was shallow and raspy, and her skin was flushed and damp. Her eyes were closed, and beneath them were grayish circles.

"I knew she wasn't feeling pert," Stephen went on, scooping up Charity's limp hand. "So I told her we didn't have to . . ." Ivy felt Stephen's swallow as a gulp in her own throat. "But she—we—you know Charity. She has to have her way. Said she'd be just fine." Stephen glanced uneasily over his shoulder, then edged closer to Ivy. "What'd I do to her?"

Ivy spared her brother a long, incredulous look. Was this the same young man who, days before, had argued his maturity with her? When he was sure of himself, Stephen Wingate was formidable evidence of his adulthood. Just now, however, tense, pale, plainly worried, he looked so much like the little boy she'd tended that Ivy felt a shiver from the past. That he could be so naive as to believe he had something to do with Charity's condition might even have made her laugh, had she not felt such apprehension over his wife's sudden, unexplained illness.

"Get a hold of yourself," Ivy scolded him, deriving an odd but welcomed courage from his childlike uncertainty. "Charity needs you, and you'll be no good to her if you worry yourself to a thread. I doubt this is a result of—of anything you did. She's feverish and weak." Ivy returned her attention to Charity again, who lay upon the scattered blankets with her eyes closed in a grimace of discomfort. A sigh slipped away from her. "She's ill, Stephen. Some sort of ague, I expect. I wish Noble were here; he might know what's wrong with her, and how to make her more comfortable. But he isn't, so we'll simply have to do the best we can, until we can get help for her."

"I am not liking this."

Ivy started at the sound of Braman's quiet voice in her ear. The freighter regarded Charity with puckered lips, an expression that made the gray streaks of his beard stand out like the quills of a bothered porcupine.

"Was influenza in Laramie and Cheyenne last month," Braman reported, scrutinizing Charity as if she might be bearing a sign of some sort. "Was influenza in Petersburg many years ago. Spread like rash. From town to town, over mountain, river, sea. Many people die. Many more run away from cities. From each other." He shook his big head.

255

Influenza! Of course. A few of her students had been taken ill with symptoms a few days before she left town. They'd been quarantined, and some families had even fled town. Running from it was the best defense a healthy person could mount. Apparently Charity and Stephen had not run fast or far enough.

Panic sent a wild notion to Ivy's lips, and she spoke to Braman again before she thought.

"You don't mean to abandon us out here because of this, do you?" The sharpness of her challenge surprised her. Apparently it surprised the mule driver as well, for his round eyes widened and he drew his short bulk up stiffly.

"Many run," he repeated stiffly. "But influenza run faster. It catch you, maybe." He shrugged. "Maybe not. No matter. Is my job to take you to Rawlins." He rolled his "r" like distant thunder and sent a glare her way that made her blush. "I take. Sick or well." He held her gaze for another moment before heaving a deep sigh from his capacious chest and walking away.

"Oh, Lord, now I've offended him," Ivy muttered, half to herself. "But at least he's good to his word. It's still a long way to Rawlins, and we'll have to make Charity as comfortable as possible in the meantime."

"She's—she's not going to die, is she?" Stephen whispered his question as though loath to apprise the Angel of Death of a potential candidate for his services.

Of course not, Ivy wanted to say. But she kept the words inside of her, unwilling to promise her brother what she knew she could not guarantee.

Stephen attended Charity through the night, persuading water into her when she stirred, holding her hand when she did not. Ivy knew this because she herself had been unable to sleep for worry over the girl. Neither Pa nor Stephen had ever been sick. Ivy herself had only suffered illness when she'd carried Laurel, and that was a different sort of malaise altogether. For what Charity had, Ivy could think of nothing more than to try and keep her comfortable, and to keep her fever from rising. And she had the uneasy feeling that those simple kindnesses would not be sufficient to help Charity outlast the endurance of so formidable an enemy as influenza.

The wagon ride had previously seemed slow to Ivy compared with horseback travel, but with Charity failing, it wound on interminably. The following day they threaded the canyon to the outskirts of a town at the first bend of the Wind River, called, unimaginatively, Riverton. Stephen rode the mare ahead into town to try and determine if there was a doctor who could see Charity. He came back within the hour, grim-faced.

"The doctor backed away from me like I was covered with horse shi—manure," he panted as Braman drew the mules to a halt for him. "There's no help for us in Riverton. We'll have to try farther down the trail."

Ivy, sitting in the back with Charity, wanted to say a prayer, but she couldn't think of any. Stephen seemed determined not to look at her as he dismounted. Solly, silent as ever, got out and hitched the mare up behind the wagon again.

"Is nothing farther down trail except for Green Mountain Pass, and then Rawlins," Braman informed them, chucking to his team. "Four, maybe five days."

The wagon jolted to a creaky start that snapped Ivy's frayed nerves.

"Didn't you tell him this is important?" she challenged Stephen as he settled to a crouch on Charity's other side. "Didn't you tell him—" She stopped herself with a glance at Charity, then lowered her voice. "Didn't you tell him she's dying?"

Stephen's already ashen, haggard face went a shade whiter.

"Well, criminy, Ivy, what do you think?" he retorted. "I'd a' dragged the drunken old bastard out here by his hair, except he got the drop on me. Told me he was going to get me some medicine, and instead he pulled a shotgun out of his cabinet. He ordered me out of his clinic with blood in his eye. He warned me not to try and bring Charity into town; said he was goin' to report us to the sheriff so he could post a lookout to keep us away. They didn't want no epidemic in Riverton, he said. Prob'ly just as well, though. His place didn't look any too clean, and it smelled like a flop house. And like I said, I could tell he'd been drinking."

That last did not surprise Ivy. Alcohol was a way of life for people who had too much work and too many spoiled dreams for one lifetime. That was why there were more saloons than there were schools or churches in every town she knew of. But an epidemic? True, Braman had mentioned far-off Laramie and Cheyenne, two of the biggest towns in Wyoming, having been struck by the killing sickness. The disease was widely known to be spread by people, and people travelled, thanks to the trains and stagecoaches. Ivy herself had never experienced an epidemic, but she remembered Ma telling her of a typhoid outbreak that had wiped out half of her family and town when she'd been a girl. Typhoid was an ugly illness, Ma had said, and would not speak of it more when pressed. Influenza was not typhoid, Ivy knew, but it often was a killer, nonetheless. Ugly or not, it often left its victims just as dead.

The thought drifted into her mind: Suppose the epidemic had already reached Rawlins? Or suppose it had caught up with Noble, wherever he was?

"How's she doing?"

Stephen's question, voiced in a gentle whisper, drew Ivy back from her grim, unwanted musings. His big, roughened hand was on his young wife's pale cheek, and the anguish in his green eyes as he studied her was palpable. His love for Charity was so plain that it reminded her, painfully, of Noble, and of how much she missed him. She had to look away. She shook her head, wishing she had better news for him.

"I don't know for sure, although I'd guess she's no better," she replied, uttering a weary sigh that caught in three places. "The fever hasn't broken. She mostly moans, when she makes any noise at all. I have to tell you, Stephen, I'm scared. I wish—"

She stopped herself. What she wished was that Noble was there, but something prevented her from saying it aloud. She longed for Noble desperately, but she knew Stephen did not entertain any sentimental feelings about her husband, Charity's brother. Quite the opposite, in fact. They still had that confrontation ahead of them, providing Charity survived her ordeal.

Ivy shuddered to think of the alternative. How could she account to Noble for having failed to keep his sister alive?

"Are you all right, Sis?" Stephen's concern for her was so unexpected that she could not reply right away. She was touched by it. Stephen had not expressed such consideration for her since he was a child, when she'd been ill with pregnancy. She sat straight up and concentrated her stare on Charity, again. She did not want to think about the past. She did not want to think about how she felt, either. She had managed not to think about how she was feeling, other than worried, until Stephen asked. Forced to it, she became aware of a dull, throbbing ache that covered her head like a tight cap from her brow to the back of her neck. She pinched the bridge of her nose and squeezed her eyes tightly shut.

"I'm all right," she lied. "Just tired. I wish we could stop under a shady tree and rest for a while. This bumpy ride can't be doing Charity any good, but we can't stop until we find help for her. God, I just wish it were all over!"

She opened her eyes, wishing she'd see Noble's face. She pictured him wearing his wide, crooked, teasing grin, telling her it had been nothing but a bad dream. What she saw instead was Stephen's anxious expression.

"Tired?" His interrogation was abrupt. "You're sure that's all?"

She nodded, unable, she knew, to repeat her falsehood aloud with any credibility.

"Charity said she was just tired, too," he muttered, still scrutinizing her in an unsettling manner. "Only I think she had a headache, besides. She was holding her head the same way you are now."

Although the afternoon was warm, Ivy felt a shiver go through her.

"When was this?"

"Two nights ago," Stephen told her. "At Wind River Canyon."

Between them, Charity moaned. It was an eerie sound, as if her soul were trying to escape from her slender, limp body by way of her throat. Stephen's attention was diverted immediately to the care of his ailing wife.

"I'm here, honey," he murmured, taking the damp cloth from her forehead. Ivy watched as he refreshed it with water from the keg and tenderly bathed her brow. "I want you to drink some water for me. Can you do that?"

Ivy felt useless after Stephen took over the care of his wife. She mumbled an "excuse me" and accepted the hand Solly offered in assistance as she made her way up to the front to sit with Braman. He transferred the leather reins to one hand and helped her over.

"Young miss is better?" He sounded more polite than hopeful.

"I don't know," she admitted, reaching under the seat for her hat. The sun hurt her eyes nearly as much as the constant bumping of the wagon hurt her head. "She doesn't seem any worse, although I don't see how she could, short of—"

She'd been about to say "short of dying." The words stuck in her throat. For several minutes thereafter, she said nothing. Neither did Braman. Presently he extended one arm and gestured toward the horizon.

"Green Mountains," he told her, as if conducting a tour. "Pass is good. Wagon is light. We make Rawlins in four days. Maybe three."

Four days, she thought, her heart sinking. It might as well be a lifetime. Perhaps it would be, for Charity.

"I hope Charity has four more days in her," was what she said aloud, hoping she did not sound as discouraged as she felt. None of this was Braman's fault. He'd done everything one could expect of him. Which reminded her of something else, something she'd forgotten in the ordeal of the past two days.

"I believe I owe you an apology," she said lightly, looking straight ahead at the sweating backs of the laboring mules. "I insulted you the other day, when I suggested you might be considering deserting us because of Charity's illness. It was wrong of me to say such a thing. I'm sorry."

He gave her a brief, sideways look, his beard working thoughtfully.

"Is never wrong to say what you think," he allowed. "And never wrong to believe worst. My papa lose his home because he believe only best of people. Is hard way to go through life, believing worst, but is better to believe worst and be surprised by best than to believe best and be surprised by worst. Your Benjamin Franklin say that, I think."

Ivy could not help but smile despite her headache, remembering the timeless wisdom of Poor Richard.

"Something like that," she agreed. "Mr. Braman, you said you've seen influenza before. Do you think that's what's wrong with Charity?"

The driver shrugged his bearish shoulders.

"At first I think maybe she is bitten by snake," he replied, considering the trail ahead of them as he drove. "She become ill—" He snapped his fingers. "Then I am remembering, influenza is funny sickness. Sometimes is quick. Sometimes is not so quick. I lose my mama and my sister to influenza. My mama nurse my sister. My sister sick for long time. Then Mama get sick, she die first. Boom." He shook his head as if he still could not believe the events. "Papa, he is sick, but he get better. Is no way to tell. Young miss, I think she is strong. But my sister was strong, too. And my mama. Papa was not so strong, but influenza leave him for the czar."

Braman chuckled softly at the memory, and Ivy detected a hint of irony filtering through as he stroked his beard. "Me, I am never getting sick."

Yet, Ivy thought, studying his profile. Suppose the driver did become ill? Would Solly take over management of the wagon? Then what if Solly became ill, besides? They could end up being marooned in the Green Mountains, a crippled wagon of death.

Her head hurt to think about these things, yet think she must. Noble would be waiting for her in Rawlins. She must get them through somehow, no matter what.

Then she had a terrible thought: Suppose Noble had contracted the influenza, and was even now ill, dying of it, alone somewhere in the wilderness?

"Can't we go any faster?" she asked, watching the mules plod along. She knew the answer before he gave it.

"Maybe," Braman allowed, shifting his weight on his seat. "Maybe one go lame, too. Maybe more than one. Then we get to Rawlins in six days instead of four."

Ivy said nothing else. Her head hurt. And her heart.

By the following afternoon, the Green Mountains surrounded them like prison walls. Ivy knew she was sick, too, as her headache had not abated and she shivered with the chills of fever. She looked at Charity, still delirious with fever, and fought for every moment of strength. By evening, she realized she was going to lose the battle.

"Noble will be waiting for me at the hotel in Rawlins," she told Stephen as he tucked his own blankets about her, his young face looking tired and old. "Promise me you won't take Charity on the train before you both talk to him. If I die—"

"You're not going to die, Ivy." Stephen cut her off gruffly. "And I'm not taking you to Rawlins. We're going to hole up at the MacDonalds until you and Charity get well—"

"No!" Ivy sat up and grabbed the lapels of her brother's shirt, ignoring the protest of her throbbing head. "Stephen, we can't endanger them! I won't allow it!" The very thought of Laurel being exposed to this awful sickness made Ivy weak with terror.

Stephen's brow furrowed. "They're Pa's kin. Our kin. They're less likely to turn us away than some old doctor in Rawlins, or anywhere else. Anyway, I can't worry about putting them in danger. You and Charity are my concern. And if kinship don't buy us favor with them, maybe a little gold will." Stephen got that glint in his eye, the one he always got when he mentioned his treasure. Ivy shuddered.

"No, Stephen—"

"You just hate not being in charge, don't you?" There was a note of humor in his teasing question that sounded forced. "Ol' Noble's gonna have his hands full with you, that's for sure. Never saw two people who liked to manage things more than you and him. Now lie down. You don't have a say in this, anymore. All you have to do is get well . . ."

Stephen's singsong voice droned on, but Ivy was no longer able to concentrate on the words. Get well, he had exhorted her. Lying there in her misery of aches and chills, she no longer remembered what being well felt like.

There was an odd, pinging sound near the fire where Solly was stirring up supper. Ivy squinted through her pain as Solly looked up wearing a startled look. Another ping struck the coffeepot in the big man's hand. A stream of liquid arced away from the noise and hissed as it hit the fire. There was a third pop, and Solly jerked like a marionette in an unskilled puppeteer's hands before falling face first on the rocks by the fire. Stephen reached for the Colt at his hip.

"Don't, Wingate!" A nearby male voice shouted into the darkness. "I can't kill you yet, but we got a bead on your sister and your wife. Put your hands up slow. You too, mule driver, unless you wanna end up like your friend."

Ivy trembled in the bedroll. She knew that voice. The last time she'd heard it, its owner had been about to rape her.

Chapter Twenty-two

A pair of boots Ivy also recognized swaggered into the campsite and stopped by the lifeless Solly. Her side hurt as if her ribs remembered them, too.

"Where's the gold?" Whatever Jack Murray lacked in imagination, he more than compensated for in directness.

"Solly?" Braman's voice was thin with panic and dread as he called to his partner. Answer him, please, Ivy begged silently, although she knew he would not. The driver knelt by the fallen man, a dark shape quivering with grief.

"Whatsa matter? Don't you understand English?" Another man taunted, entering the campsite with his rifle cocked. "Get 'em up! High!" He emphasized his order by poking Braman with the smoking muzzle.

Braman betrayed no fear with the look he directed at the man with the rifle, only a kind of stolid resignation.

"He is dead," he announced with a heavy sigh. "You have killed him. For what?"

"He got in the way," Jack told him in a sardonic tone of warning. "You don't do as you're told, and you'll join him in heaven, or hell, or wherever you Jews go when you die. Understand? Now put your hands up!"

As if Braman's cooperation were a foregone conclusion, Jack turned his attention once again to Stephen.

"The gold," he repeated, sounding less patient than before. "Where is it?"

"What gold?" Stephen's counterquestion was as insolent as the sneer on his young, angular face. Ivy shuddered at the crunching sound made by the impact of Jack's balled fist against Stephen's jaw. Stephen spun away with the force of the blow and fell flat out on his stomach beside Solly. He lay still for several seconds.

"The Indians sometimes cut a feller's wrists and let him bleed a bit, Jack," another voice advised as Stephen roused himself. Another face appeared by the fire. Three men, Ivy counted, struggling to hold onto her consciousness. "I seen a feller hand 'em his own ma oncet on account o' that."

As if to emphasize his suggestion, this new man withdrew a long knife from a sheath at his belt. The broad blade shined like silver. The man glanced over his shoulder, and Ivy trembled as his cold-eyed gaze caught hers.

"Or maybe we ought to try it out on the ladies. From the look of 'em, it might be a mercy."

"They are sick with smallpox," Braman, rising slowly from Solly's side, spoke up in a voice that surprised Ivy for its calm lie. "Dying. You leave now, maybe you don't get sick, too."

Ivy wondered why Braman had embellished

267

their illness, but his plan became clear when the second man took three steps backward. Jack briefly looked at her, then at Charity, through narrow slits. Ivy knew, watching him, that the thought of a contagious, possibly fatal disease did not frighten him, any more than God or man might.

"I'll leave when I get that gold," he countered, flexing his fingers as if he itched to knock Stephen down again. "Now where is it, boy? You led us a good chase, I'll admit, but it's over now. You hand it over, and we'll go easy on you and yours, even though I owe your sister some."

Ivy wondered if Stephen could hear the lie in Jack's voice. Stephen got to his feet with effort. A ribbon of crimson glistened at the corner of his mouth and his eyes were dull.

"You'll go easy on us," Stephen mimicked faintly. "Like you did on Solly? You can go to hell, Jack," he breathed, squaring his broad shoulders.

Ivy braced herself as if the blow Stephen expected would strike her instead. Jack delivered it, this time to Stephen's midsection. Her brother doubled over and grunted from the impact, but he stayed on his feet.

Ivy recognized the next series of sounds as a chorus of guns being cocked. From her position on the ground, she saw two more men join the others, making an effective ring of guards about them.

"I expect you know where it is," Jack said, jerking his head in Braman's direction. "Or didn't Wingate tell you your cargo was sixty-four thousand dollars in gold?"

"Is no cargo," Braman said woodenly, glancing once more at his dead friend. "Is only three passengers."

"Tie 'em up, Carl," Jack ordered, as if he'd lost interest in bandying words. "We'll take the damned wagon apart, if we have to. Then we'll take them apart, one by one, starting with the women."

"Them women is sick," one of the men reminded Jack, sounding nervous. "Didn't you hear the Jew? They got—the pox." He spoke the last two words in a whisper.

Jack spun on him. Ivy saw his face, ugly with rage, by the changeable light of the small fire. "You turnin' lily-livered, Moss?" His voice was hard and flinty. Ivy felt his casual derision as if it were aimed at her, instead of the sensible, if apprehensive, Moss.

"I can't spend no gold if I'm dead of pox, now can I?" Moss masked his fear with gruff impatience. "I ain't goin' near 'em. I'll help with these two." He gestured toward Stephen and Braman with his Colt. "They don't look sick. But I ain't touchin' the women. No, sir."

Jack drew himself up, and by a trick of the fire he looked like an ominous shadow of doom.

"You'll touch 'em if I say so," he growled, and Ivy thought of the coyotes she and Noble had heard howling several nights ago. Noble, she thought, where are you?

"They look near dead, to me," another voice offered diplomatically, pulling Ivy back from her brush with delirium. "Don't look like we need to bother with them, anyway."

"They damn well better not be dead!" His observation did not please Jack. Jack took three steps toward Ivy and jerked the blanket away from her. She gasped.

"I don't see no pox," he muttered, staring down at her. "I don't see nothin'! Carl, have a look at the other one."

Ivy let out a moan of protest as Carl performed a similar gesture to Charity's still form.

"This one ain't movin' at all," he reported. "I think she's already dead."

Ivy could not hold back her cry of despair. Stephen's broad shoulders slumped forward and his green eyes were naked with pain.

"Char . . ." A sob cut off the cry in his throat. Ivy could not bear his anguish, and she could no longer fight the pain in her head, luring her to welcomed blackness.

"Ivy, if you can hear me, I'm sorry." Stephen's voice whispered in her ear. Ivy was not immediately sure whether it was real or part of a fever dream. She was bumping along, sitting up. The motion made her dizzy and ill.

"Where are we? What's happening?" The question sounded garbled in her own ears; she hoped he understood her. It was an effort to open her eyes, but she did so. They were surrounded by darkness.

"Shh," he advised her. "They'll hear us. There's something I have to tell you."

This was a dream, or a nightmare. It could not be anything else. Charity was dead from her illness. Solly was dead, shot in cold blood by the men looking for their gold. Ivy ached so she wished she would die. Would this hell never end?

"Steph . . ." she moaned.

"Shh!" he cautioned again. "They're all around us. They want me to lead them to the gold, and they made me bring you along just to be sure I wouldn't double-cross them."

Some part of her understood what Stephen was saying: They were together on horseback, probably on the mare, and they were riding through the night to a destination only Stephen knew. Hell, as far as she was concerned.

"The gold, Ivy." Stephen commanded her attention again, rasping in her ear. "They think I'm taking them to it, but it's back with Braman in the wagon. They couldn't find it, because the wagon has a false floor. It's under there. I wanted you to know, in case you make it and I don't." His voice fell on the last word, as if he did not care one way or the other.

How could he think the men would let her go, she wondered through her dizziness, if they did not get what they wanted from him?

"Charity," she murmured. "What about Charity?"

"Back there with Braman." Stephen's voice went suddenly stiff as a gentleman's shirt collar. "They said she was dead. There's nothing I can do for her now, and I don't much care what happens to me anymore. But if you get away, if you get better, I want you and Noble to have that gold and make some kind of a life for yourselves. You'll do that for me, won't you, Ivy?"

Ivy didn't think there was much use in pointing out to Stephen that the chances of her making it back to Braman's wagon alive by herself were next to none. She felt as if death were but a shout away, and not a very loud one at that.

But Stephen was her brother, and she had always taken care of him.

"I will, Stephen," she managed, allowing her head to rest against his chest. She'd sooner toss the whole pile of it down the Wind River Canyon, she knew, and she would do so in a moment if only it meant she could see Noble once more. She ached so, and she was so profoundly weary, that she closed her eyes and prayed for death. *Our Father, Who art in Heaven . . .*

When next Ivy was aware, she was no longer

moving. There was dirt in her mouth; she assumed she was lying on bare ground. She had no idea how much time had passed or where she was. She hoped she was dead, but if she were, this was Hell and of no consolation to her. She had no strength to speak or to move, except to open her eyes.

Daylight was a rose-colored band of velvet that rimmed the dark-green mountain range around her. A few feet away there was a dying fire, and beyond that the figure of a man huddled. His knees were drawn up to his chest and his arms curled about them, making a nest for his head. She recognized the soft rattle of a man's snore.

Where was everyone else?

With effort, she rolled onto her back. In the thicket beyond, perhaps ten feet away, there were horses hobbled. She could hear their placid grazing and the occasional snort. But there were no other human beings about.

If you get away . . . Stephen's words echoed from some half-remembered dream. Could she drag herself ten feet without alerting the sentry no doubt left behind to guard her? She could scarcely see for the fever delusions swimming about her brain, but she had to try. For Stephen, she had to try.

And for Noble.

She rolled to her side and propped herself onto one elbow. A dizzy, punishing pain in her head was her reward and she sank back to the ground. She smothered a cry. *I can't give up,* she told herself. *I must get through this. I must live* . . .

The howling January blizzard wind rattled the four-room MacDonald cabin outside, and inside Ivy was certain she was going to die. She felt as if her body were being torn asunder by the steady, unre-

lenting pains that the doctor said were going to bring her baby into the world. Beside her, Cousin Ciely gripped her hand with both of hers.

"Tighter," Ivy gasped. "Tighter, Ciely. It still hurts. I can't feel you."

"Any tighter and I'll squeeze your fingers off, honey." Ciely's voice, and the gentle humor behind it, possessed the power to calm her. Ivy had learned gaiety from her older cousin in the months since coming to the MacDonald place. Gaiety and tenderness. In Ciely, she had unexpectedly found a friend, a sister and a mother, all three in one kind, loving woman. Ciely nurtured her in a way Pa never had, even spoiled her with attention. It was the least she could do, she'd told Ivy once, not long before her confinement: It was a way for her to take care of the baby Ivy carried for her, and to repay Ivy for her kindness in giving the baby to her and Tom.

Another cramp throbbed like a speeding locomotive through Ivy's insides.

"It's too much," she gasped, when she regained her breath. "I can't, anymore. I'm so tired, so tired." But the pain came again, not caring whether she could bear it or not.

In the days before she had begun to feel the first pangs of labor, the pale, phantom contractions that only hinted at the violent exercises to come, Ivy had found herself thinking about Noble again, and the moments spent in Witherspoon's grass that had brought her to this. As the baby moved and stretched inside her enormous belly with the snow flying in Rawlins, she wondered where Noble was. She wondered if he had any thoughts to spare for her, and if he was paying anywhere near the price that their imprudence had exacted upon her.

Another one. Dear Lord . . . All of her prayers had long since been reduced to that one terse phrase.

"*Just a little while longer, Miss Ivy,*" the calm voice of the doctor soothed her. "*Steady, now. You can do this. God made you for it. Just try to rest between the pains.*"

They weren't pains, really. They were the most amazing, exhausting sensations of her body trying to turn itself inside out to expel the human being trapped within her. But they were coming so quickly that she scarcely had time to draw a breath between them, let alone to rest. And it had been going on for so long, so long . . .

Another wave. Striations from her neck to her knees. Her back arched off the bed and the sound of the wind was joined by the gravelly howl from her throat.

"*That's it.*" How could he sound so calm, when she was being torn apart before his eyes? "*Good girl. I see the head, now.*"

In the intervening months, there had been times when Ivy had wanted to be rid of the burden inside of her, or at least to set it aside for a time. There had been times, too, when she cherished the life inside of her, and had marvelled at such a miracle that produced those feelings when she thought she could never care about anything again. In either case, it had begun to feel as if she was going to carry this child inside of her forever, and never give it up to the couple who waited so patiently for it.

The next contraction was not pain so much as it was relief. Even her body sensed the end of its labors was near, and it felt marvelously good to push.

"*Oh, God, Doctor, the cord—*"

The panic in Ciely's voice gripped Ivy's chest. Something was wrong!

"*Breathe, Miss Ivy!*" The doctor rasped. "*Breathe, and don't stop! That's it! Now push.*"

Something tore, and now a low burning accompanied the ungodly pressure of the child between her legs. Ivy thought she must be dying. *Noble,* she thought, not knowing whether the name came out of her mouth or merely remained fixed in her mind. *Noble, I'm dying. I love you, Noble. Please don't forget me . . .*

Then it was over.

"Oh, Ivy," Ciely sobbed over the small but lusty cry of an infant. "She's beautiful. A perfect little girl, honey. Sweet and perfect."

"She's—she's all right?" Ivy ventured, half afraid to ask.

"All right?" Ciely's echo was a breathless laugh. "Oh, she's perfect. She's perfect and she's precious, Ivy. Her little fingers and toes. . . ."

Despite her weariness, Ivy was overcome by an urge to see for herself and to count them. The doctor was doing something else between her aching thighs, but Ivy was beyond shame, beyond caring. She was sore and exhausted, and the cry of the infant tugged on her heart.

"Let me see her," she begged. "Please."

Ciely brought the swaddled newborn close, and Ivy looked upon the face of her daughter. Noble's daughter. Her thatch of hair was nearly the same shade of chocolate brown as his. Her pinched-up face was indelibly stamped in the same angular mold as her father's, and her eyes, when she opened them to regard Ivy for the first time, were the color of midnight.

"Name her, Ivy," Ciely said softly. "She'll be mine to raise, but she's yours to name. Name her, sweetheart."

Ivy had known her name at once, as if the babe had introduced herself.

"Laurel," she murmured, touching the bit of heaven before her with a tentative tip of her finger.

Ivy crawled across the warm rocks toward the hobbled horses, who made no sound. The sentry's soft snore did not change. Just a few feet farther, and she would reach the nearest horse. Her hands were sore and her body ached with fever, but she groped ahead, thinking of Laurel, and of Noble, trying not to think of what would happen to her if she was caught.

The horses nickered and milled about restlessly. Ivy covered her head with her arms and closed her eyes, hoping she would not be kicked. The animals quieted and she allowed herself to breathe again. She longed to rest after her arduous crawl, but she knew she could not afford the luxury. There was no way to tell where the others had gone, or when they would turn. She speculated that Stephen had led them away on purpose to give her a chance to escape. The Lord alone knew what price he'd pay for that. But he had granted it to her, and it would be a terrible injustice to her brother not to take advantage of the opportunity. Especially as it was unlikely that there would be another.

The horse's hobble confounded Ivy in her lethargic state, and it took far longer to solve than it should have. Her fingers working frantically, Ivy was sure that at any moment the men would come back into the camp, or that the sleeping sentry would awaken and be alerted to her activity. She longed to lay her head down again and sleep, but she kept at her mission until the horse's legs were free of their restraints. Breathing a sigh, she reached up for the stirrup dangling above her head.

The saddle slipped as she pulled herself up, but it did not slip far. Trying to stand, she realized just how weak she was, and she was obliged to lean against the saddle for what seemed a very long time to clear her head once again. Climbing onto the horse seemed no less daunting a task than scaling a mountain. She slipped her foot into the stirrup.

"Oh, no, you don't!"

Ivy was seized from behind and thrown to the ground, as if by a great gust of wind. She could not breathe. She cringed against the rock, waiting for another blow like the one that had knocked her aside, but it never fell. Surprised, she opened her eyes to see the man who had been guarding her until he fell asleep secure the horse's hobble again. Apparently he thought pushing her aside was enough to stop her escape.

Apparently, he was right. She had no energy in her even to weep with bitter disappointment, although she felt it keenly. She lay still on her side, overcome by pain and by the failure of her undertaking.

"Guess you wasn't as sick as they said you was." There was disgust mingled with satisfaction in the man's low, ugly tone. "Jack ain't gonna be happy to hear about this when he gets back; no ma'am, he ain't. Or Carl, neither." A rough hand grabbed Ivy's collar and a handful of her hair and gave her an excruciating jerk to bring her to her feet. "What kinda game you playin', girlie, you and that harebrained brother o' yours?" The man's face was in hers; his stench was an insult to her stomach. "Don't you unnerstand? We want that gold, and we don't much care who gets hurt, or kilt, on account of it!" She tried to twist away from him, but he held her fast.

"You ain't goin' nowheres," he told her in a harsh whisper, pressing his unshaven face still closer to hers. The spiny bristles rubbed her cheek raw. "My name's Charlie. You and me is gonna get to be friends, honey. You feel so hot, and it's been too long since I had me a soft, sweet-smellin' woman—"

"And it's going to be longer still." A new voice cut the air, close by.

Chapter Twenty-three

"Let the lady down. Now. Real gentle. Like you're holding glass, and you don't want to break it." Noble kept his voice low and steady, which was no easy task. He wanted to squeeze the life out of the thing that had a hold of Ivy, and it required every shred of self-control he possessed to prevent himself from doing just that. He contented himself with the thought of slicing Charlie's throat open with the hunting knife he had pressed against it.

When Charlie swallowed, his Adam's apple strained against Noble's blade.

"Can't breathe," he choked out.

"I'm not asking you to," Noble replied as reasonably as he could. "I'm just telling you to let the lady go."

After a moment's hesitation, Charlie dropped down a bit, loosening his hold on Ivy, holding his head high in respect for Noble's knife.

"That's it. See? I'll come with you." Noble sank down too, slowly, but did not ease up on the knife. "No quick movements, now, or my hand's liable to slip. Good."

Ivy was on the ground again, and she lay still as death. Noble forced the thought from his mind. She's all right, he told himself. She had to be. If she were, he had time to take care of this poor excuse for a human being on the blade of his knife. If she weren't, none of it mattered anyway.

"Where are the others?" he queried, yanking Charlie to his feet again.

"What others?" his captive croaked.

"You can't be as stupid as you look," Noble growled, pulling the knife up against Charlie's throat again. "God doesn't have that much of a sense of humor."

The man in his uncharitable embrace reeked of fear, and it was not a pleasant odor.

"Yonder," he replied vaguely. "Lemme go. I'll tell you."

Noble loosened his hold and relaxed his grip on the knife.

He had no time to regret his imprudent action before he doubled over from the shock and pain of Charlie's sharp elbow in his ribs. Charlie was not a big man, but he was wiry and deceptively strong. The knife flew from Noble's grip and clattered on the rocks somewhere behind him. Charlie's quick uppercut caught him on the side of the jaw, setting off a shower of sparks in his head. He shook it off in time to see Charlie reach for the Colt at his hip.

No! Noble's mind raced ahead: If he gave Charlie the chance to draw his weapon, he, Noble, was dead for sure, and so was Ivy. Desperation made him seize Charlie's gun arm with both hands and shove with every bit of his strength. There was a dull but distinct cracking noise. Charlie gave a choked off cry. Noble suspected he'd broken Charlie's arm, and the thought was surprisingly satisfying.

Noble pushed until Charlie fell backward to the hard ground, and he fell on top of him. Quick as light, he sat up, sliding his knee up to his squirming adversary's chest, to the hollow just below his windpipe. But was that enough to ensure Charlie's cooperation? Panting, Noble punched him in the face as hard as he could for good measure.

Charlie was a bloody, ugly mess after that, and he stopped trying to twist away. Noble's jaw ached, and so did his hand, but he felt full of fight vigor. Remembering how insolently the man had held Ivy, he was almost sorry Charlie had taken away his reason to strike him again.

"Where are they?" he demanded. He jammed his knee into Charlie's neck. Charlie, beaten, gasped for a breath.

"Yonder." He coughed, and blood issued from his swollen mouth and his newly reshaped nose, which was no more attractive and no less repulsive than previously.

Noble dug his knee in harder. "You tried that once," he warned in a growl.

"Get your damn knee off my neck!" Charlie begged.

Noble smothered a derisive laugh. "Last time I let go of your neck, I got your elbow in my ribs for thanks." But he eased his knee back an inch. Charlie gulped air, and his eyes, which had begun to bulge, sank back a little into their dark sockets again.

"They climbed up them rocks," Charlie rasped out. "The kid said he took the gold back there and hid it in a cave. Jack, Carl, Moss and Ruby went with him and left me to watch the woman."

Noble considered the man whose face was at the end of his knee. Charlie was in no position to dissemble. He doubted Charlie even knew what the word meant. He wanted to ask him more, but a startled cry beyond the rocks took his questions away from him. He recognized the sound of a man in pain. But which man? He looked up.

Charlie was fast as an eel, and twice as slippery. In an instant Noble was on his back with the wind knocked out of him and Charlie's forearm wedged up against his chin.

"I ain't so stupid that I couldn't get the drop on you twice, boy," Charlie sneered. "You a friend of Wingate's? If y'are, I guess it means you got a mourner. At least until we gut him, anyway."

Son of a bitch! Noble thought, enraged, impotent. *Why didn't I kill you when I had the chance?*

Charlie leaned on Noble's windpipe with the whole weight of his body, effectively pinning him to the ground. Noble's vision grew frayed and black about the edges like a tattered old coat. If St. Peter refused him entrance to heaven, he decided, it would be on account of his stupidity rather than his not having attended regular church services. And if this was how the Lord rewarded those who turned the other cheek, Noble was just as glad he hadn't wasted all those Sunday mornings anyway.

The weight was gone. Everything went white, then black again. He coughed, shook his head, and felt sick. He opened his eyes and saw Charlie again, only he saw his back, as if he were looking at Charlie choking him from some vantage point a distance away. His head cleared, and he realized he was, indeed, looking at Charlie, but it was not himself that Charlie was assaulting, this time. Dizzy, aching, Noble groped about, struggling to gather his strength and his wits.

Ivy!

Noble's hand found the knife he'd dropped. A feral sound grated his throat and he launched himself at the figure straddling Ivy, possessed by a bloodlust.

Noble had never used his knife for anything other than skinning or gutting an animal. He was fascinated by the first shock as the blade of his weapon penetrated human flesh, striking bone. His arm jolted with the force of it. His quarry reacted like a stung beast, twisting away from the pain. Noble struck again, and this time his blow was slowed by the deep thrust of the blade into Charlie's unprotected side.

Then he pulled upward. Hard.

The heat engulfing his hand was Charlie's blood, he knew. Its faint metallic scent permeated the still night air. The gurgle of death welled in Charlie's throat, an odd accompaniment to the sound of the breeze in the cedars. Noble released the knife, but it stayed where it was, as if it had become part of Charlie's body, like a useless extra limb. Charlie fell, testament to a power Noble never realized he possessed. He grew ill again at the thought, but he pushed his musing aside in favor of attending to Ivy.

"Noble?" She was lying on the ground, her eyes staring at him with an empty look that convinced him she did not see him, or did not know him. His own eyes grew hazy with fast-gathering tears he had no time for. He shook his head and blinked several times to dispel them.

"It's all right, sweetheart," he told her, wiping his bloodied hand against his pants before he pressed it against her cheek. "Jesus, you're burning up. I have to get you out of here, before . . ."

"But Stephen . . ."

Ivy's plea faded to fevered unconsciousness. Damn it, he didn't want to leave Stephen, but he had to get Ivy away from there. He tried to stand but quickly realized that his contest with Charlie had taken more out of him than he cared to admit. He would not get three steps with Ivy in his arms, he realized, tasting a bit of blood in his own mouth. And she sure as hell couldn't walk herself.

A noise in the thicket drew his attention. It sounded as if the others were returning. And there he was with blood on his clothes, and Charlie's dead body on the ground beside Ivy.

It was so inane an idea that it had a chance of working. In any case, he didn't have a better one and he had to try something.

He kicked dirt over the fire and traded hats with the dead man.

"Why the hell'd ya let the fire go out, Charlie?" one of them groused as three men trudged into camp prodding a sluggish fourth. Stephen, Noble thought. But another man was unaccounted for. Where was he?

"Ruby took a snake bite in that pit. A rattler. He's dead." One of them answered his unasked question, sounding more annoyed than regretful over his companion's demise. Noble grunted, a reply he deemed not only safe but under the circumstances suitable, as well. He doubted that sentiment ran deep in these men, except where the gold was concerned. Even though it was considerably darker with only the glowing embers of the fire lit, he took the precaution of hiding the lower portion of his face with his hand.

"Who the hell is that?" Another man cursed as he tripped over Charlie's body, shrouded in darkness.

I know you don't owe me, God, Noble thought, flexing his hands and feet to keep his blood moving. *But if you could just make Stephen smart enough for one minute to know what's going on right now, I'd be obliged. Maybe even enough to start attending church regular with Ivy.*

"That other fellow come bustin' in here a little while ago to rescue the woman." Noble tried to mimic Charlie's voice and manner of speech, although he felt like an actor caught onstage without a cue.

"Whatsa matter, Charlie? You losin' your voice?"

Like an actor onstage without a cue, and without clothes on, Noble amended.

It was time. He could not wait any longer.

He stood up slow as another man bent over the dying fire, and he drew his Colt from the holster with a clean, silent motion that he hoped no one noticed. He needed every second he could beg for.

The man at the fire, he thought, holding his breath. *Then the fellow who tripped over Charlie. And maybe Stephen can take care of the one behind him before he can pull his gun on me.*

Firing at a man, even in the dark, was so little different from firing at an animal that Noble was amazed. The fellow fell over the fire in a heap. Noble could not wait to determine if he had done his work effectively; he turned at the waist and fired again in the darkness, where he'd seen the other man standing a moment earlier. An instant later he heard another shot. He jolted, but quickly realized he had not been hit, and that Stephen and the remaining man were grappling on the ground before him.

The darkness lent a nightmare quality to the scene, and the groan of a wounded man accompanied the spectacle. It seemed that shadows fought at Noble's feet. His gun hand was numb from the shock of having bestowed two bullets into human flesh. He felt incapable of any kind of movement more than breathing, and even that was difficult. He was trapped; time was going on around him, without him.

One phantom pinned the other on the ground, straddled him like a calf about to be branded, and raised his joined hands high above his head in preparation for a crushing blow to the face of the specter beneath him. Noble moved. Shifting his gun so the hot muzzle was in his grip like the hilt of a sword, he whipped the butt end quickly about and caught the superior figure on the side of the head. The fellow was knocked to the ground, his final, killing blow undelivered.

The campsite was now not only dark, but quiet as well, except for the sound of Noble's own panting breath.

"That you, Noble?"

It was Stephen Wingate struggling to sit up, still breathing hard from the weight of the man who would have crushed his windpipe.

"It is," he answered, after he'd given himself time to steady his voice.

Stephen gave out a low whistle and sat still, bracing his elbows against his knees.

"How'd you know it wasn't me on top?" he asked, eyeing the bodies about them.

"I didn't." Noble had not realized the truth of that statement until he uttered it.

Stephen laughed, and the hollow echo mocked him. "Help me up. That bastard beat the crap out of me."

Noble automatically extended his arm to the younger man. Stephen took it and hauled himself to his feet, shakily. Noble was startled by the strength of his brother-in-law's big-handed grip, and by the weight of him pulling at the end of his arm. It was dark, but not so dark that Noble could not see the sober, direct look in Stephen's eyes.

"Criminy," Stephen muttered, massaging his wrists. "We were in a hell of a mess here before you showed up. How's—"

Noble did not realize right away that the reason why Stephen was on the ground again was because he himself had put him there with his punch. It took Stephen rather longer to stir from that than from his previous difficulty.

"I had that coming from you, I guess," he growled, rubbing his jaw. Noble did not offer him an arm up, and he did not ask. "Especially since— aw, hell, Noble." Stephen's young voice broke, and his broad shoulders shuddered with a sob. "It about kills me to tell you this, but—Charity's dead. She took sick, like Ivy, and she . . ." He trailed off as if unwilling, or unable, to embellish his forthright statement.

Noble felt Stephen's grief as if it were his own, and he was instantly sorry for the boy. The remorse in his young voice was so genuine that Noble savored it a moment longer than he otherwise might have. Despite the satisfaction he felt from his punch, he still felt he owed Stephen Wingate for what he'd put Ivy through, and for what he'd done to what was left of Noble's own family. Stephen deserved to suffer a little longer. The news would keep.

"We can't stay here." Noble choked off what he'd started to say in favor of his concern for Ivy. "Get the horses. Your sister needs looking to."

Noble knelt by Ivy, not wanting to look at her brother. They had to put distance between themselves and these men, and he had neither the time nor the desire to think about anything more than that.

"Come on, Stringbean," he entreated her in a broken whisper as he gently rolled her onto her back. "Got to get you someplace safe and warm, where I can take care of you." He slipped his hands beneath her knees and her neck and lifted her into his arms.

Ivy was no burden, even helpless as she was, but fighting had taken its toll on Noble's constitution. As he struggled to his feet, he staggered under her weight.

"Here; I'll help." Stephen's voice beside him was husky, as if he'd been crying.

"I'll do it myself." Noble pulled Ivy away and willed the strength back into his knees. He hadn't meant for his reply to be so brusque, but as Stephen shrank away from him again, he could not regret it. If Ivy did not survive, it would be another mark to tally against the careless young fool.

"Jesus, Noble, I said I was sorry!" Stephen was plaintive, a boy needing reassurance.

"You'd best gather all the horses and bring them along, or you'll be sorrier still," Noble retorted, holding Ivy close to his breast, away from her brother's contrite gestures.

"It'll take too much time," Stephen argued. "They're scattered anyway, and unsaddled. Besides, to leave 'em out here without horses would be nothin' less than pure murder."

"Trust you to argue the point," Noble grumbled, aware that Stephen was right. He knew that he himself had not one further act of savagery in him; he could hardly demand more of Stephen. But neither could he bring himself to let the boy off so easily, yet. "There's at least one dead body here already, not counting that fellow that got snakebit. That's two more souls to your credit by my tally, Mr. Wingate. Now let's move, before you make your sister number three."

Noble was damned if he'd ask Stephen for help lifting Ivy up on the pie, even if it killed him, and it damn near did. He knew it would have been easier for him to have Stephen hold her while he mounted, then to have him lift her up before him, but his pride and his anger refused to acknowledge his need for help, even to Ivy's own brother.

While Stephen gathered the reins of the other horses, Noble struggled to set Ivy in the saddle. His limbs trembled from the strain, and Ivy was unable to help. No sooner did he have her up than she slipped sideways and fell into him, sending them both to the ground. Noble cushioned the fall for her, but he had the wind knocked out of him and ended up gasping for a breath.

"Criminy, Noble," Stephen muttered, stooping over him to pick Ivy up in his arms. "You're a stubborn son of a bitch, just like Charity said you were. Can you get up?"

Noble could not speak, but he could nod, and he did. It took him a full minute to start breathing regularly and get to his feet. It took another minute of holding onto the saddle horn and resting his head beside the saddle before the world stopped spinning. With a grunt, he climbed into the saddle, trying to ignore his various hurts, each vying for his attention in their own sharp way. His expression of thanks never made it past his heart.

"You're welcome," Stephen said sourly, handing Ivy to him. He started to walk away.

"Stephen." Noble stopped him. Stephen turned in silent expectation.

"Charity's not—she's alive. I followed the sounds of the gunshots and found Braman. He's taking care of her. She's going to make it, I think."

The words weren't out of his mouth before Stephen let out a whoop of joy and cut a caper right there among the dead and unconscious men. Noble started to caution him to be quiet, but he stopped himself. Whom was he afraid Stephen would wake? Besides, much as he still grudged Stephen, he had to admit the boy loved Charity. And like it or not, it looked as if their lives, Charity's, Stephen's, Ivy's and his own, were destined to be linked like creeping vines.

That is, assuming Ivy pulled through.

Noble gathered her close in his arms, making sure she was secure before him. She made a small, whimpering sound in her fevered delirium and Noble cursed virulently under his breath, hoping his sharp words would drive away his dread. He was sure the fall hadn't done her any good, even if he had been the pillow for it. Ivy was sick, and if she made the ride back alive, it would be nothing short of a blessed miracle.

Noble dared to ask God for a miracle.

Chapter Twenty-four

Ivy never saw sunshine so bright. The whiteness of Laurel's pristine pinafore hurt her eyes. Ivy heard a voice call: "Laurel! Laurel!" and the child turned toward her with a fistful of Indian Paintbrush flowers in dazzling colors. She was so like Noble in her features that Ivy caught her breath. "Come home, Laurel!" The voice called again. "Your mama's come for you. Time to go!" The girl broke into a run. The sight filled Ivy's heart and she knelt down in the long grass to receive her daughter's embrace.

"Laurel! Laurel!"

"Mama!" The child ran past her as if she had not even seen her, toward the voice that called, a voice filled with such love that it broke Ivy's heart. "Mama! Mama!" Laurel had passed her by without a look, and the sun faded behind a bank of dark clouds, as threatening as a blue northern.

Noble's back ached. His head ached, and his arms and legs, as well. Come to think of it, there wasn't anything about him that didn't ache. That was the only reason why he knew he was still alive. It was dusk, but he could not remember of what day. They'd ridden too hard and too long without more than a rest and food for the horses, mules and themselves. In his half-dream state, he looked down to check on Ivy. She'd been lying beside him all night, or had she? He started. He was on his horse and Ivy was gone. Panic jolted him wide awake, and he heard the creak of the wagon behind him.

"That's Tom and Ciely's place up ahead, I guess," Stephen called, and Noble's heart slowed again to a normal pace as he remembered that Ivy was in Braman's wagon, being tended by Charity, who had recovered more smartly than she had a right to. He hadn't had it out with her yet, but he meant to. Just now, though, he had bigger concerns.

He looked up and followed the line from the brim of his hat along the horizon. Sure enough, in the distance he saw a rambling cabin with a dark band of smoke decorating the sky above its tall chimney. There were lights in the windows, bright lights. There were several darker outbuildings some distance from the house, including a small bunkhouse. There were corrals and pens and the distant sound of a busy ranch settling down for the night. The MacDonalds, it appeared, were prosperous.

Stephen rode up beside him and slowed to a walk. Something inside Noble told him that Ivy's brother had come up to tell him Ivy had not survived the trip in Braman's wagon, after all. He could not even bring himself to ask.

"Charity says Ivy's holdin' on," was what Stephen

reported, sounding as if he didn't believe it himself. "What say we ride on ahead and warn them about what's on the way?"

Stephen did not wait for a reply before he chucked to his mount. "Giddap!" And the animal was off at a lope, kicking up dust. Noble glanced over his shoulder once at the wagon, then decided against looking in on Ivy. He'd tempted fate enough. They both had. He dared not risk it again. The pie still had a lope left in him, if not a dead run, so Noble followed Stephen up the trail, the first real road Noble had ridden since they'd departed from Basin ten days earlier. The lights and smoke ahead of them promised a civilization he hadn't seen in as long. If the reality lived up to the promise, he suspected he'd never want to leave it again.

The wagon and its passengers were half a mile behind when Noble and Stephen gained the house. Noble could smell fresh-baked bread and roasting meat, luring him like a temptress from inside. As he and Stephen dismounted, a woman appeared on the porch. Noble could not see her clearly, but he saw enough of her to know she was holding a rifle, and along with her full apron, she was wearing a frown of suspicion on her lined face.

"Cousin Ciely?" Stephen spoke up before Noble could. "I'm Stephen. Stephen Wingate, from up at Peaceful." He sounded hopeful and enthusiastic. Well, why not? If the woman was, as they expected, Ciely MacDonald, Stephen probably figured Ivy was off his hands, and he could take Charity and run just like they'd planned. Noble felt a spark of irritation at the thought, and was barely able to prevent himself from scowling in Stephen's direction.

"Wingate?" the woman's frown deepened, and

Noble's heart slid lower into his empty stomach. "We don't know no—"

"Stephen Wingate?" From inside the doorway came a lyrical voice high with surprise. "Ivy's baby brother? Matthew's boy?" With the last word, a second woman joined the first on the porch, shorter, plumper, with none of the harshness about her pleasant face that characterized the other's blatant distrust.

"Yes, ma'am," Stephen supplied, pulling off his hat respectfully. "Ivy's with us. Well, she's not with us exactly yet, but she's coming right along in that wagon yonder." He gestured back with a jerk of his thumb. "Are you Cousin Ciely?"

A movement, quick as a cat, behind the woman caught Noble's eye, and he tensed. His fingertips felt for the reassurance of the Colt at his hip, but otherwise he kept very still, watching. The movement was shrouded in shadow. Perhaps it was a cat, he thought, chiding himself for his wariness born of exhaustion. Or a trick of the light. Or merely a child.

"I'm Ciely," the woman murmured, pushing the barrel of the rifle aside. "Put that up, Lizzy. These folk are my kin."

"But how do you know—"

"They're kin, Lizzy. You say Ivy's in the wagon?" Ciely looked past them, then Noble felt her gaze on him. "And who's this?"

"This here's Noble Smith," Stephen told her. "He's my brother-in-law. He and Ivy, they got married. And I married his sister."

But Ciely's gaze never left Noble. It made him uncomfortable, but he offered a polite greeting.

"Noble Smith," she repeated after acknowledging it, as if storing the name in a safe place in the event of future need. "You're much welcome.

You're all welcome; I'm pleased to offer you our hospitality, such as may be, with Tom sick and myself not feeling so spritely as I might."

"Just why they should head straight into town," Lizzy asserted, grumbling. "I don't like havin' two strange men and who knows who all else here while the mister is sick—"

"Oh, Lizzy, you heard him! They're kin. Now let be and see them inside. They must be hungry, and they look tired."

Noble wondered if she guessed how true her observation was.

"That isn't the worst of it," he heard himself say, and he was dismayed, but not surprised, by the worn-out sound of his voice. "Ivy's sick too, ma'am. Maybe with the same sickness as your husband."

"Ivy? Ill?" Ciely's alarmed interrogatory forced a halt to his explanation. "Oh, then you must bring her here at once. Lizzy, I'm sorry, but she'll be needing your room. Lizzy sent 'round for the doctor today for Tom," Ciely addressed Noble again. "So he should be here sometime this evening; tomorrow the latest. Is she very bad off?"

Noble started to answer, but a swell of emotions caught him off guard and choked him up. His eyes burned with sudden tears he didn't dare shed. They had arrived safely at the MacDonald ranch with Ivy still alive. That was one huge burden lifted from his heavy heart. But all that meant was that he was free to bind all his worry tight to Ivy and his concern for her recovery. And at the moment, tired, hungry, aching, he felt as if he was going to break under the weight of that single worry.

"She's bad," Stephen acknowledged hesitantly, as if he realized he was covering for Noble's inability to speak. "But she's made it through this far, and it's been a rough trip."

295

An understatement, Noble thought, swallowing his bitter amusement along with his pain. Stephen was good at that.

"They're coming," Ciely observed, wringing her hands in her apron. "We'd best get to work, Lizzy. Stephen, you and Noble can wash up out back, for now. Then come in to supper."

She must have known she sounded abrupt, for she offered a sigh that passed for an apology.

"I don't know why you've come," she told them with a sober nod of her head. "We can talk of it later. But you did right to bring her here. Ivy has given me so much. There's nothing so great that I wouldn't bend heaven and earth to do for her." Ciely fidgeted as if she might have something more to say, but instead she reached behind her and hastily shunted something before her into the cabin. A shy child, Noble decided, dismissing it. The squeal of the freight wagon in the distance reminded him that Ivy needed him.

He washed up quickly if not thoroughly and returned just as Braman reined the mule teams to a halt. Several ranch hands had taken charge of the animals, although Braman himself insisted on seeing to his mules. Noble helped Charity out of the wagon and climbed in to fetch Ivy.

"She's not changed," Charity reported, wooden with fatigue. "Except she stopped taking water a ways back. Just as well; it doesn't smell so good to me. I kept the compress fresh on her brow, though, just like you said."

Noble did not answer. He knelt down beside Ivy. Wrapped in fusty, sweat-dampened blankets, she was still and pale and clammy as a corpse. Gently he lifted her into his arms. After so many days burning with fever and taking in no nourishment save water, she weighed scarcely as much as a ghost.

"Hand 'er down to me, Noble."

Noble looked up, startled, to see Stephen again, waiting by the wagon, with Charity right beside him. By the light coming from the MacDonald cabin, Noble saw the simple, undisguised compassion in their young faces. A sigh reached deep into his chest, felt around for his heart and squeezed. The only answer he could give was to hand Ivy over the side to the waiting arms of her brother.

"Noble." Charity stopped him with a word and a touch of her hand on his arm when he'd climbed down himself and began to follow Stephen to the house. Meeting her steady gaze, he realized he hadn't spoken to his sister about all of this since he and Stephen had joined them at the wagon, who knew how many days earlier. Indeed, he'd hardly spoken at all, to any of them. He would want to, eventually, he guessed wearily. But not now.

"Charity," he started, but she held up one small, fine hand in gentle protest.

"This won't take long," she told him, in a more grown-up voice than he'd ever heard her use. "I just want to tell you I'm sorry for everything. I know you have some things to say to me, and probably to Stephen as well, but I thought you should know first that I'm sorry for all the trouble we put you through, you and Ivy. She's a fine, dear lady, and I hope she's going to be all right. No, I know she will be. And I thought you should know . . ." She lowered her gaze for a flicker of an instant, then looked at him again, more resolute than before. "I thought you should know that I've come to appreciate everything you've done for me since I was a little girl. Since Pa left us. I know we were never much for saying it around our house, but—I love you, Noble."

He didn't think anything could surprise him more than that, but then she leaned forward, closing the short distance between them, took hold of his sleeves and, raising to tiptoes, kissed him lightly on his cheek. He must have looked as stunned as he felt, for when she backed away again, she was grinning like the prankish, school-girl little sister he knew. Still smiling, she slipped her hand in his.

"Come on," she entreated. "Ivy needs us."

Noble followed her guidance to the house in a lighter step than he would have dreamed he possessed.

The MacDonald house reminded Noble of his own, except for the distinct air of contentment about the place that was as obvious as if it were a living, breathing person. The house was well-ordered and homey, right down to the wondrous smells of supper emanating from the kitchen and crisp gingham curtains framing the glass window in the front door. There was no man in evidence, but there was a long coat hanging on a peg by the front door, along with a hat. He remembered Ciely saying that her husband was ill. The rag doll he spied abandoned in the hall confirmed his suspicion that it had indeed been a child hiding out behind Ciely MacDonald's voluminous skirts. He was too preoccupied with Ivy to notice more than that as he followed Stephen through the one-story house.

Ciely fluffed out a feather pillow in the small back bedroom that looked as if it had been hastily abandoned by a previous occupant. Probably the housekeeper, Noble decided.

"We don't want to put anybody out . . ." It was

more out of politeness that Noble offered his remark than anything else. The truth was he didn't
care who had to be inconvenienced, if it meant Ivy
was going to be properly looked after at last.

Ciely waved a hand at him as if she'd divined the
true meaning of his remarks. Stephen put Ivy in
the middle of a small but clean bed whose pristine
linens served to illustrate the contrast with Ivy's
trail-stained appearance. Ciely shooed Stephen
and Charity out of the room and tried to shoo Noble as well.

"With all respect, ma'am, I'll stay right here," he
told her, undertaking to remove Ivy's boots.

"The name is Ciely," Ciely corrected him
warmly, placing a gentle hand on his wrist that
reminded Noble of the touch of his own mother.
"And you're worn to a thread yourself, Noble. Get
you to the kitchen. Lizzy will set you up some supper, and then you get some rest. Ivy doesn't need
you getting sick on us, too."

Noble paused and met the woman's gaze. By the
light of the two lamps in the room, he saw that she
looked a bit older than he'd first thought; perhaps
even older than forty. Her face was round and her
eyes clear and merry, but there were deep, distinct
lines about her eyes and mouth that spoke of ad-
vancing years. The thought struck him: She looked
a bit old to have a child who would play with rag
dolls, and there were no older children apparent
in the household. He liked her easy, familiar manner, though, and the fact that she seemed to want
to care for Ivy elevated her still higher in his opinion.

"I can't allow you to put yourself out any more
than you already have for strangers," was what he
replied, slipping his arm away from hers politely
and continuing with his task.

"But you're not strangers, Noble. You're kin." She spoke with such conviction that Noble felt warmed, although used as he was to standing for himself and his little family, he found it somewhat unsettling, too.

"Your Lizzy said your own husband is sick, and you admitted to feeling poorly yourself," he argued, not looking at her. "I'm fine. Just hungry, and a little tired, but not so tired I can't take care of my wife."

Ciely made a sound as if she meant to contest him, but then she stopped. Noble continued to peel away the dusty blankets wrapped about Ivy like a cocoon, but he knew Ciely was looking at him. Her scrutiny made him uncomfortable. He could not tell why. Much as he felt a warmth and kinship for the woman and for her obvious affection for Ivy, he suddenly wished she would leave him alone with his wife. He wished it so hard, he felt a burning in his back where her gaze was no doubt concentrated.

"Noble Smith," he heard her say in a measured tone as he worked the buttons of Ivy's shirtwaist. "Yes, I think you'll do just fine."

For what? Noble wondered in weary amusement.

"Ivy Wingate has about the most generous soul of anyone I've ever known, and it would take a special man to be deserving of such a bounty from the Lord," Ciely answered his unasked question with sufficient conviction to leave him utterly nonplussed. "You just may be that man. I have some broth made for Tom," she went on matter-of-factly, obliging him not to brood long on her puzzling remark. "I'll bring some back for Ivy, and supper for you. I'll have Lizzy draw some fresh water to bathe her, and I'll fetch some fresh linens."

Ciely seemed to be talking more to herself than to him by then.

"I'm obliged for all your help, ma'—Ciely," Noble murmured, peeling away Ivy's soiled outer clothes.

"Not at all, Noble. It is we who are obliged to Ivy. Eternally."

Ciely's declaration sounded as true and as genuine as if she were professing her feelings before the throne of God Almighty. Her vehemence baffled him so that he turned to meet her gaze again, hoping to gain a clue as to her motivation. She merely met his gaze with a nod, glanced at Ivy as if to assure herself that she was faring well, and left the room. Noble caught sight of the anxious face of a girl child, whose worried dark eyes met his own for an instant before the door closed behind her.

Ivy was cleaned up, wearing one of Ciely's fresh nightdresses and she had half a cup of good, strong broth in her by the time the doctor arrived. Noble, established by the side of her bed, abandoned his own supper to attend him.

The doctor, whose name was Cannel, looked in her eyes and listened to her chest with his stethoscope while Noble supplied him with the important details of the last several days.

"I don't like it that the fever hasn't broken," the older man said in a stern voice, as if Noble were responsible for that state of affairs. "And she's too weak and dried out. But her lungs are clear. That's good." He rolled down his sleeves and fastened his cuffs. "She still looks strong, though. She's lasted this long; I'd guess she'll pull through."

She still looks strong . . . Noble had a thought.

"How long have you been here in Rawlins, Dr. Cannel?" he asked as the surgeon packed his equipment away.

Carole Howey

"Close to twenty years," the doctor replied. "I've seen plenty of epidemics, too: Typhoid. Smallpox. But this damned influenza's the worst. Can't confine it. It jumps around like a flea, and there doesn't seem to be one thing that can stop it, unless maybe it's a change of the weather. People either die of it, or they don't. But I don't think your wife's going to die, Mr. Smith. If she were, she'd have done it already. And you have your own good care to thank, for that. You kept her taking water and nourishment. I'm only sorry there isn't more I can do for her. For any of them." He shook his head, and a lock of tired gray hair fell into his face.

Noble allowed the compliment to pass unanswered.

"My—Ivy had a child here, in this very house, I guess, about nine years back," he pursued, keeping his voice low. "I wonder if you—if you might have been with her then."

Cannel looked up. His arms were halfway into the sleeves of his coat, and they stayed that way for a few seconds as his pale blue eyes squinted speculatively.

"I remember," he said at last, and Noble wondered why his reply should sound so studied.

Chapter Twenty-five

After a full minute of waiting for the doctor to tell him more, Noble realized, to his chagrin, that he did not intend to say anything else. He felt obliged, therefore, to say something, although he had no idea what.

"Was she—I mean, do you remember anything particular? About the birth, I mean."

Before him was a man who had known his daughter, had held her, even if only for a few moments. Noble found that he was hungry, starved, in fact, for a word about the child, and to share a part of Ivy's past he'd been denied. He waited, holding his breath.

Cannel finished shrugging on his coat in a slower, more deliberate gesture, without looking at Noble.

"It was a long labor," he conceded, choosing his words with care. "And hard. The contractions went on for hours. That child just didn't seem to want to be born."

As if it knew it hadn't a proper father and mother to be born to, Noble thought, a bitter taste in his mouth. He thought of Ivy travailing, perhaps on the very bed upon which she lay now, her face contorted with the strain of childbirth. He wished he hadn't asked the doctor, but it was too late for that.

"The child was born breech," Cannel went on in a clinical tone. "A girl."

Noble waited for the word "dead."

It did not come. Part of him was relieved; part of him needed to hear Cannel say it. He forced his next question.

"What happened then?"

Cannel took a deep breath. His brow gathered in a frown like gray storm clouds over a distant mountain range, and he sent his piercing gaze straight into Noble's eyes.

"Would you be this baby's father?"

The quiet, blunt question caught Noble unawares, and his own sudden sense of shame was even more unexpected. He wanted to answer with a clear, honest "yes," but the best he could manage was to nod.

Cannel appeared satisfied with his admission, bold or not. He grasped the well-worn handle of his black medical bag and started for the bedroom door. Confused, Noble started to repeat his question.

"You'd best talk with Tom and Ciely about it." Cannel cut him off, not unkindly, but firmly. "Tom and Ciely, and Miss Win—your wife. Excuse me; I have another call to make before I can head home myself."

The doctor could not seem to leave the small bedroom quickly enough. Noble saw him to the door and found Stephen waiting for him on the other side of it, wearing an anxious look.

"Will she be all right?" His question was hushed, as if quiet ensured an affirmative response. Noble reported all that the doctor had told him of Ivy's condition, leaving out the tag of his conversation with the man, about the child Ivy had had. Stephen's features sagged with relief.

"That's good," he said, still whispering. "Because me and Charity are leaving, and I didn't want to go before I knew if Ivy were——"

"What!" Noble exploded, then quickly pulled the door closed behind him so as not to disturb Ivy. "Leaving! Over my dead body! This isn't over just because we made it safely to Rawlins," he informed Stephen sourly. "In case you don't remember, we left at least two, maybe three men alive out there who'll still be looking for you and your damned gold. And if they don't find you, Ivy'll be the next one they come looking for. And anyway, if you think I'm going to just let my sister——"

"My wife," Stephen corrected him, his jaw setting like cement. He grabbed hold of Noble's sleeve, not roughly but with purpose. "Come on. We can settle this outside, so we don't disturb the whole house."

Noble knew Stephen did not mean to fight it out with him, which was a good thing, because angry as he was, he just might kill the young upstart. He yanked his arm away from Stephen's hold and delivered his most hostile glare. Stephen did not retreat from it, but nodded toward the door.

"Noble, I thought we'd settled this," Stephen began, ambling toward the corral alongside the house, a distance away.

Noble passed him with a hard stride and placed himself in front of the younger man like a barrier.

The moon, nearly full, was over his left shoulder and he was able to see Stephen's face perfectly. Perfectly enough for Noble to imagine his fist in Stephen's cheek.

"We settled nothing," he seethed, grinding his knuckles into his hips. "You told me how you came by the gold, and I believe you. You married Charity right enough, whether I like it or not, so there's not much can be done about that. But what I can do something about is your determination to break your sister's heart, and to keep you and Charity— my sister—from remaining in danger until either you or those men out there are dead. You know that's the only thing that'll stop them, don't you?"

Stephen looked away beyond Noble to the deserted corral.

"We hurt 'em pretty bad," he observed, sounding only half-convinced. "I doubt they'll be anxious to follow us after we gave 'em the slip like that."

"You don't really believe that, or you wouldn't be in such an all-fired hurry to quit this place," Noble argued. "I don't like being here, putting your kin in danger when they've been kind enough to take us in, especially with Ivy sick. But just the fact that you were here puts them in danger. Running out makes it ten times worse on them. And on you."

Stephen scowled. He shoved his hands into his pants pockets, drew them out, then thrust them in again.

"I wasn't planning on leaving without giving them something," he grumbled, not meeting Noble's gaze.

Noble shook his head with a single, incredulous laugh. "You still think this is about gold, don't you? About money, and about buying things, people. Where'd you learn to look at life like that, Stephen? Not from Ivy, that's for sure. And I don't remember your pa much, but he didn't seem the kind to put more stock in money than people."

Stephen's head jerked up and his chin stiffened. "You don't know nothin' about my pa," he said in a low, warning tone that Noble could have sworn was hurt. "You don't know what it was like growin' up without your ma, living with a man you couldn't seem ever to please no matter what, or with a sister who tried to make a baby out of you."

Noble did not answer. He thought of the girl-woman Ivy, returned from Rawlins with an empty place in her heart and in her arms where her—their—child should have been. The image lanced him. But Stephen had been seven then, or eight. The age when boys start thinking about growing up, not about being their mama's little babies. Still, Stephen's mama had pushed him out of her arms when she'd left them nearly a year earlier. A boy, or even a man, doesn't ever like to be pushed away. He likes to walk away himself, when he's ready. And he likes to know that, even though he's walked away from them, those arms are there ready to take him back, whether for a minute, an hour, a day or a lifetime.

"She loved you, Stephen," Noble said at last, quietly. "She needed you. She still does."

"Criminy, I know that." Stephen growled his angry retort. Noble guessed he was trying to mask a deeper emotion. He was filled with an unexpected sense of empathy for the younger man. He did not speak, and Stephen did not fill the void.

Noble spread out his elbows on the uppermost fence rail and leaned on it. He could not look at a fence that he didn't think of that day in Wither-spoon's meadow, and the sweet young girl who'd fallen into his arms and into his heart. Ivy. Ivy, who was about the age then that Charity was now.

"Charity's not after you about leaving, is she?" The thought that his sister might want to place distance between herself and him opened another old wound.

"N-no." Stephen's reply was guarded. "At first, back in Peaceful, she was all set to turn her back on the whole blamed territory. Couldn't wait to get to Chicago, she said. I thought that trip south through the mountains, especially with her bein' sick, would have made her all the more anxious to light out for the big city as soon as she could. But just tonight—" Stephen stopped.

"What?" Noble prompted.

Stephen issued a sound through his nose that might have been disgust, or at least impatience.

"I don't know, Noble. Women. There she was back in Peaceful, all excited about goin' to Chicago, and havin' a little brick house all our own on a paved street, and me maybe settin' up in some business. Now here in Rawlins, she's settin' there in Ciely's kitchen with Lizzy, Ciely, Lulu, and—"

"Lulu?"

"Tom and Ciely's little girl," Stephen explained with a restless wave of his hand. "Pretty little thing. Kind of shy. Don't look nothin' like Ciely, but she says the girl takes after Tom. Anyway, there's Charity talkin' away with these women, teasin' the little one to come sit by her. I mention Chicago and our plans, kind of tryin' to remind Charity of all we'd talked about, and she looks up at me with those big blue eyes of hers and—hell, you know how she does, Noble—and she says she thinks she'd like to stay, after all. And I know her well enough to know she don't mean just stay for the night."

Noble's heart lightened at the thought, and he felt closer to his baby sister than he had in a very long time. Suddenly he was no longer angry with them. Either of them.

"I hope you don't mind my saying," he began, pressing his lips against his joined hands. "But it doesn't sound to me as if you're all that excited about the idea of going anymore, yourself."

Stephen toed the dirt at his feet, his head down.

"I thought I was," he defended himself. "I thought Charity wanted it."

He left his remark hanging like an old door on a single leather hinge. Noble felt a smile tease his mouth.

"Comes a time when you have to stop thinking and start feeling," he said through his hand, thinking of Ivy again, and their schoolhouse confrontation a scant two weeks before. He'd thought that out hard before doing it. He'd thought and thought, till he thought he had every word planned down to the last why and wherefore. Then he'd seen her standing there, the light-hearted girl staring at him through a woman's eyes, the air scented faintly with violets, and every thought abandoned him, leaving only the certain feeling that he still loved her with all his heart and soul . . .

" . . . for you, Noble?"

"What?" Noble started at the sound of his name, and he realized Stephen had asked him a question. "What? I wasn't listening." He regretted that admission and waited for Stephen's teasing laughter. He was relieved when it was not forthcoming.

"You said sometimes you have to stop thinking and start feeling," Stephen reminded him, crowding beside him at the fence. "When did that happen for you and Ivy?"

"A few years too early, like you and Charity," Noble muttered, aware of a tightening in his chest. "Then about ten years too late."

He regretted his revelation at once. Stephen knew nothing about his history with Ivy except that they'd been sweet on one another when they were children. Noble felt, despite the fact that Stephen was now his brother-in-law twice over, that he'd rather keep it that way.

"What are you going to do about Charity and about Chicago?" Noble thought it best to redirect the conversation. He gazed expectantly at the younger man, whose stark features were light and shadow by the almost full moon.

"What do I . . ." He echoed, trailing off weakly. "But I thought you said you'd try and stop us from . . ." He did not seem able to finish.

Noble could not hold back a rueful smile.

"You sound as if you were hoping I'd try."

"Well, damn it, won't you?" Stephen sounded confused. Angry, even. Noble remembered just enough of his own youth to know that his brother-in-law was no doubt feeling annoyed by his own indecision regarding his immediate future. In a moment of clarity, he realized that what he said, or did not say, in the next few minutes might make the difference between whether Stephen and Charity remained or departed. He bit his lip to prevent himself from blurting his feelings, and he drew blood doing so.

"No, I won't," he declared, closing his eyes. "You decided you were a man, and by going ahead and marrying you, Charity decided she was a grown woman. What you do, where you go, is all up to you. It's not for me to like it or disapprove of it. And God knows, I've made plenty of my own mistakes without helping anybody else along in theirs."

"Who's to say which is the mistake?" Stephen retorted defensively. "Staying or leaving?"

Noble shook his head. "You're the only ones who can answer that. You and Charity. The only piece of advice I'll give you, even though you didn't ask for it, is this: If you're going to make a mistake in life, at least let it be your mistake, and not one you can lay on somebody else's doorstep when things turn sour. Because there's one thing I can tell you from personal experience: There's no regret more bitter than the one you get from piling your mistakes on top of somebody else's. And no mistake is harder to undo.

"I'd be lying if I told you I wouldn't care if you stayed or went, or that Ivy wouldn't care. But I'd be doing you and us an even bigger disservice if I tried to talk you into doing something you and Charity really didn't want to do. And I know Ivy would feel the same. But in any case, I don't see why you have to decide this in the next five minutes. That gold's going to keep. Whatever you think it's going to buy you, it can buy you tomorrow just as easily as today."

There was more that Noble wanted to say, but he stopped himself, judging that he'd given Stephen more than enough to chew on for a time. By his ensuing silence, it was apparent that Stephen thought so, too.

"Laurel!" a woman's voice called in a singsong, a voice that sounded a lot like Ivy's own, except she knew it wasn't. "Laurel! Mama's here. And Daddy. Don't keep them waiting!"

Ivy scanned the landscape frantically, but she was alone. She saw no sign of the little girl. She tried to move, to look for her, but her feet seemed sunk in some imprisoning mire, like quicksand. She tried to call out, but her mouth was full of some gummy substance that sealed her lips together.

311

"Laurel?" It was a man's voice calling that time, deep and low, as if he were standing right beside her. *"She's not here, Ivy. She's gone. She died. Don't you remember? You said she died, and she did. She had the influenza, just like you and Charity, only she died from it—"*

"No!"

"Whoa, there."

Ivy opened her eyes to discover that she was not mired in quicksand after all, but in clammy, twisted bedclothes.

"Easy, Stringbean."

She was not standing in an expanse of space, but sitting up in bed, in a small room that was vaguely familiar. Confusion made her head throb. "N-Noble?"

The touch of two warm, firm hands on her shoulders answered her weak cry.

"It's me, Ivy." Noble's hushed voice was right beside her. "I'm here. You're all right. Take some broth."

A spoon magically appeared before her eyes. She could not see Noble, but she felt the strength of him around her and smelled his wonderful, clean, male scent. The support behind her back was Noble's arm, she knew, and he was sitting beside her on the bed. Her mouth felt thick and tasted like a week of sickness. She grimaced and shook her head.

"Come on, sweetheart, you have to eat." The spoon floated closer to her mouth. "Eat just a little, then you can go back to sleep, if you like."

Sleep? But where? Where was she, anyway? And Noble, how had he gotten there, wherever "there" was?

She took the mouthful Noble offered, figuring he would be more likely to answer her flood of questions if she first obeyed his simple request.

"And another."

A second spoonful of warm, flavorful broth stopped her mouth. She realized she was ravenously hungry.

"More," she begged.

"You're better, Ivy!"

The surprise in his declaration made her look at him. There were smudges of sleeplessness below his dulled dark eyes and at least two days' growth of beard shadowed his chin and jaw. She touched the stubble with her finger and smiled.

Then her stomach revolted.

"Oh, God—"

She got out that much before the broth she'd just swallowed came back up again, burning her throat raw. She was mortified to display such behavior before Noble. She closed her eyes in shame. Too weak to apologize, she sank back against the pillows and listened to Noble's hurried movements about the small room.

"No, don't feel bad about this, Ivy. It's my fault. My fault. I shouldn't have forced you to eat if you weren't up to it. Lie still. I'll get this cleaned right up. It isn't so bad."

Ivy stopped listening to his words and allowed herself to be reassured by his soothing voice. She thanked God that Noble was not a squeamish man who looked with distaste at another's illness. In any case, she knew she was in no condition to care, even if he were.

"There. Better? Ivy?"

A damp cloth cooled her brow and cheeks. She managed to open her eyes again and saw the concern in his face.

"I'm sorry, Noble." Her voice was as weak as she felt.

"Sorry? For what?" He sounded incredulous. Jovial, almost. But she detected the false heartiness behind his lopsided grin.

He was worried for her.

"I'm—I'll be all right," she murmured, reaching for his cheek only to have her hand fall limp into her lap from the great effort. "I'm feeling much better." Her stomach protested the lie, but the pain in her head was subsiding. "Where—what place is this, Noble? It looks familiar."

"Your cousin Ciely's," he told her, rolling up the soiled bedclothes. "We got here last night, with Stephen and Charity."

"Charity," Ivy echoed, struggling to remember. "She was ill, too. Is she—?"

"As well as if she'd never been sick," Noble informed her with a wry grin Ivy found very reassuring.

"Stephen . . . ?"

"Everyone's fine, Ivy." He propped one leg on the edge of the bed beside her. He took both of her hands in his and shook them once with gentle impatience. "We're all fine. Trust you to worry about everybody. Except—"

Laurel's dead. She died of the influenza . . . Ivy dreaded what Noble was about to tell her. She forced herself to maintain his gaze, and she held her breath.

"Your cousin Tom," he said, looking at her hands. "There was a Dr. Cannel here last night who said of the two of you, you were in the better shape. Ciely said she'd been nursing him for several days by the time we got here. Ciely herself hasn't been feeling well, but as soon as she heard your name, she started bustling around here to make sure you

314

were treated like a queen. She thinks very highly of you, did you know that?"

Ivy's hands turned to ice and she felt the sensation drain from her face as she looked into Noble's fond but serious dark eyes. *Do you know why she thinks so highly of me? It's because I gave her your child.*

"You'd better lie down again," he told her. "You're all pale."

"You said—you said we got here last night?" Could he not know the truth about Laurel, yet? Could Ciely not have told him? Ivy prayed that Noble could not detect the hysteria threatening to erupt as her sickness had moments before.

"Lie down," Noble said soothingly. "I'll take these dirty things and find out if Ciely has a fresh blanket for you. If she doesn't, I expect she'll make one. Rest now, Stringbean. Time enough for us to talk later."

"But—"

"Shh." Noble touched his finger to her brow and gave her another quick smile. "I'll be back directly."

The door had hardly closed when Ivy's stomach roiled again, giving her scarcely enough time to reach the chamber pot. She dragged herself back to bed, certain that this alarming new symptom had nothing whatever to do with influenza.

Chapter Twenty-six

Noble sensed a shadow following him through the house, a scant half step behind his own. He guessed it was Lulu. He paused at the end of the hallway and pretended to adjust his burden of dirty laundry, thinking she might reveal herself to him. But she was no doubt too canny for that.

Charity, he knew, had already made friends with the little girl whom he'd seen only briefly in passing, and even Stephen spoke of her familiarly. He felt left out, somehow, as if the child, like some fairy creature, ruled an invisible circle to which he had not yet been invited. He found himself wishing that Ivy was with him. She was wonderful with children. Everyone in Peaceful said so. Why, she'd no doubt have had Lulu out of hiding and into her arms quicker than a kitten into cream.

He wanted to say something to draw the girl out, but he had no idea what might do it. He thought of saying aloud, as if to himself, that he had a sweet in his pocket. But aside from the fact that he had no such thing, he knew he'd feel foolish and re-buffed if that ploy did not work. He thought of one or two more things to say and rejected each of them. Soon he realized he'd been standing in the hallway like a stump for nearly a minute.

"Damn," he muttered, and his face quickly heated: Ciely would not thank him for using pro-fane language in front of her child, he was sure. Disgusted by his ineptness, he proceeded through to the kitchen where, to his surprise, Lizzy, not Ciely, was busy preparing breakfast, and his own sister, Charity, appeared to be helping her. The sight so astonished him that he nearly dropped his bundle.

"Close your mouth, Noble, unless you expect to catch some flies," Charity teased him with a twin-kle in her eye. "I guess Ivy's better, or you'd still look like some old spook. Is this thick enough, Lizzy?" She dropped a ladle-full of pale yellow bat-ter onto a griddle on the stove. It hissed agreeably and spread into a circle.

Lizzy glanced away from her fry pan. "That's fine. Just don't make 'em so big. Lulu likes hers the size of silver dollars, and the rest of us ain't Paul Bunyan." Lizzy looked over her shoulder and grunted a grudging greeting to Noble. He sus-pected she still did not trust him.

Lizzy had lost little of her gruff suspicion from the night before, but Charity was obviously trying to work into her good graces. That did not surprise Noble; Charity had a way of winning people. What did surprise him was that his engaging sister seemed to want to win the aloof woman's approval, although why, Noble was at a loss to explain.

"Ivy's better, except her stomach seems a bit

touchy. I don't recall the last time I saw you smile before noon," Noble teased his sister right back, heading for the door with his armload of soiled linens. "Much less wearing an apron. You figure on learning how to cook before Stephen realizes he married a woman who's a stranger to the kitchen?"

"You leave her be." Lizzy was quick to Charity's defense. "And where do you think you're going with those bed things?"

She sounded for all the world as if she thought Noble were trying to steal them. He could not help laughing. The exercise felt good, and he realized this was the first time in days he'd had anything to laugh about.

"Out back to wash them, I thought," he replied, meeting the cook's doubtful gaze with a grin. "They're, uh, soiled. I expect Ciely keeps her wash-tub on the porch?"

It was Lizzy's turn to look surprised. "You? Wash? A man?"

"Oh, Noble's real good at doing laundry," Charity asserted, happily making circles of batter of wildly varying sizes all over the griddle. "He can press with a hot iron, too. Except once he burned a hole in an old calico of mine. Other than that, he makes a great ma."

A giddy, childish giggle answered from under the kitchen table beside him. Noble curbed an impulse to stoop down and peek beneath the gingham-skirted tablecloth.

Lizzy looked him up and down, as if he were someone she hadn't seen before.

"Well I'll be," she muttered, as if she meant it was a surprise to find that men were good for anything at all. "It's out there. And there's soap in a tin, and a washboard. You'll see the pump, too."

Noble nodded his thanks and made for the door.

"Oh." He paused with his hand on the doorlatch and turned to the unlikely pair of chefs. "If you see anyone about that's never seen a man do wash, charge 'em a nickle for the privilege and send 'em on out back. I'd be glad for the company." He directed a look to Charity, then a glance at the kitchen table. She nodded quickly in understanding. "And look in on Ivy for me, would you? Tell her I'll be back as soon as I finish."

Noble strolled through the yard past the mule driver's ready wagon carrying everything he needed in the big tub. It had been a while since he'd done washing, but not so long that he didn't remember how. It was a good morning for the work: dry and warm, but not hot, with a decent breeze that would have the things drying in no time.

If the half-dozen or so ranch hands washing up for breakfast thought it odd that a man was up to his elbows in suds and hugging a washboard, none of them said so. If they had, Noble would have invited them to try it. Laundry was hard work he'd been doing for ten years, off and on, when there was nobody about whom he could hire for the task. He was accustomed to the labor by now, but he could still recall the abiding ache in his arms and shoulders when he'd first undertaken the chore. The notion that it was considered to be women's work had amazed him from that very first sleepless night of discomfort. He figured he had laundry to thank for much of the muscle in his chest, arms and shoulders, and for the strength in his hands. It took a strong grip to wring the water out of soaked bed linens, that was for sure.

His hands were tender and wrinkled from the work and the water before he realized he was no longer alone. He could not see her, but he could hear her breathing behind him, as if she half wanted for him to turn around and catch her spying on him. It was a surprisingly good feeling, yet a scary one as well. He felt as if a rabbit had stopped to watch him, and if he moved too quickly it would take flight and leave him alone again.

"Why don't you come on around in front, where you can see better?" He tried to sound offhand, as if he held conversations with little girls every day, even though the last time he'd done so was when Charity was younger. "I bet you never saw a man up to his elbows in a washtub before."

The first real look he had at Lulu MacDonald was the hem of her pink-striped pinafore, in a finer material than the usual homespun and trimmed with a fancy, zigzaggy kind of lace. His first thought was that Ciely indulged her only child unabashedly. He wondered if he'd be that kind of parent.

Lulu edged out from behind him, keeping a distance, as if she expected him at any moment to reach out and try to grab her. Soon she stood before him with the tub between them, studying him with solemn brown eyes set wide in a pretty face that startled him for its grown-up, angular proportions. Her hair was dark and thick, the color of strong coffee, and it was tied back off of her face with a bright pink ribbon. She looked older, and bigger, than he'd expected, although why he'd expected anything at all of her, he could not say.

Words formed slowly on his tongue.

"You'd be Lulu, I guess." He felt wondrously stupid, looking into her eyes.

She nodded, biting her lower lip, keeping her gaze trained on him in a way that made him feel somewhat uncomfortable, as if she knew him, even though they'd just met.

"Well, I'm Noble," he said, resting his elbow on the washboard. "I'm Charity's big brother. You already know Charity, I think."

Lulu nodded again, and a breeze pulled at a lock of her hair. It looked like silk. Noble wondered if it felt as soft as it looked.

"I'm also your aunt Ivy's husband." He went on with his scrubbing, more for effect than for results. "That makes me your uncle, doesn't it?"

The girl clasped her arms behind her back and pressed her lips together, giving no sign that she intended to speak to him anytime soon. Noble wished she would.

"Well, what do you think?" he demanded, gruff in his awkward impatience. "Am I doing this like your ma would?"

She dropped her steady gaze. "Mama's sick." Her small voice betrayed both her youth and her distress. Noble was gripped by a bewildering urge to put his arms around her in a reassuring embrace.

"Your aunt Ivy was sick, too," he told her, letting his wash slip down into the tub again. "And she's on the mend. Your ma'll be well soon, too. You see if she isn't."

Noble could see she was not convinced, and he realized he'd stopped short of promising. He wished suddenly that he could. He would have given quite a lot to see the pretty child smile.

"Papa's sick, too." There was real worry in her voice, and her dark brow seemed heavy.

"I know," Noble commiserated. "I haven't met your pa yet. Do you think he'll like me?"

One eyebrow came up again, and Noble, amused, would have sworn she was mocking him with the look.

"Papa never does laundry," she observed, glancing down at the suds as if wondering whether Noble was truly doing laundry as well, or just making a show of it for her.

"That puts me one up on your pa, then, doesn't it?" Noble pretended to retort, retrieving the bedclothes from the suds again to prove himself. For an awful minute, he could think of nothing further to say. Lulu continued to monitor him with a most unsettling complacency, as if the silence troubled her not at all.

"How old are you, Lulu? Ten? Eleven?"

"Nine," she said smugly. "I'm big for my age, Mama says."

"Shouldn't you be in school?" Noble asked, wringing the soap from the bed linens with a deft twist.

"No school. Teacher's sick, too." Lulu did a little skipping dance in the dust about the washstand. Her shoes, he noticed, were sensible lace-ups, but they looked as if they were lovingly polished to a high shine every night.

"Your shoes are so shiny they're blinding me," he teased, dumping the used water into the ditch. "You buff them like that all by yourself?"

"Nope," she replied blithely, stooping to watch the river of suds sluice down the ditch until it disappeared into the dirt. "Papa does it, mostly. Mama did it last night."

"Humph," Noble observed. "If you were my little girl, I'd teach you how to take care of things for yourself, instead of having someone else do everything for you. I knew another little girl like that, and she was a spoiled br—"

He stopped. He was being disloyal to Charity with such a declaration, he knew, but worse, he was admitting to his own mistakes in his care of his sister. He did not finish his remark. Lulu did not press him.

"Mama didn't get out of bed this morning." Lulu had obviously not been paying much attention to his comments. She was more concerned about her ma, just as she should have been. Noble set the empty tub down before the pump.

"Want to help me?"

You need help? her doubtful look said. Noble laughed. "Come here. You know 'London Bridge?'"

There was an awkward moment when Lulu positioned herself on the opposite side of the pump and she reached for the handle at the same time as he did. He felt an odd tingle as they brushed hands, making contact for the first time, but he took hold of the pump and began to sing.

"London Bridge is falling down, falling down, falling down,"

It was a well-oiled pump, and it gave easily in time with the song.

"London Bridge is falling down, my fair lady."

Her high voice found its place beside his baritone and she pumped with him. Fresh water splashed into the tub.

"Find the key and lock her up, lock her up, lock her up,"

A guarded smile appeared on Lulu's face as she looked up at him.

"Find the key and lock her up, my fair lady."

"You have a funny voice." Lulu laughed. "It's deep, like an echo, but it shakes at the end."

"Well, thank you very much." Noble could not help feeling a little embarrassed by her candid, childlike observation, especially as he'd always thought he had an adequate singing voice. "Here, toss these in there. They're ready to rinse."

The three twisted bundles splashed into the tub,

sending a spray of water all over Noble's shirtfront. Lulu giggled.

"Why, you little—" Noble reached out to grab her but she danced just past his reach, over near the corral.

"Hey, Noble, why don't you go pick on somebody your own size, instead of botherin' little kids?" Stephen interrupted their play with a scolding tone. "Go on up to the house, Lulu. Lizzy says breakfast is ready."

"I'll go tell the hands." She raced off to the bunkhouse, eager, it seemed to Noble, to follow her own itinerary rather than to quietly yield to the wishes of the adults. He watched her go with a smile on his lips, feeling as if he had made a friend.

"Tell them I'll be in after I string up these wet things," he said to Stephen. "And Lulu'll get there when it suits her, but I guess Lizzy's used to that."

"It's uncanny, isn't it?" Stephen said, his voice filled with surprise.

"What the hell is wrong with you?" Noble growled. "You look spooked." If Stephen made one comment about his occupation, Noble was going to flatten him, and he knew he would enjoy doing it.

"Spooked?" Stephen echoed faintly. "I . . . yeah, I guess I was. I hadn't seen the two of you together before, and it kind of threw me."

"The two of who?"

"You and Lulu."

"It surprised you? Why?" Noble was incensed. "Did you think I'd take a bite out of a child? What kind of a monster did Charity make me out to be, anyway?"

"No, no. It isn't that." Stephen seemed eager to reassure him. "It was—I mean, Lulu looked so much like you when the two of you were pumping that water. Her face is the same shape, and her coloring. I thought for a minute that, I mean, hell, Ciely and Tom's girl could be your daughter, Noble."

Your daughter.

If Laurel had lived, he thought, *she would be just about Lulu's age.*

"Well, I guess we know she's not," he muttered, feeling as if Stephen had just carved his heart out of his chest with a dull, rusty blade.

"Yeah, I know," Stephen agreed with a little laugh.

"Here, make yourself useful," Noble growled, wringing out a bedsheet. "Hang this up over Ciely's clothesline."

"How?"

Noble rolled his eyes. He realized, disconcerted, that they were wet.

"Lord, what a pair you and Charity make!" he declared with a shake of his head. "Helpless as babies. Here, I'll do it. You just squeeze the water out of these, as much as you can, then bring them to me when you're through. And don't take all morning about it; I'm hungry."

Stephen looked clumsy handling the wet laundry. Noble guessed he'd have been better off taking care of it himself, but he figured Stephen might as well learn. A man never knew when such an unlikely skill might come in handy, particularly if that man were married to Charity Smith. Which reminded Noble of another topic he needed to broach with his brother-in-law.

Stephen brought two log-hard twists of muslin. One sheet was already billowing in the breeze like the proud banner of an unconquered stronghold. Noble took one, purposely leaving the other one in Stephen's possession.

"Find the ends," he instructed, loosening the twist. "Then shake it out. Mind you don't drop it, or I'll make you wash it all over. You decide what you're going to do, yet?"

"What?" Stephen fumbled with the thing he'd twisted, wearing a look that said he'd rather be riding straw on a herd than trying to solve the seemingly simple domestic mystery of wash. "Oh, where we're—oh, crimin—" He dropped a corner and just caught it before it dipped in the dust. "I mean, whether or not me and Charity are goin' to Chicago? No. I sort of brought it up last night, or tried to, but Charity said pretty much the same thing you did. She's not in any hurry." Stephen sounded more resigned than annoyed. "And you know what, Noble? Neither am I. I can't explain it to you, 'cause I don't understand myself. All I know is, for so long I wanted to get away from Pa and from Peaceful that it sort of got to be a habit with me. You know how habits are? Good or bad, they're damned hard to shake."

Noble said nothing. He knew exactly what Stephen meant.

"Maybe it was bein' away from Charity when I thought she was . . . she was dead," Stephen went on in a lower tone, looking at the sheet in his hands. "Or maybe it was somethin' you said to me last night. But I got the feeling there's some good here, and there's got to be some good in me for Charity to have taken me for a husband. I'm sorry I didn't ask you proper for her, and I guess you know she's a sight better'n I deserve. Oh, hell," he wound up, blushing to his hairline, "We talked about takin' a place in Rawlins for a while until we decide where we want to be. Maybe at a boarding house, or over a store. I don't know, for sure. All I know is that I don't want to pile up a lot of misery

that Charity'll have to help me plow through later."
Resolutely, Stephen jabbed a clothespin into the
upper corner of the sheet. "It was one thing when
I was on my own. I got her welfare to think about
now. And maybe a little one, soon. Now, where'd
Lulu get to?" Stephen changed the subject. He
called to her.

"She ran off to the bunkhouse," Noble reminded
him. "I'll go get her."

"Darned kid should come when she's called,"
Stephen grumbled. "Lulu!"

"Like you did when you were a kid, right?" Noble, guessing Stephen's gruffness was all for show,
elbowed him in the ribs, unable to prevent himself
from grinning. "Leave her be. I'll fetch her."

"Like you always fetched Charity, and made her
into the 'spoiled brat' you think she is." It was Stephen's turn to elbow him, and he winced at the
surprisingly sharp dig. "Lulu!" he called louder.

There was no sound from the bunkhouse, not
even the noise of half a dozen ranch hands. The
eerie silence made Noble uneasy. He started toward the low clapboard building.

"Lulu! Laurel Ann MacDonald! Lizzy said for
you to come out here right now!"

Noble's feet halted in the middle of the quiet
yard and refused to carry him any farther.

"What did you call her?" His question strangled
him, and he dared not look back at his brother-in-
law.

"Her real name's Laurel," Stephen informed him
with a laugh of amazement. "Criminy, you didn't
think Ciely and Tom would name their kid 'Lulu,'
did you? Ciely said that's what she called herself
when she was learnin' how to talk, and it kinda
stuck."

Noble heard, but in his mind he was listening to

the words Stephen had spoken earlier: *Ciely and Tom's girl could be your daughter.*

But Ivy said Laurel had died. Could it merely be an eerie coincidence?

Could be your daughter. Noble felt as if he were suffocating, or drowning, and he could not even consider moving from where he'd stopped. Everything felt wrong, as if he'd been hurled smack in the middle of a strange world where nothing was as it seemed to be, as if he'd just realized, after two weeks of this harrowing adventure, that he should have stayed out of it, should never have paid Ivy that visit at the schoolhouse, should have stayed at home after all.

But it was too late for that. Far too late. His feet had already started down that path, first at a tentative step, then a trot, and finally a dead run until they brought him to this very place at this very moment. Only he didn't know whether he'd caught up to something, or something had caught up to him.

His mind, to his amazement, still functioned with remarkable clarity, and he found himself remembering every minute detail of his exchange with Dr. Cannel the night before, down to the reedy sound of the old man's voice. Cannel had not said that Ivy's child had died. In fact, he had avoided the subject entirely by suggesting Noble take the matter up with Tom and Ciely themselves.

Had Tom, Ciely and the doctor conspired to persuade Ivy that her child had died, and then undertaken to raise the girl themselves? It was an absurd, ghastly notion. Still, the alternative to that preposterous idea was even more unthinkable: that Ivy herself had lied to him about their daughter.

You'd best talk with Tom and Ciely about it. Tom and Ciely, and Miss Win—your wife.

Noble and Ivy

Ivy knew. She had known all along. Laurel Mac-Donald was his daughter, after all. His and Ivy's.

Noble felt dizzy. Faint. He wanted to be sick, suddenly, but there was nothing in his stomach to bring up.

"What's the matter, Noble? You turn to stone, out there?"

And Stephen, blithely ignorant Stephen, seemed to think it a great joke that Noble faltered in his undertaking. Noble tried to speak but found that his tongue had gone as numb as his limbs.

"Noble?" There was a note of bewilderment in Stephen's prompt. Noble did not turn around.

"Either one of you move, and I'll put you both under a stone," a new voice called casually from the direction of the bunkhouse.

Chapter Twenty-seven

When Ivy heard the gunshot in the yard, her heart froze even as her limbs became miraculously energized. She threw off the fresh covers Noble had left her and stumbled to the window on the far side of the room, knocking over the nightstand in her haste, scarcely feeling the pain when she skinned her shin.

The first thing she saw was Noble standing by the pump, his face drawn and pale. He was staring at the ground some distance away, nearer to the house. She started to the other side of the window to follow his gaze, to discover the source of his dismay, but her attention was redirected by the crash against the door behind her. She spun around in time to see a man charge into the room, a man she recognized at once.

Jack had returned. And third time, as her mother used to say, pays for all.

She screamed, but it was a pitiable sound, more like the yelp of a whipped cat. Weak with terror and with the remnants of her illness, she was unable to fight the big man as he caught her about the waist and slung her over his shoulder like a sack of grain. She grew dizzy and nauseated again as he carried her through the hall in that fashion, and she would have fallen down when he deposited her in the kitchen if it were not for Charity catching her. As her vision cleared, she saw that Charity and Lizzy were under the eye and gun of one of the outlaws she recognized as Moss. They stood together and quickly took Ivy to them.

"Carl couldn't wait," Moss informed Jack, not taking his eyes or the muzzle of his gun from the women. "He's so mad, he knee-capped that boy."

"I know. I heard." Jack stared hard at Ivy, a look that offered her no succor. "But at least it means he took care of the bunkhouse. Damn fool. He ain't much of a shot. He could've killed him."

Beside Ivy, Charity whimpered. The girl's grip tightened about Ivy's shoulders.

"Shh," Ivy whispered to her. "Don't let them see your fear."

"Shut up," Jack ordered curtly. Then, to Moss: "Check the rest of the house. I'll take these three outside. I'd guess it's gonna be quite a little show, and I owe those two bastards outside plenty." He paused for a long, leering look at Charity. "Little Miss Yellow Hair and the schoolteacher, maybe we'll keep them for some fun, 'less we have to hurt them." He turned to Ivy, and for the first time she noticed that his ugly face was mangled further by a bruise that looked to be a few days old.

Lizzy and Charity had to help her out into the yard, and she squinted against the glare of the mid-morning sun. Charity abandoned her at once and

331

ran to Stephen with a cry of dismay. Ivy, leaning heavily on Lizzy's unfailing support, saw that her brother was writhing in the dirt some distance away from Noble, clutching his bloodied knee in both hands and sobbing like a child.

Child—Laurel! Where was Laurel? Filled with a paralyzing terror that stuck in her throat like a sob, Ivy sought Noble's gaze. She was further distressed to find him already staring at her with cold, empty eyes, as if a part of him had already died. She longed to go to him, but that look seemed not to want her near. The thought filled her with fresh dread, and she had to look away.

"What took you so long, Jack?" Ivy heard another familiar voice from the vicinity of the bunkhouse, but she saw no one. "You diddle those ladies while you was inside?"

"If I did, it would've taken me a whole lot longer," Jack growled in reply. He straddled the porch rail in a lazy, arrogant pose, his revolver still cocked. "But we'll have plenty of time for that once we get the gold. And there's one for each of us now. We can flip a coin to see who gets the old hag. You get those bunkhouse boys settled in?"

"Nice and tight, just like bugs in a rug," Carl crowed, appearing at last in the doorway of the ranch hands' quarters. "Got me an extra prize, too. Looky here." He emerged fully from the bunkhouse, and Ivy could not restrain a cry: He was pulling Laurel along by her thin little arm, although the child was struggling against him and protesting.

"You let me go!" She demanded in her imperious yet childish voice, with more anger than fear. "I'll tell my papa, and he'll make you go away!" Laurel beat against him with her little fist, but Carl dragged her along unnoticing, as if she were no more of a nuisance than a fly.

"Brat," Jack observed, uninterested. "Still, somebody might just be fond enough of her to talk. Where's the Jew mule driver?"

Carl shrugged. "Didn't see 'im. Where's Moss?"

"Inside lookin' around." Jack eyed Stephen with no fondness. "He tell you anything?"

Stephen's gold. Ivy remembered something . . . Stephen's voice, talking low and earnestly. Telling her where he'd hidden it. If only she could remember.

"Told me to go to hell; that's why I knee-capped him. I've had about as much from these people as I can stomach, and I ain't in the mood to play games no more." Carl's voice went hard, and he gave Laurel a jerk designed to make her keep still. The child struggled harder. Ivy felt faint watching, and the cloudy memory of Stephen's revelation was still maddeningly out of reach. It was all she could do to keep herself from pleading for the girl's release when Noble spoke.

"Let her go. She doesn't know anything, and she's done you no harm," he said in a deliberate voice that shook once near the end, but Ivy was sure only she could detect it.

"Like hell, she hasn't," Carl retorted with a snort. "My shins is bruised on account o' this half-pint. Brat. Somebody ought to take a strap to her." He shook her until her dark hair came loose from its bright pink ribbon. Laurel aimed a kick at him again, but he danced away from it awkwardly. He grabbed a handful of her abundant hair and pulled until she cried out.

"Noble, make him stop!" Ivy was stunned by the sound of her voice, and even more shocked by the cold, penetrating look Noble sent her way.

"Damn you, Ivy," he muttered, shaking his head. "Damn you to hell!"

He knew. He had found out her lie. Her reasons would not matter to him, now. They no longer made any sense to her. Ivy felt the force of Noble's words, and of his hatred, as if they were indeed capable of sending her to hell. She sank to her knees, feeling as if her heart could not go on.

"Nobody inside but one man in bed, and he's dead," Moss reported, circling around front near Carl. *Tom is dead,* Ivy thought, but she was unable to summon any grief. But where was Ciely? Surely she would have been with him!

"Where's the mule driver?" Jack brayed the question.

"Ain't seen 'im."

"Me neither."

"Prob'ly hidin' out under a rock somewhere," Jack said with satisfaction. "We got rid of his watchdog out on the trail, and he's got no spine without him. No matter. I think we got us everything we need right here to get that gold at last. Bring the brat over here, Carl. Anybody does anything sudden, you shoot 'em, Moss. I don't care who. Won't take us much to burn this whole place down after they're dead and dig the gold up out of the ashes."

The look on Jack's mutilated face said he'd enjoy the chore. Helpless, Ivy watched as Carl dragged the whimpering Laurel to the fore by her hair, about three yards from where Noble stood clenching and unclenching his big hands.

"I'll tell you where it is," Stephen called out, his voice clear but tight with pain. "But first you let them go. All of them. Then you can take me with you, and do whatever you want with me."

"Stephen! No!" Charity's plea was the cry of a

little girl. She sounded almost as young as Laurel.

"Hell, I'm going to bleed to death anyway, Char." Stephen tried to laugh, but it was a frenzied sound that did not fool Ivy, or, she suspected, Charity. "How much more can they hurt me?"

"Oh, you'd be surprised, boy."

Ivy watched from the ground as Jack sauntered toward her brother. Charity wore an expression of pleading that might have melted someone less greedy or more human. Jack, however, delivered a sharp, neat kick to Stephen's injured knee. Ivy covered her ears at the sound of Stephen's scream of pain.

"What I didn't know before, I learned for myself, all those years in prison. And you can't make no bargains with us," he told him, wearing a sickening grin. "It's too late for that by far. We still owe you for Charlie and Ruby, although splittin' that gold three ways 'stead of five'll be nice. But Boyd owed me for six years in the Territorial, and since he ain't around, I'll take it from you, instead. You," he paused for a long look at Charity, sobbing by Stephen's side, "and your kin."

"Let that child go!"

Ivy jerked her head up at the clear command from the back porch. Indeed, everyone turned in the direction of the new voice, including the three men. It was Ciely, holding a rifle in her hands and wearing a look of cold challenge on her usually tranquil features that said she meant to use it. Ivy felt a thrill of hope mingled with dread.

"Mama!" Laurel called, her child's voice full of terror and joy. "Mama!"

Mama! Ivy heard the echo of a troubling dream she could not remember. *Mama!*

"The hell I will," Carl retorted, pulling Laurel in

front of him like a human shield. "Shoot her, Moss!"

Ivy heard the cock of the rifle, and of the revolver. She saw the maelstrom of pink as Laurel broke free at last of Carl's grip and hurtled herself past Ivy toward the porch. "Mama!"

As Laurel gained the steps mere inches from Ciely, two weapons discharged almost simultaneously with an awful roar. Laurel pitched forward into Ciely's arms and they both fell over on the porch. The air hissed and exploded with more shots; too many for Ivy to count. She was deafened by them anyway, with no way to know whether the explosions were real or merely echoes of a hideously vivid bad dream. It did not matter, she knew. They were dead. They were all dead, and beyond care. And if they were not, they would be, very soon. She closed her eyes and waited for the light.

Noble felt as if he'd been cemented to that spot in the yard for time uncounted, and as the air stilled and the sulfur smoke dissipated, he realized that he had not been hit by the lead that had torn great holes in the air about him. He wondered, looking about at the bodies decorating the barren landscape, how many others with him this day could make the same claim.

No one moved. No one spoke, if anyone was able to. Carl lay on his face a few feet away, a huge red stain spreading over the back of his dirty shirt from a great, gaping hole in the center. Dead, Noble knew instinctively, feeling nothing at all. Not far away from him, his companion Moss was sprawled on the ground. Half his face was gone; the other half, lined with rivulets of crimson, stared lifelessly at the dirt beside it.

A choked, coughing sound broke the stillness, so quiet that Noble's first thought was that it was coming from a great distance. He blinked in the sunlight, which suddenly seemed an inferno, and found the source of the gasping noise.

It was Jack. He was not dead. He was on the ground, though, twisting and writhing like a hornworm, his bloated, ugly body governed only by pain. Noble watched, unable to do anything else, as the outlaw flipped onto his back. He saw at once the source of Jack's distress.

He'd been shot in the throat, just at his Adam's apple. There was a small, red hole gurgling blood and air. Jack's eyes were bulging and his lips were blue, except for the blood streaming from the corners. He was suffocating, Noble guessed. And there wasn't one thing anybody could do for him, even if they wanted to.

Noble shook his head. The scene was a nightmare. He'd felt so damnably helpless, without his gun, without any kind of defense whatever. Stupid, he berated himself, for thinking they were safe, for acting as if there wasn't a trio of dangerous men with nothing to lose so close on their trails. But what Providence had saved him from his own carelessness?

As if managed by a will other than his own, Noble shifted his gaze in the direction of the privy by the bunkhouse. Moishe Braman walked toward him from that edifice, his dark eyes stripped of any emotion save utter exhaustion. The revolver at his side was still smoking. Noble's glance seemed to remind him of the weapon, and he raised it as if he'd never seen it before.

"Solly's," the mule driver offered, giving Noble a faint smile through his beard. "I take it when he die. I don't think he mind." Braman looked about him, bestowing a glance on each of the bodies in unspoken, belated apology, although Noble sensed the apology was aimed at Solly rather than the men Braman had slain. "I hope he don't mind."

Noble wanted to answer him, but found that his tongue was not yet ready to move. He wondered if the rest of him was. He tried his hand, flexing his fingers. He groped for Braman's shoulder. Braman nodded with a sigh that shook his big chest.

"I think your wife need you," he said with a quiet calm Noble envied. The very mention of Ivy sent a shock of pain through him that made him want to double over. But somehow he knew that would not help.

Charity looked up at him but did not speak as he passed her. Stephen lay still, his face contorted in the agony of his painful wound, but he was alive. Noble forced his gaze to the porch. Ivy was there, in her torn, soiled nightdress, lying beside the prostrate Ciely. Her eyes were closed and her fingers were entwined with Laurel's. Neither of them moved. Laurel's pink dress was decorated with spatters of blood, as if she'd been finger painting and had carelessly spilled an entire jar of crimson on herself.

The day seemed suddenly very far away to Noble, although the bright sunshine, near and immediate, hurt his eyes. There was a hardness in the back of his throat, as if he'd tried to swallow a board. Could he have found his daughter only to lose her forever? Could God be so cruel? And Ivy. Ivy, whose deceit had very nearly cost him the knowledge of his child . . . He wanted to hate her with all his heart, but he could summon only a dull void that was nearer to pity than to loathing, and nearest of all to pain.

And Ciely.

Lizzy, kneeling, lifted Ciely's head of tight, graying, wound braids into her lap. The housekeeper looked up at Noble with a tearless stare that surpassed sadness.

"She's dead," Lizzy uttered in a hoarse, toneless voice.

Noble said nothing. He thought that he might be dead, too, only the Lord had not seen fit to tell him so, just yet.

"Dead?" Ivy's brittle echo questioned. She struggled to a sitting position and felt Laurel's little body with shaking hands. "But she called. I heard her call me. Noble?" The plea in her eyes was stronger than the one in her voice, and both made him ache.

Ivy had no business being out of bed, Noble's rational, practical side realized, even as he stood there, unmoving. She was obviously still weak from her illness and from shock. This was too much for her. God knew it was too much for him. He knelt on the other side of mother and daughter because he knew his legs would not support him much longer. He refused to meet Ivy's gaze as he placed his hands tentatively on Laurel's small back. What he felt both amazed and elated him.

"She's breathing," he reported with clinical woodenness. Encouraged by his finding, he probed further and quickly determined the source of the blood staining her pretty dress.

"It's only her shoulder," he pronounced, going lightheaded with joy at the thought that the child—his daughter—would live, after all. "And the bullet went all the way through. That must be what killed Ciely." He looked into Lizzy's eyes as he said that, still not able to look at Ivy. "Help me get her inside, Lizzy. And Stephen, too. Plenty of time to take care of the dead. It's the living who need us now."

"I go in town for doctor," Braman volunteered, looking only too pleased to be quit of the vista of death around him. "And sheriff, too."

Of course. The sheriff needed to be notified. Noble was glad that his practical nature had shoved his sentimental one aside. He suspected the former would be of far more use to him and to everyone else than the latter, at least for the time being.

"Best see to the fellows in the bunkhouse, first," Noble said, rising with Laurel in his arms. "I'll need their help getting Stephen inside."

"Noble." It was Ivy whispering his name. It hurt. He made himself look at her, but he could not force a reply. He was too angry for that.

"I'm sorry." Her apology was even fainter than her invocation of his name. Ignoring her, he carried his daughter into the house.

Chapter Twenty-eight

Charity's dress was not the proper black crepe for mourning, but it would do. It had to. Ivy suspected the girl did not own a better one. She'd been younger when her own mother died, Ivy recalled, and doubtless her woman's figure would no longer fit into such a garment in any case. But at least her dress was her own. Ivy had nothing suitable to wear to a burial, so Lizzy said it would be all right if she wore one of Ciely's.

"This is going to be too big for you," Charity fretted, fastening the back of the black woolen dress for Ivy. "But there isn't time to fix it. Maybe you shouldn't be outside for the burial, anyway. It's gotten to be hot again, and Noble says you might not be strong enough yet."

Ivy winced. Noble had not been to see her since that awful day that had crippled Stephen and made Laurel an orphan. That Charity mentioned him to her now as if he still cared about her, when his avoidance made it obvious to Ivy that he did not, made a mockery of the love they'd shared briefly.

"Are you all right, Ivy?"

So Charity had noticed her fresh pain. Ivy looked away from the mirror, not wanting to see the evidence of it herself. The black wool mourning dress itched her. It reeked of camphor and it was stiflingly hot, besides. She felt as if she were wrapped in a shroud.

"I . . ." Ivy hesitated. Should she ask again, having listened to polite, evasive excuses from Lizzy and Charity for two days? She had no choice. "Would you please tell Noble that I need to speak with him before the—before they bury Tom and Ciely?"

Charity, she noticed, pretended to be busy with pins, fussing at the hem of the heavy gown.

"He's tending Laurel," Charity murmured. "She wanted to come see them buried, but Noble thinks it's better she doesn't. Her shoulder is fine," Charity added hastily, anticipating Ivy's concern. "Healing up faster than it has a right to, Noble said. But she's so young. She—" Charity stood up, and Ivy was surprised that the girl was nearly as tall as she. Her blue eyes were direct and unreadable, a sapphire version of her brother's sable ones.

"Noble hasn't said," she began in a lower tone, as if afraid someone might overhear, although they were quite alone in the bedroom. "And I haven't dared ask, he seems so distant. But the night it—the other night, he got to drinking—he never does that. He said some things. . . ." She glanced away, and in that short space of time Ivy prayed her sister-in-law would lose her nerve and leave the dreaded question unasked. When she looked up again, Ivy knew that her hope was in vain.

"Lulu—Laurel—she's your child, isn't she, Ivy? Yours and Noble's."

"Yes." The admission did not pain her as much as she'd feared, but it was nevertheless enough to cause her to look away again, this time without looking back. She walked a space across the small room toward the door.

"Stephen guessed," Charity murmured, half to herself. "You must have been very young." It was a statement, but the inflection of her voice implied a question.

"I was your age." Ivy knew she did not have to answer, but she realized, having spoken the first words, that she wanted to. That it felt good to do so, in fact. "It happened once. We were on our way home from school. It was the day we found out that my mother and your pa ran off."

The silence told her that Charity was pondering this.

"Your pa sent you away," the younger girl mused at last. "Why didn't you and Noble run away together, like Stephen and me?"

It was a child's answer to a grown-up problem. Ivy sighed.

"Even if it weren't for the fact that our families were depending on us, I don't think either of us would ever have considered such a thing," she said. "I can't explain it any better than that, because I'm not sure I understand it myself. People needed us. My father and brother. You and your ma. Noble and I were raised to be responsible, and I think we tried too hard, as a result, to see to it that you and Stephen had a childhood. We tried to make up for the misery—" No, she did not want to start down that trail. She'd been there too many times, and she was tired of it. Sick to death of it, in fact. She drew herself in and reduced the story to its most elemental components.

"I was forbidden to see Noble, and he the same. Pa sent me here when he—when he found out about the baby. I had no choice. No choice."

God, she hadn't meant to cry, but the tears were choking her again, all the same. How many times, and in how many ways, was she to be called upon to answer for one lapse of good sense? Some people barrelled through their entire lives, and the lives of others, come to think of it, piling mistake upon mistake, leaving a trail of misery in their wake and yet escaping unscathed themselves. It hardly seemed fair that she and Noble should be subjected to so much pain for a simple accident of timing.

"And you never told him." The words were not accusing, merely wondering. Probing.

The probe stung like an angry hornet.

"I—" Ivy started to present her defense, her litany of very solid reasons why she'd never told Noble, or anyone else, but she choked them back, too weary after ten years and hundreds of miles to dissemble. "No." The single word sounded dead and flat in the tiny, airless room. "At the time, I couldn't. Later, it was too late."

Charity did not speak, and the silence weighed on Ivy like the dress in which she was imprisoned. She longed to escape the room, but she sensed that she was somehow waiting for Charity's dismissal. She felt, oddly, as if she were the fifteen-year-old and Charity the older and wiser. Her breast hurt with every breath.

"Noble would have wanted the baby." Charity was thoughtful. Ivy read her quick calculations in her serious frown. "He'd have moved mountains to get her back; you know he would. She was his, his

344

responsib—" Charity's frown deepened with understanding, and she slowly met Ivy's gaze again. "God, Ivy, what a mess!"

Charity's unexpected understanding was like a sudden, blinding light in a dark hole. Ivy felt a burden evaporate from her soul, all the more lightening because she had borne it for so long, she had become accustomed to its ponderous weight.

"How you must hate your mother," Charity went on with a new hardness to her voice. "And your father. And my father. And how you must have hated Noble, for bringing this on you."

"Charity."

"What?"

"Charity," Ivy repeated, taking the girl by the shoulders. "I never blamed Noble. I never hated him, either. That would have been harder than hating myself. And as for the others, this isn't their fault, either. It's nobody's fault. I can't go through my life blaming others for my troubles. Sometimes things just happen. Things we can't do anything about, except live with them. We do our best not to make mistakes, but sometimes we do. We can only hope to learn from them. They're hard truths, but truth, nonetheless. Like Laurel losing Tom and Ciely, who have been her ma and pa all these years. Who should she hate for that?"

Charity looked away. "Stephen," she said, as if the confession cost her a limb. "And me."

There was one hard lesson Charity was learning already.

"Learn from it," Ivy advised, placing her hand on Charity's slumped shoulder. "But don't let it be a cross you bear. Tom was dead of influenza already, the same thing that might as easily have killed you or me. Ciely was ill. All this might have happened anyway. It just might have happened differently. In any case, it's happened. Leave it. Learn from it. But leave it."

"How do I do that?" Charity was plaintive.

Ivy turned her around and pulled her into her arms. "You'll find a way," she assured her. "You have a good heart, and that's a beginning. So does Stephen. And you love each other. There's a few more steps in the right direction. Now if you could only get him to stop thinking of that gold as his salvation—"

"I guess he hasn't told you." Charity loosed herself from Ivy's embrace. Her face brightened. Ivy marvelled at her mercurial recovery. "Well, how could he have? He's still an invalid, although Dr. Cannel said Noble did a fine job patching up his knee. He may limp for a time, but if we can keep an infection from setting in, he will walk again. Anyway, he and I talked about this last night. Stephen feels badly about everything, including what happened to Solly. He gave Mr. Braman both their shares of gold, and wants to use a third of what's left to set up in business with him in Rawlins. And he means to give a third of it to Laurel, sort of in trust, for her future. And the rest of it is for you and Noble. I know he doesn't want for money, but a little extra never hurt, especially now that you, Noble and Laurel will be a family."

Charity's assumption brought a renewed stripe of pain like the lash of a whip through Ivy's insides. She knew it showed in her eyes, but she saw no use in trying to conceal it from Charity.

"I don't know that for sure," she said, the uncertainty of the future looming suddenly like a great, black chasm before her. "I've hurt Noble badly. I don't know if he can forgive me."

"But you're husband and wife, now. Laurel has

you and Noble both," Charity pointed out, as if that fact should solve the whole predicament. "You're going to take her and raise her together, aren't you, Ivy? How much you must want to!"

"That's all I've ever wanted from the day I learned I was pregnant," Ivy admitted, tasting an old bitterness in her mouth.

"Oh, Ivy, of course you did!" Charity's sudden rush of emotion threatened to flood Ivy with tears again. "It's sad that Tom and Ciely had to die for you to have your dream, but that's the way of it. Noble loves you, I know he does. Surely he'll come around—"

"Noble is angry with me," Ivy cut in, unable to bear Charity's bubbling enthusiasm. "He has a right to be. Honorable as he is, he expects absolute integrity from everyone else. I hurt him deeply. I lied to him. Why I did it doesn't matter, in his eyes. I'm not even sure it should."

"Ivy, listen to you!" Charity shook her, stirring the odor of camphor from the dress. "You stand there and tell me in one breath that we can't blame others for our troubles, and then you tell me you'll let Noble punish you for something he had as much to do with as you did! You talk about being fair to people. How are you being fair to yourself? By letting Noble be unfair to you?"

There was something wrong with Charity's reasoning, but Ivy was hard put to determine what. She realized, abashed, that she was staring at the floor.

"Put yourself in Noble's place," Charity went on, sounding more vehement by the moment. "Or better yet, put him in your place. If he were you, and he'd had the baby, don't you think he would have done whatever he thought it took to make things the best he could all around?"

Ivy was so startled by the notion of Noble, or any man, having a baby that she laughed once, nervously. Charity continued to stare at her without smiling. Her forceful argument harkened back to a time not long ago, although it seemed so distant as to have actually happened to someone else.

"He would have put me in jail," she murmured, before she'd intended to speak.

"He what?" Charity was incredulous. Ivy's face heated.

"He intended to put me in jail back in Basin," she repeated. "To keep me from coming along. To keep me out of danger, he said. I've no doubt that he meant to do just that. But then he—he thought the better of it, and we married, instead. He said he was sorry."

Charity shook her head, still eyeing Ivy with a prim, purse-lipped expression.

"Well, by golly, we all make mistakes then, don't we?" she intoned. "Even my big brother Noble, who thinks he's always right. Only I expect it must be a little harder on folks like him when they have to admit to one."

Charity flounced toward the door, and Ivy had no doubt in her mind that Noble's sister was headed straight for her brother to tell him what she thought of his double standard.

"Charity!" Ivy employed her best stern schoolteacher invocation.

The girl halted at the door in midstep and turned. Ivy softened at her sister-in-law's guilty look.

"Noble is my concern," she said, stressing each word. "I appreciate your intention, and I'm grateful for your insights. You reminded me of some very important things, and I'm obliged. But I think it would be better if you let Noble and me fix our fences ourselves." If we can, she thought, but did not add.

Charity looked at her sideways. "He can be pig-headed," she warned her.

"I know."

Charity's grin seemed reluctant, but not forced. "And remember, he does love you, Ivy. I know he does."

Ivy was close to tears again, but she held them back, nodding.

"I know that, too."

Smiling in earnest, Charity slipped from the room.

Noble kicked a clod of hard clay dirt with the toe of his boot. He wished he had his suit. It didn't seem right to be wearing work clothes, however clean, to a burial. It seemed disrespectful. Oh, he didn't care that it might look that way to the other mourners who were milling about the makeshift graveyard avoiding his eyes. He just felt he should show more regard for the couple who had raised up his daughter. Lizzy had very practically suggested he try Tom's suit, but Tom was much shorter and heavier in the middle than he. It hadn't taken but one look in the man's wardrobe to determine that.

The MacDonalds did not have many close neighbors, so Noble was amazed at the number of mourners who showed up at the ranch, from as far away as Sinclair. They arrived singly, in pairs and in groups, in wagons and buggies and on horseback. Each one brought a silent offering of food, whether cooked or not: cakes, stews, cold roasted game, bread. At least there was no worry about what to feed them after the burial. Lizzy had her hands full in the kitchen, even with Charity helping. And Ivy. . . .

Noble had not allowed himself to see Ivy in three days, since the tragedy that had taken Ciely's life. There had been plenty enough to keep him busy, what with tending to Laurel and Stephen until the doctor arrived, helping with the laying out of Tom and Ciely MacDonald, and answering, with Stephen, Charity and Moishe Braman, a spate of questions from the Rawlins sheriff about the dead outlaws. Now there was no avoiding her.

Damn.

A man brushed by him and Noble looked up with a guilty flush. Had he spoken the word aloud? There was no way to tell from the fellow's bland, unsmiling expression, although he did stare a moment longer than Noble felt comfortable with.

Damn again.

Ivy was back at the house, patiently explaining to the restive, recovering nine-year-old girl who was their daughter why it would be best if she stayed in bed rather than attend the burial. He'd tried all morning to persuade the child, doggedly answering her every pleading "why." And there'd been so many of them! He let loose a sigh, remembering.

Then Ivy was there. He had not heard her enter, would not have known she was in Laurel's little room at all except for the faint, sweet scent of violets. The familiar aroma had been squelched at once by the odor of camphor and old wool, but the damage had been done, nonetheless. There was Laurel, his daughter, in her rich little bed like a queen, and beside him was his wife, Laurel's mother, the woman he loved so hard he couldn't see straight.

He had not been able to look at her. He'd wanted

to. But something—pride, anger, hurt, who knew what?—prevented him.

Hurt! Noble swallowed dust. He might have died from it, standing in the hot sun that morning, hearing the words from Ivy's own lips. *I'm sorry. . . .*

He squeezed his eyes shut tight. He loved her, and he hated what she'd done to him. To them. He escaped from Laurel's room without speaking to her, for he knew he could not govern what words might come out. Words of love, or words of hatred, he'd mean them both. And just now, he could not live with that paradox.

"They're ready."

He started. It was she, beside him. He felt her, heard her, smelled her impossible, incongruous blend of violets and camphor, although the odor of camphor was weakening and the scent of violets was becoming stronger.

Just as your anger is weakening, a gentle voice in his head prodded.

No, by God. This was worse than any deception she'd contrived to save her brother from his anger.

And where's that anger now? the voice wondered congenially.

Clumps of mourners, like black crepe sagebrush, gathered about two holes in the ground. Noble wondered how much time had passed since Ivy had spoken to him.

"Laurel?" He deemed the one-word question enough.

"Inside," Ivy murmured. "We talked. She agreed it would be best."

He felt her warm, soft fingers slip into his, and he had neither the will nor the desire to pull away from them.

"I told her she was to live with us, now." Ivy's voice was soft and low. He knew, despite the press of mourners, that he was the only one who could hear her.

The company parted, and two plain pine caskets came forth on the shoulders of MacDonald neighbors, men who sat in church with Tom, Ciely and Laurel, every Sunday.

Guess I'll have to start going now, to set the example for my girl.

A curious shimmer, part pain, part yearning, tingled in his gut. Forgive. No. The hurt is still too great. Too raw. Too—

"She's frightened," Ivy went on, her hand still in his, not invading, not retreating. "But she knows me, a little. And she trusts you. You should feel very good about that."

His traitorous heart crept into his throat, and he had to swallow twice before it slipped back where it belonged.

"Did you—" Damn his throat! It would fill up. "Did you tell her—" He had to stop. He prayed she'd think he meant to, and that she would take his meaning without further clarification.

The minister, in a black cassock that the morning breeze took like the wing of a raven, opened his prayerbook. The pages fluttered.

"No." Ivy's answer came at the end of a little sigh that made him want to squeeze her hand. "We'll do it together, when the time comes."

Together. We did it together, didn't we, Ivy-Girl? We found each other again, and were smart enough to hold on to it, this time. We found Stephen and Charity, and saw them through. We found our way back to Laurel, as sure as a bird finds its nest. But long before any of that, we found that we could work our way through whatever God or man put in our path, and do it all the better if we were together.

The minister laid Tom and Ciely to rest in sonorous tones like the distant bells of a church. Noble, squeezing Ivy's slender fingers, knew that a part of him was just coming to life. Somehow, he knew it was the best part. And he knew, as Ivy's hand answered his with a gentle, secret tug, that it planned to live a long, long time.

Epilogue

Laurel was asleep. Ivy tucked the blanket up to her daughter's chin and allowed herself the delicious luxury of gazing at her as she had every night since she and Noble had claimed her, nearly three months before. The more she looked at her, the more little things she noticed. This evening, she observed the peak of Laurel's upper lip, one of the few remaining traces of infancy that the nine-year-old bore. She did not need to touch it with her fingertip to know that it was soft and pliant, but she did anyway, and Laurel's nose, the mirror of Noble's, wrinkled at the resulting tickle.

"You'll wake her." Noble rested his chin on Ivy's shoulder and closed his arms about her from behind.

"Will not. Your daughter could sleep through Armageddon. She's like her Aunt Charity in that regard, I expect." Ivy rubbed her cheek against his bristled one, loving the coarse but sensuous feel of it. Noble decided he'd like to grow a beard so he could look like a respectable married man, now that he'd sold off his and Ivy's places in Peaceful and made the MacDonald ranch their home. Ivy never lost an opportunity to suggest that it needed more than a beard to make a man respectable, although she had to admit that loving a man with an abundant, soft down on his jaw yielded certain unexpected advantages.

"Hmm." Noble's chuckle was a pleasing rumble deep in his chest. "Think she'll sleep through this one's caterwauling in the middle of the night?" He placed a gentle, protective hand on the swelling of her belly that was his child growing there.

"Behave yourself." She put her hand on top of his, but did not pull it away. She grew serious again. "Will we ever be able to tell her, do you think?"

"I think you just ask me that because you like to hear me say yes."

In the aftermath of Tom and Ciely's deaths, Ivy had tried to be a mother to Laurel without demonstrating any desire to replace the one she'd lost. Laurel had recovered remarkably quickly; the neighbors had all been kind and encouraged them to stay on at the ranch. Stephen and Charity, free at last from persecution, were set up and content in the dry goods business with Moishe Braman in Rawlins. They were eager for Noble and Ivy to stay as well, a fact that pleased Ivy and gratified Noble.

She and Noble had decided to stay, as much to keep their family together as to make a difficult situation for Laurel as painless as possible. One day they would tell Laurel the true story of her parentage; it remained for them to discover the best time to do that.

"Let's go sit outside a while." Ivy discovered she did not want to think about it.

"I have a better idea: let's go to bed. I have something I want to show you."

Ivy turned toward him, giggling. "I bet it's nothing I haven't seen there once or twice already," she whispered, touching his wide mouth with the tip of her finger.

He shushed her.

"Now who's misbehaving?" he scolded her with a grin. "Do you want your surprise, or don't you?"

Of course she did.

The low August moon was nearly full and it shined in their bedroom window like a great, unseeing eye. Ivy wanted to draw the curtain and light a lamp, but Noble stayed her.

"Don't yet." He stood before her. His hands moved upward languorously until they brushed her breasts. She started with a familiar shiver of want.

"I've seen this before, Mr. Smith," she told him with a sigh. "Was there something else?"

"Be patient." He nibbled her earlobe as if it were a rare, succulent confection. "All things in their own time."

"Biblical wisdom. That's what I get for seeing that you go to church regularly."

"Would you have me any different?" His dark eyes were bright with a characteristic yet always irresistible blend of devilment and expectancy.

She moved forward into his waiting arms, figuring that would be answer enough for him. It was a cool night, but his embrace more than warmed her, and his long, lingering kiss made her feel downright combustible all the way to her toes.

"Ah, sweet," he murmured, nipping her lower lip

gently with his teeth. "There's strong magic here for us. Feel it?"

She didn't know about magic, but she did feel his hands charm the buttons of her shirtwaist with the art of a sorcerer. She was not without accomplishments of her own, though. She knew his buttons and buckles as well as her own, perhaps better, and she gladly demonstrated her facility.

"Whoa," he halted her with a little laugh as she commenced to push his loosened trousers down his buttocks. "Got to get something from my pocket."

"Are you afraid I'll rob you?" she demanded in a throaty whisper, licking the sweet saltiness from his breastbone.

"No.—Lord, I—don't do that, sweetheart. Not yet, anyway." He took hold of her arms.

Her breasts swayed between them, their tight nipples dusting the hairs on his chest. Her fingertips found some interesting territory. She wanted him. She'd wanted him forever, and every night he gave to her, often more than once, and she still wanted more. There was magic, all right, she decided, gazing appreciatively at the contour of his fine chest muscles. They were lightly painted with perspiration in the bright moonlight, and they begged for her touch.

There was magic between them for certain, but it had nothing to do with where they were. The magic was all their own. She hoped they would never lose it.

"I have something for you." His voice was nothing more than a ragged plea to the night.

"I know," she replied, wanting to be helpful.

"Lord, Ivy, stop a minute."

Ivy was a fast study, and she'd quickly mastered the questionable skill of teasing Noble as he so often did her, although he might have wished it to be otherwise, particularly now. Obediently she put her hands at her sides.

"All right. What is it?"

He blew off a shuddering sigh.

"Thank you," he huffed. "Lord, but you're maddening sometimes, Ivy-girl. I swan, a man tries to give you a gift, and you're all over him like ants on honey."

"Mmm, honey." She pressed close to him again.

"Ivy—" This time his growl was a warning.

She giggled. "I'm sorry." It was a lie, but he didn't call her on it.

He fumbled in the pocket of his trousers, which were sliding ever farther from their original position. He withdrew a bit of cloth, a small sack, and they dropped all the way to his knees.

Oh, but he was splendid.

"If you can be serious for just a minute—"

"I can."

"Don't pout, now. Here." He slipped a small, shiny bit of a star from the pouch, and Ivy gasped. Looking closer as he held it up, she saw that it was not a star at all but a gleaming golden circle cut and braided like a miniature crown.

"It's a wedding ring," he explained. "Remember? I promised you one in Basin. There's been a lot of water under the bridge since then, hasn't there?"

The best she could do was nod. She'd all but forgotten his promise on their wedding night. She was pleased, though, that he had not.

"You'd best breathe, or you'll be fainting on me." It was Noble's turn to tease as he took her left hand. "Do you like it?"

"It's . . ." Ivy's eye caught something peculiar in the delicate design. She held it up to the bright moonlight.

What she'd first thought was merely a pretty, flower-like embossing in the gold face was in reality a clever weaving of laurel and ivy.

"Braman helped me track this down." Noble anticipated her amazement at finding such a treasure in remote Rawlins. "It took some doing, too. It came all the way from Chicago."

"It's beautiful." She was moved by his care. "But there's nothing of Noble in it!"

"Sure there is," he asserted, tracing the circle of gold with the tip of his finger. "This is me. All around you. Always. With this ring," he whispered, his face gone serious, "I thee wed." He slipped the band on her fourth finger.

"With this body," she replied, feeling as if she were under another intimate spell, "I thee worship." She leaned into him and found the kiss he had waiting for her.

"Mmm," he answered, then tore his lips away from her again. "And this one?" He placed his hand against her belly and she felt the tenderness and throbbing of the life they'd started there together. Suddenly she did not want to tease him anymore.

"And the one in the other room," Noble added with unmistakable satisfaction, taking his lips from hers just long enough to say it. "Provided she doesn't wake up just now."

"She won't," Ivy promised him again, pulling him down onto their bed.

Maybe Noble was right, she mused as his lips found the places of her secret pleasure. Maybe there was magic here, after all.

Sheik's Glory

Carole Howey

Bestselling Author Of *Touched By Moonlight*

Missy Cannon is a woman who doesn't have time for fancy dresses or sweet talk. The no-nonsense horse trainer is looking for a brood mare, and she is bound and determined to get the best money can buy. Then a run-in with a riled filly leaves the untouched hellion as skittish as the animal itself—especially after a charming rogue rescues her and stirs a longing she cannot deny.

But Flynn Muldaur isn't after Missy's heart: He wants her South Dakota ranch. Gambling has won him half the spread, and she fears he will use any conniving trick or seductive strategy to get the rest. Yet the harder Missy fights Flynn, the more she realizes she wants him, needs him, and will risk all she possesses to have him.

_3903-6 $5.50 US/$7.50 CAN

Sheik's Promise

CAROLE HOWEY

Bestselling Author Of *Sweet Chance*

Allyn Cameron has never been accused of being a Southern belle. Whether running her own saloon or competing in the Rapids City steeplechase, the brazen beauty knows the thrill of victory and banks on winning. No man will take anything she possesses—not her business, not her horse, and especially not her virtue—without the fight of his life.

An expert on horseflesh and women, Joshua Manners desires only the best in both. Sent to buy Allyn's one-of-a-kind colt, he makes it his mission to tame the thoroughbred's owner. But his efforts to win Allyn for his personal stable fail miserably when she ropes, corrals, and brands him with her scorching passion.

_51938-0 $4.99 US/$5.99 CAN

Touched By Moonlight

CAROLE HOWEY

Bestselling Author Of *Sweet Chance*

Terence Gavilan can turn a sleepy little turn-of-the-century village into a booming seaside resort overnight. But the real passion of his life is searching for Emma Hunt, the mysterious and elusive creator of the tantalizing romances he admires. When he finds her, he plans to prove that real life can be so much more exciting than fiction.

To the proper folk of Braedon's Beach, Philipa Braedon is the prim daughter of their community's founding father. Yet secretly, she enjoys swimming naked in the ocean and writing steamy novels. Philipa has no intention of revealing her double life to anyone, especially not to a man as arrogant and overbearing as Terence Gavilan. But she doesn't count on being touched by moonlight and ending up happier than any of her heroines.

_3824-2 $5.50 US/$7.50 CAN

DEBRA DIER
LORD SAVAGE
Author of *Scoundrel*

Lady Elizabeth Barrington is sent to Colorado to find the Marquess of Angelstone, the grandson of an English duke who disappeared during an attack by renegade Indians. But the only thing she discovers is Ash MacGregor, a bounty-hunting rogue who takes great pleasure residing in the back of a bawdy house. Convinced that his rugged good looks resemble those of the noble family, Elizabeth vows she will prove to him that aristocratic blood does pulse through his veins. And in six month's time, she will make him into a proper man. But the more she tries to show him which fork to use or how to help a lady into her carriage, the more she yearns to be caressed by this virile stranger, touched by this beautiful barbarian, embraced by Lord Savage.

_4119-7 $4.99 US/$5.99 CAN

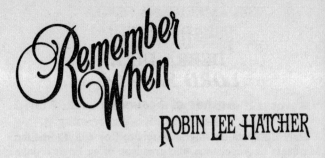

Remember When

ROBIN LEE HATCHER

Bestselling Author of *Forever, Rose*

"Robin Lee Hatcher writes lively, tempestuous romance!" — *Romantic Times*

Certain that her destiny doesn't lie in her dull hometown of Homestead, Idaho, Sarah McLeod wants to shake off the town's dust and see distant lands. But as long as her ailing grandfather needs her, fantasies of exotic cities and dashing noblemen have to wait. Then Jeremiah Wesley returns from years of wandering around the world, looking for a steady job and a peaceful home. He is the last man Sarah thinks she'll ever love. Yet as she gets to know Jeremiah, she finds herself dreaming less of a far-off prince—and more of a virile lover only a heartbeat away.

__3683-5 $4.99 US/$5.99 CAN

Dorchester Publishing Co., Inc.
65 Commerce Road
Stamford, CT 06902

Please add $1.75 for shipping and handling for the first book and $.50 for each book thereafter. NY, NYC, PA and CT residents, please add appropriate sales tax. No cash, stamps, or C.O.D.s. All orders shipped within 6 weeks via postal service book rate. Canadian orders require $2.00 extra postage and must be paid in U.S. dollars through a U.S. banking facility.

Name _____
Address _____
City _____ State _____ Zip _____
I have enclosed $_____ in payment for the checked book(s).
Payment <u>must</u> accompany all orders.☐ Please send a free catalog.

Captive Legacy

Theresa Scott

"**Theresa Scott's captivating writing brings you to a wonderous time and shows you that love inself is timeless.**"
—*Affaire de Coeur*

Heading west to the Oregon Territory and an arranged marriage, Dorie Primfield never dreams that a virile stranger will kidnap her and claim her as his wife. Part Indian, part white, Dorie's abductor is everything she's ever desired in a man, yet she isn't about to submit to his white-hot passion without a fight. Then by a twist of fate, she has her captor naked and at gunpoint, and she finds herself torn between escaping into the wilderness—and turning a captive legacy into endless love.

_3880-3 $5.99 US/$7.99 CAN

Dorchester Publishing Co., Inc.
65 Commerce Road
Stamford, CT 06902

WEST WIND

Linda Winstead

Annabelle St. Clair has the voice of an angel and the devil at her heels. On the run for a murder she didn't commit, the world-renowned opera diva is reduced to singing in saloons until she finds a handsome gunslinger willing to take her to safety in San Francisco.

A restless bounty hunter, Shelley is more at home on the range than in Annabelle's polite society. Yet on the rugged trail, he can't resist sharing with her a passion as vast and limitless as the Western sky.

But despite the ecstasy they find, Annabelle can trust no one, especially not a man with dangerous secrets—secrets that threaten to ruin their lives and destroy their love.

__3796-3 $4.99 US/$5.99 CAN